The Ladies of Rosings Park

A *Pride and Prejudice* Sequel
and Companion to
The Darcys of Pemberley

Shannon Winslow

A Heather Ridge Arts Publication

www.shannonwinslow.com

Cover design by Micah D. Hansen

For my daughters-in-law

Ann and *Kristy*

For your beautiful spirits.
For your delightfully unique personalities.
But especially for loving my sons as much as I do.

Soli Deo Gloria

Author's Foreword

The Ladies of Rosings Park expands *The Darcys of Pemberley* series laterally, the events agreeing with and the majority of the action paralleling the timeline of that book. However, when I set out to tell Anne de Bourgh's story, I immediately realized that the important events shaping her life began earlier. Everything changed for Anne when Elizabeth Bennet came to Hunsford, so that's where I started with Part One, during the timeline of *Pride and Prejudice*. Part Two covers the gap between the end of that novel and where *The Darcys of Pemberley* picks up. Then Part Three continues on from there.

Since I enjoy writing in first person, I had intended to charge Anne de Bourgh alone with telling her own story (as I did with Georgiana in *Miss Georgiana Darcy of Pemberley*). But the chance to get into Lady Catherine's head and translate her warped perspective onto the page was just too tempting to pass by! So I began alternating chapters between mother and daughter, entertaining myself with how differently the two of them viewed things.

Then I thought about who else qualified as one of the ladies of Rosings Park. That's how Charlotte Collins and Mrs. Jenkinson got into the act. I discovered they each had valuable contributions to make as well. So take careful note of each chapter's heading as you go along. It will identify which of these four *ladies* is telling the next portion of the story. Happy reading!

Shannon Winslow

Prologue

Two things Anne de Bourgh understood from a very early age: first, that she was loved by her father, and second, that she would one day marry Fitzwilliam Darcy.

These unalterable facts served as the sure foundation of her young life. If her mother censured some weakness in her character or deportment, Anne could depend on finding unconditional approval in her other parent. When she might have been tempted to fret for her future prospects, she was reassured that an excellent match had already been made for her. Her continued social consequence and connubial contentment were secure.

"My sister and I arranged it all between ourselves," Lady Catherine frequently told her only child, sometimes varying her exact words but never her conclusion. "And the men mean to make no difficulty about it. When the time comes, you shall marry your cousin. It is not only the cherished wish of your mother and aunt, it is a solemn promise between us, and therefore to be considered a settled engagement. The two great estates will thus be united. There could be no connection more highly desirable on either side, no alliance more perfectly natural."

Anne, being still too young to understand the mysteries of love between a man and a woman, could see no reason to question her mother's decree on the subject, especially since her dear papa concurred when pressed.

"It will be a fine thing for you," he had said with conviction if not enthusiasm. "A very fine thing indeed, my pet."

No evidence to the contrary, Anne believed she should be as happy with her cousin as with any other man. Had he not always been kind to her?

But nothing lasts forever, it seems, not even sure foundations. One pillar of support crumbled when Anne's father suddenly died a month shy of her fourteenth birthday. A few years later, the other – her betrothal to Fitzwilliam Darcy – was cast into serious jeopardy upon the arrival at Rosings of a young woman by the name of Elizabeth Bennet.

PART ONE

Times of Pride and Prejudice

- 1 -

Anne

On Envying Elizabeth

I often wonder what might have happened had Elizabeth Bennet never come to Rosings.

That occurrence is laid to the charge of Mr. Collins; he must have the credit or the blame for it. One does not like to speak ill of the dead, but why Mama should have taken a liking to that odd gentleman, I shall never entirely comprehend. Then as now, it is a enduring mystery to me.

From the beginning, Mr. Collins made it clear by his servile manner that he would always be entirely at my mother's disposal. He made good on his implicit promise too. He was, for his short tenure as rector, Mama's eager lapdog and an ever-willing hand at her card table. His deference to her in all things never failed. I suppose that personal devotion (even more than religious piety) was her chief requirement for the office, and no one before or since has satisfied her half so well.

Looking back, it seems to me that Mr. Collins's installation as rector toppled the first brick, after which all the others fell in an inexorable chain of events that has brought us to this point. He came. Upon Mama's advice, he obligingly married. He brought Charlotte Lucas home to the parsonage as his wife, and she in turn invited her friend (who was also his cousin) to Hunsford.

Then one day, there she was: Elizabeth Bennet in all her glory – arrived at the parsonage, sitting in church on Sundays, and by repeated invitation, within the very walls of Rosings time and again.

There was nothing to give me any alarm at our first meeting, when she came with Mr. and Mrs. Collins, Sir William Lucas, and his daughter – nothing to awaken the slightest feeling of dislike within me, only the mildly envious sensations I often experienced upon being introduced to a person in whom all the extraordinary benefits of good health and good humor reside. Miss Bennet was everything I was not – strong, blooming, self-possessed, and with an exceptional liveliness of mind.

But perhaps I overly demean myself. For I consider that I too possess a very lively mind, although few if any would notice. Most of the feverish activity remains secreted below the surface, as unseen and unheard as a flowing underground stream. Within, I entertain myself by a nearly continuous private dialogue, with stories of unguarded imagination, and sometimes with very cutting but silent remarks.

None of it is allowed to come out into the light. Therefore, no one appreciates the long and clever debates I carry on inside my head. My companions have no suspicion of the fanciful tales to which I make them a party while I sit quietly with my hands folded in my lap. Neither can they perceive the witty comments and the occasional merciless barb I imagine myself dispensing.

Usually these samples of wit come to my mind too late to be of any practical use. Even if they did not, I would be far too timid to speak them aloud. Besides, although Rosings is an extremely large house, there is room for only *one* person to exert the force of her will and opinions. And that person is my mother, Lady Catherine de Bourgh.

Mama was entertained by Elizabeth. *I* did not know what to do with her. So I did nothing. Externally at least, I became more stupid and more insipid than usual in the face of Elizabeth's vivacity. I barely managed to utter a word in her presence that first day, all through dinner and afterward. It was not because I found her objectionable in some way – in truth, I did not – but because of my general lassitude and the fact that nobody quite like Miss Bennet had come my way before.

My silence was not entirely wasted, however; I turned it to a useful purpose. I studied Elizabeth, for she intrigued me, especially how she kept her courage under the heat of Mama's interrogation (for it was little short of that). When we ladies withdrew from the dining table to return to the drawing room, the questions thrown Elizabeth's way commenced in earnest. 'How many sisters have you, Miss Bennet?' 'Are they handsome or plain?' 'Is there any reason to suppose you or your sisters will marry well?' 'What kind of carriage does your father keep?' 'Who are your mother's people? What was her maiden name?' 'Do you play and sing, Miss Bennet?' 'Do you draw?' 'Do your sisters?' And so it went.

Elizabeth could not have failed to feel the impertinence of these probing questions, and yet she answered them composedly, without apology, demure, or much visible resentment. Extraordinary. She was respectful but not overawed by the great Lady Catherine, despite Mama's imposing posture, superior rank, and grand house.

"Has your governess left you?" Mama continued.

"We never had any governess," Elizabeth explained.

"No governess! How was that possible…?"

Ordinary families do it all the time, Mama. They have little choice.

"…Five daughters brought up at home without a governess! I never heard of such a thing. Your mother must have been quite a slave to your education."

Elizabeth smiled. "I assure you, Madam, she was not."

As I silently observed, I tried to picture myself behaving the same in similar circumstances – arriving somewhere I had never been before and calmly answering an imposing stranger of superior rank. *"Yes, Your Grace, that is correct… I assure you, Madam, it is quite possible, for it has been done that way in my family for generations. I am sorry if that fails to meet with your approval…."* Only in my imagination, for in reality, I cowered before my own mother! Thus, I discovered that I must envy Elizabeth's self-confidence as well.

"Are any of your younger sisters out, Miss Bennet?" asked Mama.

"Yes, Ma'am, all."

Oh, dear! That will not sit well with Mama. It just isn't done in 'good' society.

"All! What, all five out at once? Very odd! And you only the second. The younger ones out before the elder are married! Your younger sisters must be very young?"

"Yes, my youngest is not sixteen. Perhaps she is full young to be much in company. But really, Ma'am, I think it would be very hard upon younger sisters that they should not have their share of society and amusement because the elder may not have the means or inclination to marry early. The last born has as good a right to the pleasures of youth as the first. And to be kept back on such a motive! I think it would not be very likely to promote sisterly affection or delicacy of mind."

Hearing this, Mama expostulated on Elizabeth's daring to have an opinion at her young age. And then Elizabeth went on to answer more questions about the Longbourn family. Meanwhile, I made another mental note to this effect. *I must add a point of envy to my growing list. I now must envy Elizabeth having a father alive and a large family of sisters, all of whom she clearly adores.* It was not so much the words she used as the way she expressed herself – the warmth in her voice when she mentioned her father, the crinkles at the corners of her eyes when she spoke of her sisters.

I had never spent a great deal of time bemoaning my lack of siblings, but the truth is I had been lonely for years, ever since Papa died, really. He had been my closest companion and truest friend. He loved me – as most fathers love their children, I suppose – but he went beyond. His attention was not limited to fifteen or twenty minutes every evening as I have heard is typical. He took the trouble of including me in his day-to-day affairs as much as possible.

He made a place for me alongside him in his library, for one thing, with my own more diminutively sized desk. While he dealt with business correspondence or examined the estate finance books, I would pretend to do the same, completing little tasks Papa set me to and signing my name to imaginary contracts. I routinely accompanied him on his periodic tours of the park as he inspected the fields and spoke to the tenant farmers. He often took me along on ventures to the outside world as well, thinking up little games to amuse me along the way.

I can still see him in my mind's eye, robust and merry. Bending down to my level, he would say, "Annie, my dear girl, how would you like to take a drive with me today?"

Barely able to contain my excitement, I would ask, "Where are we going?" It hardly mattered, you understand. We could be going to the bank or the solicitor's offices for all I cared. It was enough that I would be spending the day with him.

"I cannot tell you that," he might answer with mischief in his eye. "It is a surprise. Now, run get your bonnet and kiss your mother, and then we shall be off on an adventure."

Those were happy times.

Papa's invitations to adventure still echo down the halls of Rosings, although more faintly with the passage of the years. My spirit still longs to answer that call, but now my explorations must take place in my imagination, often sparked by what I discover within the pages of books. That realm has been my one true solace, my refuge, my ever-reliable escape from the disappointments and oppressions of life. Only there do I find freedom without bounds. Unlike my body, my mind knows no limits. And books reveal their secrets to anybody who takes the trouble to open them. Man, woman, young, old, strong, or frail: they make no distinctions or judgments. They hold no prejudices. "Come on an adventure with me," they freely beckon, and I am happy to follow.

So I have climbed mountains without my health or sex holding me back. I engaged in high finance, solved mysteries, and faced powerful foes – on the battlefield and in a court of law – all with no anxiety for safety or decorum. I sailed the high seas and visited far-away lands. Paris. Madrid. The Alhambra. The pyramids of Egypt. Bombay. Even the New World. These are places my father mentioned, places he had already been or promised to take me one day.

And since my travels occurred only in my imagination, there was nothing to stop me imagining my father went with me, just as originally planned. In this way, I kept him fresh in my mind, for the idea that I might eventually forget him altogether filled me with dread. How could I successfully pattern myself after my better parent, my wisest and truest friend, the one who loved me most and who well earned my love in return? How was I to be trained by his example if I could no longer remember it?

He was the very best of men – highly principled, and kind to everybody regardless of position or class. I do not believe he ever disappointed or harmed another living creature in his life. In truth, I fairly worshipped the ground he walked on and still do to this day.

My mother has good qualities too, I suppose. I would do well to incorporate some measure of her confidence into my character, for example. There is a certain rigidity about her, however, an unrelenting severity which I do not wish to emulate. It is well to know one's own mind, but I believe firmness must be moderated by reason and charity to prove a true virtue. Papa knew the proper balance between kindness and resolve; I fear my mother does not.

With the loss of my father, light and warmth vanished from my world as surely as if I had been plunged into a place of perpetual winter. A cold cloud settled over Rosings, and darkness reigned unchallenged for months.

For a long while, I knew very little beyond my own sorrow. I should have been thinking of my mother's pain, but I confess I was not. Youths of thirteen and fourteen are extraordinarily selfish creatures in general, I believe, and I was no different. I only knew that Mama offered little comfort to *me*. In any case, it would have been impossible for me to judge my mother's state of mind during that period – whether she sincerely grieved for Papa or not – for she was stoically inscrutable. She never betrayed any trace of emotion, even then.

And so we went on, the two of us in that vast house, now feeling cavernously empty bereft of my father and his ability to fill it with warmth and laughter. We rarely left home anymore, my spirits declined, and then so did my health.

We had few visitors, Mama and I, for it had always been Papa who initiated plans for balls and parties. We occasionally made or received calls from our closer friends. The ancient rector, Mr. Ludington, and his wife dutifully came to pay their respects once a week. A steady procession of medical men arrived, one at a time, to apply their various theories and potions towards improving my health, all without result. Other than these, my only companions were my paid attendant and teacher, Mrs. Jenkinson, and occasionally my cousins.

Yes, my cousins. I could surely count William Darcy, Georgiana, and Colonel John Fitzwilliam among my friends too…

My mental wanderings had arrived at this point when Mama's voice called me back to the present.

"Ah, here are the men at last," she said as they joined us in the drawing room. "Cards next, I think. We have just enough to make up two tables." A wave of her hand was sufficient to send servants scurrying to adjust the furniture arrangement accordingly. "Sir William, Mr. and Mrs. Collins, I must have you with me for quadrille. Anne, you take Mrs. Jenkinson and the two young ladies. What will you play? Name your game."

"Casino, I think," I murmured.

"What did you say?" Mama asked. "For heaven's sake, child, speak up!"

I tried again, a little louder this time. "We will play casino, Mama, if everybody finds that agreeable." It was the longest speech I made the whole night and probably the only complete sentence. With Mama's scolding, however, I was more embarrassed than before.

The others at our table were nearly as taciturn, even Elizabeth. Dear Mrs. Jenkinson was the only one amongst us who ventured any remark much beyond the necessary business of the game, for she was in the habit of inquiring after my welfare, moment by moment. Was I too warm or too cold? Was the light bright enough for me, or did I find it too glaring? Did I desire any alteration in the position of the fire screen?

I could not blame her; it was her assigned duty to do so. And yet I wished I could kindly explain that I was not nearly as fastidious as Mama's potted orchids in the conservatory. Despite all opinions to the contrary, I knew I would not die if the temperature were to waver by a degree or two. I would not wilt away to nothing if briefly exposed to the direct heat of a fire or the unshielded rays of the sun.

Although Mrs. Jenkinson's solicitous chatter relieved the terrible weight of silence at our table, it drew more attention to me and to my accursed weaknesses than I liked. What a relief when Mama decided we were finished with cards! The carriage was sent for, the weather discussed until it arrived, and then finally our guests departed.

I spent much time in contemplation after they had gone, considering our new acquaintances, how they had behaved, and how I had behaved in return. I could not reflect on the latter with any satisfaction. Although not without some excuse, for I really had been dreadfully tired that evening, I had been silent to the point of rudeness. I had in all probability offended Maria Lucas and Elizabeth Bennet. As Mrs. Collins's intimates, they would be recurrent visitors to the parsonage, and so I would no doubt be obliged to see them again and again. They may even have become my valued friends had I behaved better by them.

That night I vowed to make what amends I could, to learn from Elizabeth's example, to acquire (and soon) some courage, fortitude, and social grace, whatever it might cost me. Perhaps then I would be more content within myself and have less cause to envy others.

I did not know it at the time, but before long I would be given yet one more significant reason to envy Elizabeth. It became apparent as soon as two of my cousins arrived.

- 2 -

Lady Catherine

On Eyeing Elizabeth

It matters little what others may say on the subject of Elizabeth Bennet. *I* stand ready to set the record straight. Around one indisputable fact, however, the opinion of every person of sanity must unite. It is that the disaster encompassed in her unfortunate presence among us was entirely Mr. Collins's fault.

To be scrupulously fair, as I always am, I looked at the question from all sides. Was I in any way to blame, I asked myself. After all, Mr. Collins may have brought Elizabeth to Hunsford, but I had brought Mr. Collins. No doubt that is what a shrewd barrister would argue. And yet no one would dare convict me on such grounds, not when my spotless character and irreproachable motives are considered. Christian charity and the principle of *noblesse oblige* govern my actions at all times.

I am no fool; I knew there was nothing exceptional in Mr. Collins to justify my singling him out for such a valuable preferment. He had done nothing to earn my especial favor. If I am not mistaken (and I *never* am), that is the very definition of grace, the stooping down to bestow a gift on the undeserving, the giving of kindness to one who does not merit it. Perhaps that was my crime after all – being more charitable than what was prudent.

And how was I repaid for my goodness? Mr. Collins unwittingly delivered a viper to my bosom, one come from *his* family to destroy *mine*. I say 'unwittingly' because I do not for one minute believe he understood the danger. I did not see it myself in the beginning. The possibility that my own nephew, my dear dead sister's only son, could fail to keep his solemn engagement was the farthest thing from my mind. That Darcy might forsake Anne for a young woman without family, connections, or fortune… Well, it was inconceivable.

So, I welcomed Miss Bennet into my home for the same reason I frequently did the Collinses – in a spirit of kind condescension. I held no illusions that my daughter and I could meet her on any kind of equal footing. Considering she was a relation to Mr. Collins, I expected to find her birth inferior, her manners marginal, and her education suspect. This, by skillful questioning, I soon confirmed. Indeed, the unfortunate tendency of her information went beyond anything I had expected. She actually admitted to her family having kept no governess, despite five daughters being brought up at home. Five!

"Then, who taught you? Who attended you?" I asked, somewhat incredulous at the news. "Without a governess you must have been sadly neglected."

"Compared with some families, I believe we were," Miss Bennet replied. "But such of us as wished to learn, never wanted the means. We were always encouraged to read and had all the masters that were necessary. Those who chose to be idle, certainly might."

This and more she confessed without apology. No doubt I was more ashamed for her than she was for herself, and you may be sure I did not fail in my duty to give her benefit of my opinions on these and other subjects. Had I known her mother when it might have done some good, I should most strenuously have advised her to engage a qualified governess. In fact, I might have been able to go so far as to recommend someone to her. I have lost count as to how many families I have been the means of supplying in that way.

I am always glad to step in where I can be of service, whether it be to settle some dispute within the parish, to see that a young person is well placed out, or by giving wise and timely counsel to keep a weak sort of character on the straight and narrow. There seems to be a general want of gratitude and common sense roundabout, which I make it my business to correct whenever possible. Oftentimes a word from me is enough to restore harmony and contentment.

I believed Miss Bennet had been brought to me for this same reason, that she was yet another one who might benefit from my guidance. Although she expressed her mind too freely and without sufficient deference to her superiors, I put this down to the deficiencies of her upbringing and did not consider her faults beyond remediation. Left in the proper hands, I thought something useful might very well be achieved.

Here again, I allowed my kindness to lead at the expense of what would have been, in hindsight, a justifiable vigilance where the cunning Miss Bennet was concerned. But instead of raising my guard, I was thinking only of being of use to a misguided girl, of allowing the advantages I had in my gift to take their due effect.

Sir William Lucas departed after a week's stay, but I knew he soon would be replaced by a person of real quality. This was yet another benefit I could provide our visitors – exposure to better society than they would ordinarily encounter. They could not help but be impressed by the contrast and edified by such superior examples.

One evening when the diminished party from the parsonage was dining at Rosings again, I decided the time was right for my announcement. Clearing my throat first to be certain I had their attention, I began.

"Miss Bennet, Miss Lucas, I am pleased to say that I will have it in my power to improve your society by the addition to our party of my nephew Mr. Darcy, who will be arriving the week before Easter. I understand from Mr. Collins that you may have met him some once or twice in Hertfordshire, but now you will be seeing him nearly every day. He is a young man whom you cannot help but admire, for he embodies everything that is best about the upper classes." Miss Bennet smiled in such a way that I could not decipher what she meant by it. Nevertheless, I continued my thought. "You would do well to observe and learn from him. I daresay you do not often see a man of his quality in your usual society, confined as it must be. Are not you pleased with this news, Miss Bennet?"

"Oh, yes," she said. "Mr. Darcy is very welcome, I am sure, and I shall be happy enough to see him again. But in truth, Madam, he is well known to me already."

"How can this be?" I asked her with justifiable indignation. Mr. Darcy was *my* nephew, after all, and the right to introduce him should have been mine as well.

"Mr. Collins may be unaware that Mr. Darcy spent a good deal of time in Hertfordshire before his arrival," said Elizabeth. "We were very often seeing Mr. Darcy in Meryton and at assemblies of one kind or another. Were we not, Maria? In fact, I spent several days in the same house with him, at Netherfield, while my sister happened to be convalescing from an illness there. So you see, Lady Catherine, why I say he is well known to me."

There was nothing more to be said on that subject for the moment. However, you may be sure I put the question to Darcy himself when he arrived a week later, bringing Colonel Fitzwilliam, my brother's younger son, with him. Now I would know the truth of the matter.

After welcoming them both in the drawing room, I hastened to ask, "Darcy, what is this I hear of your acquaintance with Miss Elizabeth Bennet? She tells me you are well known to her. Can it be so?"

The change in his appearance was marked and immediate. His face first went white and then grew quite red as I waited for his answer. Clearly, he was not expecting to hear that person's name spoken at Rosings. That must account for his bewilderment.

"Elizabeth?" he asked, all at attention. "Is she here?"

"She is staying with the Collinses at the parsonage," I explained. "But you did not answer my question. What is your level of acquaintance with this young lady?"

When he hesitated, Colonel Fitzwilliam added his urging. "Yes, Darcy, who is this Miss Bennet, and how well do you know her? Do tell us."

"Oh… not well at all," he said finally. "I… I met her in Hertfordshire, Fitzwilliam, while I was visiting Mr. Bingley at Netherfield. The Bennets are one of the principle families of the neighborhood, so naturally we were often thrown into company with them. Still, I would not say I know Miss Elizabeth Bennet particularly well. If she is here in Hunsford, however, it would be right for me to pay my respects to her… and to the Collinses, of course." He rose as if to go at once. "Come Fitzwilliam. When one has a duty to perform, it is best to do it without delay, and you may as well accompany me."

"A duty, is it?" Fitzwilliam remarked. "Are you sure it is not a pleasure? You seem very keen to be at it."

"Stay where you are, both of you," I said firmly. "Tomorrow or the next day will be soon enough to begin paying calls of duty. For now, you must rest from your travels and give your attention to those who have a higher claim to it. Ah, here is Anne."

I had sent for her as soon as the gentlemen arrived. Now, however, I could have wished she had been less prompt answering my summons and taken more time attending to her appearance first. Mrs. Jenkinson would be reprimanded for allowing Anne to come down in such a state – in a very ordinary gown, hair mussed, and spirit not fully composed.

Fortunately, Darcy and Fitzwilliam seemed not to notice anything amiss. They both rose to cordially welcome Anne, each taking her offered hand in turn. Fitzwilliam, I knew, would flatter and make jokes, but I was much more interested to observe Darcy's interactions with my daughter, to watch for some advancement in their courtship. I intended they be given every opportunity for that progress to occur. Indeed, that was my purpose in sending for my nephew. It was high time some definite plan for their wedding was made.

"Darcy, you sit beside Anne," I directed. "Fitzwilliam, I will have you next to me. I am pleased you have come. You must tell me how my brother does, and all your family."

He was in good spirits, and I allowed him to chatter on, following his banter as well as possible while at the same time keeping one eye on the other pair. There was very little of a satisfactory character going forward there, however.

- 3 -

Anne

On Making Oneself Agreeable

Fitzwilliam Darcy, whom I had always known as William, was coming to Rosings. Mama had informed me of this, but not that she had summoned him. She let me believe it was his own idea.

"His attachment to Rosings and to you increases month by month," she told me. "Still, you must do everything in your power to make yourself agreeable when he comes."

My bewilderment as to how that was to be accomplished must have shown, for Mama sighed and went on, slowly, as if speaking to a small child or an imbecile.

"Smile at him. Compliment him on some aspect of his person or character. Show your interest by asking him questions about himself and about Pemberley. Few men are secure enough within themselves to make an offer without encouragement. And although it is a mere formality in this case, we are dependent on his doing so before moving forward with the wedding plans. Do you understand?"

"Yes, Mama," I said.

Make myself agreeable. That was a tall order. I was not unwilling to do so, nor was I disinclined. I liked William very well indeed, and I did wish to marry him, just as was intended from the beginning. Though I had been of a marriageable age for months without his formal proposal having come, I was not particularly worried. I considered it probable that my cousin was unready to give up his bachelor ways quite yet. He knew where to find me when he was. Then I would become his wife and mistress of his estate in Derbyshire.

When we were all children together, I looked forward to my visits to Pemberley with great anticipation. The vast, untamed country of the north, the enormous park, along with the less stuffy tendencies of the Darcys themselves, set a relaxed tone. I could breathe more easily as we left the heavy atmosphere of Rosings farther behind and then the greater distance beyond London we passed. My nerves unwound mile by mile like a tight ball of yarn being released to run across the floor where it would. When gathered together again, it would be remade into something new and beautiful, something fresh and useful. Likewise, I felt recreated each time I traveled north. It was not that I disliked my own home. It was more that Mama did not rule at Pemberley. That was the largest part of the attraction.

Georgiana was like a sister to me. Being a little younger and just as painfully shy as I, she presented no threat. I could be at my ease in her company. We could romp and play with abandon. And we did. While I had my health, we rambled across hill and dale. I even learned to ride and also to drive a donkey cart in those idyllic days at Pemberley.

Georgiana tried to share her interest in music with me on more than one occasion, and I remember her mother gave me a few elementary lessons at the piano-forte when I was very young. Later, I wished that I had taken advantage of the opportunity to learn while Lady Anne was still alive and I still had the ability to apply myself. But there were simply too many other things to do and places to explore at Pemberley for me to settle down to anything so studious. Georgiana did not despise me for my lack of dedication, and Aunt Anne made no scolds that I should be a true proficient if only I would practice. I understood I was among friends who accepted me as the imperfect person I was and still am.

My relations with Georgiana's brother are not quite so simple to characterize. It is a complex thing with which I never entirely came to terms.

With the young Master Darcy being nearly a decade my senior, it is hardly surprising he should have been no playfellow to me when I was a child. He treated me in much the same manner he did Georgiana – benignly indulgent but largely disinterested in a young girl's concerns. My clearest and happiest memories of him during that period come from time spent out of doors. He was often assigned as guardian, guide, and escort to his sister and myself on our rambles throughout the park, whether on foot or on horseback.

He saw we came to no harm, and he did not interfere with our pleasures any more than necessary. Sometimes he even contributed to our enjoyment with little games and other kindnesses.

Looking back, I honor his patience. I can see how irksome such a duty must have been to a boy on the verge of manhood. But he never complained, at least not in my hearing.

He treated me as a sister, and yet sisterly affection does not adequately describe my feelings for *him*, either then or now. Nor does the idea of friendship tell the whole story. The knowledge that he would be my husband one day made a distinct difference from the beginning, and the importance of that fact only increased as I grew older. How could it be otherwise? Even had he been a very ordinary man – plain and utterly undistinguished – I could hardly have banished our future connection from my mind. But this was William Darcy. With his superior height, maturity, and good looks, was he not exactly the type of romantic hero to inspire a young girl's imagination?

From the age of eleven or twelve, my daydreams were filled with proposals and wedding scenes. In these imaginings, William was always perfectly handsome, and I was always graceful and completely at ease, no trace of my perpetual timidity evident. As for how this transformation in me was to have taken place… Well, these were dreams, after all. Logic does not enter in.

I often I pictured myself strolling on William's arm by the lake at Pemberley, he having cleverly maneuvered to leave the others behind so that he could have me to himself. My fanciful daydreams went something like this:

He smiles down at me and presses my hand. I wonder if this could be the moment. But then a pheasant startles from the brush and flies, the noisy distraction breaking the spell.

We laugh and stroll on again in contented silence.

"Such a beautiful day!" I say spontaneously minutes later. "It is pure perfection – the sky, the lake, the grounds. I do not think I can ever remember Pemberley looking finer."

William stops and turns to me, taking both my hands and looking earnestly into my eyes. "Dear Anne," he says, "I must agree with you. Never have I seen more beauty here than I do at this moment. But if you ever leave, the picture will be spoilt. Say you will stay at Pemberley always... with me."

"Why, William, what can you mean?"

"I mean that I love you, hopelessly and passionately. Say you will marry me, my darling. Be my wife, mistress of my estate and of my heart."

"Yes, yes of course I will," I cry, collapsing into his arms, prostrate with joy.

This is the point at which the daydream typically began to fail. William leant down as if to kiss me, but the picture always faded before he could accomplish it. It seemed my youth and naïveté were insurmountable obstacles; even my overactive imagination could not fill in the places left open by my complete lack of experience.

These melodramatic fancies seem foolish to me now, especially in light of all that has happened since. But at the time, I stood in considerable awe of William Darcy. It is an impression I never completely outgrew.

~~*~~

Brushing aside these remembrances, I came down as soon as Mama sent for me, informing me of William's arrival to Rosings. It was an added bonus to discover that my other cousin, Colonel John Fitzwilliam, had accompanied him. John I found less intimidating, and I expected that his presence and jovial manner would ease conversation all the way round. In consequence, perhaps I would be less profoundly reserved and appear more "agreeable" in my intended's eyes, more the competent lady of my imagination. At least I hoped. But Mama, probably thinking she did me a favor, immediately took up conversation with the colonel and left William to my share.

After an awkward, silent minute, during which time I thought of Elizabeth Bennet's example, I bravely ventured an opening comment. "I hope your travel was comfortable, Cousin," I said, immediately wincing for how completely unremarkable my remark sounded. *This* was no very good imitation of Miss Bennet's wit or even the best of my own.

"I thank you, yes," he answered. "We suffered no complication of either weather or equipage. And Fitzwilliam is always excellent company."

"Yes, of course."

A long pause reigned until he presently continued, "May I inquire after your health, Anne?"

I inwardly sighed at the question. Although usually a mere courtesy – the one asked expected to answer, "I am very well, thank you" – for me it was not so easy. I was *not* very well, in general or at that specific moment either. But I preferred not being reminded of that fact… and reminded that everybody else remembered my sickly constitution too. Still, I knew the question had been kindly meant.

"I am well enough, I suppose," I said and thanked him.

He nodded and offered nothing more. Neither could I think of anything to say. William turned his attention to Mama and Cousin John, listening – or at least pretending to listen – to what was passing between them. *They* were not sitting in silence. Neither of them struggled for words.

Once again, I had failed. If I could not hold William's interest for five minutes, how did I propose to keep it through long years of marriage?

Mama must have had marriage and proposals in view as well, for she wasted no time making sure to arrange conditions amenable to that very thing taking place. "Fitzwilliam, come with me," she said before a quarter of an hour had elapsed since my arrival downstairs. "I have something very particular to show you in the conservatory."

He rose, and I began to as well, saying, "We will come with you, Mama." A cold hand of fear had clutched my throat as soon as I realized what she had in mind. I was afraid it was all too obvious to William, but mostly I was afraid of the long, awful silence that would most probably ensue once we were alone together.

"Stay where you are, Anne," she ordered at once. "This business concerns no one but Fitzwilliam. I wish you to remain and keep your cousin Darcy company. No doubt he has things to say to you that could benefit from a degree of privacy." Then she and John quit the room, he giving us a backward sympathetic glance on his way out. Or perhaps John's sympathy was meant only for his friend's unenviable position.

If someone with a pallid complexion is capable of going red in the face, no doubt I did, for my cheeks were burning. I was humiliated, and it seemed the only way to rescue myself – and my cousin too – from the mutually mortifying situation would be by my speaking first, though it ran contrary to my every natural impulse. I felt far more like retreating to the safety of my own apartment than standing my ground. But I was quite sure Elizabeth Bennet would never be so cowardly.

Gathering my courage, I said abruptly, "I am sorry, William. Mama should never have placed you in such an untenable position. Please be aware that I had nothing to do with this." It seemed somehow insufficient, so I went on, hardly knowing what I was saying. "And furthermore, you should know that I neither want nor expect anything from you."

His head tipped to one side, he looked at me quizzically for a long moment. Then his expression softened to understanding. "Ah," he said, nodding. "Yes, of course. I see how it is. I see now that you are as much a victim of my aunt's misplaced ambitions as I am." Here he rested a hand over my own, saying, "Be not alarmed, Anne. Despite what your mother has decreed, you shall have nothing to fear from me, I promise you."

That is when I realized the truth. Fitzwilliam Darcy would never propose marriage to me… and it was at least in part my own fault.

- 4 -

Lady Catherine

On Doing One's Duty

I kept myself and Colonel Fitzwilliam away from the drawing room for a considerable length of time – long enough that I fully expected matters to be favorably settled at last. Therefore, I was seriously displeased to discover no sign of progress upon our return. Anne sat alone and silent where I had left her, and Darcy, also silent, stood across the room gazing out of the window. I wondered if Anne had even listened when I told her what to do. And what of my nephew? Was he so dense that he failed to understand my pointed hints?

The matter should rightly have been completed months before. This hesitation was something I could not fathom. It certainly would not have been tolerated in *my* day!

My father, without my knowledge or consent, arranged what was thought to be a highly suitable match for me. I was told of my 'good fortune' only after all had been decided. When the senior Mr. de Bourgh informed his son of the news, he did what was expected of him. He came to call on me; the question was asked and answered; and we were married within three months.

I had seen him exactly five times before the wedding: first at a dance during the London season, then on his two brief courtship calls, at our engagement party, and once more a week later. And I had never seen his house. Yet I knew enough to do my duty, for better or for worse.

Darcy and my daughter had been dealt with far more generously. They had known whom they were to marry since early childhood. They had been allowed to become well acquainted with one another, and she with her future home. Anne was even to remain within the comfort of her own extended family circle. Nothing could have been more agreeable than these arrangements. And yet the two of them behaved almost as if they were strangers.

Well, if they did not know how to do their duty after all this time, they must be *made* to know it.

~~*~~

Mr. Collins called early the next morning, so early that he had to wait whilst we finished our breakfast. Then we joined him in the drawing room – Anne, myself, and our two houseguests.

"Mr. Collins," I said, "what can you mean by coming at this unseemly hour? Most people have better things to do at this time of day than bothering their neighbors."

"A thousand pardons, your ladyship!" he said, bowing low. "If my early visit is inconvenient to you, I am mortified indeed. But as for myself, I consider that I never have anything better to do than to be of service to others. I could not help but notice yesterday the arrival of your noble guests," here, nodding to Darcy and Fitzwilliam, "and I felt it my highest duty to pay my respects as soon as possible. I am but a humble parson…"

"Yes, yes, Mr. Collins, that will do," I said, cutting his speech short. "Now you are here, I suppose we might as well all sit down so you can accomplish what you came for."

At least Mr. Collins was properly impressed with the quality of the gentlemen before him, one whom he had previously met and the other whom he had not. The rest of his remarks are not worth repeating; they were such as what anybody who knows the man might expect him to say. I must give Mr. Collins his due, however. Though he has his faults, he certainly understands the importance of preserving the distinctions of rank. That is something of value… and something increasingly rare, it seems, in this rebellious age.

Again to his credit, Mr. Collins did not exceed his time. After twenty minutes, he saw his opening in the conversation and announced, "Unless I can be of any use to you by staying, your ladyship, I will take my leave now before I overstay my welcome."

"You may go, Mr. Collins," I answered. "I shall send for you and those of your household when you are wanted again. However, I think it most likely we shall be very much occupied amongst ourselves, keeping to a family party for a few days at least. You understand."

"Yes, of course," he said, beginning to back his way toward the door. "It is only natural and right that the larger share of your gracious hospitality be reserved for those within the bonds of blood. Family ties strained by long separation must be tended and mended on such occasions as may present themselves. There can be no higher priority than preserving good family relations, as I have often heard you say. Your ladyship always judges exactly what is wisest and best."

I gave him a nod to acknowledge this piece of civility and waited for him to be gone. But to my surprise and consternation, he was not the only one to go. Darcy stood also.

"Since you are so eager to be of use, Mr. Collins," he said. "Perhaps you will be so good as to show me the way to the parsonage. I wish to follow your example by paying my calls promptly also."

"You are *most* welcome, Mr. Darcy," Mr. Collins said, bowing and looking very pleased with himself. "I should be gratified indeed to have my humble abode honored by your distinguished presence. I daresay the ladies will be equally delighted."

"Thank you," said Darcy. "Let us be off, then. Are you coming, Fitzwilliam?"

"I would not miss it for the world," he said cheerfully and rose to go. "Please excuse us, Aunt."

And just like that, they were gone, leaving us alone again. Matters were not proceeding at all as I had hoped. First yesterday's failure, and now this premature desertion in favor of the parsonage! I would need to keep a closer rein on the young men, I decided, lest they began to think they could do exactly as they pleased.

Clearly, they still had much to learn. Fitzwilliam was the more tractable of the two, I perceived. Darcy had been without parental supervision too long. He had grown used to being his own man, with no one to answer to but himself. He *would* have to answer to his conscience, however; that is the one guardian we, none of us, ever outgrow. With a little prompting from me, it would speak to him loudly enough of duty and honor. That plus the other inducements…

I looked at Anne with an appraising eye, trying to put aside a mother's prejudice to achieve a more accurate picture. In point of true beauty, she was not deficient – far superior to most, in fact. I thought it a pity that Anne's features were more delicate than my own, her frame more diminutive – the unfortunate de Bourgh influence – but I understood that many men actually preferred a daintier appearance in a wife. So this presented no barrier. Her want of complexion was nothing; it would naturally mend when her health improved. The unmistakable mark of good breeding was upon her; that was the most important thing, that and a handsome fortune. She could be perfectly amiable, too, when she chose to exert herself.

"You must try more diligently, Anne," I told her when I had concluded my silent evaluation.

"What do you mean, Mama?" she asked.

I thought it perfectly obvious, but I patiently explained. "What I said before about making yourself agreeable. You must apply a more concerted effort. You saw how the gentlemen could not wait to be gone! Do you suppose there is really anything at the parsonage to tempt them? No, it was but an excuse for a change. They are young. They want constant novelty and entertainment. You must give it to them, or they will go elsewhere."

"But Mama," she complained, "you know that I cannot play and barely sing!"

"Lively conversation will do, and yet you keep silent."

"I cannot help that I am shy, especially with men."

"Now, Anne, you are perfectly capable of talking and acting as sensibly as any other girl. These are not strangers, after all; these are your cousins, whom you have been in the habit of seeing all of your life. You only want a little more exertion. I will do what I can to assist, but you must play your part. You must give the gentlemen a reason to stay and your cousin Darcy a reason to propose. You do your duty and he will do his."

I expected this encouragement would have the proper effect on my daughter. I was prepared to take Darcy aside and give him a similar exhortation if it proved necessary. How often I have observed that when a thing wants doing properly, I must take it in hand myself.

- 5 -

Charlotte Collins

Receiving Visitors at the Parsonage

I took some small satisfaction in preventing my husband from running off to Rosings the moment he saw the expected visitors arrive. But I could not make him listen to reason the following morning when I diplomatically suggested it was far too early in the day for a call to be considered polite.

"Nonsense," he said. "When the compliment of a call is required, it cannot be paid too soon. Indeed, were I to delay another moment, it would be an insult to my esteemed patroness and to her honored guests. I am very far from fearing I will be turned away. I flatter myself that I am on such a footing at Rosings that I shall be very welcome. Her ladyship is always 'at home' to me."

A wife owes it to her husband to do what she can to elevate him, so that his prospects are better for having her at his side. I believe in the sagacity of this universal truth. Consequently, since my coming to Hunsford, it had been my chief aim to direct, by subtle means, sounder judgment and more sensible behavior in the man I had married. I was not always successful, however.

What occurred when Mr. Collins arrived at the great house, I do not know in full. He never seemed conscious of having blundered in any way. And he could not have offended very greatly, I suppose, since when Mr. Collins returned to the parsonage he was accompanied by Mr. Darcy and his cousin Colonel Fitzwilliam. Mr. Collins took this triumph as a compliment to himself, I believe, but I gave the credit for it entirely to Elizabeth. No doubt *she* was the one the gentlemen were eager to see.

When I espied all three of them from the window, crossing the road in our direction, I informed her and Maria what an honor was in store for us.

"I may thank you, Eliza, for this act of civility," I concluded. "Mr. Darcy would never have come so soon to wait upon me."

"You are mistaken, Charlotte," she said. But that was all she had time for before the gentlemen entered to pay their compliments.

Since a suspicion of Mr. Darcy's being partial to my pretty friend had already been awakened within me, I was on alert for any confirming signs. He barely spoke, however, to Lizzy or to anybody else. He sat composedly but silently, allowing Colonel Fitzwilliam to bear the weight of the conversation. The only sign that I might not have been entirely wrong was that I noticed Mr. Darcy's gaze, if little discourse, was very often directed at Elizabeth.

Meanwhile, Elizabeth largely ignored him for the more amiable company of the colonel, whose manners one could not help but admire.

At length, however, Mr. Darcy's courtesy was so far awakened as to enquire of Elizabeth after the health of her family. She answered him in the usual way, and after a moment's pause, added, "My eldest sister has been in town these three months. Have you never happened to see her there?"

Understanding Elizabeth and her ways so well as I did, I knew there was more to her question than what the words themselves revealed. She was testing Mr. Darcy to see what he would say. She was tormenting him with the trouble of constructing an answer. She meant to tease him. She meant to place an irritating pebble in his shoe. My guess was that she wanted to remind him of Jane and his presumed interference there, for Lizzy had always believed Mr. Darcy responsible for removing Mr. Bingley from her sister's side.

I believe Lizzy's question hit home; Mr. Darcy looked taken aback and his answer was not very articulate.

"I.. I cannot recall. That is, I cannot recall that I did see Miss Bennet. Well, in fact, no… No, I was not so fortunate as to have the pleasure of meeting with your sister in London. But then, that is hardly surprising, is it? There are so very many people, and one tends to only come across those who move in one's own circle."

"Quite so, Mr. Darcy," Lizzy answered with a satisfied smile, as if she had made her point. "That is exactly what I thought you would say."

Their eyes held for another moment or two, and I had the impression that Mr. Darcy was deciding whether or not to say anything more. In the end, he only walked off to the window in silence.

The gentlemen soon went away, but we would see them several times more while they remained at Rosings. I was interested to observe what, if anything, would develop. There was very little intrigue in my own life, but I had high hopes for finding more in Elizabeth's.

- 6 -

Anne

On Being Eclipsed

I kept my suspicions to myself. It would only have upset Mama unnecessarily to hear that I believed William would never propose marriage to me, regardless how agreeable I made myself henceforth. I was even less inclined to tell her I had the blame for it by inadvertently convincing him that I did not desire his attentions.

No doubt I should have corrected this misapprehension as soon as I realized what I had done. After it occurred to me what he meant by promising I had nothing to fear from him, ever, I should have instantly responded with something like this. "*Oh, no, sir. You mistake my meaning. I would not find your attentions the least bit unpleasant. In fact, I should be very glad of them. I only desired that you should not feel obligated to bow to Mama's machinations.*"

I doubt it would have made any difference even had I done so that day. Elizabeth Bennet was already come into the neighborhood. That was the material point. That was the thing that must have changed to produce a different outcome. Although William had become acquainted with Miss Bennet in Hertfordshire, it might have come to nothing if she had not been thrown in his way again… thanks to Mr. Collins.

In that case, would William have done what Mama proclaimed to be his duty and married me instead? Would he even now be my husband, and should we be tolerably happy together? I shall never know, for Elizabeth *did* come to Hunsford parsonage, and thither also went William as surely as a moth drawn to a flame.

What exactly transpired during that visit, I know not. At the time, I had no reason to suppose William's hurry to call at the parsonage had anything to do with Elizabeth. I had got used to hearing Mama's interpretations of events and too often accepting them. It seemed perfectly reasonable to me, therefore, that, just as she suggested, the men had been bored by my silence and left because they desired a change – any change, even if it were only the modest society a humble parsonage could provide.

In any case, I did exert myself when they returned. Mama was off tending to some conflict among the servants, so I had little choice. "Had you a pleasant visit to the parsonage," I asked them when they joined me in the drawing room again. "How did you find the Collinses?"

"The Collinses are well," said William, looking dissatisfied, "and our visit was tolerable, I suppose."

"Tolerable, indeed! Darcy, you astonish me," cried my cousin John. "I have not been so well entertained in an age. Your Miss Bennet is delightful!"

"She certainly is not *my* Miss Bennet, Fitzwilliam," came the peevish response, "and I will not have you referring to her as such. It is a gross impertinence."

"I only meant that you knew her first, old friend, but I am happy to hear you make no proprietary claims. I would hate to come to blows with you, and yet I could never concede to giving up the pleasure of Miss Bennet's conversation. And what eyes! They fairly sparkle. Surely you noticed, Darcy, or you would have done if you had made some effort to speak to her yourself. I shall never understand why you are so grave and taciturn when we come into Kent. But Anne," he continued, turning to me. "You must tell us your own opinion of the lady. You know her somewhat better than I do."

"Oh… well… I cannot really say. As yet, we are not well enough acquainted."

"Come now," he coaxed. "You must have formed some impression. Tell us what you think."

"Yes, do," added my other companion.

They were both looking at me now, as if they were genuinely interested in what I might say on the subject. After hearing her so lavishly praised, I admit that I felt a sudden inclination to disparage Miss Bennet. "*She may have beautiful eyes and good conversation, but she has no fortune to speak of and some very low connections. Her education has been sadly neglected as well. Do you know, she actually admitted to never having had a governess, though she comes from a family of five daughters. Have you ever heard of such a thing?"*

Were such uncharitable thoughts proof of Mama's influence asserting itself? Or perhaps the answer was something equally sinister but less complicated: simple jealousy.

Holding my tongue came easily enough to me, and on this occasion at least, it was for the best. Saying anything of the kind would only have made me appear mean-spirited. So, after a pause to consider a better response, I gave my honest opinion instead. "She is a very pretty creature, and I admire her liveliness of manner. Would that I had a portion of her self-possession."

"There," said John with satisfaction. "I knew we should have an insightful assessment from you, Anne. You may be quiet, my dear, but I daresay you are the more observant for it."

Based on the evidence of this one conversation, if I had suspected either of my cousins of forming a design on Miss Bennet, I would have suspected the wrong one. This early impression, however, seemed further justified by the fact that John called at the parsonage more than once in the week that followed while William stayed away. I was curious to see where it would all lead. Toward that end, I awaited the chance to observe John and Elizabeth together in the same room.

At last the opportunity to gather more direct information came. Mama, upon leaving church Easter Day, invited the Collinses and their guests to come to Rosings later to form a small evening party. When they arrived, Mama directed where everybody should sit, and in so doing, who was meant to talk to whom. With nine of us in all, it was more practical to separate into smaller groups than to attempt maintaining one conversation. Mama claimed William for herself and for me. John took up with Elizabeth directly. The other four – Mr. and Mrs. Collins, Miss Lucas, and Mrs. Jenkinson – were left to themselves.

In our threesome, Mama talked with little intermission, William and I speaking only when asked some question requiring a response. Every minute, however, my attention was drawn across to the other side of the room, where Elizabeth and John were entertaining one another in so spirited a manner that it could not be ignored. I was hardly the only one to have noticed either. William's eye repeatedly turned that way, I observed, and finally so did Mama's.

"What is that you are saying, Fitzwilliam? What are you telling Miss Bennet?" she demanded.

"We are speaking of music, Madam," he answered.

This solicited from my mother a long speech on the subject, ending in a query as to how Georgiana was getting on.

"She was very well when I left her, and her playing improves apace," her brother said. "I never grow tired of hearing her and often tell her so. She is very modest of her own talents, though, and will not believe me."

I thought it a fine sentiment that needed no supplementation. Mama, however, would add her unnecessary advice that Georgiana should practice daily. Then she found a cautionary illustration conveniently close to hand. She said, "I have told Miss Bennet several times that she will not play really well unless she practices more."

Mama may as well have pointed at Elizabeth and said, *"Look. Here is a sad example of the sorry state to which a person who does not heed my counsel is doomed to descend. Make very sure such a pitiful end does not befall you!"*

It was all the more remarkable, then, that after such an insult Elizabeth consented to play for us later that evening. Having come about by Fitzwilliam's particular request, he settled in a chair beside her. But then my other cousin broke from our group to position himself for a better view of the performer as well. Or perhaps it was only to separate himself a little from Mama after her rudeness. In any case, the three of them were soon carrying on together, Elizabeth's music punctuated by pauses for conversation.

From my location, I heard no more than an occasional word. I could see quite well enough, however: an arch look from Elizabeth, some explanation from one of my cousins, a laugh in return, a comment to the other, a smile exchanged between two or all three. The gentlemen were clearly enthralled.

I was suddenly very weary. "Mama," I whispered weakly, "I have a headache. May I retire? I shall not be much missed, as you can see."

My headache was not the primary problem, of course. It was a renewed attack of envy brought on by the sight of Miss Bennet doing what I could never hope to: captivating not one man but two at the same time. It was being forced to watch as I was thoroughly eclipsed by another in the eyes of the man who was supposed to have become my husband. How effortlessly Elizabeth had managed it too!

Although I had asked to withdraw – a request that my mother flatly refused – that would not have been my *first* choice, to be honest, just the most practical solution. If all things were somehow possible, I would have wished for the strength and confidence to join the group round the piano-forte instead, to be part of their talk and laughter. Possibly even to flirt a little as I had seen others do, for it looked very much to me like that was part of what was going forward in the next room.

I knew exactly what I would say, too.

I would walk right up to them, as bold as you please. Shaking my head, I would give my cousins a look of mock disapprobation and tell them, "I have come to stand beside my friend in her time of need, for it seemed to me as if the two of you were teasing her without mercy. I think you will behave better, now I am here and our numbers are equal. Elizabeth, how can I be of service? We ladies must look out for one another's welfare, to face down every attempt by men to intimidate us. Is not that so?"

I would laugh playfully. Elizabeth would smile and join me, our friendship forever secured. The gentlemen would be left quite speechless, amazed (and impressed) that timid little Anne had the temerity to behave in such a way. Perhaps I would then ask Elizabeth to play something I could sing to, so that I might contribute to the evening's entertainment and receive my share of the company's admiration.

But of course, I did none of these things. Instead, it was Mama who interposed herself. She walked in, listened to Miss Bennet play for a few minutes, and then began speaking to William. Her voice raised to be heard above the music, she reminded him, "Miss Bennet would not play at all amiss if only she would practice more…"

I averted my eyes from the scene to find Mrs. Jenkinson looking at me. She was a very keen observer. I wondered how much she could guess of what I was thinking and feeling at that moment. We could not speak of such things, but I always had the impression she understood me very well indeed.

- 7 -

Mrs. Jenkinson

Making Keen Observations

Poor Miss de Bourgh. What agonies she suffered that night, and there was very little I could do to assist her, much as I had wished to. I could not even openly sympathize with her lot, for that was not my place. But I made (and would continue to make) every possible effort for her comfort, everything up to the point of siding with her against her mother. Not that Anne would ever ask it of me. She knew I could ill afford to lose my position, and Lady Catherine, not her daughter, paid my salary.

So we communicated in a circumspect mode, Anne and I. We chose our words judiciously. We commiserated without speaking plainly, each careful not to involve the other in a culpable disloyalty.

"You are tired," I said to Anne as I escorted her upstairs that evening. With the visitors from the parsonage gone and the young men adjourned to the smoking room, Lady Catherine had dismissed us for the night as well.

"Yes," Anne answered without elaboration.

"You are not strong, and having so many people about can be taxing. Do not you find it so?"

"It can be, especially when there is much excitement and noise. But Mama is very fond of company, and she is determined to provide some lively society for my cousins while they are at Rosings."

"I daresay it is very good of her to do so. Do you think the gentlemen were well entertained tonight?"

"They seemed to be enjoying themselves, especially Colonel Fitzwilliam."

"Yes, indeed. I think Miss Bennet knows how to be quite amusing. And although she does not play so very well, it is always pleasant to have music in the house."

"Mrs. Jenkinson," Anne said with concern, "I hope you do not mind too much that Mama invited Miss Bennet to practice on your piano-forte whenever she pleases. I am sorry she should have done so without asking you first."

This was as close to an actual criticism of her mother that Anne ever made to me. "How could I mind?" I said, even though I had in fact felt a twinge of resentment at the time. I thought Anne perceptive to have noticed. "I am beholding to your mother for every good thing. Even my pianoforte is here only by her kindness. Besides, Miss Bennet does not seem disposed to make use of the offer. Perhaps we will not see so very much of her during her stay after all."

That is what I hoped, for I believed it was not only Colonel Fitzwilliam whose interest had been stirred up by Miss Bennet. I worried for my young mistress – that perhaps her unofficial engagement to the handsome Mr. Darcy (of which Lady Catherine spoke so sanguinely) might be in considerable jeopardy.

Although the gentleman was kind to Anne, I certainly had not ever noticed in him any symptoms of peculiar regard for her, any indications of a progressing courtship between them. His countenance did not glow when looking at her. His eyes did not light up when she entered the room. No, I had begun to think that any such positive signs of love existed entirely in Lady Catherine's mind.

It was only that night, in the presence of Miss Elizabeth Bennet, that Mr. Darcy seemed roused from his indifference. There was nothing overt in his speech or actions, but I noticed he watched her very narrowly. And in the end, he could not allow his friend to monopolize the lady's time. He must have his share, though he had seemed to resolutely resist until then. I put it down to some inner turmoil, perhaps the struggle between will and inclination, between head and heart. No doubt one told him he must marry his cousin while perhaps the other led him in another direction?

I could waste no sympathy on Mr. Darcy's struggles, whatever they may have been; he had to look out for himself. My concern was only for Anne, that she not be passed over and left behind. I could not tell for certain if she was aware of the danger or not. In either case, I knew it was doubtful there would be anything I could do to save her. My ambiguous position in the household gave me little influence. Although I was set a step above a common servant, I could never be fully family either. My opinions carried no weight. My concerns were not considered. Indeed, it would be more accurate to say that my opinions and concerns were never heard. I had to keep them to myself. And yet I could not help feeling them. One does not live a long time within the bosom of a family without beginning to care what happens to them.

I had been with the de Bourghs for several years by then, ever since the governess left them. I was not employed to be a replacement for her, nor did any other title neatly define what I did. I was part paid companion, part teacher, part nurse, part waiting lady, and, I flattered myself, part friend to Anne de Bourgh. I saw to her food and encouraged her to eat more than the bird-like portions she would otherwise have taken. I administered whatever physic and health regiment the latest medical man prescribed to cure her longstanding illness. I accompanied her on every outing, making arrangements, taking charge of coats and parcels, protecting Miss de Bourgh from weather and every other danger.

My tasks did not seem odious, as one might expect they would to a lady of some refinement who had once been mistress of her own household. When my husband died and I was left with almost nothing, I considered myself fortunate indeed to find a respectable way of keeping body and soul together. Anne was a sweet girl and undemanding, and I was happy to be of service to her. Although it is an undeniable blow to one's pride to lose one's independence, to be required to always bow to the authority of another, this is a situation most women must come to accept in some form or another. The change for me was not very shocking. Before, I had a husband telling me what to do; now, I had Lady Catherine de Bourgh.

Lady Catherine was not an especially cruel taskmaster, as husbands or employers go. In many ways, she was quite generous to me. She provided me an extremely comfortable apartment when I came, allowing me to bring many of my own things (including my beloved piano-forte), to make me feel at home. She was comparatively liberal with my compensation as well. With the preponderance of daily expenses eliminated by my residing at Rosings, I was able to save nearly all my pay for a rainy day… or for when I was no longer needed in my current position. If it meant that Anne had recovered her health and was happily disposed in marriage, I should be glad to find myself unemployed in the end.

I prayed for that day's arrival. Until then, I intended to stand faithfully at my post, doing what I was called upon to do in service of my young mistress, and ready to go beyond my prescribed duties if and when an emergency arose.

- 8 -

Anne

On Being Well Out of It

I went to bed that night with every intention of having a good cry, of exasperating myself as much as possible over my lot and what I had lost. Although I was not yet convinced of William's being in love with Miss Bennet, after seeing him (and John, too) so amused by another, one so different from myself, I was more convinced than ever of his never being able to love me enough for us to marry.

Despite my determined resolution, however, I produced very few tears that night, hardly enough to dampen my pillow. And of those I did shed, even fewer were over William himself.

It was true that I liked my cousin well enough; I had entertained naïvely romantic fantasies about him in my youth; I respected him as a man; and I would have been confident entrusting my future to him. But upon serious reflection, I knew I was not truly in love with him. Perhaps we might have learnt to be happy together had we wed, and yet I did not desire that either of us should be forced to marry against our inclinations. Even *I* had too much pride for that. If a man proposed to me, I wanted it to be of his own free will. If I accepted him, it should be on the same terms. Anything else would be a humiliation.

Once I became accustomed to the idea, a portion of my mind felt almost relieved to know I was released from my peculiar engagement, at least so far as any obligation to William was concerned. Mama was another matter. She would never give up. The only sanctioned release from her expectations that I could possibly envision would be if another gentleman with claims superior even to William's were to come along. A duke perhaps? Mama might accept that. Mr. Collins was always spouting some flattering nonsense about how I seemed born to be a duchess. So that would please him as well, to have his prediction fulfilled.

The idea diverted me, and so I let my mind wander further down that path.

Where I was likely to fall into company with an unclaimed duke, I could not say. As for how I might secure him, though... Well, at least there I had no difficulty. It often happened that an ancient and noble family became impoverished over time, requiring a fresh infusion of funds to remain solvent. The titled gentleman's solution was simple: marry an heiress. My other attractions were perhaps few, but my inheritance would be far from trifling.

With a little thought, it was easy enough to envision how it might come to pass.

A gentleman in significant distress of circumstances peruses a list of suitable candidates his solicitous mother or aunt has compiled for his consideration.

"...No, no, I will certainly not have Miss Eversleigh," he says. "With her long face, I should be afraid of our children all looking like they came from the stables."

His elderly female advisor shakes her head. "Tut-tut. You exaggerate, sir, and you should consider that beggars cannot be too choosy."

"I am hardly a beggar! I have a very fine estate and a very distinguished title to offer. All I ask in return is a reasonably attractive lady with the money to afford them. Now, what about this Miss de Bourgh? She seems by your account to be rich enough."

"Oh, yes! She is the sole heir to all Rosings Park and considerable other assets besides – a London house in Bellgrave Square, an excellent stock portfolio, and a deal of money in the funds. Very eligible, I should say!"

"But what about the rest? Is she at least tolerably handsome and able to construct coherent sentences?"

"She is not a great beauty, it is true, but neither is she unpleasant to look at, for I have once seen her myself. I cannot testify anything as to her conversation, however." A pause yawns, after which the lady resumes with less confidence. "There is one more thing to consider. Observe my final notation, just there," she says, pointing to the list of her own creation. "It seems Miss de Bourgh

has a somewhat sickly constitution. Could you bear that, your grace? It might be seen as a disadvantage... or as an advantage, although it may be indelicate to allude to such a thing."

"Indelicate, but true. Once we are married, her fortune becomes my own. What transpires after that..."

"Yes, I see that you take my meaning. Well then, shall we keep Miss de Bourgh on the list?"

"By all means."

Enough! Such a fate was too horrible to ponder. Sometimes my active imagination did me no favors.

Given the choice between this lamentable scenario and the original plan, I would have preferred marrying my cousin after all. At least there I would know he did not only covet my money, having plenty of his own. At least there I could be sure he held me in some genuine affection and, presumably, was not wishing for my early death.

But if these were my only alternatives, it seemed best that I should never marry at all. I considered the picture this raised in my mind for a minute. I did not need a husband to be content; I was quite certain of that. I had interests and inner resources enough to keep me happily occupied for years, and my large fortune kept the possibility of remaining single from being something to fear. If only my health improved, I could live and move about in society, completely respectable and doing just as I pleased. I would spend part of my time in London and part at Rosings. And I would by all means travel – to every corner of England that interested me, to the continent, and perhaps even beyond Europe. With my father's cherished memory in mind, I would pursue all those exotic places I had read about. In my father's honor, I would travel to Italy, Israel, and India. I would go wherever my fancy took me. I could afford it.

My situation was not so dreadful after all, I concluded. It was certainly nothing to sob myself to sleep over! But the tears did come eventually. They came when I remembered one more thing. If I did not marry, I would remain under Mama's thumb as long as she lived... and I had heard her say more than once that she intended to live forever.

~~*~~

I watched with a sort of detached fascination to see how events would unfold. While my cousins remained, visits between Rosings and the parsonage house occurred nearly every day in some form or another. One or both of the gentlemen would venture out of doors 'for some exercise,' and inevitably it would come out later that they had taken in the parsonage on their tours. Sometimes Mama and I would visit briefly as well, or the others were invited to Rosings instead, giving more opportunity for me to observe how matters were progressing.

All this careful observation led to very few firm conclusions, however, my opinion frequently vacillating as to how it would end. At first I was convinced John would marry Miss Bennet. Without question, she seemed to like him best of the two, and their conversations were always light-hearted and cordial. But then I wondered if there could be any true passion between them, or if the match could even be eligible from a pecuniary standpoint. My guess was that Cousin John could ill afford to marry without some attention to money, and I doubted very much that Miss Bennet could have enough to satisfy his needs.

William had no worries of that kind. Still, I did not understand his behavior at all. He certainly looked at Elizabeth a great deal, but the meaning of his look was impossible to decipher. It was an earnest, steadfast gaze, although whether it derived more from admiration, disapproval, or simple absence of mind, I could by no means be certain. He spoke to her so little that it was difficult to believe he wished to solicit her good opinion. He frequently sat beside her for more than a quarter of an hour without opening his lips. When he did speak, it seemed to be more of a sacrifice of necessity rather than as a pleasure to himself. No doubt Elizabeth was just as puzzled by William's behavior as I. Sometimes, in fact, it seemed to me as if Elizabeth asked him a question just to vex him, requiring of him the inconvenience of forming an answer.

And yet on rare occasions, I caught a glimpse of something like a quickening in William's expression when Elizabeth happened to turn his way, something that to me spoke of longing. It was as if in that moment the sun had broken from the clouds, and he found the thought of its never smiling on him again unbearable.

I admit to feeling a pang whenever this occurred, not so much from regret that William would never look at me the same way as for my being thoroughly convinced that *no* man was likely to ever experience that kind of anguish on my account. Was it morally wrong that I should feel thus, that a part of me should want another human being to suffer over me? The obvious answer was yes, but I could clearly see the other point of view as well… which always made for a more spirited debate.

One side proclaims, "It must indicate a serious flaw in character for anybody to desire an innocent human being to suffer torment!" The other argues back just as zealously that perhaps the person in question is not so innocent. "Perhaps it is only God's way of teaching the guilty a lesson about the like pain he had previously inflicted on another." Upon further reflection, I rule that the true motivation is actually the universal desire to be deeply loved by another human being, not a desire to inflict suffering, and therefore I am acquitted of guilt.

I should only desire the sting to last a moment, after all, that the situation would be such that I could quickly relieve the suffering soul with the assurance of his love being returned. The initial grief could thereby be said to have served a beneficial purpose, heightening the following joy by contrast.

Having successfully worked this out in my head, I applied it to the case before me. Would William's current anguish quickly turn to joy when Miss Bennet accepted him? If asked, surely she could not refuse Fitzwilliam Darcy. Even if Elizabeth had no great affection for the man, who could reject such an exceptional offer? Oh, how dreadful for William if she did, or worse yet, if my two cousins should come to blows over love of her! But perhaps I had misinterpreted the signs completely.

The only thing I could say for certain at the time was that I stood to be vastly enlightened by observing this drama close at hand. Although on the surface, the dance proceeded as calmly and politely as anybody could wish, I believed that, underneath, dangerous currents pulled emotions to and fro. I could see the potential for disaster everywhere, and I did worry for my friends.

As for me, I considered myself well out of it. None of this could touch me deeply. Once I resigned all claims to my cousin, I no longer feared any personal ramifications at the outcome of these events. With no expectations, I escaped being disappointed and also the worry of being seen as a disappointment myself. With nothing at stake, I could not be injured. I was entirely safe.

Consequently, I grew considerably more at ease – with myself and with the others as well. With this deliberate alteration in my thinking, I finally felt able to take Mama's advice about making myself agreeable to my cousin William. I knew it would not produce the results *she* desired, but I did not do it for her; I did it for myself. I decided it would be good practice for me. Besides, I truly was interested in William and his concerns.

"Tell me, William, what is new at Pemberley since last I was there?" I asked him the next time we were seated side by side. "Have you any improvements underway?"

He seemed surprised by my question but not unwilling to reply, saying, "There are always improvements of one kind or another underway, but can you really be interested, Anne?"

"I am. I have such fond memories of Pemberley, especially from when I was a child."

"Very well. Here is something you will remember less fondly, I think. Do you recall that swampy area off to one side of the stream? It was down the hill from the house a fair distance. You and Georgiana often walked that way along the path."

"Oh, yes! I know the place you mean. Because of the foul smell, we used to hurry past it, holding our noses all the way."

"Yes, exactly. The stagnant water that collected there was good for nothing but breeding insects, disease, and rot. I always considered it a blight on the landscape, and now it is no more. I have had it drained and filled in. As soon as the grass covers a little better, it will be as if it never existed."

"That sounds like an excellent improvement indeed. Has Georgiana seen it? I had regular letters from her while she was at her London establishment, and I know she went on to Ramsgate last summer. But I have heard nothing from her since. I suppose she has returned home to Pemberley by now."

William glanced at me in a peculiar way, and then answered solemnly. "Yes. The situation in London did not suit, and now Georgiana is at Pemberley again."

I wondered what I had said to spoil my cousin's previously cheerful mood and, more pressing, if there was anything I could do to restore it. "It has been a great responsibility you have shouldered," I said, hoping for the best, "looking after your sister these last years. I am sure Georgiana is very grateful for all your benevolent guidance and care."

He was quiet so long that I thought perhaps he would not answer. I was silently blaming myself for once again saying the wrong thing when he began to speak, not looking at me but away, as if he were talking more to himself than to anybody else.

"It is true; the responsibility has been great, certainly more than what I was prepared for. My father trained me up from an early age in how to manage a vast estate, but I believe that is child's play by comparison. I was not taught how to raise my sister, for nobody expected it to be necessary. Although I have always done what I thought was best, I have made mistakes. Georgiana has suffered for them. A young girl needs her parents to protect and advise her; that is the simple truth. Anything else is a poor substitute." After a moment he seemed to remember me. "You must forgive my ramblings, Anne."

"There is nothing to forgive, William."

"You are a sympathetic listener, but I should not have burdened you."

"Not at all. I have some understanding of the problems associated with growing up deprived of a parent. You know that is so."

"Yes, of course you do. At least you still have your mother, though."

"True. At least I still have Mama."

- 9 -

Lady Catherine

On the Serious Business of Marriage

I was happy to see that my serious talk with my daughter had some helpful effect. Although still too reticent for my taste, Anne made much more of an effort to be agreeable to our guests afterward. She ceased to be always cowering in silence, wringing her hands and asking to be excused. In addition, there was more in the way of easy conversation going forward between herself and the gentlemen than when they first arrived. She even extended overtures of friendship to Miss Bennet and Miss Lucas.

I considered it wise to enlist Mrs. Jenkinson to the cause as well, instructing her to make sure Anne was always rested and in her best looks before presenting herself. "Take care not to shield my daughter away from our guests," I also told her. "I know it may go against her natural reticence to put herself forward, but it is important that she avails herself of every opportunity to make a good impression on the gentlemen, especially Mr. Darcy. Do you understand? I expect you to encourage her in this, Mrs. Jenkinson."

When dealing with one's subordinates, it is important to make one's expectations clear.

There was just one more thing required; I decided I must speak to Darcy himself, to be sure matters stayed on course. So I watched for an opportunity for a private exchange with him. This was more difficult to find than expected, with him keeping Fitzwilliam always by his side or going off on some ramble or another. Finally, one day I saw my chance.

Fitzwilliam yawned, clapped his hands together, and then a-bruptly stood. "Well, I have clearly stayed sedentary too long. I believe this will be as good a time as any for me to take my annual tour of inspection round the park. The weather is fine. Darcy, will you come?"

Darcy glanced up from the newspaper he had been studying. "You must excuse me, John," he said. "I really ought to finish reading this before doing anything else. It could be important, and it is my duty to stay informed. Please go ahead without me."

"If you wish. I tell you what I shall do. I shall commit every one of my insightful observations to memory and enlighten you with my report later this evening. I will, of course, make very free to embellish the facts quite extensively in order to render my report more entertaining for you all," he added with a bow. "Just see if I do not."

So off he went. Then I sent Anne and Mrs. Jenkinson on an errand upstairs, leaving Darcy to me.

I began without hesitation. "Now then, Darcy, I know your stay is soon coming to an end, and I must have some assurance from you for how things stand before you go."

He raised his eyes from his paper, looking instantly uncomfortable, possibly even annoyed – without reason, I maintain – but he pretended ignorance instead. "I cannot imagine what you mean, Lady Catherine. Assurance of what?"

"How can you be so obtuse, Darcy? You must know that I am thinking of your intentions toward Anne. I have been extremely patient, you must admit, and so has she been. But we grow weary of this waiting game you seem to be playing."

A look of real concern crossed his countenance. "Has Anne complained? Is she vexed with me?"

"Anne? Why, you should know that she is the mildest creature in the world. She would never dream of saying a word against you, to me or anybody else. But even she cannot help but be distressed by this perpetual delay. It is not a flattering thing for a young lady to be kept waiting. I am very fond of you, Nephew. You are the only son of my dear dead sister, and for her sake I am loathe to criticize you. However, this has gone on long enough. You have a duty to perform, and you had best get to it."

"I am perfectly aware of your wishes in the matter, Aunt."

"And of your mother's? Remember, it was her earnest desire as well as my own that our children be united in marriage."

"I have not forgot. You may believe that I shall always endeavor to do my true duty and also to please my family wherever possible. In that, I know we will never disagree. However…" Here, he paused, whether from some distraction of mind or otherwise, I cannot say. "However, I am not a child. I am a grown man, and I reserve for myself the responsibility of deciding what is right for me to do, including when and how to do it. As for my cousin, what I can assure you is this. Anne possesses my true affection and highest respect. My coming to Rosings this time has been of great benefit, for I believe she and I now clearly understand each other as we did not before. That will have to be enough for you, Madam. I have nothing more to say on this subject and no apology to offer."

So saying, he left the room.

His reply was not everything I could have hoped for, but I decided to be satisfied. The young people had an understanding, which was as good as an engagement. Most likely, I thought, they had also settled on an approximate date for the wedding. I wondered when all this had transpired, for rarely had they been together out of my sight.

When I put my questions to Anne afterward, she was peculiarly circumspect. "It is as William has told you," she said. "We have arrived at a mutual accord as to how things stand between us. That is all I may say for now."

"Why this need for secrecy?" I asked.

No answer.

"You needn't worry that I shall intrude into your private affairs, Anne. I only wish to know what was said between you and when the wedding will take place."

Not another word would she utter on the subject, however, not for all my coaxing, then ordering, and finally threatening. Perhaps I should have been made suspicious by her sudden obstinacy, which was not consistent with her usual behavior.

Here is another instance of how I am sometimes led astray by my generous nature. Against my own better judgment, I am at times too trusting, too yielding, too forgiving of the follies of others. So I put the most charitable construction possible on Anne's behavior that day. I interpreted it as another symptom of her shyness.

From my position of greater wisdom and experience of the world, I recognized the marriage contract for what it was: a piece of serious business. I imagined Anne saw it very differently. In her innocence, she was probably thinking of it purely as an affair of the heart, something her maidenly modesty would not allow her to speak of before others, even her mother. "Poor sad girl," I thought. "We shall allow her to preserve her fairy tales a little longer. She will find out the truth about marriage soon enough."

- 10 -

Anne

Getting to the Crux of the Matter

What I had told my mother was strictly true; William and I did have an understanding for how things stood between us. I understood that he had no plans to marry me, and he understood that I had released him (albeit unintentionally) from any obligation to do so. Eventually Mama would learn the truth, but I was in no hurry to undeceive her and invite the furor that would surely follow. Besides, the visit was nearly over, and my cousins would soon be gone.

Little did I suspect that the climactic portion of our little drama was still to come.

The inhabitants of the parsonage were engaged to drink tea with us at Rosings that same day, but when they came, they were only three – Mr. and Mrs. Collins and Maria Lucas.

"Where is Miss Bennet?" Mama asked at once.

"She is indisposed, your ladyship," said Mrs. Collins, "and she begs to be excused."

"A severe headache," added Mr. Collins. "I questioned her myself, your ladyship, and I am convinced she really is quite ill. Indeed, nothing less could keep any person of sense from partaking of the pleasures of Rosings and of your gracious presence…"

"That will do, Mr. Collins," said Mama. "Well, I suppose we shall have to get on without her. But who will play for us? We must have some music. Mrs. Jenkinson, would you be so good as to oblige us?"

Mrs. Jenkinson nodded her acquiescence.

We did as my mother had suggested; we got on without Miss Bennet. She was definitely missed, however, our party being noticeably diminished by her absence. Although Mrs. Jenkinson filled her place at the piano-forte more than adequately, no one could compensate for Elizabeth's normal share of the conversation.

William was more grave and silent than usual, I noticed. He sat nearby me, so I quietly asked him, "Is anything the matter, Cousin? You seem uneasy."

He looked doubtful at first. Then he must have decided he could safely confide in me. Leaning closer, he said in a low voice, "I am concerned about Miss Bennet. She has a vigorous constitution, and I have never known her to be the least bit unwell before."

"All the more reason not to worry, William. A headache can be a serious thing in someone of delicate health, but not to a person who is strong."

"I suppose that is true. Thank you, Anne."

He held his peace after that, but he still seemed restless to me. Finally, I whispered, "Perhaps you would feel easier if you were to call on her, to see for yourself that she is in no danger."

"That is a very good thought," he said with suppressed excitement in his voice. "Perhaps I might at that. It would be terribly rude of me to desert you all, however. Your mother…"

"You leave her to me. Just say you need some air and go."

He could not have been gone much above half an hour, and yet he did not rejoin us that evening. Upon hearing the door, we waited, fully expecting his return to the drawing room.

When after several minutes he did not come, Mama sent John after him. "Fitzwilliam, go and discover what detains your cousin. This will be our last evening all together and I must have Darcy with us."

John obediently went, and in a few minutes he returned with a message for the whole company. "My cousin begs forgiveness of you all, but he has just recollected some urgent business that requires his immediate attention. While he is sincerely sorry to give up the pleasure of your company tonight, he promises to call at the parsonage tomorrow to take proper leave of you then."

William was out the door early again the next morning. I did not see him until one o'clock, when I happened to have a minute alone with him upon his returning to the house. "Did you find Miss Bennet well when you saw her yesterday?" I asked him.

He shook his head once and smiled ruefully. "I found her well but left her vexed and agitated."

I had no reply for this cryptic statement.

His forced smile melted away and his shoulders sagged. As if he did not know what else to do, he lightly took my hands in his, speaking distractedly. "She will not have me, Anne. God help me, but I have been a conceited fool, and she will not have me."

The two gentlemen left Rosings the next morning, but not before William took me aside for a few more private words. His spirits had clearly not yet recovered.

"My dear Anne," he began. "Allow me to apologize for imposing on you yesterday by relating somewhat of my disappointment, words that had much better have been left unsaid. Please forgive me."

"Of course, but it was no imposition."

"Thank you, and I know I can depend on your secrecy as well. There can be no occasion for upsetting my aunt or dwelling on such vain wishes…" His courage failed him, and it was several moments before he could go on. "These things bring no pleasure to anybody and cannot be too soon forgotten. Promise you will waste not another thought for it."

"I freely promise to say nothing to anyone, William. It is more difficult to promise I can forget something that has made you so unhappy."

"You are too good to me, my dear, and not just in this. You gave me the clear conscience to try for happiness. My gratitude is not diminished in the least for how it has turned out. You have been kinder to me than I have been to myself. Why do you suppose it is that one wants those things one is not meant to have and not… Never mind. If I am to conquer this foolish inclination, I must stop asking questions with no sensible answers. I am glad at least that we now understand each other, Anne, and I wish you far better success when your turn comes."

He looked so miserable, poor creature, that I could not help feeling very sorry for him indeed. There seemed no doubt now that William was in love with Miss Bennet, that he had made her an offer, and that for some reason she had soundly rejected him. He confessed to wanting what he was not meant to have (Elizabeth), and then he caught himself before finishing his question, which would have been to ask why one so often does not want what is offered, available, and intended (in this case, myself). Although there was some insult in it, there was also a compliment in the implication that he might have been wiser to prefer me.

~~*~~

It felt very odd to see Elizabeth again after that, knowing what I did. When she and the others came to dine with us that afternoon, I thought I saw some new feelings of consciousness in her as well, especially in the odd way she smiled when greeting my mother. Perhaps she was thinking how differently the scene might have played out if she had accepted my cousin. Instead of receiving a civil welcome, she would no doubt have been thrown out the door once the truth was known.

"How nice to see you again, Lady Catherine," Elizabeth might commence. "Now that I am to be your niece, I am sure we will be great friends."

"My niece! What can you mean?" Mama demands, a look of horror overspreading her face at the mere suggestion. "Do you have some delusion of marrying Colonel Fitzwilliam, the son of an earl? You have no family or fortune to make such a connection even remotely eligible. It is unthinkable. Every feeling revolts!"

"Have no fear, Madam. Although he is perfectly charming, I do not mean to marry Colonel Fitzwilliam."

"Thank heaven for that!"

"No, it is your other nephew to whom I am engaged, to Mr. Darcy."

Mama staggers backward at the news before gathering herself to retaliate. "Miss Bennet, you gravely deceive yourself. If Fitzwilliam was unthinkable for you, Darcy is impossible! The obstacles to such a match are too numerous to list, but the most insurmountable is this. Darcy cannot be engaged to you, for he is already engaged to my daughter and has been for years!"

"Apparently not, for he has just proposed marriage to me, and I have accepted him. We will be wed by special license just as soon as one can be procured, which will make me the next mistress of Pemberley."

"Silence! I will not hear another word. Out of my house, you... you... you ungrateful hussy!"

Oh, dear! As much as it might amuse me to imagine somebody finally getting the better of Mama, I would not be in Elizabeth's shoes at that moment for the world.

But no such calamity took place. When I returned my attention to the conversation, in fact, Mama was insisting that Elizabeth and Maria Lucas should extend their stay at Hunsford, attributing Miss Bennet's being out of spirits to her dread of soon leaving for home. Elizabeth held firm to her original plan, however, saying that her father had written to hurry her return to Hertfordshire.

Mama, finally resigned to this loss, duly compensated herself (and punished Elizabeth) by conducting a full inquiry into when and how the journey was to be made, and dispensing detailed instructions on every aspect of the formidable undertaking.

I would be sorry to see Elizabeth go as well, I realized. Although I could not yet say we were the best of friends, some progress had been made. I would have been glad for the opportunity to continue our acquaintance… and to continue my study of her. I had learnt much by her example, and now my interest had been further piqued by her rejecting a man I would have believed impossible to refuse anything.

How I would have loved to inquire about the proposal and the reasons for her negative answer! It had even occurred to me that she might have held back partly out of delicacy on my account, which would be admirable but unnecessary. I could not ask directly, since I had sworn to say nothing to anybody about what William had confided, and I was sure that included most particularly the object of his unrequited affection. Still, I did think I might discreetly query her, possibly even put in a good word for William. It might do no good in the end, but there would be no harm in trying.

The night before Elizabeth's intended departure, therefore, I so far exerted myself as to invite her to sit beside me. Then, after a few exchanged pleasantries, I opened the topic of William. "I am curious as to your opinion of my cousin," I said lightly.

"Which one?"

"I believe I can guess your opinion of Colonel Fitzwilliam. He is universally liked because of his easy manners. Mr. Darcy is more difficult to know and appreciate. It is your opinion of him that interests me."

Elizabeth gave me a quizzical look, causing me to worry I had been too transparent. In the end, though, she only answered, "My opinion of *him* has of late been vacillating rather violently. His character, as you say, is difficult to make out."

"Oh, no, I see you have misunderstood me, Miss Bennet. I believe Mr. Darcy's character to be irreproachable. It is only his manner that sometimes gives offense."

"It is to your credit I am sure, Miss de Bourgh, that you avow such unshakable confidence in your cousin. But that is hardly surprising, since he is a near relation… and may one day be nearer, or so I have heard it said."

"No doubt you refer to a wish expressed long ago by our mothers. Although that arrangement is still sometimes spoken of, neither Mr. Darcy nor I myself feel bound by it. I believe our inclinations will likely take us in very different directions."

"Is that so? Hmm. I pity your mother when she finds out."

"Yes, you have deduced the difficulty, Miss Bennet. It will no doubt come as a cruel blow to Mama, for she considers it quite a settled thing."

We delved no deeper into the issue; we ventured no nearer the crux of the matter. Still, I was pleased to have made the attempt on William's behalf, whether or not it would have any effect on the ultimate outcome.

- 11 -

Lady Catherine

On a Scandalous Falsehood

How dull the house seemed with all our company gone! Still, I consoled myself that it would not be long before we saw Darcy again. He and Anne both admitted to having an understanding between them. Even more promising, I had caught them in whispered conversation more than once before he went away. An excellent sign! Surely, it would be only a matter of a little more time… and a little more patience on my part.

Weeks passed, however, and then months. My letters – sent to encourage Darcy's return and addressed alternately to Pemberley and his house in town – all went unanswered. Neither could I find out that Anne had any correspondence with him. Then one day – it was the middle of September – my first intelligence came from a most unlikely source.

Mr. Collins called at Rosings. There was nothing unusual in that, of course, except it was for the second time in the same day. I could see he was near to expiring under the weight of some kind of agitation.

"Forgive me, your ladyship," he said, half out of breath for having hurried. "I would not presume to impose my humble presence on you again so soon, at least not without a definite invitation, except I thought it my solemn duty to relate some surprising information to you at the earliest possible moment."

"What is it this time, Mr. Collins?" I asked mildly annoyed, for I was ready for my tea, and I could not imagine he could have anything to say that I was in a rush to hear. "Is it another unsavory tale about the youngest Miss Bennet? Has she given up her shoddy marriage and run off with somebody new?"

"No indeed, your ladyship. It is something quite different!"

"Very well, Mr. Collins," I said, resigned. "Deliver your information, and I will decide if it warrants all this anxiety."

He glanced about himself. "I see Miss de Bourgh is not present, which is all for the best, considering what I have to say. You shall judge for yourself how much of this news she can be told."

"Yes, yes, Mr. Collins. Do get on with it."

"The news is this. Mrs. Collins has had a letter today – within the last hour in fact – from her mother. Well, Lady Lucas informs us that my cousin, Miss Jane Bennet, the eldest, is very recently engaged. It will be a most advantageous marriage for her too!"

"I am sure her parents are very happy, although I pity the man who is foolish enough to marry into such a family. But you begin to try my patience, Mr. Collins. Why should any of this concern me or my daughter? *Do* come to the point."

"The point is this, your ladyship. Miss Bennet is to marry your nephew's great friend Mr. Bingley, and the rumor is the business will not end there. Mr. Darcy has also been seen in the neighborhood, staying at Netherfield and visiting repeatedly at Longbourn. As Lady Lucas tells it, it will be just like the old song; one wedding is sure to bring on another. People are saying that friend will follow friend into marriage; sister will follow sister to the altar; and it will not be long until Miss *Elizabeth* Bennet changes her surname as well… to Darcy."

It may be imagined how I felt at this vile insinuation. I was for a moment too stunned to speak. Mr. Collins evidently took my silence as permission to continue talking.

"Miss Bennet's allurements are far from trifling. I have to say, your ladyship, that I saw signs of a burgeoning attachment when she and your nephew were together here in the spring. Perhaps I should have said something at the time, but how could anybody ever have suspected this? Still, I shall be of what service I can. I shall write to my cousin Mr. Bennet, just to give him a cautioning hint…"

"Be quiet this instant, Mr. Collins!" I ordered, and he stifled himself at once. "It is impossible that this will turn out to be otherwise than a scandalous falsehood spread by tongues that have nothing better to do than idly wag back and forth about their superiors. Still, it cannot be allowed to persist. Slander, however it gets started, must be ruthlessly dealt with; it must be quickly put an end to. Even the suggestion of such a disgraceful match injures my nephew and the entire family! You say that an engagement between Mr. Darcy and this… this adventuress cousin of yours is considered a *fait accompli*?"

"Yes, your ladyship."

"Very well. I shall soon see about that!"

I sent Mr. Collins on his way, and then I formulated my plan. I would speak to Miss Bennet myself; nothing less would do. I would make my sentiments plainly known to her and demand that she universally and unequivocally refute this revolting rumor. Most likely it would take some considerable persuasion, seeing that she had probably started the report circulating herself in an attempt to increase her importance, falsely attaching her name to a family of nobility. But my celebrated frankness would serve me well in this situation. It would have its due effect on Miss Bennet. She would soon come to know what it would cost her to persist in such evil pretensions.

Accordingly, I made arrangements to depart the next morning for Hertfordshire by way of London. Anne could accompany me as far as our house in town, but no farther. There would be no benefit in having her with me when I confronted my adversary. I would tell her all she needed to know after the fact.

- 12 -

Anne

On a Little Family Drama

Mama would not tell me much about why we must suddenly be off, only that she had business of some urgency in Hertfordshire and that she was taking me as far as London, where I was to patiently await her return. Fortunately, though, I called at the parsonage before we left and received a helpful dose of information from Mrs. Collins.

Taking me into her parlor, she invited me to sit, and then said, "How kind of you to call, Miss de Bourgh. I am afraid you must content yourself with my company alone, for Mr. Collins is studying for Sunday's sermon in his book room and asked not to be disturbed. Although for *you*..."

"No, no," I interrupted. "I would not have you bother him on my account. Mama only sent me to tell you we will be away for a few days. Some urgent business in Hertfordshire, she says, but that is all I know."

Mrs. Collins glanced about and then got up to close the door. Returning, she looked me straight in the face and spoke quietly. "Miss de Bourgh, my husband would not like me interfering, but I think you have some right to know what this is about. I also feel some responsibility since it was a letter from my mother that has been the cause. Will you allow me to enlighten you?"

"By all means," I said, instantly intrigued. "Do speak freely, Mrs. Collins."

"Very well then, I apologize if what I say will injure you, for my motives are exactly the opposite. My feeling is that it will go better for you – any disappointment – if you are prepared." She paused. "It concerns Mr. Darcy."

"Oh! I hope he is not unwell!"

"No, he is quite well. I will come right to the point, Miss de Bourgh. There is a rumor circulating – how credible it is, I cannot be sure, but I am inclined to believe it – a rumor that Mr. Darcy and my friend Elizabeth are very soon to be engaged. That is what has Lady Catherine so vexed. No doubt she means to put an end to it, but I think little of her chances for success, if indeed the couple themselves are very determined to marry."

All I could say was, "I see."

"I hope I have not shocked you too severely, Miss de Bourgh."

"No, not at all, Mrs. Collins." I wanted to say more. I wanted to compare what I was already aware of with what she knew or suspected. I wanted to assure her it would not break my heart if the rumor about William and Elizabeth should turn out to be true, for I had indeed received prior warning already. But I was afraid of revealing too much, of violating my promise to William, so I kept silent. I only thanked her and departed.

Alas! I seemed doomed to miss all the best dramas playing out round about me – first the scene of William's proposal being made and rejected, and now Mama's confronting Elizabeth, for that was surely why she was going into Hertfordshire.

Oh, how I would have loved to witness it, to be a fly on the wall! Although I could imagine well enough how it must have unfolded between them, especially when further informed by Mama's foul mood upon her return to me at our house in town.

"Get your wrap, Anne," she told me when I asked how her business had gone. "We are off to see Darcy. Fortunately, I happen to know he is in town. For there is trouble brewing, and it seems it is up to me to steer my nephew clear of it. You may be of some use to remind him where his duty lies."

So I would *not* miss all the drama after all.

We were lucky enough to find William at home when we arrived in Berkeley Street – lucky for Mama, that is, but unlucky for him. Although it was bound to be unpleasant, it could not be helped. Sooner or later the truth must come out. Even if William were not so fortunate as to succeed with Miss Bennet, he still had no intention of marrying me. And I had much rather that information came to Mama's ears from his lips instead of mine.

William seemed surprised to see us but not particularly distressed. Judging from the conversation that followed, I collected that he had no prior idea what Mama's business was.

"Lady Catherine, Miss Anne," he said upon receiving us. "Please do sit down. To what do I owe this pleasure?"

"Anne may sit," said Mama, which I did, expecting to be a mere spectator for whatever followed. "I will remain standing," she continued, "for I am far too provoked at present to be comfortable."

She thus obliged William to remain on his feet as well, watching her pacing and her other displays of displeasure. "I am sorry to hear it, Aunt. How may I be of assistance?"

"You may be of assistance by giving me the assurances I require. I have just returned from Hertfordshire where I had some serious words with Miss Elizabeth Bennet, who, I am sorry to tell you, was as perverse and contrary as any person I have ever encountered. I am not accustomed to such language as she inflicted upon me."

William ignored Mama's complaints to ask, "Miss Bennet? What business could you possibly have with her?"

"If you do not know, perhaps you are indeed ignorant and innocent in this contemptible affair. Very well, then, allow me to inform you. I received a report of an *alarming* nature two days ago, and it concerns you, sir. I was told that the whole countryside surrounding Longbourn is waiting in confident expectation of soon hearing the announcement of your engagement to Miss Bennet! There, now you see what has me in such a state. I naturally took the report as a scandalous falsehood and went straight to the source to silence any further gossip."

William apparently required a moment to take this in, but he looked far less displeased than one (at least one disgruntled aunt) might have expected. Instead of outraged exclamations, as Mama obviously required, he only said, "I take it your efforts were somehow frustrated."

"Darcy, how can you be so calm while the family name is being dragged through the dirt?"

"I have heard no evidence of that as yet, Lady Catherine, but I am ready to listen to whatever else you have to say. Miss Bennet failed to give you satisfaction?"

"Yes, in the extreme! I rue the day I distinguished her with my notice and condescension, receiving her at Rosings as I did. I surely would *not* have, had I suspected her true character. She has presumed upon my kindness and yours. And when I questioned her, she refused to oblige me at every turn. She not only denied she had originated and circulated the rumor herself – when common sense clearly shows that to be the obvious explanation – she even claimed to have never heard such a rumor before."

"Perhaps that is true; I have never heard it myself."

"If that were the case, then why would she make such a point of defending the idea?"

"Miss Bennet defended the rumor?"

"Not the rumor itself. I did finally force her to admit that no engagement currently existed, but she argued against its being an impossible match and flatly refused to promise never to accept you. And *this* after I informed her of your understanding with Anne! Can you imagine?"

"Yes, I believe I can," William said slowly. He turned to look at me and winked in a way Mama could not see. "What about you, Anne?" he said. "You have seen enough of Miss Bennet to form an opinion. Can you imagine her behaving in such a disobliging way?"

It was pleasant to be treated by my cousin as a trusted co-conspirator, a valued friend and confidant with a shared secret. I quickly apprehended that Mama's information was not having the effect she intended. Instead of being appalled by Elizabeth's reported conduct, William appeared… Well, I suppose he appeared hopeful.

Although I had intended to stay out of the fray, looking at William, I found myself saying, "Miss Bennet is a spirited young lady. I believe she is not one to be easily intimidated when she feels herself to be in the right."

William smiled at me. "Exactly," he said.

"But she is most definitely *not* in the right in this case," countered Mama, "and her failure to admit it shows a very unbecoming obstinacy, a dangerous degree of willfulness, and a total disregard for the claims of duty, honor, and gratitude. And so I told her. The idea of such a girl having pretensions to marry into a noble family is... Well, I refuse to lower myself by using such language. You must have nothing more to do with her, Darcy. She has shown herself to be an unprincipled person; that should be reason enough to shun her. Beyond that, visiting Longbourn or even Netherfield again will only fuel these noxious rumors."

"I think you overestimate their power, Aunt," William said calmly. "If there is not foundation, rumors of this sort die away soon enough."

"I wish I could agree with you, Nephew, but I will not have the honor of the family subjected to such a test. I will not have my daughter's name or yours sullied by the gossip of the lower orders. No, the only solution is a clean break. Promise me you will never see that young woman or any of her relations again. Since she refused to give me satisfaction, sir, you must!"

Whereas Mama had stopped her pacing before making her final demand, my cousin now commenced his. William did not reply at once. His looks in my direction showed me he understood that how he answered could put me in an uncomfortable position, even more so than himself. He could walk away in the end and never see Mama again if necessary; I did not have that luxury. Still, I gave him a little nod of encouragement. There would be unpleasantness whenever the truth came out; it mattered little whether it was that day or another.

"Come now, Darcy," Mama prompted. "This is not a difficult thing I ask of you, only what you owe to yourself and all the family. Not long ago you acknowledged the careful designs set in place for your future and assured me of your good understanding with Anne. This is simply the necessary extension of that commitment."

At last, William came to rest. He drew a deep breath and spoke respectfully, but firmly. "Lady Catherine, in that conversation to which you refer, I told you I would always endeavor to do my duty and also to please my family whenever possible. I still stand by that statement."

"There, now," Mama said with a firm nod.

"But that does not mean I concur with all the rest you have said. I will on no account allow you or anybody else to dictate to me where my duty lies and how I must perform it. Nor will I allow any person to tell me whom I may see and whom I may not. In fact, I agree with Miss Bennet in standing up to this kind of interference, whether it comes from a stranger or a near relation."

Mama opened her mouth with an objection, but William held up his hand to forestall it.

"You have had your say, and now it is my turn." When he was certain she was listening, he went on. "I am truly sorry if it pains you, Aunt, but it seems there is no avoiding it now. Since you press the issue, it is time you became aware of the nature of my understanding with your daughter. It is something other than what you have presumed. Out of our mutual respect, Anne and I have agreed to each free the other from any perceived obligation to what our parents once planned for us. Therefore, Anne is not to consider herself bound to me, and I am also at liberty to make a different choice if I like. I hope I shall choose wisely. What constitutes a wise choice in a mate, however, may depend on factors beyond what you can comprehend.

"Miss Bennet has been truthful with you; we are not engaged. I agree with something else she told you, however. There would be nothing impossible or disreputable in such a match. She is the daughter of a respectable gentleman, and I have never seen anything in her own conduct to censure. That is all that I require. Anything more speaks of avarice and unbecoming ambition."

Mama could be held at bay no longer.

"But her nearest relations – low connections everywhere, a mother totally in want of decorum, and a sister whose marriage came too late and only at the behest of others. Heaven and earth, Darcy! Are the very shades of Pemberley to be soiled by such as these? Are these people to henceforth make up the chief part of your innocent sister's society?"

"These are things for me to decide, Aunt, not you. Perhaps I shall marry Miss Bennet and perhaps I shall not. That is really none of your affair. It is just possible, you know, that she would refuse me. Same as you, she may be put off the match for fear of acquiring unpleasant family connections."

After an exclamation of disgust, Mama turned to me in desperation. "Say something, Anne! It is your future being thrown away here. Everything I have planned, everything I have hoped and strived for… I have done it all for you and your happiness. Think carefully before casting it aside like so much rubbish."

Here was my last opportunity to change my mind, to attempt to correct the course William and I had recently diverted to. If I had any hope of saving my supposed betrothal to him, I must speak now. Otherwise, the chance to wed my cousin would be gone for good like so much castoff rubbish, just as Mama had said.

But no, that was untrue. I was not treating my connection with William as rubbish. By releasing him to follow his heart, I was doing a far better thing.

So I said, "I appreciate your solicitude on my behalf, Mama, but I will not be made happy by my cousin marrying me against his will. If he chooses to wed Miss Bennet or somebody else, I shall be the first to wish them both joy."

His eyes shining, William took my hand and kissed it.

The confrontation having run its course, with little more to be gained on either side by its continuance, Mama and I abruptly departed.

Back in the carriage, I braced for the angry lecture I knew was sure to come. To my surprise, however, I escaped mostly unscathed. Although Mama's wrath for William and Miss Bennet seemed unlimited, judging from her continuing tirade on the way home and beyond, she appeared to have exempted me from more than a token share of the blame. She seemed to believe that all this had come about against my will, that I was either too weak or too accommodating to prevent it, and that I was simply resigned to accepting the inevitable consequences.

There was a deal of truth in that, of course. I had not meant for it to happen at all, William's departure from the plan. A few short months earlier, I would have married him if he had offered, and I felt some lingering regret over losing him. But I had no power to prevent his falling in love with Elizabeth and no inclination to try, by pressing my own feeble claims, to keep them apart once he had, even though the result was an uncertain future for me.

I only wished Mama could reconcile herself, as I had, to this fact. Despite its long history and hallowed treatment, the match between William and myself was never meant to be.

- 13 -

Lady Catherine

Celebrating Frankness

I do not know what this world, and more particularly the British Empire, is coming to when young people no longer respect their elders, when members of the next generation no longer care to do their duty and obey the rightful heads of their families. The country shall surely fall into wreck and ruin, and the only crumb of comfort I find is in thinking that the final disaster may not descend upon our shores in my day.

I thanked heaven Anne had not yet been touched by this fever of rebellion. I could not be entirely satisfied with her behavior in the recent affair, but I believed her failures stemmed from weakness rather than obstinacy. While that might be just as provoking, it was more easily excused, since she could not help it. I have to continually remind myself that she has neither my excellent constitution nor my crusader's heart to sustain her in the long fight, but I believed she would have abided by my wishes if it had been within her power. Moreover, the concessions she made, the things she said the day I confronted Darcy, were by way of saving face – a natural enough response. No, it is the other two who must shoulder the blame for this debacle.

I should not have been so surprised that Miss Bennet failed to recognize my authority, even after all my kindness to her; she was obviously very badly brought up. But Darcy has not the same excuse, which makes his downfall – caught, as he was, in the web of that young woman's arts and allurements – all the more tragic. Still, I held out some hope that he might meditate further on my frank advice to him that day and come to his senses in time, that is, until I received this communication from him not long afterward.

Dear Aunt,

I am a most fortunate man. Miss Elizabeth Bennet has done me the great honor of accepting my proposal, and we are to be married in November. I do not delude myself into thinking you will receive this news gladly. However, now that everything is definitely settled, I pray you will endeavor to adjust your mind toward accepting my decision, that you will determine to put aside your former prejudices and welcome into the family the lady who is soon to be my wife. All further intercourse between Pemberley and Rosings depends on it, for my sister and I will by no means continue to associate with any person who persists in insulting someone we both care for so deeply. The matter is entirely in your hands, Madam.

Fitzwilliam Darcy

Words fail to adequately describe what I felt upon receiving this letter. Righteous indignation? Incensed? Livid? Outraged? Yes, all of these things and more. And when I considered that one who had been near and dear to me was the cause of my suffering… Again, the English language does not contain anything equal to the task.

Yet language was all that was left to me at that point. Therefore, I immediately sat down to get on with the job of making my position clearly known to my nephew, in order that I might have done, once and for all. There was nothing to be gained by delay. I wrote as follows:

Darcy,

I can no longer address you as 'my dear nephew,' for by your actions you have forfeited your right to any such regard. With this disgraceful marriage you plan to perpetrate upon the family, you spit in the face of everything I hold sacred. I only thank God your father and your sainted mother did not live to see this day!

As for your suggestion that I meekly accept your decision and your intended bride, this can never be! My character, which has been ever celebrated for its frankness, will not permit it. I shall speak my mind as long as I draw breath, and my opinion is this. Miss Bennet has behaved disgracefully. In total disregard for honor and right, she has forced herself in where she was not wanted. She has entered through the back door like a common thief and carried away the peace and integrity of a noble family, treating these things as cheaply as dirt. She has shown herself to be selfish, devious, and irreverent. Mark well my words, Darcy. She lusts after money and status. She cares nothing for you, your sister, or for your beloved Pemberley. She will ruin all three in the end.

If intercourse between our households must now cease, so be it. However, I refuse to take the blame. I lay it instead where it rightly belongs, at Miss Bennet's feet. This is her doing. I warned her what she could expect if she succeeded in drawing you in – that she would never receive any notice from the family, that she would be censured and despised wherever she went, and that she would drag you down with her in the eyes of the world. That you were (and apparently still are) too blind to see it is most regrettable, but it in no way acquits you of responsibility.

I am most seriously displeased! But beyond refusing to see you again or to ever acknowledge your wife, it is not for me to mete out the punishment you deserve. Nevertheless, punishment is surely coming. The course you have set for yourself makes that certain. You are bound to suffer the inevitable consequences of this decision for years to come. Perhaps painful experience will finally teach you to repent of this foolishness where reason failed to do so. Unfortunately, by then it will be too late. I have done my best, but I now wash my hands of you.

C. de Bourgh

I folded the letter, wrote the direction, sealed and posted it the same day.

- 14 -

Mrs. Jenkinson

On Taking the Heat

It was Anne herself who gave me the news about Mr. Darcy's engagement. Her ladyship had been in a particularly foul mood all evening long, and then Anne delivered the explanation later in private.

"We have just had a letter from Mr. Darcy," she said as I brushed out her honey-colored hair that night before bed.

Her tone was unalarmed. In fact, I thought it sounded a bit overly controlled. "Have you, now?" I asked cautiously, continuing with my work.

"Yes, and with such good news, too. Miss Bennet has accepted him, and they are to be married in November."

After a moment to recover myself, I said, "This is surprising news indeed, Miss, and yet you sound pleased. Can it be so?"

"Oh, yes, Mrs. Jenkinson. You must not imagine me shocked or made the least bit unhappy by this announcement. I was aware in what direction Mr. Darcy's inclinations were leading him. And he is perfectly free to marry whomsoever he chooses, you know. I made that clear to him when he was here, admiring Miss Bennet. So you see, I was not surprised, and I expect they will be very happy together."

I almost believed her. "That is very generous of you, Miss," I said, weighing my next words carefully. "I hope her ladyship received the glad tidings with as much equanimity." I kept my face a blank, taking great care to give the impression of innocent inquiry. But when our eyes met in the looking glass, they held a long time – one of those moments of silent communication we sometimes shared, where much truth and feeling were exchanged without a single word.

If she read my thoughts accurately, she heard me saying, *I am so sorry, my dear! How can you be so calm, though? Are you truly uninjured? Is there anything I can do for you? This must be killing your mother, as much as she counted on his marrying you instead.*

I studied her at the same time, having the sense that she wished to convey something like this to me. *I am well. It was a minor blow, not a devastating one. I will soon recover. I cannot say the same for Mama, however.*

Anne actually said, "I trust Mama will come to terms with the change in time, Mrs. Jenkinson."

Despite her sanguine words, you may be sure I watched my young charge carefully in the weeks that followed, feeling it my duty to redouble my efforts to see that she came through this latest misfortune unscathed, that she had enough sleep, that she ate sufficiently to support life and health. She seemed to weather the crisis better and more peaceably than I could have expected. Yes, there was melancholy, but not of an extreme sort or anything more worrisome.

Conversely, Lady Catherine stormed and blustered for days on end, snapping at anybody who got in her way or did anything to catch her notice at all. The servants began to wince every time she opened her mouth and cringe in fear if they did anything clumsy like rattling the china or allowing a door to slam shut. They quickly became more adept at walking on tiptoe and noiselessly going about their business, hoping to be unseen and especially unheard.

I could not hide, however; I was required to be wherever Anne was, which meant usually within view of her ladyship. This made me an easy target. In an attempt to spare her daughter, I suppose, Lady Catherine seemed to redirect her criticism my way instead. "Mrs. Jenkinson, do something about the pillows. How is Anne to sit up straight when you have arranged them so awkwardly?" "Anne looks quite red in the face. How could you have allowed her to get over warm, Mrs. Jenkinson? If you must drape her with so many clothes and shawls, then for heaven's sake place the fire screen where it will do some good!"

I nodded meekly, doing my best to take Mr. Collins's place as lap dog and chief whipping boy. "A thousand pardons, Madam. How stupid of me. I shall correct the problem at once."

Mr. Collins himself was conspicuously absent during this period, no doubt afraid he would receive the brunt of Lady Catherine's wrath, since Elizabeth Bennet was his relation and had been his guest at the parsonage when the chief of the mischief was done.

I did my best to soothe her ladyship's offended feelings. I tried to pet down the bristling hairs of the wounded animal, for so she seemed to me – snarling as much out of pain as spitefulness. Not that she had the right to take out her misery on others, but I could comprehend her wanting what she thought best for her daughter. According to her perspective, her careful arrangements for her only child's security had been cruelly and unexpectedly crushed. Now Anne's future hung in a precarious balance.

I had had a child once, and I could understand somewhat of that mindset. I would have done nearly anything to secure a safe and happy future for my Robbie. I would have fought tooth and nail for him. I would have begged, borrowed, or stolen. I would have gladly given my own life if it could have saved his – so young, so innocent – from that murderous fever. What mother would not?

But I suspected Lady Catherine's motives were not entirely unselfish. I suspected the source of her consternation went well beyond desiring what was truly best for her daughter. Whatever match Anne ultimately made (or failed to make) reflected on her ladyship. Loss of a prize like Mr. Darcy was a blow to her pride, and so was loss of control. I was afraid *that* was the real issue – the damage to Lady Catherine's pride and prestige. That is what she would be willing to fight to the death to protect, and beware to anybody who happened to get in her way, including her own daughter.

- 15 -

Charlotte Collins

On Facing the Music... Or Not

I had begged Mr. Collins to keep quiet about my early suspicions that I might be with child, but he could not contain himself. Before I could stop him, he had published the news of his expected "young olive branch" to those he most wanted to impress – to Lady Catherine and the Bennets. Thankfully, it went no further because, when it all came to nothing, we were obliged to publish that news to the interested parties as well. We had to correct my husband's erroneous – or at least premature – announcement.

I clearly was not carrying a child anymore, if ever I had been. There was no reason to despair, however; our marriage was young and we had plenty of time. No, my main mortification stemmed from the fact that it had not and now could not remain a strictly private matter.

The necessary information was related as simply and quietly as possible. I saw to that myself.

The timing could not have been better; that is one thing to be grateful for. Since both families were soon afterward in uproars of different sorts – the Bennets in preparing for the marriage of two daughters, and Lady Catherine in a storm of anger against Mr. Darcy – no doubt they became completely occupied by their own concerns and found my trifling news dull by comparison. I trust they soon forgot to think of it altogether.

Toward that end – that Lady Catherine should think of us as little as possible – I recommended to my husband that it would be an auspicious time to pay a long-overdue visit to Lucas Lodge. He had just returned from Rosings and looked rather shaken.

"Perhaps you are right, my dear Charlotte," he said with an uncharacteristic tremor in his voice. "I did try to console her ladyship on her grievous affliction, but she only yelled at me, if you can imagine it. 'This is all *your* fault, Mr. Collins,' she said. 'Now, get out of my sight!' Those were her exact words. I believe I may take that as permission to absent myself for at least a few days, just until her ladyship is more herself again. She is too affable and fair-minded to hold to such an unjust accusation for long, and I trust I will soon be back in her good graces."

Thus, we suddenly decamped in favor of Hertfordshire, and I was glad for it. I would no longer have to hide my true feelings about the engagement between Mr. Darcy and my friend. I rejoiced at it and at my happy reunion with Elizabeth. Mr. Darcy was very civil, but he did not seem to view the meeting with as much pleasure. I took no personal offense, since I was quite sure it was my husband, and not I, who was the source of this hesitation. Some people simply are not comfortable with the clergy.

- 16 -

Anne

On Considering the Episode Closed

"We are to consider this reprehensible episode closed," Mama told me, "and I can foresee no need of us ever mentioning it again. Darcy and everything associated with him are as dead to us now. No, it is more than that. It will be as if they never existed."

"Mama!" I objected. "What of Georgiana? She is my friend, and she has done nothing at all. Must we give her up as well?"

"I regret that for now it is necessary. Perhaps we may admit her to our society again in time, when she is no longer under her brother's control. Then it will be for her to decide who her true friends are and where her loyalties lie."

I was very cast down by these developments. Although I had anticipated some unpleasantness, this was more than I had allowed for. I felt the loss of my cousins exceedingly – that and my lack of any say in the matter. I had few enough friends as it was, and the thought of never being permitted to see either William or Georgiana again hit me hard. I did not know how to support myself under the weight of this affliction.

In an attempt to relieve my feelings, I surreptitiously wrote this letter.

Dear Georgiana,

Although Mama has forbidden any contact with you or your brother, I could not in good conscience abide by this separation without at least saying goodbye. Your brother and I parted on good terms, I believe, and I am truly pleased for the happiness he has found. Although you and I have not seen much of each other in the last year or two, I continue to value your friendship. I shall sincerely miss our correspondence, and the thought of never visiting you at Pemberley again fills my heart with sorrow.

Please know that I hold no ill will against you or your brother. I hope you likewise will harbor no resentment against me for the actions of my mother. Her sentiments, as I trust you now understand, do not reflect my own.

I shall hope for an earlier reconciliation between our households than there currently seems any reason to expect. In the meantime, should either of you wish to contact me, send your letters through Mrs. Collins at Hunsford parsonage. She will be posting this letter for me and has promised to watch for anything that might come in return. I believe Colonel Fitzwilliam would also be willing to carry a message whenever he comes to Rosings. I pray he will still be prepared to visit us, for losing his company would be the final blow.

Your faithful friend,
Anne

I could not hide my ongoing melancholy. Mama, who I am sure believed I was grieving the loss of my engagement instead, left me in peace for a time, for which I was grateful. We sat very quietly together at home the day the wedding at Longbourn church took place, neither of us mentioning one word about it but unquestionably thinking of little else.

Once the event had come and gone, however, Mama apparently determined I had been sad long enough. Her idea of encouragement was to scold me into a better humor. "Do pull yourself together, Anne," she told me firmly the following day. "This attitude of despair is most unbecoming, and it is your duty to struggle against and overcome it, just as I have."

I did not find this advice helpful.

These things are all well in the past now, however. Mama's dire predictions came to nothing. Neither the order of the world as we knew it nor the security of our nation crumbled due to this so-called calamity. Even the Pemberley estate survived and prospered. The Darcys, from everything I have since learnt about their period of estrangement from us, suffered no punishment or ruin. They were not shunned by their neighbors and former friends. They did not soon regret their decision to marry. In fact, I believe they were very happy together, right from the beginning.

I ask no sympathy for myself; I truly wished them well. And I would live to enjoy much better days, although I had no assurance of that fact then.

You see, I did not yet know I would soon meet a gentleman who would utterly transform my prospects. I did not know that I could learn to consider another, one whom I had been acquainted with all my life, in a very different role. I still had no notion that I might find greater courage within myself and, alongside it, a new independence. And I could never have imagined that compelling echoes from long ago would shortly arrive to rewrite the past as well as the future of my family.

Mama battled on. However, I am not sure she ever completely recovered from the shock of her plans being so thoroughly frustrated – in this instance and in a second similarly disagreeable (that is, to her way of thinking) circumstance still to come. It must have been a bitter revelation and a severe assault on her pride to find there was, after all, a limit to the power she was able to exert, and that occasionally other forces might overrule her wishes.

Looking back, I marvel at how, with no design to do so, Elizabeth Bennet diverted every one of us from our previous courses, changing the direction of our lives forever. Considering what it ultimately meant for me, I thank her. We are all the better for it, I am sure… with the possible exception of Mama.

PART TWO

The In-Between

- 17 -

Anne

Taking Medical Advice

With William and Elizabeth's wedding past (and ordered to be forgotten), a long, bleak winter loomed before us. But Mama promised brighter days ahead if only I would exert myself.

"Your situation is far from hopeless, and I shall not stand idly by," she declared. "You may be sure of that. I have already begun making plans. Once word gets out that you are free, there are any number of eligible gentlemen who will take an interest. Then it will only be a matter of choosing the best offer."

And of course, I knew who intended to do the choosing.

In my mind's eye, I could already see the line forming – through the hall, out the door, and down the front steps – for a chance at my tremendous fortune.

Mama would be very organized and systematic about it this time. She would designate a day (or perhaps two if the pool of suitors were too large). Each gentleman would sign his name when he arrived, present his documentation of pedigree and prospects, and then take a seat in the drawing room with the other contenders. There, he could view my portrait as he waited, to see what it was he was competing for, what the victor must be prepared to accept along with the money.

Our solicitor would first examine the evidence of eligibility provided, judging according to Mama's stated minimum requirements. Those who failed to qualify would be sent on their way at once, while the successful candidates were passed on to Mama to be further scrutinized and interviewed, one by one.

Where would I be all this time? No doubt closeted away upstairs somewhere, playing no part in the process. If I were lucky, I might catch a glimpse from an upper window as the gentlemen came and went. I could expect nothing more. Perhaps even that would be enough for me to form some opinion, though. If I liked the look of a man in a green coat with an elegant yet manly way of moving, I might, by concentrated effort, induce him to pause and turn his gaze upwards. I would then observe his fair hair and excellent countenance. Our eyes would meet, and he would smile in a knowing way. In that instant, I would instinctively and accurately appraise his character. He was entirely honorable. He understood me and sympathized with my predicament, and he would always treat me kindly. We would surely be very happy together. Or at least we could have been.

No doubt Mama would decide on somebody else – probably a gentleman with a title, better connections, and old enough to be my grandfather. Then she would inform me who I was to marry and when. In an attempt to soothe away any protest, she might offer to entrust some minor detail into my hands – deciding what color flowers I preferred, for example, or choosing between two eligible dates for the ceremony. Should I like to be married on a Tuesday or on a Wednesday? I could not see that it much mattered, so I considered the choice again. Tuesday or Wednesday?

"Tuesday or Wednesday, Anne? Are you listening to me?" asked Mama.

I tried to gather in my straying thoughts. "Tuesday or Wednesday for what?" I inquired, coming back to the present.

"Sometimes, child, you do try my patience! Tuesday or Wednesday for the doctor? I must send word which day we want him. Did I not tell you that I have another medical man coming to consult on your case?"

I sighed. "No, Mama, you did not tell me. What is *this* one called?"

"He is Mr. Essex – a younger man this time, university educated with all the latest knowledge and newest techniques. He sounds very promising to me, and he comes highly recommended. Mrs. Metcalf says he is the toast of all London."

"Then, by all means, let him come on Tuesday," I said sardonically. "The sooner he begins my cure, the better."

I had been down this road a dozen times before. Most recently there had been Mr. Conner, and before him Mr. Stewart, Mr. Plowright, Mr. Parrish, and Mr. Silverwood – all tried and ultimately dismissed. A new man – always someone highly recommended – came to Mama's attention one way or another and was called in. After he examined me, he invariably claimed to know just what the problem was and how to solve it. Six months later, however, after enduring all manner of abuse at the fellow's hands, I was no better. Then it was on to the next, who was just as confident of a cure. I had been through it too many times to allow my hopes to be raised again.

Nobody seemed to know what the trouble was, and I remained as ignorant as all the rest. I told each one who came to consult, "I am always tired, often to the point where I can manage nothing more than getting dressed before I am exhausted. I sometimes feel terrible pains in my head that last for hours, and I often have no appetite. One day might be better and another worse, but the sickness never entirely leaves me, and it has been going on like this for years." Ever since my father died, in truth, although I had stopped mentioning that fact since no one seemed to think it relevant.

I told the same to Mr. Essex when he came.

He was so dissimilar to all the others that, against my own better judgment, I felt a glimmer of optimism – optimism and discomfort too. I was accustomed to old, bearded men of fifty or sixty examining me with an air of detachment, and I thought my modesty long done away by them. This Mr. Essex, however, was no more than thirty, unless I missed my guess, and much more attractive than any of his predecessors – tall, lean, with a pleasant, clean-shaven face and fair coloring. I at once perceived that he also possessed somewhat the appearance and air of a gentleman, although that was inconsistent with his having such a profession.

In any case, to have a young, good-looking man hovering near, lifting my lids to look into my eyes, listening to my chest, and palpating various other parts of my body through my thin chemise was completely different. It seemed far more personal. The experience unnerved me, even though Mr. Essex did nothing at all out of the ordinary to cause me embarrassment. His manner was entirely professional. And I suppose he could not help his age, his appearance, or their effects on me. So I endured his examination without complaint, trying to conceal my discomfiture as well as possible.

Mrs. Jenkinson stayed in the room to support me, although I could hardly decide if that made the circumstances more or less awkward.

"I am finished. Please make yourself comfortable again," Mr. Essex said at last, turning his back and walking away to the window to allow me some privacy.

I was mightily relieved to hear it. When I had redressed, with Mrs. Jenkinson's help, and settled into an armchair, he returned, drawing another chair up close for himself.

"I am sorry to have taken so long with my examination, Miss de Bourgh. I fear I have fatigued you. Can you bear another few minutes – conversation only this time – and then I promise to leave you in peace."

"No need to apologize, Mr. Essex," I said. "But should I not call for my mother so she can hear your findings as well?"

"Not just yet," he answered. "I wish to put a few questions to you first, and that will best be done without any… any interference." He looked at Mrs. Jenkinson. "Perhaps, my good lady…"

"Of course," she said, preparing to leave us.

"No," I said quickly. "I desire Mrs. Jenkinson to stay. We may speak freely in her presence."

"As you wish, Miss de Bourgh. Then, could you please tell me more precisely when your illness began?"

"I first noticed the symptoms about seven years ago, when I was almost fourteen. They came upon me very suddenly."

"Had anything peculiar occurred at that time which might have contributed to the onset of your troubles?"

"I have been told by others it is of no account, but it was in fact very shortly after my father died."

I braced for the awkward moment that inevitably followed whenever I gave the information that my father was dead. There was always an averting of the eyes, a nervous hesitation, and then some expression of sympathy, often clumsily conveyed. People meant to be kind, of course, but I found the doctor's matter-of-fact reaction refreshing.

"Oh, I see. Tell me, was his death long expected or did it come as a shock?"

"It was entirely unexpected, Mr. Essex. He was killed in a carriage accident in London."

"Tragic. And you were very close to him, Miss de Bourgh?"

"Yes, very close. He was my champion and my chief companion. He took me nearly everywhere he went, except that last day. It was devastating when he… when he did not return. And even now…" I could not go on.

"Yes." He paused to make a few notes in the book he kept with him, but I had the feeling it was mostly out of kindness to me – an excuse to give me a moment to regain my self-command.

Presently, he said, "I am sorry to have pained you with unhappy recollections, Miss de Bourgh, but that information may have a bearing on your case. Now, satisfy my curiosity on one further point, if you will. Did your father have a brother? The reason I ask is that I was lately introduced to a gentleman by the name of de Bourgh in London, a gentleman of about fifty just returned from the West Indies. He had his young son with him. This was before I knew of your existence, you understand, or I should have asked him about a connection to the Rosings Park family. De Bourgh is a name that one does not meet with every day."

"It is unusual, yes, as you say, Mr. Essex. But my father had no brothers nor any other living relations that I am aware of."

"Ah, just a coincidence, then. Well, and so now your mother is your chief companion, I collect. From my conversations with her, she seems exceptionally solicitous for your health and future well-being."

I hesitated, hardly knowing how to respond to this characterization. It seemed important to be honest but loyal to Mama at the same time. This man was a stranger, after all, and he had no right to our family secrets. "She is a very attentive mother," I said. "No aspect of my life is so small as to be beneath her notice."

"Ah, that is just what I would have guessed." He made another notation in his book. "Now then, I am especially interested in your headaches, Miss de Bourgh, since I suspect they are at the root of the problem. Your lack of appetite, for instance, is that more pronounced when your head is bothering you then when it is not?"

"Oh, yes! When the headache comes upon me, I cannot bear even the thought of food."

"And does it ever happen the other way round? You are off your food and then the headache comes?"

This one had me puzzled. "I could not swear to it, Mr. Essex. I have never considered the question. Is it important?"

"Perhaps, and perhaps not. Have you a diary of some sort? I would like you to begin at once taking down daily notes. Write what you eat and drink, including when, and how much. Rate how tired you feel at intervals throughout the day. And then mark down the time whenever you feel a headache coming on, as well as what has occurred just beforehand, if anything. It may seem a bother, but can you do that?"

It seemed a reasonable enough request. "Of course," I said. "What do you think the trouble is, Mr. Essex?"

"It is much too early to say, Miss de Bourgh. It would be inexcusably premature of me to hazard a guess with incomplete information. Now that I have seen you, I intend to do some further study on similar cases and also to see what light your diary may shed on the situation. Then perhaps we shall have a more accurate idea. I will return in one week's time to continue. Will that be agreeable to you?"

"Perfectly, although Mama will undoubtedly have an opinion as well, and some questions for you."

"I will speak to her on my way out. Goodbye, Miss de Bourgh," he said, rising. After a slight bow, he was gone.

I looked at Mrs. Jenkinson for her opinion, and she looked at me, waiting for me to speak first. "What an impressive young man," I said in an effort to keep my praise vague. "Did not you think so, Mrs. Jenkinson?"

Being just as vague, she said, "Oh, yes. He seems very… very impressive, just as you say, Miss. Perhaps he is the one who will finally help you."

"I do feel somewhat encouraged that he might be. Let us hope Mama likes Mr. Essex well enough to let him try."

- 18 -

Mrs. Jenkinson

On an Impressive Young Man

I did, in truth, think Mr. Essex an impressive young man, but I could have vouchsafed some additional opinions on the subject. For example, I could have said that I had a lot more respect for a man, young or old, who admitted to not having all the answers than for those who pretended they did. That placed this medical man far above the others in my book. He was infused with youthful energy as well, which is often contagious, I have observed. If he could pass even a little of it on to my young mistress... Well, I knew I should not allow my feelings to run away with me, but I thought there was at least a chance of this one doing Anne some good. Heaven knows she deserved a change in her luck.

I felt only one moment of anxiety during the whole course of his lengthy visit, and that was when Mr. Essex mentioned to Anne about his meeting another Mr. de Bourgh in London. But the moment passed quickly enough, and my young lady seemed to think no more about it. Perhaps it was only a coincidence after all, just as the doctor said. Yes, that must be the case. How could it be otherwise?

- 19 -

Lady Catherine

With Work to Do

I had not quite made up my mind about Mr. Essex. Although he spent considerable time with my daughter, he had very few answers for me upon his quitting her room. When I asked for his diagnosis, he would only say, "Your daughter's condition requires further study," and "I will return in one week to continue my work." Then he changed the subject, inquiring about my family, my late husband, and the circumstances surrounding his death. What possible bearing that distant event could have on the present case, I could not imagine. I gave him no more than the most superficial of answers. The rest was clearly none of his business.

Nevertheless, I supposed I must give Mr. Essex his try, just the same as all the others, but I made certain he knew I would not continue paying his fees indefinitely without seeing some results.

In the meantime, I had important work to do as well. A husband needed to be found for Anne, and the sooner the better. She had waited upon the shelf far too long as it was. Now there was no time to lose. She must be settled within a year – two at the most – to avoid any perception that she had drifted, unwanted, into the years of danger. With her inheritance, surely it would not come to that. But youth is always an added inducement, which should not be wasted.

It could be no ordinary match either. It must be something equal to or better than what was planned for her before – the alliance with a certain person whose name I will not dignify by mentioning it ever again. The new match could not be seen as a coming down, as a settling for less.

I determined to cast a wide net. I would write a letter for the purpose of getting the process underway, varying it slightly as necessary according to each recipient. I would be extremely judicious as to whom I sent it. It must go only to a handpicked group – the very best of my society, trustworthy friends of impeccable quality and great discretion. The situation had to be tactfully explained, too. Something like this, perhaps…

Dear friend,

It is possible you have heard the rumors of my nephew's unfortunate marriage. Sadly, it is all too true. Although I am sorry for his bad judgment, for which he is bound to pay the price for years to come, it may end by working in our favor. Anne was not much inclined to marry her cousin, I discovered, so that is all very well. And now she is free to pursue better options.

I cannot depend on the usual methods to introduce her to a range of suitable gentlemen, for Anne is unequal to the fatigues of going out much into company just now. A London season is out of the question. Again, this may work in our favor, since I can maintain superior control over whom she sees within my own house. And as you know, these things can scarcely be left to the management of the young people!

I am sure you feel as I do, that there is great satisfaction at our time of life in helping to get a young person properly placed out or disposed of in marriage. With your excellent connections amongst the gentility and nobility of England and Ireland, you may well be in the position to recommend someone who would be worthy of my daughter's hand, and at the same time to drop a good word for her here and there throughout your vast acquaintance. You know I would do the same for you, my dearest friend, without a moment's hesitation.

Yours, etc…

I would work on the wording a little more to get it just right. It was important that the letter evoke a helpful response without planting any suspicion in the reader's mind of the situation being desperate. It was not, of course. However, I knew I would sleep easier at night once Anne was creditably settled. My clear duty as her remaining parent was to see it accomplished, and my uncompromising character never allowed me to shirk my duty in any way.

While these measures ran their course, however, which would take some little time, I continued to press for Anne's improved health and spirits. Mr. Essex had to be trusted with the former, I supposed, but I thought perhaps Colonel Fitzwilliam might assist with the latter. Just because one nephew had failed me, that was no reason to sacrifice the company of the other. As far as I knew, Fitzwilliam was in no way to blame for… for what went amiss on his previous visit. And I was inclined to think Anne liked him at least equally well. In any case, he was certainly the more cheerful and lively of the two, which must have been seen as an advantage at such a time.

"I was thinking of sending for Colonel Fitzwilliam," I told Anne one day. "It has been a few months since he was last here, and I think we might persuade him to call again. Would that be agreeable to you?"

"Oh, yes, Mama!" she replied. "How kind you are to think of me. I would like to see Cousin John again above all things."

So there I had my answer – my answer to the immediate question and perhaps something more. Yes, I would send for Fitzwilliam at once.

- 20 -

Anne

Looking Forward

Mama was up to something, no doubt something to do with getting me well married. After all, she had sworn she would not sit idly by, an assertion which I could well believe. Though I begged her not to meddle, she would be sure to anyway. I prayed she would at least be discreet. News of my situation would travel fast enough on its own, I feared, without anybody helping it along.

"The matter is well in hand," was all she would say. "It is not for you to worry about."

I did worry, though. It mortified me to think that I and my romantic status might become fodder for every gossip in the county, for every wagging tongue with nothing better to do.

"Did you hear about poor Miss de Bourgh? She got the jilt, you know. They say that the gentleman she was supposed to marry – a very rich man from the north, he were – he threw her over for somebody else."

"Well, I suppose it was to be expected. She isn't much to look at, is she, so thin and pale as she is? And I hear there is nothing accomplished about her."

"There is her money, though. That must be seen as a definite attraction."

A knowing laugh.

"It may be a temptation to a poor fellow, but not a rich one. A rich man can be as choosy as he pleases, thinking of more than money. He can marry a girl of beauty, good health, and good family. One with a cheerful disposition."

"True, and there are any number of young ladies who would rank higher in those categories than poor Miss de Bourgh. I do feel sorry for her. She will lose her bloom, if she ever had any, and then what will become of her? She might sit alone with her mother in that big, empty house until she grows old or goes completely off her head."

No, I had to stop thinking like that. I was not a helpless victim. I had not been abandoned… not exactly anyway. And I had much to offer besides my fortune – as an independent person, as a friend, or even as a prospective mate. I knew this even if no one else did. I believed it was true even when I saw little evidence of it. Even when my confidence waned, I clung to that fact so as not to lose hope. Every creature, no matter how weak or badly flawed, had value in God's eyes. Not a single sparrow fell to earth but that He knew of it. My life was worth something to my creator. That is what signified. The opinions of ignorant strangers, wholly unconnected with me, were of no consequence. Here again, I believed these words even though I did not always live up to them properly.

At least I had my cousin John's visit to anticipate with pleasure. I always felt more cheerful when he was about. Months had passed, though, and I had begun to be afraid he would never come again. But apparently Mama's very particular invitation served to allay any fears he might have had about his being warmly received at Rosings again. His response said he would gladly come in late January or February.

I began looking forward to Mr. Essex's weekly calls as well. When he came the second time, he asked if I had developed any new or worsening symptoms (which I had not), and then he spent the greater share of his time studying the diary I had faithfully kept for him, rather than examining me. I just sat there, fully clothed, with Mrs. Jenkinson by my side while he read, making occasional comments to which he did not seem to want any reply.

"This is interesting, this note from Thursday… Good appetite at breakfast, but later… hmm… A headache the next day… Yes, as expected… Retired early to bed without dinner… Unfortunate… Feeling well all Sunday, though… Then the next day, lethargic again… I see… Yes, I see… Very interesting."

"What does it all mean, Mr. Essex?" I finally asked when he had grown quiet.

"Oh, Miss de Bourgh!" he said with a start, as if he had quite forgot I was present. "My apologies. I sometimes plunge myself so deep into thought that I become abominably rude. My mother would be appalled at my bad manners. We both beg your forgiveness."

"Then you surely have it, Mr. Essex. But can you tell me anything about what you have learnt? I am most curious, as you might imagine, to discover what is the matter with me."

"Yes, of course, although I still have no simple answer to your question. What I believe is that a combination of factors, not one single ailment, is to blame. And we must approach the treatment accordingly. But I continue to think your headaches are at the heart of the matter. They may have begun as a result of the trauma you received upon your father's death, or possibly consequent to the disruptive changes that take place in the body during the adolescent years. Regardless of the original source of the trouble, our efforts must be directed toward relieving, or preferably preventing, these headaches, since they seem to spoil your appetite and leave you tired for days afterward. We must break the cycle that has kept you its prisoner. Once broken, you can begin climbing upwards again. Does that make sense to you, Miss de Bourgh? You need not be afraid to speak up if something I say is confusing or if a course of treatment I recommend contradicts your own intuition. You are the true expert on your own body, after all, and therefore you have a very important role to play in improving your health."

I allowed myself time to think through all that he had said before responding. "No, I believe I understand what you mean, Mr. Essex, and it makes perfect sense the way you have explained it, which is quite different from what any of the other medical men has theorized."

"Good. If this approach has not been tried before and failed, then I think we have every reason for optimism. It will be a matter of trial and error to see what is most effective in your particular case – various combinations of rest and exercise, diet and medicinal herbs, and removing whatever elements tend to strain your nerves. It may take some time, but I believe that together we can achieve considerable improvement."

"What am I to do?" I asked. "You say I have an important role to play."

"And so you do. Let us start with the basics. Establishing a wholesome routine will serve as the foundation to everything else. Nothing additional can be tried and tested until these fundamentals are in place.

"First, I want you to eat frequently and regularly – every three or four hours. Even when you have no appetite, you must take at least a small amount of some simple food. Avoid exotic spices, and you are to have no wine or spirits at all for the time being. Agreed?"

"Very well, sir," I said.

"Such privations may not always be needed, Miss de Bourgh, but they are a necessary precaution in the beginning."

"I understand, Mr. Essex, and I will not consider it a hardship. These things I count as small sacrifices to be well again."

"I am pleased you feel that way, Miss de Bourgh, however I am not quite finished yet. Can you bear more orders from me?"

"I believe so."

"Excellent. You have a strong heart for the work ahead, I perceive, and that often makes the difference between failure and success. Now secondly, you must have plenty of sleep nightly, rising and retiring as close to the same times every day as possible. And take some exercise every day as well – out of doors whenever weather permits. Fresh air is very restorative. Otherwise, walk the halls of this great, old place," he said, looking up toward the ornate ceiling and making a sweeping gesture with his arm. "There must be rooms and corridors enough to keep you occupied exploring for weeks at times of rain or snow. On the occasions when you feel too weak to go alone, I am sure Mrs. Jenkinson will lend you her arm." He looked at her and she nodded. "Shorten your route if you must, but never omit your exercise completely. And continue keeping your diary faithfully; your attention to detail there has been most helpful."

He wrote something in his book, tore the page out, and handed it to Mrs. Jenkinson. "Brew a cup of this for Miss de Bourgh every morning and evening, and again at the first sign of a headache. Ginger, lemon, and few other things you probably already have stocked in your larder or at hand in the conservatory."

Mrs. Jenkinson scanned the recipe. "Yes, sir. No trouble at all. I will do my best," she promised.

"I am sure you will, Mrs. Jenkinson," Mr. Essex said, rising to his feet. "I am sure you *both* will. Oh, and one more thing, Miss de Bourgh. Do try to remain as calm as possible – no emotional outbursts, no fretting over what another person says, does, or may be thinking. I know this is not an easy charge, but when you remember that nothing is more important than the improvement of your health, it may help to keep these other petty annoyances in proper perspective.

"I shall speak to Lady Catherine before I go, to inform her of my findings and elicit her cooperation in these measures. No doubt she will wish to do all in her power to assist us."

Saying he would return again in another week, he bowed and was gone. For a moment, I just sat where I was, unable to move or say a word. Other than Mama, I had rarely heard a person talk so much with so little intermission, and I was still trying to digest all the doctor had said. I was staggered by the sheer volume of his instructions and the enormity of the task before me. As poorly as I usually felt, what might appear simple tasks to others seemed quite daunting to me.

Forsake your bed on schedule, although you are still too tired to move. Eat frequently, even if your stomach rebels at the very thought. Drink medicinal tea until you are afloat in it. March a vigorous mile or two every day, rain or shine. And in your spare time, keep a detailed account of everything you consume, think, feel, see, and do – every time you sneeze, turn around, stand up or sit down. Oh, and do ignore your overbearing mother's presence and criticisms too.

Perhaps these were not precisely Mr. Essex words, but they may just as well have been for how insurmountable the assignment sounded to me at first. It might be the same as telling a strong, healthy man to hoist a heavy pack upon his back and climb an enormous mountain… on his knees… in a driving snow… blindfolded.

Despite my confident pledge of cooperation and the faith Mr. Essex had expressed in me in return, I was by no means certain I was capable of scaling the mountain before me. And yet, I could not let him down somehow. Neither could I let myself down.

I was not only daunted by the task ahead; I was thrilled as well – by Mr. Essex's apparent command of the situation and by the very real prospect of my health finally improving. As much as my head cautioned me not to allow my hopes to run away with me, the feelings of my heart would not be suppressed. I *did* feel hopeful; there was no denying it. I felt more hopeful than I had in a long time, thanks to Mr. Essex.

"Some of these things will be difficult for you," ventured Mrs. Jenkinson, breaking the silence.

"Yes," I agreed, "I imagine they will be. I am very determined now, but no doubt there will be times ahead when I will lose my resolve. When I am tired or weak, I may feel like giving in. You must not allow me to do so, Mrs. Jenkinson. You must not allow me to fail of following every one of Mr. Essex's instructions to the letter."

"But Miss! How am I to do that?" she objected. "I have no power, no authority, and no magic potions."

"I am giving them to you, Mrs. Jenkinson. Well, all but the magic potions, of course." She still looked mystified. "Mrs. Jenkinson, I know you are accustomed to always deferring to the wishes of others. In this case, however, you must not. Now, while my resolve is strong, I hereby empower you to act as my warden in this matter. I make you Mr. Essex's deputy to enforce all of his rules, even against my will. This is your duty and charge. Let no one bully or deter you from it – not me, and especially not Mama."

"Very well, Miss, but hadn't you better speak to your mother about this too? I wish to serve you faithfully; however, I cannot afford to lose my position by going against Lady Catherine."

"I will, Mrs. Jenkinson, I promise. Although my guess is that Mr. Essex is himself at this moment laying down the law for Mama. Nothing further may be required to ensure her cooperation."

Mrs. Jenkinson took her new responsibilities extremely seriously, as I expected she would. And I soon discovered that underneath that mild, accommodating exterior resided a will of iron.

The very next day, I awoke with the beginnings of another headache. I wanted nothing more than to close my eyes again and keep to my bed all the day long. My strength seemed at a very low ebb and my appetite nonexistent.

My new warden, however, was having none of it. Mrs. Jenkinson immediately swung into action. First she administered a cup of Mr. Essex's special tea. (It was not undrinkable, I had to admit, and it seemed to settle my insides a little.) Then I was got out of bed and dressed by my maid, over my objections and by Mrs. Jenkinson's firm command. A tray came up from the kitchen by her order as well – toast with marmalade, a soft-boiled egg, and more 'Essex' tea. I took a little of these things at her urging.

It was all done with gentleness, but there was no getting round Mrs. Jenkinson. She was immovable. By the middle of the afternoon, she even had me by the arm, escorting me back and forth along the upstairs corridors for my daily exercise. I had obviously selected the right person for the job of my bulldog.

- 21 -

Lady Catherine

Meeting Frankness with Frankness

Imagine, presuming to lecture *me* on what was best for my own daughter, telling me what I may and may not do in my own house! After delivering his report on Anne's condition and his proposed line of treatment, Mr. Essex came to the impertinent portion of his remarks.

"Lady Catherine, I am a man of science," he said to me. "Although I was raised a gentleman and still consider myself to be one, I find that social niceties often get in the way of practicing good medicine. They waste time, at the very least. So I ask your indulgence as I state the situation plainly. Anne herself, with Mrs. Jenkinson's assistance, will have the greatest share of responsibility in implementing the regime I have laid out for her improvement. However, you must be willing to do your part as well."

"Of course," I said somewhat indignantly, knowing what was coming next. It was always the same. My *part* consisted of procuring the medical man's attendance to begin with and then paying his bills promptly ever after. Although I thought it rather vulgar that this new fellow should mention his fees so soon, especially in the same breath as claiming to be a gentleman, I resigned myself and asked, "How much do you want, then?"

Mr. Essex had the decency to look offended and confused. "What? Oh! No, this is nothing to do with money, Lady Catherine."

Now I was confused as well. It was not to be supposed that this one was really any different from all the rest. "Then what, pray, do you want from me, Mr. Essex, if not money?"

"Do not misunderstand me; I would be very much obliged if you will pay my bill by and by, your ladyship. I cannot afford to continue indefinitely without some remuneration. But all I meant to ask at the moment was your cooperation. It is vital that we find a way to get the upper hand over these headaches of Miss de Bourgh's."

"I agree, but what you expect me to do about them, I cannot imagine. My daughter has consistently failed to respond to my constant encouragement and to the best medical advice available. That is why *you* are here, sir."

"Quite. Then, as we all have your daughter's best interests at heart, may I be frank with you, Lady Catherine?"

Now *here* was a subject on which I was particularly expert. "I always speak my opinions frankly myself," I told him. "However, I cannot say it is equally advisable for everybody else, especially one so young and inexperienced as you seem to be. Pray, what *is* your age, Mr. Essex? And at the same time, I might as well inquire, what are your family connections?"

"My age and my connections are immaterial, your ladyship. You have summoned me here not for these but for my other credentials. Now, as I was saying about Miss de Bourgh's headaches, you are her mother and you have the very strongest degree of authority in this house. Therefore, I believe you to hold the strongest degree of influence over the circumstances surrounding Miss de Bourgh's daily life as well – whom she sees, what situations she is expected to confront, whether there is tranquility or great turmoil around her. All these factors can have an effect on your daughter's health, especially when it comes to the mysterious maladies of the head. They are not like other illnesses; they seem to have as much to do with the sufferer's emotional state as with her physical condition. I wish to enlist your help in keeping Miss de Bourgh's emotional state calm."

There appeared to be some error in the young man's logic. "Surely our emotions are something that we each have under our own regulation," I said, "or at least it should be so. Perhaps you should be having this conversation with my daughter and not myself, Mr. Essex."

"I have spoken to Miss de Bourgh about this very thing, and she has vowed to do what she can. Some things are beyond her power, however. That is where I must charge you to use your superior position in this household to maintain a peaceful home… and to govern your own behavior so as to vex your daughter as little as possible."

"Vex her as little as possible! How do you mean, sir? Do you suppose I lay awake at night devising plans to thwart the happiness of my only child? Tell me if that is what you accuse me of doing. If so, you may leave my house at once and *never* return."

"Not at all, your ladyship. I only mean to acknowledge what is already clear to me from our brief acquaintance – that you are a woman of exceptional abilities and exacting standards…"

Well, at least there, he was right.

"…and although these are admirable traits in general, they may do more harm than good in this instance. Let us be forward thinking, Lady Catherine. Let us be willing to try something new, since the old ways have proved useless. For the sake of your daughter's health, I would respectfully ask you to redirect your abilities toward finding ways to praise instead of correct her, to support instead of rule over her, to trust that she knows what is best for her own well-being, and to allow her to have her own way about it as much as possible."

Dumbfounded, I thought how very unlikely this was to be true. Anne knowing what was best and doing it? How little this young man knew about her! Why, for all her life it had been necessary for me to step in and guide her. Without me, she should have been as helpless as a lamb among the wolves.

"Lady Catherine? Have you heard what I said?" he asked.

"I have heard you, Mr. Essex. I have heard your questionable diagnosis and every impertinent word of dubious advice that followed! I am not accustomed to such language as this, especially from an inferior, and I have a good mind to dismiss you here and now."

I paused to see what he would say to this, expecting either a humble apology or perhaps more impertinence. He offered neither.

"That is, of course, your ladyship's prerogative," he said calmly. He then waited in silence, looking me coolly in the eye, showing neither fear, penitence, nor anger. This one was not to be so easily intimidated, I perceived.

Well, two could play at that game. If he could be silent and self-assured, I could be more so. I was the one in the position of power, after all. Despite all his bluster, in the end he would dance to my tune or not at all. So I left him dangling, uncertain of his fate for a full minute, which is a long time to do nothing but wait for the ax to fall.

Meanwhile, I considered what my next action should be, whether to retain his services or summarily dismiss him. Could I abide his offensive manners, or had they already forfeited his right to come among us again? He was young, I reminded myself, and *some* allowance might be made on those grounds. And his excellent credentials were, I supposed, ultimately more important in this case than his manners. After all, he was here to perform a service – hired help, like the groundskeeper or a dancing master – not as a candidate to be considered for acceptance into our exclusive society. Finally, I decided that sending the man away might also be judged closed-minded, and never let it be said that Lady Catherine de Bourgh was incapable of progressive thought!

"Very well, Mr. Essex," I said at last. "I have decided to overlook your offenses just this once for the sake of my daughter, and we shall try it your way for now. However, henceforth you should remember whom you are addressing and make a concerted effort to speak with proper respect. If you claim to be a gentleman, you must comport yourself like one at all times, without exception."

"Duly noted, Lady Catherine. No doubt my mother would appreciate your reminding me."

Mr. Essex wasted no time departing after that. I imagine he was greatly relieved to get away with his employment and promise of future remuneration still intact.

Although I was confident it would come clear to me with further study, I could not at first make him out. Was Mr. Essex a principled man, I wondered, or a charlatan? He seemed sincere, but his methods were unusual to say the least. I expected some tablets or draughts for my money, but he prescribed little more than tea and fresh air. And why had he been so interested in Anne's father and the manner of his death the first time he came? I did not like it. He seemed to imply some prior knowledge or suspected relevance to the case.

The biggest puzzle, though, was why Mr. Essex should be a physician in the first place. If indeed he were the son of a gentleman as he claimed, I reasoned that he must be at least a fifth or a sixth son at that. All the other respectable occupations – the church, the army, the navy, the law – having been claimed by those born ahead of him, he was forced to attempt something different. For what else but an expendable excess could ever induce a proper gentleman to allow any son of his to go into the suspect field of medicine? There was no prestige in it, certainly, and I should think very little money to be made either… except perhaps off a wealthy and gullible patron. Well, if Mr. Essex aspired to make his fortune by picking *my* pocket, he would be sadly disappointed. The sooner he understood that, the better.

- 22 -

Anne

Seeing an Encouraging Trend

I tried to faithfully discharge my duties toward improving my health, according to the doctor's instructions. And Mrs. Jenkinson was always there to be sure I did so. Mr. Essex came periodically to check on my progress and offer suggestions, refining his recommendations according to what appeared to be helpful and what was not.

At first, I was afraid I had imagined the change. I feared it was only wishful thinking that told me my headaches were a degree or two less severe and coming slightly less often than before. After so many months and years, and after so much disappointment, it was difficult to trust that it could be true, to believe that something was different this time.

But my diary told the story. The plain truth was there to be read. I was glad, then, that I had been required to keep a record, for evidence enough to convince any skeptic could be found in that account written in my own hand. My decreasing symptoms were available to be counted and measured, as much as things without physical substance can be measured. How does one accurately quantify pain? Can one attach a number to fatigue or appetite? I did my best, and over the weeks a clear pattern of improvement developed. I was feeling a little better, and then a little better still.

The progress was slow but soon marked enough as to be undeniable. Although I still had dark days – days when I would have as soon given in and given up – my burgeoning success was generally enough to convince me to stay the course. Good health is something undervalued by those who have always possessed it. Having known the unhappy alternative all too well, however, I understood it was a treasure worth any price one had to pay. As with the parable in the Bible, I would have been prepared to sell all I had to possess that pearl of exceptional value. Other gems were nothing by comparison.

So I carried on. The hope of being free of debilitating headaches was the strongest of motives. The chance to live a normal life, the promise that urged me on. If I ever wavered, Mr. Essex or Mrs. Jenkinson reminded me what I was striving for.

I cannot say that Mama contributed a great deal towards my recovery, except I must acknowledge that she did very little to hinder it in those early days either. That is all I could reasonably have hoped for, I suppose. She mostly played the part of a silent observer to the process, which was quite remarkable in itself.

I knew her to have strong opinions on every subject under the sun and, ordinarily, she scrupled not to share them at length with whomsoever fell within the range of her voice. My new doctor, my new health regiment, and how competent or incompetent was the manner of everybody's carrying it out: these things could be no different. Doubtless, Mama longed to take control of it all, to overrule where she thought she knew better than Mr. Essex, to pronounce my efforts and Mrs. Jenkinson's deficient on one point or another.

I could see the exertion it required to hold her opinions and criticisms back. I could imagine what it must have cost her to bite her tongue. It should have come easier for her as time passed and she observed my improvement, but I saw no evidence of that. I particularly remember her obvious discomfort one morning shortly after Mr. Essex first laid out his plans for my amendment.

"Good morning, Mama," I had said when Mrs. Jenkinson and I finally joined her in the drawing room – after I had dressed, taken my medicinal tea, some breakfast in my room, and a spot of exercise in the garden.

"Good morning," she returned, frostily. "Anne, what is the meaning of…" Here she broke off, as if she suddenly thought better of what she had been going to say. Her face took on a sour expression while she fidgeted a minute in silence. I could clearly perceive she was struggling. I could almost hear her mind at work. Did her debate with herself go something like this?

Would it be considered critical to inquire about Anne's late attendance? Surely not. I am only asking for information, not rendering a judgment.

But perhaps it might be taken as a judgment, even if it is not meant to be one.

Only a person who is over-sensitive would think so.

And have you never known your daughter to exhibit signs of that failing?

Well, yes, frequently in fact. Although I have attempted to break her of the habit, it persists.

Then you would do well not to ask your question about tardiness, lest you risk "vexing" the girl. Is not that what the impertinent doctor warned you against?

Oh, very well! Do you suppose it would be safe for me to comment to her on the weather, or might she find that vexing also?

There is no knowing, but it must be an altogether safer subject than the other.

"…I mean, how did you enjoy your walk?" she asked instead, sounding as if the words nearly caught in her throat. "The weather looks very fine for a December morning."

"Yes, very fine, Mama. It is cold, of course, but dry. And no wind to trouble us."

"I hope you remembered to wear… That is, I hope you were dressed warmly enough that you did not much feel the cold."

Poor Mama. It was no trouble at all for *me* to hold my tongue at times; I was accustomed to it. But I make no doubt it was painful as a toothache for her to do the same, and oh, so difficult to practice diplomacy with her own daughter, whose feelings she had been used to never taking into consideration.

I marveled at her restraint… at her restraint and at Mr. Essex's apparent ability to command it. What had he said to elicit her cooperation, I wondered? One day I would have to ask him.

Had he made her malleable with heavy threats of some kind? That seemed unlikely. What power could a man like Mr. Essex possibly exert over a woman of Mama's strength and position? Or had he persuaded her with a liberal application of tact and flattery? My mother liked to be flattered as much as anybody I knew, although she would hardly admit it was so, preferring to see any forthcoming compliments as simply her due. But perhaps Mama was not beyond the reach of masculine charm. Mr. Essex had all the necessary tools at his disposal – good looks, intelligence, ease of speech, a ready smile – and yet I could hardly imagine him demeaning himself so. I could hardly imagine him taking the trouble… or being that disingenuous either. He seemed a very straight-forward, plain-spoken sort of man – no arts, no demurs, no kowtowing.

Most probably it had been a bit of one thing and another, including an appeal to her latent maternal instincts. Mama had her share of them, presumably, although well-concealed and not of a sentimental tendency. And she did want me well, I believed, as much for selfish as charitable reasons. Her purposes and her pride would be better served by having a daughter who was the model of well-bred womanhood, whole and brilliantly married, than one who was a permanent invalid. And so there really was no mystery in her efforts to further my cure. Even Mama could be made to see the value of temporary sacrifice to achieve a worthwhile end.

So, thus we finished out the year and faced the bleak month of January, when the nights are long and the sun is too lazy to mount more than a half-hearted assault on the sky each day.

But January held the promise of further improvement in my health, and then Colonel Fitzwilliam would be coming round toward the end of the month, which was a definite matter of cheer.

~~*~~

It was awkward at first having John Fitzwilliam to Rosings on his own. He had hardly ever come without his cousin, who was no longer welcome. However, I would wager that the phantom presence of William Darcy was felt by us all. It permeated the atmosphere. It was apparent in what we did and did not say. It shouted from the conspicuously vacant place on the sofa where he had always used to sit when we gathered together in the past. Still, with two such proficient talkers as my mother and my cousin John, we soon moved past these early difficulties, and all became easy again.

I was gratified when John noticed my improvement that very first day, confirming once more that I had not imagined it. He gave me a quizzical look and then said, "Do my eyes deceive me, or are you in better health than when last I saw you, Anne? I know you are in very fine looks today, if that is any indication. Why, there are roses in your cheeks. I am sure of it."

He was always a flatterer and yet in such a pleasingly innocuous way that it never failed to lift my spirits. I smiled, and I am sure I colored as well. "You are too kind, Cousin," I said.

"I arranged for a new doctor to attend her," explained Mama. "It is too soon to tell, but he may be doing her some good."

"I say there can be no doubt about it, Lady Catherine! You are too close to see clearly. Being with your daughter every day makes it difficult to notice the incremental changes. I have a better view. Coming in from afar after a prolonged absence, I observe a distinct improvement."

"I do feel better, John, day by day."

"Excellent! And what is this miracle worker giving you? Has he brought some magic elixir from a far corner of the globe?"

"Not at all," I answered. "There is nothing the least bit exotic about his remedies. It is nothing much beyond proper food, rest, and exercise. Oh! That reminds me, I have not yet taken my exercise today, and soon the sun will be setting. Mama, would you mind terribly if Mrs. Jenkinson walks with me while it is still light out of doors? We would be no more than half an hour."

Before Mama could reply, Colonel Fitzwilliam stood. Coming across the room to me and stretching out his hand, he said, "Might *I* have that pleasure instead, Cousin Anne?"

Mama might very well have refused my request, but she did not deny my cousin's

"Out of doors?" he asked when we had exited the drawing room together. "It *is* early February, in case you forgot."

It was true that the air would be frosty. It would fill my chest with sharp prickles of ice. The sensation could not be considered entirely pleasant, and yet I had come to look forward to it. The cold against my warm skin made me feel alive, which was worth anything else.

"I am much stronger than before," I explained, "and Mr. Essex says that fresh air is very restorative."

"Mr. Essex's wish is your command, I see."

"It is by meticulously following his instructions that I have come as far as I have, John."

"Then by all means, let us take a twilight turn in the garden. I shall be pleased to have you to myself for a few minutes in any case."

When we were properly attired and had achieved the back porch, he offered his arm and resumed. "I cannot tell you how relieved I am to see you looking so well, Anne – for your own sake, of course, but also for my conscience and for your cousin Darcy's. We have both been anxious for your well-being after all that happened, although what Georgiana said about the contents of your letter to her went a long way towards allaying any real fears."

"As you see, I am perfectly well. It is only the loss of my cousins' company I mourn, not the prior arrangement with William. I truly wish him and Elizabeth very well and very happy. Now, shall we set forth?"

He motioned for me to direct our course, and so I took us down the steps and onto the path that led to the right – the one that would take us into the grove.

"That is exceedingly generous of you, I am sure," he said as we walked. "Exceedingly generous."

"Not at all. Thank you for answering Mama's summons, though. I could not have born to lose you as well. I have so little family left to me as it is." In the brief pause that followed, something Mr. Essex had said came back to mind. "John, do you know if my father perchance had any brothers at all, or even a cousin of some sort? Mr. Essex mentioned happening to meet with a Mr. de Bourgh in London, and since then I have wondered. I know so little about Papa's relations, and I do not dare ask Mama. It upsets her so to speak of him. I thought perhaps, with your being so much older, you might recall something more." When he hesitated – in his step as well as with his reply – I asked, "What is it, John?"

"Oh, nothing at all," he said with a careless laugh. "As you say, I am *much* older, and it sometimes takes a moment or two for my elderly brain to find the right answer. But, no, I do not believe I ever heard tell of your father's having any brothers or other near relations. This fellow in London you mention just happens to have the same surname – a chance, a coincidence."

"That is what Mr. Essex said about it."

"He sounds like a very sensible fellow, this Mr. Essex of yours. It fills me with confidence that you have someone like that looking out for you. Now, I almost forgot." He reached to pull something from inside his greatcoat. "It is a letter from our cousin Georgiana, and I was charged to give it to you in secret."

~~*~~

Although I was thrilled to receive Georgiana's letter and filled with curiosity to see what it contained, I thanked John for delivering it and tucked it away in my pocket. I read it later in my bedchamber.

Dear Cousin Anne,

Thank you for your letter last November and for the tender sentiments expressed therein. None of us here at Pemberley holds any ill will against you, certainly. It is quite the reverse. Your behavior in this matter speaks clearly of charity and grace, putting the good of others before your own. I can only hope that, as you convinced my brother was the case, it has not been at great personal cost.

In giving William up to be happy with another, you have done a noble thing. You may be gratified to hear that they truly are happy together too – William and Elizabeth – and she is a great gift to me as well. You will remember how I have always longed for a sister. Elizabeth is that to me and more. Being older and more confident, in some ways she also takes the place of the mother I have lost. I find there is wisdom as well as kindness in her soul, and she has relieved me of acting as mistress of the house – something I always felt unequal to.

My only regret in the match is the break between our families this business has engendered. However I, like you, will continue to pray that it is only temporary, that time will have its way in softening hardened hearts and making them amenable to reconciliation. May we soon meet again on terms of great cordiality and deepest friendship. In the meantime, our covert letters and Cousin Fitzwilliam must suffice to maintain a connection between us. As you see from the hand delivering this missive, he is a willing partner in our cause.

Sincere best wishes,
Georgiana

I was indeed gratified to know I was still esteemed by my cousins, and that I had helped to promote such a felicitous outcome for them. I did, however, have to guard against my old enemy: envy. Not only had William and Elizabeth found contentment in their union, so had Georgiana. They now, all three, had each other whilst I was more alone than ever, it seemed.

- 23 -

Lady Catherine

On Plans Progressing

Fitzwilliam stayed ten days at Rosings, giving Anne and me at least a short and very welcome reprieve from the dreary sameness of the long winter months. Otherwise, Mr. and Mrs. Collins might have been our only company, and there was no novelty left in their visits. Even the one bit of promising news we had heard from them – their expectations of an offspring – had come to nothing. How like Mr. Collins to pompously announce before anything could be known for certain, to blunder when it came to something as fundamental as procreation. But perhaps in time, he might manage to remedy the situation.

In any case, the Collinses' attendance was only desirable when we could get nobody better, which was to say, nobody else at all. Mr. Essex still came down from town every week, rain or shine, and I supposed we should soon grow just as accustomed to him. Although his methods were unconventional, they seemed to be producing results. Anne's health and looks did gradually improve. She was less unbecomingly thin in her person than before, and she spent less time sulking in dejected silence, claiming to be indisposed.

As for the physician's own behavior, that was on the mend as well. If not yet solicitous, his manner had inched a degree closer to an acceptable level of civility after my frank words of correction to him. At times, he almost acted the gentleman he claimed to be. Here was proof that I had carried my point with him. He would be better for having fallen under my necessary reproof.

He could stay, I concluded, at least for the time being. He could attend Anne as her physician as long as the positive trend continued. These were the terms on which his employment depended, and so I told him. Why he should have taken offence at it, I have no idea. Surely he did not think I intended to pay him for accomplishing nothing or for seeing my daughter into a worse state of health than she had been before.

In any case, Anne's improvement came just in time to assist in my other cause on her behalf. The letters I had written to my most trusted and well-connected friends were beginning to bear fruit.

Sir Henry Stanfield was my personal favorite amongst the clutch of eligible contenders I expected to apply for Anne's hand. Not only did he have the highest rank, he was already in possession of his property while the others were still waiting to inherit. And on a previous meeting, Sir Henry seemed to agree with my ideas in nearly every particular, which indicated admirable good sense. Things regressed downward from there to Mr. Alderwood at the bottom. He was the son of a dear friend, and he would at least be a baronet one day. But I would by no means condition for anything less for my daughter. After all, she was rich as well as being the granddaughter to an earl and therefore entitled to marry exceptionally well.

Although I should have dearly liked to have been provided a grander match myself, I had at least married money and acquired a title of distinction from my father. Anne had gained no title by birth, so the only option left to her was to aggrandize her name by marriage. I could not bear to see her wed to some mere 'Mister' who could not even make her a 'Lady.' I had been prepared to overlook that disadvantage in the prior case, to see her married to my sister's son. Now, however, the situation was altered. Anne had one and only one chance to improve her position, and I would not see her waste it.

I planned to reserve final judgment until such time as all eligible candidates had presented themselves and been thoroughly examined. One cannot be too careful, especially where the male sex is concerned. Men, in my experience, are prone to many weaknesses, weaknesses that visit suffering upon others besides themselves, and I intend to do a better job deciding for my daughter than my father did deciding for his. Anne might not appreciate the trouble I take for her now, but I trusted some day she would thank me.

- 24 -

Mrs. Jenkinson

On the Parade Commencing

I had always liked Colonel Fitzwilliam, and I was glad for his visit, especially on Anne's account. He was not our only visitor that winter and spring, however, just the most welcome one, in my view.

A Mr. Alderwood first presented himself at Rosings Park the Wednesday afternoon during the last week of February. "Mr. Alderwood," said Lady Catherine when Anne and I entered the room at her summons, "this is my daughter Miss de Bourgh. Oh, and Mrs. Jenkinson. Anne, this is Mr. Alderwood."

An unremarkable man who was fast nearing forty stood before us, a stranger whom I never remembered seeing before. He was thin and only slightly above my own height with a shock of rather unruly dark hair atop his head, but he was quite elegantly turned out, especially for an afternoon caller.

He bowed and smiled at my young lady, saying, "Miss de Bourgh, how lovely to see you again."

"Again, sir?" she replied. "Have we met?" She looked with confusion to her mother, who did nothing to enlighten her.

"You do not recall, do you?" he asked smilingly.

"No, sir. Forgive me, but I do not."

"It is of little matter, Miss de Bourgh, I assure you. After all, there is no particular reason that you should remember. I visited here only once before, with my mother, when you were not much more than a child. And now I come to deliver her compliments to you both… as well as my own, of course. I am her emissary, you might say." He bowed again with a flurry of his hand to accentuate the formal gesture.

Still mostly in the dark, judging from the state of her countenance, Anne said, "How kind of you to call. Please do sit down again, Mr. Alderwood."

After all of us did so, Lady Catherine finally deigned to shed some light on the subject, saying, "Anne, Charles's mother is Lady Ethel. You have heard me speak of her many times. She and I attended the same exclusive seminary for girls together in our youth, and we have kept up a faithful correspondence ever since."

"Oh, yes. Lady Ethel. I remember," said Anne.

"To this day, I still consider her one of my dearest and most trusted friends, though we rarely see one another."

Mr. Alderwood nodded sorrowfully. "A great pity, Lady Catherine, if you will permit my saying so, for I know my mother feels precisely the same. 'Charles,' she often says to me, 'there is not another friend in the world like Lady Catherine.'"

Her ladyship looked pleased at this.

"How kind," said Anne.

When a brief silence ensued, I expected Lady Catherine to fill it, or failing that, I stood ready to lend a hand myself. In fact, I had opened my mouth to do just that when I was silenced by a stern look from her ladyship. She then nodded in Anne's direction, clearly signaling that she meant for her daughter to take up the office.

I looked doubtfully at Anne. Sustaining a conversation with a stranger had always been well beyond her capabilities and fortitude. I could not fault her for it; I understood that it must be near impossible to face down a challenge of that sort when one has barely enough reserves to get through the basic necessaries of life. And yet, things were different now. I saw a new strength in her. In fact, I saw her courage swell at that very moment. Anne had come a long way from what she was before, and speaking to a person such as Mr. Alderwood no longer held any terrors for her.

"What brings you so far south, Mr. Alderwood?" she asked. "Surely you did not travel all this way only to deliver your mother's compliments, which she could have done herself through the post – no personal emissary required."

"How perceptive you are, Miss de Bourgh, and it is just as you say. It happened that some business in London required my early attendance. Then by a happy coincidence, your mother's letter arrived just before I was to set out, giving me reason to make a small extension of my journey as far as Kent."

"My mother's letter," she repeated, looking at Lady Catherine.

"Yes," her ladyship answered quickly, as if it were a question she had been prepared for. "I had lately written to Lady Ethel, telling her how I longed to see her again and inquiring if there might be any possibility of her traveling south, perhaps escorted by her son."

"Alas!" exclaimed Mr. Alderwood. "My mother's indifferent state of health does not allow her to travel just now. It is a long way from Yorkshire into Kent. You must admit that to be true, Miss de Bourgh…"

"Of course."

"…So she urged me to come on my own, delivering her compliments and regrets in person, which I was more than happy to do. I still remembered that earlier visit to Rosings Park with considerable fondness and was curious to renew the acquaintance. Now I see you again, Miss de Bourgh, and having been received so kindly by your mother," he added with a small bow in her ladyship's direction, "I am very pleased with my decision to come."

He stayed an hour, and then Lady Catherine insisted he remain for tea after that.

"You must tell me more about how your mother and father do," Mama encouraged him, "and Anne would like to hear about your family estate, I am sure. Yorkshire is such an interesting part of the country, and she has never been, you know. Then perhaps next time you come, Anne will show you the gardens."

Mr. Alderwood was pleasant enough company, carrying his share of the conversation and more, for which I was grateful, since Lady Catherine remained comparatively quiet herself and kept me silent as well. She seemed very determined that Anne should contribute more to the social intercourse than she was accustomed to doing.

Her ladyship's reasons – for inviting Mr. Alderwood's call and for putting her daughter forward so – were immediately evident to me. The anticipated parade of potential suitors had commenced.

Poor Anne. Mr. Alderwood was only the first and the least objectionable in the procession, according to my assessment. Next came that insipid coxcomb of a fellow, Mr. Compton, followed by

Sir Henry Stanfield, whose head was bald on top and gray below. Then there was that one with the florid complexion and the nasal whine to his voice. Oh, what was his name? Bixby! That was it: Mr. something-or-other Bixby. The last (at least for the time being) was Mr. Candleford. I suppose there was nothing so terribly wrong with him, but there was nothing terribly right about him either. I saw no spark of life in him, no animation such as I would choose for my young lady.

I was present for the greater share of each visit, as was Lady Catherine. I remained at Anne's side as her companion and waiting woman, seeing to the little details of her comfort as usual. I rang for the tea. I fetched a pillow when one was wanted. If a walk in the garden were proposed, I followed at a discreet distance as watchdog and chaperone. In the drawing room, I stood ready to assist Anne with conversation, although such assistance was required far less often then what it once might have been before Mr. Essex had taken charge of improving my lady's health.

I was proud of her for how she politely bore with them all, though I could tell the exercise was very little to her liking. Here again, it was something we could not speak together about plainly, only circumspectly.

"What did you think of Mr. Candleford, Miss?" I asked after he had gone and we were on our own again. What I was thinking was, *How could you abide his listless demeanor, even for an hour? Please do not settle for him!*

"He seems a very good sort of man," she said with hesitation, "although somewhat lacking in spirit. It is perhaps unfair to judge him upon so short an acquaintance, however."

"Perhaps, but my early impression is the same as yours, so I think there is much truth in it. How is your head, Miss? Can I do anything for you?"

"Fresh air is what I require. Will you walk with me?"

"By all means." I looked out the window. "The sky does not look favorable, however. Would you not prefer to take your exercise indoors today rather than risk being caught in the rain? Fresh air is desirable, but a cold soaking is not."

She sighed. "Yes, perhaps you are correct, Mrs. Jenkinson. I have no right to put your health at peril just so I can clear my head. The picture gallery will do very well, I am sure."

"It is not my own health I am thinking of, Miss. Remember, you made me watchdog over yours in Mr. Essex's absence. When is the doctor coming next?"

"The day after tomorrow," she said cheerfully, "but first we are to receive Mr. Alderwood again."

"You liked him, did you not, Miss? Or so it seemed to me."

"More than the others, I suppose, but really the whole thing seems so…" And here she left off. "Well, I suppose I shall just have to make the best of it. Mama is simply doing what she believes is necessary for my future happiness."

"Yes, Miss. It is just as you say. The business is perhaps a bit trying for your nerves, but Lady Catherine no doubt means well by it," I said.

Then something very surprising took place; Miss de Bourgh made a sort of a joke. She leant closer to me, and with mischief in her eye, she said conspiratorially, "I have an idea, Mrs. Jenkinson. After Mama has finished practicing her matchmaking arts on me, I shall endeavor to persuade her to next find a husband for *you.* Shall I?"

"She needn't take much trouble over it, Miss," I returned in the same spirit. "I shall simply ask permission to choose from those left after you have had your pick of the gentlemen. It would be wrong to let any of them go to waste. Do not you agree?"

Anne laughed. "Yes. In that case, might I recommend Sir Henry to you?"

"That is an excellent notion, Miss! He is certainly more of an age for me than he would be for you, and I have always wanted to be *Lady* Flora." Anne laughed again, and this time I joined her.

- 25 -

Anne

Going Down the Garden Path

Mr. Alderwood came to Rosings once more before his business affairs in London were concluded and he departed for the north. During that visit, Mama made certain I spent as much time with him as possible, including, as promised, the guided tour of the garden.

It was a dry day, and I did not object, especially since I wished to be able to report to Mr. Essex that I had not neglected my outdoor exercise. So I led Mr. Alderwood through to the formal gardens at the back of the house. With the watchful Mrs. Jenkinson stationed at a distance, Mr. Alderwood and I strolled along the paths between the carefully clipped knee-high hedges, which wove back and forth, crisscrossing themselves in elaborate diamond patterns punctuated by topiary obelisks at the corners.

"Although it may not be much to look at this time of year, Mr. Alderwood," I explained, "in the summer, there are flowers blooming in all these spaces between the boxwood. It really is quite beautiful."

"Although I shall gladly take your word for now, Miss de Bourgh," he said, "I hope to see it for myself a few months hence." We continued on in silence a few more paces before Mr. Alderwood resumed in a more serious tone. "Miss de Bourgh, I realize our official acquaintance has been brief, but you should know that I have long admired you from afar, the foundation being laid by my favorable first impression years ago and built on by what I subsequently learnt of you from your mother's letters. So you see that even before I came to Rosings, I was far from indifferent to you."

I hardly knew what to think of such an assertion or how to respond, and yet I deemed some response necessary. It seemed to me that the best policy would be to make light of his rather serious statement, and so I tried to set a casual tone of voice. "I admire you too, Mr. Alderwood, but as you say, our acquaintance so far has been very brief."

"And yet I feel as if I know all I need to know, Miss de Bourgh. May I call you Anne?"

"I believe that is a bit premature, Mr. Alderwood."

"Ah, I see I shall have to earn that right." He stopped and turned to me, saying, "I hope to do so now. I dare not waste this ideal opportunity. I must speak to you about my feelings before I go. I want to leave you in no doubt as to my intentions, which are entirely honorable."

It was now obvious as to where his conversation was leading. His purport being something for which I was not prepared, I made a final attempt to forestall it. "Again, Mr. Alderwood, I cannot help but feel this kind of talk is premature. It is no pleasure to me to hear it."

"Please, Miss de Bourgh, you must allow me to finish what I have begun."

"Very well, Mr. Alderwood, if I must." The sooner he began, the sooner he would have done.

He went on to remind me of all he had to offer – his current situation as well as his lofty expectations upon his father's demise. He then took my hands. "…In short, although it may be less than you have a right to expect, I offer it all to you, Miss de Bough. If you will honor me by consenting to become my wife, I shall spend the rest of my life ensuring your happiness."

It was a good proposal, I decided, although I had little to compare it with. Looking at it objectively, what he had said did not seem deficient in either content or style. The feelings expressed were proper and possibly even sincere. They did not inspire similar feelings returned in me, however. Instead, I felt mostly vexation, more so with Mama then with the gentleman before me. This was *her* doing.

Mr. Alderwood had been perfectly charming up until this point. I had even begun to wonder if he were somebody for whom I could develop romantic feelings, given enough time. But then I was *not* given enough time. Mr. Alderwood made his intentions known without the delay that might have otherwise worked in his favor, and that promising bud of potential was prematurely blighted.

No doubt proposing was what he had meant to do all along, whether he had liked me or not. No doubt Mama's information had made it clear that there was no time to lose. I and my handsome fortune would go to the man with the best offer. Mr. Alderwood's might not be the grandest, so he was determined it would impress by at least being the first. Perhaps he could make off with the prize before the other contenders had time to get into the game – the fox stealing the hen from the henhouse before the hounds could even set up their watch.

I had no wish to be treated in such an insulting manner. I had no wish to be part of a lucrative prize package to be claimed by means of a winning bid. I could hear the auctioneer rattling away.

What am I bid for lot number eight? We have on the block the heiress to a handsome fortune and an excellent estate in Kent. It all goes to daughter when the old lady pops off. So speak up, gentlemen, before it's too late! Make your best offer...

"Did you hear me, Miss de Bourgh?" Mr. Alderwood looked expectantly to me. "Did you understand my offer?"

I could feel my newly minted sense of well-being slipping away. I feared one of my old headaches might be coming upon me. Yet Mr. Alderwood was waiting, and for all my vexation of spirit, I did not wish to be rude. I had to answer him something.

What I said exactly, I hardly know. I believe I thanked him for the compliment of his addresses. I told him that it was not in my power to accept them, however. Then, at his request, I gave him leave to call again when he was able. Despite how displeased I was at that moment, I did not wish to close that door entirely. Doing so would have been as unfairly premature as Mr. Alderwood's proposal, and I liked to think I was above that sort of meanness. My current peevishness could not be allowed to push me into making what might be a mistake. After all, I did like Mr. Alderwood, and blighted buds sometimes survived to bloom beautifully in the end.

~~*~~

I should have known better, especially with the portent of a headache hanging over me. I should have heeded the lessons I had learnt from Mr. Essex. I should have removed to the quiet of my own rooms and composed myself. Instead, when our visitor was gone, I turned on Mama. "This was your doing," I accused her. "You summoned Mr. Alderwood – him and who knows how many others – and made him propose before he should."

"Steady yourself, Anne," she said evenly. "You must not suspect me. I told you that when word got about of your being available, you would have no shortage of suitors. Mr. Alderwood's proposal is only evidence that I was correct."

"But who is responsible for putting the word about if not you?"

Mama did not answer. She just blinked at me slowly, as if she were bored, and redirected the conversation. "I take it you have rejected Mr. Alderwood's offer," she said without emotion.

"I have, although I gave him leave to call again if he wishes."

"He would not have been my first choice for you either, but you shall have to marry one of them."

Visions of my recent callers flashed through my mind. All of them, except possibly Mr. Alderwood, presented insurmountable barriers – too old, too empty-headed, too much of an arrogant coxcomb, too dull, or too something else equally intolerable. Not one of them could I imagine esteeming enough to want as a husband.

"Why, Mama? Why must I marry at all?" Then I said aloud the words I had been too afraid to speak a thousand times before. "Oh, if only Papa were here! *He* would understand my position and not see me forced into matrimony against my will. He was too good a man and too kind a father for that."

It was as bold a statement as I had ever made to my mother's face, and I held my breath, waiting for the backlash that would surely come. Instead, Mama was silent for a long minute before answering.

"Naturally, you would think so," she said with ominous calm. "In your mind, you have built your father into some brand of saint, since he has not been here to disappoint you as he surely would have otherwise. Allow me to enlighten you, Anne; your father was no saint, nowhere near it. Furthermore, please recall that before he left us, he saw to it that the arrangement for your marriage was in place, an arrangement made without his seeking your assent to the plan. If you are so determined to worship his memory, I am surprised you did not fight more vigorously to see that arrangement honored. Then you should not have been left to the mercy of my latterly efforts on your behalf. Consider *that* before you throw any more unfounded accusations in my direction."

Mama's unsettling references to my father left any further protestations caught in my throat. There was no point arguing with her in any case; she would never admit to having done anything wrong.

I retreated to my own apartment and remained there the rest of the day, drinking Mr. Essex's tea and trying to quiet my emotions as I had been counseled to do. Nevertheless, I awoke the next morning with a sick headache – the worst I had suffered in weeks.

~~*~~

Mrs. Jenkinson sprang into action once again, plying me with more tea and tempting things to eat as well as with the reminder that Mr. Essex was expected later that day.

"We cannot have you lying about in bed when he comes, can we?" she said. "You will want to show him how well you are doing. Now, give yourself another fifteen minutes and then up you get. We shall have you washed and dressed and looking your best when the young doctor arrives to see you."

And so I was up and dressed when Mr. Essex came. As to looking my best, though, that was more than what could be reasonably achieved. Although my headache may have eased a bit by that time, it still drummed a steady beat at my temples and the back of my skull, and I instinctively lowered my lids against any source of light, including the opening of the door when he entered my rooms.

"Ah, Miss de Bourgh, good afternoon," he said softly, coming over to me. "Mrs. Jenkinson tells me your head is very ill today. What has brought this on?"

"I had quite a trying time yesterday," I answered, not wanting to admit to my specific failings. "Must you have the details, Mr. Essex? They really are too tedious for words."

"If you had rather not say, then I shall not press you. Just sit quietly while I review your diary. May I?" he asked before picking up the book from the place he was by now accustomed to finding it.

I nodded, giving my permission.

As Mr. Essex studied my journal, I surreptitiously studied him. I liked the look of his face – the pleasing features, yes, but also the innate intelligence I saw in his eyes, the artless compassion. Viewing him from under my lowered lids, I watched the shifts and subtle stirrings as he read, trying to imagine what went on inside his mind. Did my incoherent scribblings coalesce into some sort of relevant pattern? Did his orderly, educated brain make sense of it all?

I thought how exhilarating it must be to have the knowledge that gave one the ability to accomplish great things, whether that took the form of building bridges or relieving human suffering. How gratifying to see the good done by the work of one's own hands! By contrast, I had been taught nothing at all useful. I could not even give enjoyment to others by providing music. My education had consisted merely of how to behave in society and how to manage a manor house. And my voracious reading habit had tended more toward my own amusement – with histories and stories to feed my imagination – rather than instilling in me any practical information.

There was nothing inherently wrong in these pursuits, I supposed, but how much better by what one has learnt to fit oneself for achieving something worthwhile. Although that was primarily the prerogative of men, of course, men like Mr. Essex, who had more important things to do than playing society's games.

He suddenly closed the book and looked up, catching me watching him. For just a moment he returned my thoughtful gaze. Then he smiled and said, "I am pleased to see from your notes that you have been very faithful with your exercise, Miss de Bourgh. What about today? Have you been out walking?"

"Not yet, sir. I have not felt strong enough for it. Mrs. Jenkinson is very reliable, but even she is not sturdy enough to bear my full weight if I were to falter."

Mr. Essex stood, went to the window, and came back again, saying, "Since I am here, what do you say to trying my arm instead? I daresay I am robust enough to carry you, if it should come to that, although I am certain it shall not. I believe you are stronger than you know, Miss de Bourgh. We can continue our discussion while we walk."

"Very well," I said, gingerly allowing him to help me to my feet, "although my eyes may be too sensitive to bear the outdoors today."

"Yes, I noticed. That is why I went to the window, to evaluate the current conditions. With the thick clouds, the light is not excessively bright. If you were to wear a wide-brimmed hat, I think you would not find it too glaring. And the fresh air will do you much good, Miss de Bourgh. Will you trust me in this?"

I did, of course. Donning my widest-brimmed bonnet and bundling up against the chill, I took Mr. Essex's arm and prepared to venture out with my eyes open no more than a slit. Even so, I could not help drawing back the instant the outer door was opened. No doubt it was a cloudy day, just as the doctor had said, but the sky seemed astonishingly bright to me.

"Is it too much for you, Miss de Bough?" he asked on the threshold. "I have no desire to push you beyond what you can bear."

"I am willing to attempt it, if you think it beneficial."

"Then I honor your courage, and I promise we will turn back anytime you say. Perhaps, once we have descended these steps, you might even close your eyes altogether and allow me to guide you. Now, where shall we walk, Miss de Bourgh?"

"Would you like to see the formal gardens, Mr. Essex?"

He looked toward them and then nodded in the opposite direction. "Let us strike off that way," he suggested. "I prefer a more natural scene to artificial beauty. To where does this path lead?"

"To the orchard, but it is a long way off."

"No matter. We shall go only as far as you wish today."

At the bottom of the stone stairs, I did what Mr. Essex had suggested; I closed my eyes and relied on his steady arm to steer me right. The gravel path was level and I had a trustworthy guide, so I feared for nothing. In fact, I found the sensation remarkably relaxing.

"Are you in too much pain?" he asked after a few minutes.

"No. Thank you for your concern, Mr. Essex, but I believe I can continue."

"Good. Then tell me anything else about your health that I should know. Have you noticed any new problems? The account in your diary looked very encouraging."

"I am encouraged as well, at least I was until this morning."

"You must not be overly concerned by setbacks like this, Miss de Bourgh. They are bound to come along from time to time. We learn as much from them as we do from our successes. So you see, you must not consider such events failures either for yourself or for the course of treatment we have embarked upon. It simply means we have more work to do, farther to travel before we arrive at our destination."

"I am disappointed in myself, though. You have told me I must learn to remain quiet within, regardless what provocation may come against me. I should have heeded the first warning sign and calmed myself before it had gone too far."

"Remaining calm is always the goal, yes, especially since you seem to pay a very high price when you become stirred up. But we can none of us expect to keep such a standard perfectly. I certainly cannot. And I daresay you did your best under trying circumstances. I can only assume you were exceptionally provoked yesterday."

I had not wanted to explain before, but now I thought better of it. What difference would it make? Mr. Essex knew every other aspect of my life. If he was to continue helping me, I should hold nothing back that could conceivably be important. It might be useful for him to know what had pushed me beyond the point of self-control. "Yes, I was," I said after a moment. "I was very much distressed by an unwanted marriage proposal and then by an argument with Mama about it afterward."

"Well! You *did* have an eventful day. No small wonder, then, that you found it difficult to deal with. You must not deem today's result a failure, though. As I said before, it is a chance to learn how to manage better for the next time. It is not unlikely that you will... That is, a young lady such as yourself, with so much to offer... What I mean to say is that you may be obliged to face similar circumstances again. Of course, it would be an entirely different matter, I should think, if the proposal were a welcome one instead."

"Undoubtedly." That was all I could think to answer, and neither of us carried the subject any further. Instead, Mr. Essex presently asked what interests I pursued or would pursue when my health allowed. "I am very partial to reading," I answered. "Novels especially, I am afraid. And one day I would like to travel."

"No need to apologize for liking novels, Miss de Bourgh. Among other benefits, they can be an excellent way to travel to interesting places, especially when no other means are available. An exploration conducted solely with the mind is not constrained by limits of time and distance."

"But still, novels can hardly be considered *serious* reading, Mr. Essex – not like the books of information you no doubt read."

"I like all sorts of books," he said, "including novels. Another time, perhaps we shall compare lists of our favorites and find those we have in common." I was about to suggest turning back when Mr. Essex continued. "You are tired now, I perceive. Let us return to the house."

- 26 -

Lady Catherine

Exercising Restraint

"Anne is still very much troubled by her headache, Lady Catherine." Mr. Essex announced when they returned from their walk out of doors. "I recommend that she spend the evening quietly in her own rooms as soon as she has taken a little something to eat."

I thoroughly expected this to be his calculated preamble to blaming me for the trouble. I did quarrel with her; I was prepared to admit that much. But it was she herself who began it. Once she allowed herself to become agitated by Mr. Alderwood's clumsy proposal, it was not in my power to pacify her. I did all I could by showing remarkable restraint when she threw her accusations at me.

I supposed what I said about her father may have been more than what was strictly necessary, but I trusted it would serve to make her calmer in the end. Dwelling on what might have been 'if only Papa were here' simply added to her unhappiness, encouraging her to continue imagining the better life she believes she was unfairly deprived of by his early departure.

However, even in this, I practiced restraint. Had I truly been bent on vexing my daughter, I could have said *so* much more. I could have smashed to pieces all her pleasant misapprehensions about her father. I could have mentioned somewhat of his disgraceful behavior over the years of our marriage. I might even have forced upon Anne the disturbing details about the day he left us, as I have sometimes been tempted to do.

It had not been easy to keep these things to myself. Knowing the unsavory truth, it had not always been comfortable to see my husband put on a pedestal and venerated by our daughter as a fallen hero, as if he had been killed in battle, bravely defending his homeland. Yet unmasking him would only have pained Anne without purpose. She would not thank me for doing so. She would not love me better for spoiling her cherished illusions.

That fact was not my guiding principle, however. Parenthood is a duty to be faithfully discharged to the end, not a competition for the affection on one's own offspring. If it were, I had lost that contest long ago.

Anne preferred her father from the beginning. That is not what worried me. What worried me was that she was so very like him. Consequently, I watched her closely from an early age for any expression of the darker aspects of his character that she might have inherited, any tendency towards his weakness needing to be extinguished before it burst into flames. If I had been critical of Anne, it was only out of my perpetual vigilance against that evil.

~~*~~

Mr. Essex did *not* attempt to reproach me for contributing to Anne's temporary turn for the worse. Very wise of him, too, for I would by no means have tolerated being treated like a recalcitrant child under the schoolmaster's discipline. It would have meant the end of our association altogether.

Instead, he only asked me, "Might I be allowed to ride down again from town tomorrow rather than waiting another week for our usual appointment? I would like to keep a closer eye on the situation until the current crisis has passed, just as a precaution."

I thanked him for his conscientious intent, but I also felt compelled to point out the illogic of his plan. "You will no more than arrive in London tonight before needing to turn round and come back again," I said. "Far better for you to remain here. We have plenty of rooms, so you can have no scruples on that account. Now that is settled, you will want to freshen up before dinner. We always dress for dinner at Rosings, but I will make an exception for you this one time since you arrived with no suspicion of extra clothing being wanted." I told the nearest footman, "Show Mr. Essex to the blue paisley room, and be sure he has everything he needs."

The doctor was quite naturally overcome by my generosity, but he could not deny that I was right. And so he agreed.

I was pleased with myself for arranging that he should stay that first night, especially when I discovered Mr. Essex to be a very agreeable addition to our dinner table. His conversation was new to us, which must have been considered an advantage. He could speak intelligently on a variety of topics as it turned out, not just medicine. In short, I found his manners surprisingly good in this new setting. Anne had no appetite, but she seemed reassured and made more of an effort with her physician present, which was another apparent benefit.

After dinner, Anne went straight upstairs, as planned. Thinking that cards would be the easiest way to entertain Mr. Essex that evening, I sent for the Collinses to make up a table for Loo. As expected, they came with alacrity – Mrs. Collins cheerful and obliging, Mr. Collins bowing and scraping and thanking me for my kind condescension in inviting them.

After being introduced to our other guest, he declared, "It is a great honor to meet you, sir, I am sure. Indeed, it is an honor to meet any person of Lady Catherine's society. In my experience, her ladyship associates with only the most refined people from the very best of families. Although I am but a humble clergyman myself, respect for my office often gives me an acceptable entrée to even the highest levels of society, as you see."

I immediately perceived that Mr. Collins had mistaken Mr. Essex for a fine gentleman, and so I had to correct him at once, giving him to understand that Mr. Essex was much nearer his own level than mine. I find it saves awkwardness and confusion when people recognize where they stand from the beginning. How else will they know how they are to behave?

"Mr. Essex is here as personal physician to Anne," I told him, "not as part of my regular society, Mr. Collins. Nevertheless, I am certain you will find his company very agreeable."

Mr. Essex bowed slightly and said, "A pleasure to meet you, Mr. Collins, Mrs. Collins. I must apologize for not being up to the caliber of those you are apparently accustomed to encountering in this house. Still, I shall do my best not to disappoint."

Mr. Essex did *not* disappoint. He continued to surprise me with more manners and air than one typically finds in a person of his less than elevated rank. In fact, his performance that night set me to thinking. As comparatively isolated as we were in our part of Kent, anybody with even a rudimentary knowledge of the social graces was considered an asset. Mr. Essex's abilities were undeniable, and he was not ill-looking either. Having such a man at my disposal could be advantageous indeed, I decided. If he continued to be accommodating, Mr. Essex could become rather valuable to me, like a pleasanter version of Mr. Collins, whose stories I had already heard and whose manners were growing tedious. One must not mistake a Mr. Essex for a person on an equal footing with one's own kind, but it might be useful to keep him standing by nonetheless.

So before he took leave the next day, I told him, "While we all hope for Anne's speedy and permanent return to good health, Mr. Essex, I can foresee that in the meantime you will likely find it necessary to stop here overnight again. Therefore, I have given orders that the blue paisley room is to be kept for your exclusive use as long as you may have any need of it. Perhaps you will find it convenient to keep a few of your belongings here as well, so you are prepared for whatever arises."

I trust he felt the compliment as he ought. He certainly said everything that was right and proper upon being distinguished by such unmerited favor. In any case, I was correct in my prediction of his finding it convenient to have a standing invitation at Rosings Park. With my encouragement, he gradually began to stop with us more often, being very solicitous of Anne and her health at all times. I congratulated myself, therefore, at having cleverly acquired additional medical attention for my daughter at no additional cost, an extra at dinner at least once a week, and a competent hand at cards whenever I needed.

- 27 -

Anne

On Being Disobliging

Mr. Essex was right in suggesting I would have more opportunities to practice remaining calm under duress, since the visits of my gallant band of suitors continued throughout the spring. I did try to keep an open mind, actually hoping that I could like one of the gentlemen well enough to marry. Alas, I could not. In the end, Mr. Candleford went away without proposing, and the others I declined as kindly but as firmly as possible, including Mr. Alderwood when he asked me a second time. I did suffer a few pangs of guilt on his account for having allowed him to continue to hope falsely, but I assuaged my conscience with the belief that neither his attachment nor any of the others had been very substantial. I would even venture to say that for most if not all, it had been purely a promising social and financial enterprise, not a matter of the heart.

There would be nothing to gain by recounting the details of that period. It is enough to report that – like the gentlemen, I prayed – I came through the entire ordeal unharmed, perhaps even better off for having persevered through it. I dispatched each successive proposal with less emotion and more composure. The second was easier; the third and fourth, easier still. None of others produced the vexation, conflict, or headache of the first. I was nearly imperturbable now. Even Mama's disapproving looks could not alarm me as much as they once had.

Mr. Essex was there to help and encourage me through it all. "See how far you have come in the weeks and months since we began!" he told me. "I must congratulate you, Miss de Bourgh, on mastering the art of self-control. I daresay no one will be able to much disturb your equanimity again, not after what you have learnt through this trial by fire."

I was more grateful than I could say for all that he had done for me in body and mind. My bouts of illness came but rarely now, and with much less severity. As long as I was careful to keep to my healthy routine and guard my mind against agitation, I got on very well.

I was glad indeed to be spared suffering – hours, even days of awful distress at every bump in the road – but I could not help feeling a small ache in my heart at the change. I worried that I might have schooled myself too well. I had learnt to remain calm in the face of provocation to the point where I could reduce a gentleman's offer of marriage (something that should have been terribly important and terribly meaningful, even if unwelcome) to a mere trifle.

Another proposal? What of it? It happens nearly every day. Nothing to work oneself up about. Certainly nothing to make oneself ill over.

I wondered, if and when the time should come that I received a proposal I actually wanted to accept, would I be capable of feeling what I ought, or had I extinguished that flame forever? I feared my natural emotions had been so quenched by my quest to conquer illness that they might never recover, they might never properly assert themselves again. That would be no way to live.

~~*~~

Despite what Mama had said in our earlier argument – that I must accept one of the offers I received – she did not renew or attempt to enforce her ultimatum. It was strange, but the remonstrations I expected from her as I sent each suitor away never came. Still, I knew she could not be the least bit happy with me. I had no doubt what she was thinking, and she could not be expected to hold back forever.

How was it that I could, first, be so careless as to lose the man I was originally intended to marry, and then, be so disobliging as to reject every other eligible candidate set before me? Was I insensible of my own good or merely an ungrateful wretch? No doubt most girls would have thanked their lucky stars for the good fortune of receiving even one of the generous offers I had rejected. How could I, a young lady brought up with the greatest care in the world, and with every advantage money could buy, be so stubbornly perverse? Was this the thanks a mother should receive for all her pain and trouble?

I never heard these accusations spoken. However, I felt every word implied in what Mama *did* say and in her disapproving looks.

"So, that is the last of them gone," she said when Mr. Alderwood departed, rejected for the second time.

"Yes, Mama."

"Well, I hope you know what you are about, Anne. You may be sure that I will be at considerable trouble to account for your inexplicable fastidiousness to my friends, to those who recommended you to their sons and others, especially when I do not begin to comprehend it myself."

That was all.

I was amazed at the mildness of her reproof. Whereas I should have been relieved by this, it made me uneasy instead. The only reason I could imagine for her so calmly accepting the overthrow of this scheme was that she already had another, possibly more unpleasant plan in mind. Either that or somebody held some kind of sway over her behavior, for it was not like Mama to take disappointment graciously.

As for my "inexplicable fastidiousness," on one level, I agreed with Mama. I was not sorry for my conduct; my feelings being what they were, I could have done nothing else. But the question remained. Why was I so difficult to please? Although it was easy for me to find something deficient in each of my suitors, perhaps that was not where the real problem lay. *I* was the common element in every equation, after all, so perhaps the defect was in me instead.

Although I could accept that possibility, I could not see myself doing anything useful with the information. I had not the determination of a careful gardener to root out the noxious weeds in my own character, and intellectual assent did little towards conquering the will. The truth was that I did not want to change, at least not in that way. I did not want to compromise on this most important point. I had no desire to settle for a man I could not truly love and esteem. And I began to deeply pity the thousands of women who had no option but to do just that.

I was one of the lucky ones, for it appeared Mama intended to allow me some choice in the matter after all, at least up to a point that I had not yet reached.

I decided this would be my strategy. Although I had not been in love with William Darcy, I had at least liked and respected him, which would have been a good foundation for a successful marriage. Until such time as another came along whom I could esteem equally, I hoped to be strong enough to continue resisting the push towards matrimony. If that made me perverse and disobliging, then I stood guilty as charged.

~~*~~

One way or another, Mama and I managed to put the recent unpleasantness behind us. Having something else to think of, something else to anticipate, was the very best help towards that end. It was summer now, and we were to receive other guests – visitors more welcome to me than those we had been entertaining of late.

Cousin John was coming again. And my Aunt and Uncle Fitzwilliam (the Earl of Matlock and Lady Constance) had decided to join him, making the journey all together. This was excellent news! I had not as much affection for the Earl and Lady Constance as for their younger son, however I would be pleased to see them nonetheless. A larger society would be a good distraction for Mama as well, I hoped. Perhaps she would even leave off conniving how to get me married for a time while she entertained our relations.

The letter from my aunt announcing their plans related that their elder son, the Viscount, would not be with them. This was neither surprising to me nor much regrettable, for Algernon had never once been to Rosings since achieving his majority, marrying, and adopting his honorary title. In fact, it had been so long since I had last seen him that I thought I should not have known him again. I am certain he should not have known me, in that I must have been only eight or nine at our last meeting. Although I had heard very little of his activities since, it was enough to convey the idea that he carried on in a way quite unpleasing to his parents. Perhaps it was gambling or loose living of some other kind. I do not know. In such cases, I supposed one could only trust to time and the impending weight of an earldom settling on his shoulders to work his eventual reformation.

Contrariwise, I would very much have liked to see my cousin Deborah again. As the youngest of the family, she was nearest my age, and I had some pleasant recollections of times spent with her when we were children. She was always kind to me, and I had grown up admiring her superior beauty and sophistication. As she was perpetually four years in advance of my own development, I looked up to her and often imagined modeling myself after her example. Now we would be more on an equal footing but, unfortunately, also less likely to meet. Lady Deborah was lately married to a man named Fortin, and her responsibilities were with her husband now. I did not know when I should see her again.

Still, three Fitzwilliams were better than one or none, so I determined to be satisfied. I was soon counting the days until their arrival.

- 28 -

Lady Catherine

On Amending One's Views

"I am quite put out with you, Mr. Essex," I told him the next time he came.

Looking not much bothered by my revelation, he said, "I am very sorry to hear it, your ladyship. What have I done to offend you?"

"You insisted I allow my daughter her own way, for the sake of her health. Now her health is improved, but she has thrown away her best chance at happiness and respectability."

"If you mean those gentlemen who came courting, Lady Catherine, I should be very much surprised if one of them had been Miss de Bourgh's best chance for anything worth having. In my opinion, your daughter is already the very picture of propriety. Were she to marry, she would not be acquiring respectability; she would be conferring it. Make free to blame me if you wish, but I shall neither repent of my advice to you nor resent you for your opinion. In fact, I must commend you instead. I honor your forbearance, Lady Catherine, for placing your daughter's health and happiness above other considerations."

"You left me little choice."

"That, I cannot agree with. I say the constraint you felt was your own conscience at work. It directed you to act according to what you knew to be right."

He certainly had an excellent command of the English language – I had to give him his due – and he knew how to make it serve his purposes. That was, in fact, one of the things I had grown to value about Mr. Essex; he was a worthy partner in conversation and a worthy opponent in a verbal joust. He was no groveling lapdog like

Mr. Collins; I had no need of another of those. As long as he did so within the proper bounds of respect – as long as he remembered his place – I no longer quarreled with Mr. Essex's tendency to speak his mind. What had at first sounded like impertinence, now often seemed an invigorating invitation to debate. After all, one must be challenged from time to time in order to keep in top form. Butter may be smooth and pleasing on the tongue, but it will not sharpen a sword. Something providing more resistance is required.

In consequence, my estimation of Mr. Essex was now somewhat improved, which is not to say that I had been in any way mistaken before. On the contrary, the first impression I formed had been accurate, so far as the limited information available to me had allowed. As my knowledge increased, I naturally… refined my opinions. A truly sagacious person is always willing to amend her views when more information comes to light.

"Now, where is my patient?" Mr. Essex asked. "I must not be negligent in my duties."

I delayed him, saying, "A minute more of your time, sir."

"Of course."

"Will you be stopping here tonight? It is all the same to me one way or the other, but it is only fair to let the servants know what to expect."

"Thank you for asking, Lady Catherine. Alas, I have an appointment back in town early tomorrow, one that I cannot miss. I may not stay."

"Very well, Mr. Essex. I have no particular need of you tonight, but perhaps you will be so good as to make yourself available a fortnight hence. My brother, the Earl of Matlock, will be visiting Rosings with his wife and his younger son, Colonel Fitzwilliam, whom you have already met. I must provide what novelty and entertainment I can while they are here, and I trust you will not despise the opportunity of mixing in such elevated society."

"In my profession, Lady Catherine, I often find myself on the most intimate terms with persons of *every* level of society. Of course, the circumstances are often quite different from what you propose."

I could see he was amused by this thought, and so I said, "Yes, I can imagine they are. However, it is my sincere hope, Mr. Essex, that on this occasion at least, you will by no means give in to any temptation to bleed anybody or to mention, even in passing, the word 'bile.' Do I make myself clear?"

He laughed. "Indeed you do, Madam. Perfectly. I promise to be on my very best behavior."

So I had secured the conversation of Mr. Essex for my brother. And the Collinses would, of course, be more than willing to come and contribute what they could in their own humble style. These would do for a night or two of cards after dinner, but I would need to gather a few more substantial personages as well. Not that I wanted extra people about all the time. I saw my brother but rarely, and on this occasion I had something very particular to discuss with him.

- 29 -

Mrs. Jenkinson

On Preserving the Distinctions of Rank

Whenever there were important guests at Rosings, I felt myself a servant more than usual. I was not free to behave as I normally did. I must be always watchful, not assuming anything. Though I was Miss Anne's companion, I could not depend on my companionship being wanted in the customary way when there were others about in the house. Instead, at these times, I endeavored to anticipate what was required of me moment by moment. I must be ever available while also remaining unobtrusive, always watchful for signs as to whether my presence or my absence was desired. Although more often than not, there was no mystery. When Lady Catherine said, "Leave us, Mrs. Jenkinson," I needed no special powers of perception to determine what to do. I went to my rooms and did not reappear until sent for.

There, I might do what odd jobs I could on my own, eating by myself from a tray, too, rather than attempting to join the servants below stairs, where I did not fit in either. Such times were not bereft of comfort, however. These were opportunities to take a precious hour or two of leisure – to read, to write letters, to play my pianoforte, or walk alone in the gardens. Other than my half day a week, I could never know when my next chance for liberty might come.

So when I heard of the expected guests, I wondered what it would mean for me. The last time these particular relations of her ladyship had come, I was included in most but not all of the goings-on. Though I had come down in life, I had not forgot my upbringing; I still knew how to behave in good society. Even so, nobody took much notice of me. My main usefulness seemed to be rounding out a card table while keeping a solicitous watch over my young mistress. Miss Anne did not need very much looking after anymore, thanks to her recovered health, but I still had the power of making an odd number even at cards.

According to my earlier observations, his lordship was very much like his sister in character: used to speaking his mind and having his way. And since he was a rich man and an earl besides, there was nobody to oppose him, nothing to curb his natural tendencies. He could indulge his dictatorial urges on every whim, and good luck to anybody who crossed him. I could not know these things for certain from my own limited information; some of my assumptions about him I based less on confirmed fact and more on the behavior of his wife. Perhaps this was an unfair judgment, however, for I knew no real harm of him, and it is possible that Lady Constance was timid and languid by nature, not because she was made so by her husband's constant browbeating. Nevertheless, I felt sympathy for *her* and no small degree of apprehension at the idea of confronting *him* again.

There was no apprehension at the thought of seeing the colonel, however. He was always a man of ease and friendliness, charmingly respectful of me and most kind to his cousin. It was for her sake that I rejoiced. Miss Anne, I knew, looked forward to the coming of her relations without reservation. Apparently, her uncle held no terror for her; she got on well with her aunt; and she very much enjoyed the warmth and diversion Colonel Fitzwilliam could be counted on to bring.

I did not see the welcoming ceremonies for the earl and his family since Lady Catherine dismissed me as soon as their carriage arrived. But I expected to have some news when I took Miss Anne her medicinal tea that night. The fact that there were guests in the house would make no difference, I knew; she would keep faithfully to her bedtime routine as she had since the day Mr. Essex prescribed it months before.

"I am come with your tea, Miss." I said, finding her in her room at the usual time. "I hope your relations arrived in safety and good health."

"Ah, Mrs. Jenkinson, you are such dear. Yes, they are very well, all three of them. I am sorry you were not allowed to stay, though. Mama is so peculiar about these things."

"Thank you, but I took no offence. I think it is only natural that her ladyship should want to keep to just a family party at first."

"You *are* family to me, Mrs. Jenkinson."

"It is kind of you to say so, Miss, but you know that can never be. I am here only by your mother's generosity, and I must remember my place. It is simply a matter of order and propriety, the same as it is for Mr. Essex. He is not invited until tomorrow, you remember, and perhaps I will be wanted then as well."

"Mr. Essex is not a permanent part of this household, so he must remember his place, as you say. But it is different with you. Why, you have spent every day in this house and by my side for years, and you know me far better than my uncle and aunt ever will! That makes you family in every way that matters."

Although I was secretly gratified by these sentiments, it seemed pointless, even unwise, to encourage them. "Never mind all that, Miss," I said. "Just drink your tea now, so you can get to bed."

Between sips, Anne informed me, "Mr. Essex has not only been invited for the evening tomorrow; he has been invited to dine."

"Is that so?"

"Yes. Mama told him to come because she needs another gentleman to balance her table. No, that is not quite right. What she actually said was that she needed a gentleman but Mr. Essex would have to do."

"I see. She will not want me, then, for that would put her table out again. Just as well. I shall plan on having a tray sent up from the kitchen. Perhaps I will be needed for cards afterward."

"Yes, perhaps."

"How do you plan on getting your exercise tomorrow?"

"You are an excellent watchdog, Mrs. Jenkinson, although you need not worry. It is all arranged. Cousin John, that is Colonel Fitzwilliam, mentioned he intends to walk to the parsonage tomorrow morning to pay his respects to the Collinses, and I said I would go with him."

"Very good, Miss. That is settled, then. Off to bed with you now if you are finished," I said. When she set her empty cup down, I gathered up the tea things. "I will see you first thing in the morning with more tea."

She sighed. "I know I said I would be willing to do whatever was necessary to be well, but I do sometimes wonder if I shall be required to drink Mr. Essex's tea forever. I do not prefer it, especially so very often."

"That is something to ask the doctor, I suppose. Still, it seems a small price to pay."

"Quite so, Mrs. Jenkinson. Quite so. Good night."

"Sleep well, Miss."

I thought about Mr. Essex later that night and how he occupied the same strange middle ground as I did – not servant and yet not accepted as an equal either. Although he seemed to have made considerable upward progress since his introduction at Rosings, earning more respect, there remained a division, an invisible line that must not be crossed. The practical reminders were easy enough to identify: the frequent insinuations that Mr. Essex was not *quite* a gentleman, my being dismissed when better company was to be had, and the compensation we each received for our services. One does not pay a family member for their attendance, after all, or a friend for a favor.

It was always so. I had even been the one to enforce the distinction of rank in my former life. Servants were to be treated with respect, but never with familiarity or true affection. The dividing lines were constantly emphasized, the unseen wall perpetually kept in good repair, lest anybody forget either its presence or its importance.

For some of us, however, the lines were not as clear. Often governesses, clergy, companions like myself, and now a person like Mr. Essex fell somewhere in between. It could be a perilous place to dwell. If roles became confused, there could be painful misunderstandings. If the lines became blurred, catastrophe might result. And if there were unpleasantness, one could be sure the consequences would not be equally born by all parties concerned. The family might be inconvenienced, but they would not lose their home or their livelihood. It was the outsider who must go. That was the inevitable solution, regardless who had been at fault. If the son and heir seduced the governess with promises of marriage, he would keep his place when it was found out, but she would lose hers. She would be cast adrift with a ruined reputation and no character reference, while the son might move on to his next conquest without a backward glance.

Although that was hardly the situation here, I had observed a worrying trend. I was concerned by what I saw as a tendency toward blurring the lines of late – Anne, by what she had said to me that very night, and Lady Catherine, by playing at having it both ways. Her ladyship wanted the convenience of assigning Mr. Essex (as well as myself at times) different roles according to her needs, and yet she expected him to remember his place afterward. One day he was dining with nobility like a gentleman, and the next he must anticipate being treated no better than the other hired help.

It seemed to me an imprudent practice, like playing with fire. Surely nothing good would come of it.

Though I might chafe against the constraints of my current situation, though I might occasionally resent the debasement thrust upon me by reduced circumstances, there was at least some security in knowing where one stood. I was old enough to comprehend this. I was too experienced to be easily moved. I would not allow Anne's recent compliments to turn my head. I only hoped Mr. Essex was as wise in the ways of the world. I hoped he would be as diligent in protecting himself from injury. I liked the man, and I did not wish to see him hurt. Still, my primary concern had to be for my young mistress.

- 30 -

Anne

Hearing of Absent Friends

"Do you carry any letter for me?" I asked Cousin John as we walked together arm in arm to Hunsford parsonage the next morning. Through Mrs. Collins, I had exchanged one more set of letters with Georgiana since I had seen him last, but I always hoped for more.

"No letter this time, Anne," he said. "I do bring you words of greeting from all your absent relations, however – those at Pemberley and elsewhere. My sister sends her love."

"Lady Deborah? How delightful! Tell me, how does she do? I have not seen her since the wedding, and then only briefly."

"She is very well, I think. She seems so to me, in any case. When she learnt we were bound for Rosings, she most particularly asked to be remembered to yourself."

"That is very kind. And your brother?"

"Algernon? What is there to be said of him other than he does just as he pleases? I am afraid he gives the old pater fits."

"Poor Uncle."

"On the contrary. You may well pity Algernon's wife, but you must not pity my father. I gather it is no more than what he earned by similar behavior in his day. Besides, it is a favor to me to have an infamous brother. When you stand us up side by side, I must be seen in a more favorable light!" He laughed. "Do not you think so? Of course, Algernon has done the one thing required of him; he has produced an heir. That is all that really signifies. Meanwhile, I am still an irresponsible bachelor, much to my father's consternation. So you see, it is not true that I am looked on with more favor than my brother. That was only my idea of a joke. I know you have often wished for a sibling, my dear Anne, but you have at least been spared the complex rivalry that inevitably comes with actually acquiring one."

I was highly diverted by his repartee, but I said, "Oh, John, do be serious. I trust having a brother cannot be half so disagreeable as you make it out to be."

"You are quite right, my dear. There are advantages enough, and you may count on my always making the most of them. Having such a notorious relation is a tremendous boon to one's wit, for example, and if the true stories of his exploits are not quite entertaining enough, they are easily embellished."

In this light-hearted manner, we passed the short walk to the parsonage. Perhaps Mr. Collins had seen us coming from one of the windows, for the door was opened to us before we could knock to announce our presence. The maid, who looked as if she had hurried, showed us into the pleasant sitting room to the right of the hall, where we found Mr. Collins ready to receive us.

"Welcome to my humble abode," he exclaimed, bowing. "It is indeed an honor to see you again, Colonel, and Miss de Bourgh as always. You must forgive my wife's tardiness. There is no disrespect intended, I hasten to declare. She is in… That is to say, she was indisposed when I perceived your presence, but I trust she will attend you just as quickly as humanly possible."

"I beg you, Mr. Collins," I said, "do not make yourself uneasy. There is no offense given or taken, I promise you."

After much reassurance on this point, Mr. Collins was at last convinced. Mrs. Collins presently joined us, and we settled into more comfortable conversation for the remainder of our twenty-minute stay.

During one of Mr. Collins's protracted speeches to my cousin John – in this case, a thorough recitation of the fortunate circumstances of his preferment to the Hunsford rectory – I gave Charlotte what I hoped was an encouraging smile.

She bore it all so bravely. No, it seemed more like the patient acceptance of a saint. Still, the day to day challenges of a sensible woman married to such a person must be many. What went on at the parsonage when the two of them were on their own, I could only imagine. Then I *did* begin to image it, that perhaps a typical conversation over breakfast might go something like this.

"What are your plans for the day, my dear?" Charlotte inquires. She asks this question every morning, no doubt in hopes of one day hearing a more interesting answer than she has come across thus far.

"I have a full slate of important work to do," Mr. Collins assures her. "I shall be in my book room for the whole of the morning, going over the discourse to be preached on Sunday. Every word of it is firmly fixed here," he says, tapping his forehead. "And Lady Catherine has already scrutinized the text point by point, giving her kind approbation... provided I make the changes she advised, of course."

"Are there many to be made this week?"

"Only so many as are perfectly reasonable and as I have grown accustomed to expecting. So you see, it is only the presentation that wants refining. A great deal of practice is required to give one's speech that unstudied air, you know, but that is what sets the really accomplished orators apart from the rest."

"Yes. So you have informed me on more than one occasion."

"Now, I think I shall have one more slice of that delicious ham, my dear, if you would be so good as to return the platter to within my reach." Charlotte reluctantly does so. "Would you care to hear it later – my sermon, I mean?"

The lady pauses to consider her answer. "I think not, my dear. I would not wish to... How shall I explain? ...to dilute the impact of your words by listening in on them prematurely. Let them overtake me at the proper time and place – of a sudden and in church."

"Of course, my dear. That is only right, and your scruples do you credit. Though you are my wife, I mustn't show favoritism." A moment later, Mr. Collins continues with a puzzling question, asking, "Why do you smile?"

"Why do you smile, Miss de Bourgh," Mr. Collins repeated, bringing me back to the present. "Said I something amusing?"

"No... no, not at all, good sir," I said, scrambling for an explanation for what was apparently an inappropriate show of mirth. "I, uh... That is, I smile for I have the happy office of delivering an invitation. We would be very much obliged, Mr. Collins, if you and Mrs. Collins would come to Rosings this evening to meet our other guests and sit down to cards."

All awkwardness was immediately forgotten, and before finally leaving off, Mr. Collins had chased us halfway home with his raptures of delight and gratitude.

Once John and I were on our own again to complete our return to the great house, I took advantage of the chance to speak freely by raising a topic I could not in front of Mama. I asked, "How is Mrs. Darcy settling in at Pemberley? It must be quite a joy to her – as well as a challenge – to have come up so far in the world. No one could object to finding herself mistress of Pemberley, but all the same, it would be an enormous undertaking for a lady not born to it."

"True enough," agreed the colonel. "Mrs. Reynolds, who knows everything there is to know about managing the house, has been a great asset to the new mistress, I gather. And Elizabeth is a game girl. I would wager she will have the place mastered within a twelve month. There is even talk of their giving a tremendous ball in January in honor of Georgiana's eighteenth birthday, something like in the old days when our Aunt Anne was alive."

This immediately brought happy scenes from the past to mind – balls where I had been too young to dance but not too young to enjoy the music and splendor. "How I should love to be there! Oh, to see Pemberley again and to dance. Lucky Georgiana, and lucky anybody who is fortunate enough to be present!"

"Then you must come. There is no question of your being welcome. And the travel will be no obstacle, not with your health continuing to improve."

"But Mama will never allow it, not if she is still determined to hold a grudge against William and Elizabeth."

"We shall work on her together to change her mind," he said, patting my hand. "Time and reason must have their effects, and the ball is still six months off. Much may happen before then."

Truer words were never spoken.

~~*~~

The remainder of the visit passed off in a very agreeable fashion, becoming almost festive when Mama could gather additional company about us, and quiet when we reverted to merely a family party. I did not mind which. It was all so much more pleasurable for me than in recent years, for now I knew I need not fear a headache resulting from the extra commotion. I could sit and talk in perfect peace. I could smell food without feeling ill and eat without worry. I could enjoy a larger society like everybody else. The only sacrifices to my delicate constitution I felt obliged to make were to continue avoiding certain food and drink as well as keeping to my early bedtime.

Mr. Essex stayed for two days only, and I thought he comported himself remarkably well in what must have been unfamiliar circumstances. The same could be said for the Collinses, I supposed – Mrs. Collins at least, for she always kept herself in quiet dignity. It was at times difficult not to lose patience with her husband, however, with his continuous genuflecting and homage paying. Not for the first time it occurred to me that perhaps his servile manner was somewhat counterfeit, that it might be nothing more than a guise he displayed for others, a show put on for those around him. I suspected he really thought just as well of himself as he pretended to think of Mama and all those who were above him. By this false humility, perhaps he expected to ingratiate himself with those who were in position to advance his own prospects. Of course, he was not the only one; many in society played at that game.

After dismissing the immediately available but inferior of her acquaintance, Mama brought on the best she could command for her brother – Mr. and Mrs. Ellerton, Sir Edward and Lady Metcalfe, and the bishop and his wife. For these and for my uncle and aunt, no effort was neglected, no expense spared. Lavish dinners were ordered, and the wine never stopped flowing.

When reduced to our smaller group again, Mama claimed my uncle's ear more often than not, taking him to one side or even retreating to the library with him on occasion. "Important family business," she called it when I later asked the topic of their private discussions. In any case, it often left John and my aunt Constance to me, which was no hardship. They were both easy enough to talk to, especially with my uncle out of the way, and if all else failed, I knew Aunt Constance had a partiality for cribbage. By my being willing to play, I could spare John one more game of something of which I suspected he had long since grown tired.

I was sorry to see them all go when it was time, especially without knowing when such a pleasure might be repeated. But then

Mama gave me a reason to hope for something sooner rather than later.

"Fitzwilliam," she said to my cousin as he and his parents were preparing to depart. "I wonder if you would agree to come to Rosings again in the autumn. It is my expectation that Anne will be well enough by then that she will want to start going out into society more. It would give me the greatest peace of mind to know that you were her escort, at least in the beginning. You understand."

What could he say? Of course he consented.

Belatedly, I offered him a way to avoid the obligation. I disclaimed both my desire to mix more in society and any need for a special escort if I should take a notion to do so. But it was no use; John was too much the gentleman to grasp after the way of escape I had thrown him or to admit that the long trip back into Kent would be the least bit inconvenient. In truth, I would be glad for his company when it came again. He was as faithful a friend as I had ever known, and I valued him all the more now for my having lately been deprived of my cousins William and Georgiana.

I tried to convey my gratitude in the look I gave him at our parting. "Thank you for all your kindness, John," I said very earnestly.

"Not at all, my dear girl," he said on the way to kissing my hand. "Not at all."

- 31 -

Lady Catherine

Congratulating Herself

I was very pleased with how my brother's visit to Rosings had come off. He seemed entertained by the company I was able to produce for him – especially the higher quality set, of course. Most importantly, though, we were now in complete agreement about the main topic of our discussions. Since the same course of action would equally serve his interests as well as mine, very little persuasion was required to bring him round to my way of thinking. It was simply a matter of laying out the facts in a logical manner and allowing him to draw his own conclusions. Even a child could see the obvious benefits of the scheme.

PART THREE

The Ever After

- 32 -

Lady Catherine

On the Difficulty of Keeping Good Help

What a bother.

It is very inconvenient for someone like myself, who lives a disciplined, well-ordered life, to have chaos suddenly thrust upon her by others. And yet, that is what has occurred. Through no fault of my own, other than perhaps excessive kindness, the peace of Rosings has been disrupted more completely than I can remember since the unfortunate departure of my late husband. I trust the consequences of *this* event, however, will be nowhere near as serious and far reaching.

It began when Mr. Collins came for our usual Wednesday appointment in hopes of receiving my approbation for his sermon text. As always, I carefully examined the content with a pen close at hand so that I could make whatever corrections or notes were required.

"You have got it completely backwards, Mr. Collins," I told him when I had finished reading what he proposed preaching on Sunday. "You will carry your message home much more effectively if you change the order. Make this second point first and your first point will neatly follow afterwards. See here?" With him looking on, I drew arrows on the page to illustrate the revision. "Also, it is much too long. There is no need to beat the congregation about their heads and shoulders. Just make your argument and have done. You can cut out this bit for a start," I explained, making lines through the superfluous passages, "and all this lot as well. That will be a great improvement."

"Yes, of course, your ladyship," he said. "It is perfectly clear to me where I went wrong, now you have explained my errors with your usual logic and insight. I will attend to your corrections immediately and rededicate myself to doing better next time. Is there anything else?"

"No, that will do, Mr. Collins. You may go, but I wish to see you back here at four o'clock tomorrow with the amended text. And *do* be on time. Tardiness is a sign of disorder and disrespect."

"Four o'clock sharp, your ladyship. I will be here. You can depend on it." He began to gather his things to depart, saying in a melancholy tone, "Now I must return to my humble abode to see what my dear Charlotte has been able to arrange for our dinner. I fear it may be only boiled vegetables from the garden today, for the hens refuse to lay and the larder is quite bare. Yet I flatter myself that nobody is better than my wife at making a little go a long way. I only wish I could provide her a bit more to work with. Just a small joint of mutton, perhaps, which is her favorite. I am not thinking of myself, you understand, your ladyship. It is Mrs. Collins. She has the fervent hope, despite our first disappointment, of soon enlarging our family. But she is lately grown so thin that I fear…" He broke off and shook his head. "Well, if God wills it, He shall provide a way. We must have faith." He bowed and began slowly making his way toward the door.

"Mr. Collins," I said, stopping him. "Do you mean to tell me that you have no meat in the house at all, and no money to buy from the butcher?"

"Well, there is a small portion of bacon remaining, but we meant to save that for Sunday. Perhaps we may have an egg or two by then to go with it. We could kill a hen, of course, but then there would be even less chance of eggs. As for money, it has all gone to some unexpected expenses this month… and to the Lord's work, of course. Nevertheless, we are content. I am convinced that some deprivation is good for the soul."

"Hmm," I said, studying him closely. He had the open, ingenuous look of a child patiently waiting for its parent to speak, ready to accept whatever wisdom comes down from on high. After a little more consideration, I continued. "Since your income should be more than sufficient to your needs, Mr. Collins, I can only conclude that this shortage is the result of gross mismanagement." But then I reminded myself that I had to make certain allowances for others, not expecting everybody to live up to the same high standards I held for myself. So, in a burst of particular charity, I said, "Nevertheless, perhaps I might spare you something extra to get by on, Mr. Collins, just this once."

"Your ladyship is too kind! Your beneficence and condescension quite overwhelm me…"

There is no telling how long he might have gone on if I had not cut him short and sent him away. In any case, against my better judgment, I spoke to Cook and instructed her to find some small joint of meat or other – mutton, if it could be spared – have it wrapped and sent the next morning to the parsonage as a present. Then I dismissed the business from my mind and moved on to more important things.

However, as Anne and I were going out that following day, I thought it prudent to stop the carriage at the gate of the parsonage so that I might have a word with Mrs. Collins.

Mr. Collins, being the first to reach us, gave a low bow and offered a tedious speech of welcome. When I had effectively silenced him, I turned to his wife, saying, "Now, Mrs. Collins, I trust you received the parcel I sent over early this morning."

"I did, your Ladyship," she said forthrightly, "and I thank you. It was a very thoughtful gift, and it is this minute in the oven under Mary's careful supervision."

"I am glad to hear it. See that she does not ruin it by overcooking. I will not have a perfectly aged joint of my best mutton spoilt by carelessness."

"No, madam."

"*Nor* will I have it said that I allowed a clergyman's family under my care go hungry," I continued with more emphasis as I came to my point. "But really, Mrs. Collins, I must insist you keep a closer watch on your budget from now on. The living I provide your husband should be more than adequate. I defy anyone to argue otherwise. So, unless a servant is thieving from under your nose, I can only conclude that this current shortfall is the result of some gross mismanagement on your part."

"It will not happen again, I assure you, Lady Catherine."

I was pleased that Mrs. Collins had not troubled me to hear whatever feeble excuses and explanations she could have produced. "See that it does not," I continued. "I take my responsibilities to this parish very seriously, and I never begrudge charity where it is due. I am no miser; ask anyone. However, there is a limit. I cannot be expected to stand in the breach for every case of negligence and bad judgment in the county. This one wants a bit of meat for the table; that one needs milk for the baby. Why, I should be quite taken in! I will not have it, Mrs. Collins. Do you understand?"

"Perfectly, madam. As I said, this error will not occur again." She turned a pointed look upon her husband. "Will it, Mr. Collins?"

From this subtle exchange between husband and wife, I immediately perceived that the purported deficit was likely of Mr. Collins's fabrication (or at least exaggeration), which made perfect sense – certainly more sense than that a lady I had always believed an intelligent and skillful housekeeper could have allowed things to deteriorate so far. Mrs. Collins did not mismanage; her husband simply aspired to a higher style of living than his pocket could currently afford. He imagined he had a right to dine at my expense every day, not merely once a week. I did not let on that I knew this, however. I trusted my words of reproof to strike the correct target, to hit the conscience of the guilty party.

Mr. Collins shook his head resolutely. "No, no, indeed, Lady Catherine. We are greatly indebted to you for your generosity in our hour of need. Such kind condescension is rarely met with. But we shall never trouble you to repeat it..."

I ignored the rest and instructed the coachman to drive on, although I might have been a bit more patient if I had known these were Mr. Collins's last words to me. For he was quite correct in saying he would never trouble me to repeat my act of generosity. Instead, he would shortly trouble me with a different sort of inconvenience.

~~*~~

As I awaited Mr. Collins's arrival for our meeting that afternoon, I received the first herald of distress. I had just checked the time again when a noise erupted from the servants' area below stairs. It came nearer by degrees until the news reached my own ears via the butler. I was told that the manservant from the parsonage had come at a run, urgently seeking assistance for his ailing master. Anybody who had thought themselves capable of lending aid had gone to the parsonage at once.

I sighed deeply, thinking what a disgraceful business it was that the whole household should be distracted from their duties by what would probably turn out a most trivial matter. There was no help for it, though; I therefore resigned myself to going to the parsonage myself, to investigate and resolve the situation. By the time I arrived, however, it was all over. Mr. Collins was gone... permanently. I was told he had choked on a mouthful of mutton – the very mutton he had by pretense induced me to send him. How careless.

It was unfortunate that Mr. Essex had not been at Rosings, for perhaps his prompt attention might have done some good. The local surgeon arrived too late to do anything more than confirm the obvious: Mr. Collins was dead.

That was only the beginning of the disruption the event created. The bishop had to be informed, funeral arrangements made, and then the arduous task of searching out a suitable replacement undertaken. Most of the bother would fall to me, of course.

- 33 -

Anne

On Being Powerless to Help

Poor Mr. Collins!

I could scarcely believe it when I heard the news, and all I could think of was what it would mean for Mrs. Collins. But there was Mama, acting as if Mr. Collins had died on purpose just to inconvenience *her*.

The household was all in confusion at the event. Mama sallied forth to tell everybody what to do, and servants ran this way and that. I was instructed to stay quietly at home, though. Mama said this would be in agreement with Mr. Essex's direction that I not be exposed to excessive stress. And as an additional precaution, she had sent for my doctor to attend me. Although I thought it more likely Mrs. Collins would be the one to need medical assistance, I should not be at all sorry to see him either. His presence always elevated my spirits.

In the meantime, I could think of nothing useful to do except that which I was prevented from by other restrictions. I felt an impulse to convey to Mrs. Darcy the news of her cousin's death and her friend's distress. But I knew I could not get a letter to the post without my mother's knowing it. So I was forced to bide my time.

With Mr. Essex's sanction, I was allowed to call at the parsonage the next morning, where I sat with Charlotte for three quarters of an hour. She was not, as I had feared, prostrate with grief; she bore her misfortune with dignity and calm. Taking my cue from her behavior, I resolved to shun an overly melancholy aspect and any gloomy talk. I aimed simply for an attitude of warmth and friendship instead.

"Might I do anything for you, Mrs. Collins?" I asked. "Perhaps I might write the necessary letters on your behalf. You could tell me to whom they must go and what to say. I would be happy to be of service."

"Thank you, Miss de Bourgh," she replied. "You are very kind. But since I could not sleep, I undertook the task myself last night. I wrote to Mr. Collins's sister Ruth, who will in turn pass the sad news on to their brother in America, I suppose. I also wrote to my mother. That is all that is really necessary; the others will hear in good time, I trust. My mother will tell our friends in and around Meryton, including Mrs. Bennet, who can be counted on to send word to Elizabeth at Pemberley without delay. So you see, it is done already."

It was some relief to know Mrs. Darcy would soon be informed, though I had been prevented from performing the office myself. I felt certain she would come, too, as close as she and Charlotte had seemed to be. A friend of so longstanding duration could sympathize more effectively with a lady in distress than I was in a position to do.

Not surprisingly, I was denied leave to go to the funeral as well when it was held a few days later. I know it is still not quite the thing for ladies to attend, but that did not stop Mama.

"If your father were here," she explained, "he would go and I would stay at home. As it is, however, I must represent the family. We cannot be seen to ignore the event. The bishop will be present, and everything will be done right and proper. I have seen to that."

She brought a report back to me later.

"Quite a creditable number of mourners," she said. "Whatever the parishioners may have thought of the man himself, they at least had the manners to show respect for his office in the end. Or it may be my influence that produced their attendance; they must have known that I would hear of anybody who neglected his duty.

"The bishop was in fine form, I must say. He had the congregation in the palm of his hand and, before he finished, each one trembling for fear of fire and brimstone. I will need to speak to him about one small point, however. I do not hold with this modern tendency toward radically improving a person's character in eulogy. Although a young man who dies is bound to be more kindly spoken of than he deserves, there is no need to make him out a saint."

"Did you see anybody there other than those in the parish?" I asked, thinking of the sister Mrs. Collins had mentioned, and the Darcys.

Mama cinched her lips tight together like a reticule closed by a firm tug on the strings. Then finally she relented enough to say that she had seen "no one of interest."

I later heard from Mrs. Collins, however, that Mr. and Mrs. Darcy had indeed come to condole with her. And I met Mr. Collins's sister myself during one of my visits to the parsonage in the week following. Mrs. Sanditon, whom I liked very much, had stayed on with Charlotte after the funeral rights were over. I was glad Charlotte would not be alone. Though she kept a stoic countenance, I still had to believe there was pain underneath it.

Whenever I heard of a death, especially an untimely one, I could not help revisiting my father's in my mind. I was not allowed to attend that funeral either, of course, and it had taken place at such a distance that I could not even observe any sign of the proceedings – people gathering or church bells tolling – for rather than having the corpse returned from town to be buried in Hunsford cemetery, Mama had decided to take care of everything in London, where the fatal accident had occurred. Perhaps that is why I had so much difficulty accepting his death. I never saw the body at the time, and I have never once been to his grave since then, my mother forbidding it, saying it would be too upsetting for me. Whether that served as a cruelty or a kindness, I cannot be sure.

In any case, without absolute proof, I could in my more obstinate moments deny the truth and fancy my father still alive. I could carry on full conversations with him in my head, discussing those things that I could never speak about to Mama. If he had been present, I would have asked him…

"Did you observe this recent visit by my aunt and uncle, Papa? Mama seemed pleased with how it came off, but I could not be entirely satisfied. My uncle was as severe as ever, and my aunt seemed rather spiritless. Did not you think so?"

"Without a doubt. I was all too glad to avoid putting in an appearance, having now the perfect excuse to absent myself from anything unpleasant." He winks and laughs at his own joke.

"Oh, Papa."

"Your cousin's being here as well would have been the only thing to make the visit worth my while. I always liked John. He does not take his own consequence too seriously, nor that of his family. He does not make too much of the rights of nobility – not like your mother. She would never let me forget which one of us was more highly born. Plus John knows how to tell a joke worth laughing at. That is my idea of good company."

"He does make me laugh," I say, "but sometimes I think he may not be quite serious enough, Papa. I am not sure it is good for a man to have no intellectual occupation, no serious pursuits. Did you know that he has no passion at all for reading?"

"The possession of leisure is something to be celebrated, Anne. If John uses this time during the peace to bring a little light-hearted cheer to himself and to others, who should criticize him for that? His leisure may not last long, after all. There is always a good chance of another war, and then he will have serious work to do again. Is that what you want for him?"

"Heaven forbid! Far better that he should be idle and merry than going to war again. He has distinguished himself in battle quite enough for any one man."

"Indeed. I admire the courage required of a military life. One tends to be impressed by those who can do what one cannot oneself. Do not you think so, my pet?"

I thought of Elizabeth Bennet. "Oh, yes, Papa. I cannot help but admire a woman of courage and spirit, one who is able to stand against whatever wrong or personal opposition she may run up against."

"But that is not something out of your reach, my dear, especially now that you are strong again."

"Do you really think so, Papa?"

"I do! It is in your blood. Though I am not a military man, I like to think I have a kind of courage – the courage of my own convictions, at any rate. And your mama... Well, what I mean is that you must have it somewhere within yourself to fight for what you want when it is most important. Did you give in and marry the gentleman your mother wanted you to – that old codger Sir Henry Stanford?"

"Stanfield."

"Yes, yes, of course. That is the very one I meant. You did not marry him, did you?"

"No, I did not. Perhaps it was very wicked of me to oppose the idea, but I could not bear to go through with it, Papa."

"That is what I mean, you see. You did not submit to your mother's tyranny when it came to something really important. I am proud of you for it. I would have been satisfied to see you married to your cousin Darcy because he is a principled, worthy sort of man and much nearer your own age. He might have given you a very good life. It was right that you should have let him go as you did, though. And now, let me advise you to not consider matrimony with anyone less worthy. Let it be a man for whom you can feel some true affection as well. Promise me that, my dear. Anything less will be entirely unsupportable. Take this from one who knows."

At times like this, I heard my father's voice as clear and true as the bell ringing in the steeple on Sunday morning. It seemed as if he were in the same room with me and not in the grave. But how could I possibly know the sentiments were true to him as well? I could not. Still, it gave me comfort to think so. If I were really tested, would I have courage enough to stand? Perhaps I would one day prove him right to have confidence in me. I hoped so.

- 34 -

Charlotte Collins

On Relinquishing Attachments

Mr. Collins is dead.

My husband was dead and buried, gone forever. Days had passed, and still I found I must keep repeating the words to myself to believe it was true. Perhaps the shock was not yet worn off, the suddenness of the thing making it seem unreal. Mr. Collins had never been erratic in his behavior before. He was an entirely dependable, even predictable man, so that I never would have guessed he would leave me so abruptly… and in such dramatic fashion too. His life had not gradually ebbed away as water seeping from a leaky jar, but all at once as if the jar had been smashed to pieces on stony ground.

Now I hardly knew what to think or how to feel.

I was extremely sorry for my husband's suffering, of course, which had been brief but horrible. One minute we were sharing a very ordinary dinner, and the next, he was in crisis. I sent to Rosings for help immediately, hoping that Mr. Essex would be on hand. And I did what little I could to dislodge the obstruction in his windpipe myself. But it was no use. In a matter of minutes, Mr. Collins slumped to the floor and expired, gone from this life and into the next, may God have mercy on his soul. If I should live to be one hundred, I shall never forget the look of dreadful surprise displayed on his countenance as he slipped away.

A premature death is always to be considered a tragedy, and this one has made me an early widow. Even so, I know I have not behaved as some might expect me to. I could not play the hypocrite, throwing myself on the sofa to sob night and day, pretending a deep despair I do not feel.

I did not love my husband, you see, not in a romantic sort of way. I did care for him, though, as is befitting a wife. And I would miss him, as one misses anything that has become a comfortable part of one's daily routine.

When Elizabeth came to condole with me after the funeral, I explained it this way. "I still cannot fully comprehend that he is gone. Every time I look out into the garden, I half expect to see Mr. Collins there, fussing over his vegetables or tending the bees. I know you did not care for him yourself, Lizzy. Yet despite his faults, he suited me well. I had, in fact, grown rather fond of him… in my own way."

"I do understand, Charlotte," she said. "One cannot help but become attached."

Attached. That was true. And although I am sure she really could not comprehend how I could care at all for a man so different from her own husband, it was kind of her to say. It was also kind of them – Elizabeth and Mr. Darcy – to come so far to give me comfort and to offer their assistance.

"I would by no means wish to intrude upon your private sorrow," Mr. Darcy told me. "Only allow me to say that my wife and I shall consider it a great honor if, should you find yourself in need, you were to think of us first. Should there be any service I might render you, please do not hesitate to make it known to me."

If I were ever tempted to tears, this had been the time – to see the compassion of such a kind friend, to witness such generous behavior in a gentleman who had no obligation to me other than through the affection of his wife. I did not doubt the sincerity of Mr. Darcy's offer, and I thought I might be forced to avail myself of it in some way, for I did not yet know what the future held for me.

My natural response was pragmatic, however; I would do what needed to be done to live modestly yet respectably. A second marriage hardly seemed likely at my age, nor was it even much to be desired. My first experience with the connubial state was hardly so satisfying that I longed to immediately repeat it. Now that I was free again, a life of self-sufficiency was more to my taste. My husband had left me a small income, which, with the strictest of economies, might be made to supply my humble needs. Above all, I needed to find a way of being useful rather than a burden to my family, whether that meant keeping house for one of my brothers or perhaps serving as a lady's companion in like manner to Mrs. Jenkinson. Under the right circumstances, these things would not be distasteful to me. As soon as my mind resumed its normal, orderly ways, I would endeavor to formulate a workable plan.

But one thing was sure; I would be sorry indeed to leave my snug, tidy little home. I had been happy at Hunsford, for the most part, or at least content with the challenge of managing my husband and household efficiently. Although Lady Catherine had not yet said anything about my vacating the parsonage, that day would inevitably come. I could not possibly stay on forever. A new cleric would be appointed, and as was his right, the house would be claimed by him.

- 35 -

Lady Catherine

On Making Smooth Transitions

I spoke to Mrs. Collins in early October, and she asked for more time to make arrangements for someplace else to live. Her sister-in-law – also a young widow, I am told – was still with her, and I gathered they got on very well. There had even been talk between them of combining their meager resources to afford a small cottage somewhere, perhaps in Hertfordshire, near Charlotte's family. It seemed an entirely sensible plan to me.

So I decided to be magnanimous and allow Mrs. Collins to stay on a little longer. The new man, the Reverend Mr. Chesterfield, had asked to be given access to the parsonage as soon as possible, but I could put him off at least until the end of the month. It might serve to demonstrate to him from the beginning who was in charge (and that it certainly was not him) as well as postponing the cost of his maintenance taking effect.

I would be glad when the transition was complete, however, and I could put the unpleasant scenes behind me.

Anne seemed to have successfully weathered this latest storm, which pleased me very much. I had been afraid the upheaval might set her health back and that she would be some time recovering lost ground. Mr. Essex came at once when I sent for him, and he saw her through the crisis with no harm done.

This meant there need be no delay. My plans could move forward on schedule.

- 36 -

Anne

Speaking of Diplomats and Invitations

Although it was no surprise, I was sorry to hear that Mrs. Collins would be leaving at the end of the month. An excellent situation for her had happily presented itself just in time. As I understood it, a relation of Mrs. Sanditon (Mr. Collins's widowed sister) had offered her a cottage in Derbyshire on very easy terms. She meant to accept the offer, and Mrs. Collins would go with her. Perhaps the place might even turn out to be somewhere near Pemberley. How nice for Charlotte if it should, to be so close to her friend Mrs. Darcy again.

The seasons continued to roll by, and with the arrival of autumn, there was once again a chill in the air. The elms and the oaks in the groves were preparing to give up their leaves, and the swallows had already flown. Always before I had found autumn such a melancholy time of year, reminding me not only of my father's death but also that months of confinement lay ahead. With my fragile health, I had barely been allowed to venture out of doors in inclement weather lest I should catch a chill and die of pneumonia. Now, however, under Mr. Essex's regime, all that had changed. I not only was strong enough go out, I was exhorted to do so. A little rain would not deter me from my outdoor exercise. Cold temperatures would not stop my accompanying Mama on her errands to the village and beyond.

With my health so much better, and the improvement holding, I wondered at Mr. Essex's continuing to come to Rosings so frequently, for he still drove down from town once or even twice a week, often staying the night. Occasionally, he did make a medical call on someone else in the neighborhood, someone to whom Mama had recommended him. I suppose that might be at least part of the explanation – that he found advantage in expanding his practice into Kent.

I did not mind his frequent presence, certainly. He was excellent company – someone with whom I could discuss books, travel, science, and whatever other topic took my fancy. I could ask him almost anything, and I did. What he knew, he was always ready to share. What he did not know, he would endeavor to discover for me from his wider acquaintance and broader resources in town. His kindness went far beyond what his duties strictly required. In fact, had any one of the parade of my supposed suitors been equally good and even half so interesting as Mr. Essex, I would have seriously considered the match. But alas, the interesting were not at all eligible, and the eligible were not at all interesting.

Still, Mr. Essex added to my experience of the male of the species. He was another man of principle against whom others could be compared. Others must now be measured against his intelligence and charity as well as his amiability. He made me laugh as no one else could, except perhaps Cousin John. It says in Proverbs that *a merry heart doeth good like a medicine*. If it is true (and I trust that it is), then a good command of humor is a valuable trait in a physician.

My opinions did not signify, however; it only mattered that Mama seemed to want to keep Mr. Essex close by, always at her beck and call. She had come to depend on him, I believe, the more so now with Mr. Collins gone. Although I really did not know, I presumed she carried on paying him too, so she must have perceived a certain value in his continued presence.

Mr. Essex would not be so much needed once Cousin John returned, however, and so I let on, expecting he might find it some relief.

"Colonel Fitzwilliam comes again next week," I told him one day while he, as was now his custom, accompanied me on my outdoor exercise, for I still strictly adhered to this and to all the doctor's other instructions.

"Again, so soon?" he asked.

"My mother has requested him to come, and he has been good enough to consent. It must be an enormous inconvenience, but John pretends not to mind. He is an excellent fellow, Mr. Essex."

"From what I know of him so far, Miss de Bourgh, I would agree with you."

"And his coming means that you may have more leisure to see to your other affairs, as Mama will not depend on you so much while she has another here."

"Another to do her bidding, you mean, to make polite dinner conversation and play whist with her afterwards." He shook his head ruefully. "I started well but then, for reasons I cannot fully excuse, I began to let her have her way more and more. You must think me a very weak and useless character to submit to such frivolous demands when I should be doing something more worth-while with my time."

"Indeed, I do not, sir! I should be the very last person to criticize on that head. It is the story of my whole life – allowing Mama to rule over me. And you have a better excuse; you must earn your living, even if it requires certain... certain compromises."

"There is some truth in that. I daresay I am as fond as the next man of a comfortable bed, a dependable roof over my head, and good food and wine on the table. But it is not that which makes me comply with Lady Catherine's wishes. Neither is it for herself. I consider it as a part of my service to *you*, Miss de Bourgh. I have sworn to get you well, and if that involves a little kowtowing, so be it. It is not very disagreeable to me to dine well at your mother's table and to spend an evening at cards from time to time. If that is all that is required to keep her content, I am happy to do it. As I have told your mother, a peaceful home is important to your full recovery."

"So your profession sometimes requires you to be a diplomat as well, maintaining the peace between two parties who would likely be at war otherwise?"

"I suppose. *I must be all things to all people*, just as Paul says in Corinthians – a dutiful son when I am with my father and mother; a man of science when I consult with my colleagues; a diplomat and more when I come here. Except this household is a rather one-sided affair; only one of the two parties is inclined to be hostile. If you will forgive me for saying so, Miss Anne, there is only one who prowls around like a roaring lion." He murmured this last accom-panied by a conspiratorial wink.

I laughed. "Do you mean you are here to soothe the savage beast?"

"Your words, not mine, and said with no disrespect to your mother intended, I am sure."

"Who said anything about Mama? I would swear an oath you did not cast her in the role of the lion, and neither did I."

"That is a fact, Miss de Bourgh," he said, taking his turn to laugh. "But soothing a savage beast – whoever she may be – that would make me a lion tamer, would it not? I think I quite like the sound of that. Perhaps I shall add it to my list of credentials."

"I think you should, by all means. If you require a testimonial, I would be happy to give you one."

"That is very good of you, I daresay. I would likewise give you an excellent reference for being an accomplished Daniel, surviving so long in the lion's den."

My smile persisted as we walked on a few more minutes in silence. Then I said more seriously, "In truth, you are a lion tamer, Mr. Essex, and not for Mama. You have tamed the savage beast of my headaches. I will be eternally grateful to you for that."

"It is all part of the service, madam," he said, bowing to me in mock formality. "All part of the service."

~~*~~

Cousin John arrived in the middle of October as scheduled, much to my delight and to Mama's. She seemed to make even more of his coming than usual. I thought I had detected a carefully suppressed current of excitement in her anticipation of the event, and then she treated him with the marked attention one might ordinarily reserve for a son. The impression was new to me, but the more I thought about it, the less surprising it seemed. Although she had never said so to me, Mama could not help but regret never having a son of her own. And, as the nephew dearest to her (since Darcy's falling into disfavor), Colonel Fitzwilliam was as close to a son as she would ever have, at least until such time as I were to provide her one by marriage.

Nevertheless, she was very far from keeping her new favorite all to herself. In fact, she wasted no time making plans to share him – with me, of course, and then with a larger society.

"I invited a few friends over tomorrow, Fitzwilliam," she informed him that first evening, "and then on Friday, if you please, you shall escort Anne to a dinner party."

"A dinner party?" I repeated. "What is this about, Mama? You have said nothing to me."

"Did I not show you of the invitation that came from the Babcocks?"

"No, Ma'am, you did not."

"How remiss of me. Well, it is just as I had foreseen. Now you are ready to go out into company, opportunities for you to do so have begun to present themselves. This is a perfect way to begin, too – just a small affair given in honor of Julia's engagement. It is not far to travel, and no doubt the guests will all be of your previous acquaintance, Anne. You cannot possibly object. Fitzwilliam, you shall not mind either, shall you?"

"Not if Anne wishes to go. You know my hearty appetite – for food and for good society – so I am always ready for a dinner party, large or small. But will you not be accompanying us, Lady Catherine? These are friends of yours as well, I presume."

"They are indeed, and I shall be very sorry to lose your company for an evening. This is a party for the young people only, however. You must go and make the most of it."

"Anne, what do you say?" asked John. "Should you like to go to this dinner?"

I had known Julia Babcock for years, and I could image who the other guests might be, so I harbored no scruples for the company. My hesitation came from my general lack of experience. Due to my chronically bad health, I had not been out much in society. While other girls – my contemporaries in age and rank – were being presented at court, I had sat at home. While one practiced flirting at an evening soirée, I had practiced patience, enduring one more sick headache. While another enjoyed a glass of wine and a full dance card, I had a cup of tea and went to bed early.

Although I did not much regret it, (for I cared little for London society or the pretentious goings-on at court), my sheltered existence had left me at a distinct disadvantage for feeling at ease doing what I might truly have enjoyed – a modestly sized party, like this one, at the home of a friend.

Still, I grew weary of always staying at home, and I was eager to test my wings, now that my health and strength had returned. Perhaps Mama was right; perhaps it was high time I got out into society more. Here was the best possible opportunity to make a start of it. I would be among friends, and John's easy manners would smooth over whatever blunders I made by inexperience.

"Yes, John," I said, decidedly. "I believe I should very much like to go."

- 37 -

Mrs. Jenkinson

Being Cautiously Optimistic

"I wish I could have consulted Mr. Essex about it first," Anne told me later while I assisted her with her bedtime preparations. "If only Mama had told me of the invitation earlier, but now I will not see him before Friday."

"Nonsense, Miss. He would tell you to go and enjoy yourself. You heard your mama; it is a small party of close friends nearby. There can be no harm in that. On the contrary, I daresay it will do you a world of good."

"You are my watchdog, Mrs. Jenkinson. If you say I may go, then I am satisfied."

"Only take care not to overdo – wine, excitement, staying out too late."

"I promise to be sensible, and Colonel Fitzwilliam will watch over me like a brother."

I was very pleased that my young lady would be going out for some pleasant social intercourse with friends, and I had confidence in her good sense and in Colonel Fitzwilliam keeping her out of trouble. The only thing that niggled at my mind was that Lady Catherine had engineered the plan. She had smiled almost triumphantly when Anne and her cousin agreed to go, and I must say she had been looking mighty pleased with herself ever since. But perhaps I was imagining things. It might be nothing more than her satisfaction at having her daughter so much improved and her amusing nephew here to entertain them. It would take no more than that to make *me* smile. And certainly we all like to have a plan of our own making turn out a success. There was nothing devious in that.

"I wish you would be going with me, Mrs. Jenkinson," Anne continued.

"I am sure I should like that very much, Miss, but you do not need me looking after you every minute anymore. And as her ladyship said, no chaperone is necessary on this occasion, not with your own cousin escorting you and your friend's parents there to assure nothing untoward happens."

"I shall miss you all the same," she said, reaching out to touch my shoulder.

I kept my countenance neutral until I could turn away to prevent betraying my emotion. "You can tell me all about it when you return, if you like. That shall be more than enough for me," I said.

It was a fact; Anne did not need me nearly so much anymore, and that was all to the good. As it must be for Mr. Essex also, my highest goal was to make my further employment unnecessary. Nothing could be more ironic, and yet it was true. I wished to see Miss de Bourgh well and independent, even if that meant I would soon be superfluous, my services – my very presence – no longer wanted or needed.

My parting gift – my final act in Anne's service – would be to break her remaining bonds of dependence on me… and mine on her. What my life would be like after that, I could not imagine. There was still time to adjust my thinking, however. I was not made useless yet, and I intended to finish my mission well.

- 38 -

Anne

Attending a Dinner

I discovered difficulty in keeping my promise to Mrs. Jenkinson not to overdo, at least in her caution against too much excitement. Once I had decided I would go to the party, my enthusiasm for the idea began to mount, my eagerness building higher and higher until it reached a fever pitch on Friday. I wanted to see my friends again, but just as important, I wanted them to see me – the new Anne de Bourgh, the one with energy to do the things other young ladies did, the one who no longer looked as if she might at any moment crumple to the floor in a dead faint.

As I dressed, my looking glass told the story. Healthy color now brightened my formerly pallid complexion, and my past gauntness had entirely fled. Instead of harsh angles and bony protrusions, I now saw a form pleasingly softened, even slightly rounded in the right places. That in itself gave me confidence.

At last it was time to go, but not before Mama could give me a tedious recitation of what I must be sure to do and not do in comporting myself like a lady. Then John, who looked almost handsome in his evening clothes, handed me into the carriage and followed after.

I took a deep breath to calm my nerves. John was perfectly at his ease, however. When the door had closed and we were underway, he asked cheerfully, "Is there anything I should know about these friends of yours before I meet them? Are you especially close to Miss Babcock?"

"Not especially close. My poor health has kept me from socializing enough to remain on intimate terms with anybody, but I know Miss Babcock tolerably well. She is marrying a gentleman called

Mr. Tallmadge, who will be a baronet one day. But his estate is in Wales, so I hardly expect to see Julia again after they wed."

"What a pity."

"Yes."

"Is there anyone else who is a particular friend?"

"Miss Diana Denton is sure to be there as well. She was a frequent playfellow of mine when we were children, since we lived not too distant from one another. Papa would drive me over to Kendlebrook Lodge or Mrs. Denton would bring Julia to Rosings of an afternoon. But it all changed when Papa died."

"Why is that?"

"It was the most tragic coincidence. Diana's mother died at almost the same moment. Both families were plunged into mourning, and we have never fully recovered our friendship since. I have always assumed it was too painful for our surviving parents to be reminded of that terrible time."

"Undoubtedly," John agreed. He tipped his head to one side a moment later. "Denton, you say? Would that be Sir Walter Denton's family?"

"Yes. Why? Do you know him?"

"No, not at all. I only recall hearing the name mentioned some once or twice, although I cannot now recall by whom or in what context." Shaking off his perplexity, he smiled at me. "Never mind. It is of no importance. This is your night, and nothing signifies but your enjoyment of it. I am completely at your service. Shall I tell droll stories over dinner, stories that make you out the heroine? Or perhaps I should pretend to be violently in love with you so all the other gentlemen will be jealous. What say you, Anne?"

I laughed. "Neither one, if you please. It is *not* my night; it is Julia's. I have neither the right nor the desire to make myself the center of attention. And let us start no false rumors. People gossip enough as it is."

"They do indeed. Very well. We shall give them no excuse to gossip about us. We shall be as quiet and dull as you like."

We arrived in good time and were received in the front hall by Mr. and Mrs. Babcock, to whom I introduced my cousin.

"Ah, so this is the legendary Colonel Fitzwilliam," said Mrs. Babcock. "We have heard so much about you, and none of it to your discredit, I assure you."

"Have you indeed, my dear lady?" he answered. "Well, I cannot imagine why; I am certainly nobody important!" He laughed. "In any case, I pray your information has not built me up too high, or I shall be sure to disappoint."

Mrs. Babcock blushed under the power of John's smile and charming ways.

"Your war record and so forth," explained Mr. Babcock. "Your aunt speaks very highly of you, sir. You are a particular favorite of hers, I collect, and no doubt soon will be more so when…"

"My dear," interrupted his wife, "How you do go on. Miss de Bourgh and the colonel do not wish to be kept talking to us; they will want to join the other young people." Turning to me, she added, "Just go on through to the drawing room, Anne. You know the way."

We did so and found most of the others already assembled – Julia Babcock and her future husband Mr. Tallmadge, Mr. George Covington, Miss Fanny Sinclair, newlyweds Carol (formerly Miss Higgins) and Henry Beaks, Miss Rosalind Monsey, and brothers Mr. Theodore and Mr. Franklin Kensington. I had met them all except Henry Beaks at least once before.

I performed my share of the introductions and was delighted with the warm welcome and compliments I received in return. Cousin John was an instant favorite. Perhaps his reputation as a soldier had preceded him with this younger set as well, for everybody seemed intrigued and very pleased to meet him.

"Dinner will be ready soon," Julia explained to the company. "We are only waiting for Diana Denton. Anne, Colonel Fitzwilliam, do come and sit with me."

Flattered by such a marked attention, I smiled and made for the seat next to her, John following to a nearby sofa.

Julia stopped me, though. "No, no, this will never do. I must have the two of you side by side, not separated. Anne you must sit by the colonel there," she said, pointing to the sofa John had meant to take alone, "and Mr. Tallmadge will sit by me."

We all obeyed. A bride's whims are to be indulged without exception, after all.

"Yes, that is much better," she said, satisfied at last. "Now, Colonel, I believe I heard that your home is in Derbyshire."

"You have been correctly informed, Miss Babcock. Derbyshire is indeed my home county."

"It is beautiful country, I understand, but I suppose you may spend very little time there in the future."

"How do you mean?"

"I naturally assumed… That is, I supposed you would be devoting the greatest share of your time to Kent, remaining near Rosings and roundabout. Am I mistaken?"

I read amusement – or was it confusion? – in John's face, and he hesitated before answering.

"Well… while it is true that I am very fond of Rosings Park, Miss Babcock, I am not free to remain there indefinitely. Alas, between my family responsibilities and my obligations to my regiment, my time is not my own."

"I thought perhaps you might be giving up your commission," suggested Mr. Tallmadge, "what with the peace and with your changing circumstances."

Just then, the butler announced Miss Denton, and everybody sprang to their feet again to greet the late arrival. I was especially glad to see her, and my impression was that she felt the same about me. "It has been much too long," I told her after introducing John one more time.

"Yes, much too long," she agreed, squeezing my hands. "And how well you look, my dear Anne! One would never guess you had been ill so long."

"That is all behind me, I trust. Now that I am stronger, may I call at Kendlebrook sometime?"

A cloud darted across her visage. "It might be better if I came to you, my dear. My father does not much care for visitors, you see, not these many years. What about your mother? Would she receive me at Rosing, do you think?"

I could not help frowning at this. "What an odd question, Diana! We have been friends since childhood. Why should Mama not receive you?"

She shrugged her shoulders and gave her head a toss. "You are quite right; it *was* a silly question. I would simply adore seeing Rosings again, and I shall make a point of calling there very soon."

What a night! Dinner was excellent and the conversation animated. John contributed more than an equal share to the company's entertainment, which was no surprise. I held my own, too, and was proud of myself for doing so.

It was delicious to be looking and feeling my best, to be returned to a society of my peers, knowing I belonged there, and to be celebrating an engagement formed by love and not obligation. No one had told me this last was the case; it was plainly evident in how Julia and Mr. Tallmadge behaved towards each other – the tender words exchanged in whispers, the covert touch of hands, the lingering glances between them. And soon their marriage would take place to complete their joy. I could not help but think how lucky they were. They were perfectly suited and had no one to object to their union. I would only experience the same if I were to have the good fortune to fall in love with Mama's idea of the perfect man for me. Judging from recent experience, that seemed unlikely.

We did not stay late; I did not wish to risk being made ill by the complete disruption of my health regiment. On the ride home, John looked pensive but I was still all aflutter and wanting to talk. "It was such a lovely evening," I began. "Do not you think so?"

"Hmmm? Oh, yes, lovely." And then he resumed his silence.

"Are you tired?" I asked presently, thinking that the most likely explanation for his quiet mood.

"Tired? No. Why do you ask?"

"It is because I have never known you to sit so long without speaking before."

"Ah, yes, I suppose that is true. I was thinking, actually. It may surprise you to learn that I *do* that on occasion."

"Of course it does not surprise me, John. Will you tell me what has your mind so thoroughly occupied, though? I might be interested."

"Certainly, although it may not make very much sense. It is just that I had an odd feeling tonight. It seemed to me that some of your friends were… It is difficult to explain, and you may think I am only imagining things, Anne. But it seemed to me that some of your friends were… shall we say, unusually interested in me? And perhaps in you too. Did you not notice it?"

No, I had noticed nothing of the kind. The evening and my return to society had been an utter triumph, according to my modest standards. It simply could not have gone better. If people had been interested in me, I was naïve enough to find it flattering, and it never would have surprised me that they should admire my convivial cousin. "How exactly do you mean, John?" I asked.

He crossed his arms and sighed. "I can hardly tell you. It is nothing I can quite pin down. It was as if they were watching us with particular curiosity – the way people look at somebody who is expected to do something out of the ordinary, like perform an acrobatic act, marry, or die. And some of their remarks seemed a little peculiar as well. *Was I not planning on resigning my commission and spending all my future time in Kent?* That sort of thing."

I thought a moment. "A bit peculiar, perhaps, but I am sure there is nothing suspicious in it. A person new to a group is always something of a curiosity, and you agreed yourself that people gossip far too much. Perhaps some inaccurate rumor has got round. It must be something flattering rather than derogatory, though, for everybody was exceedingly friendly."

"Almost too friendly, perhaps."

"Is there such a thing as being too friendly?"

"I am afraid there might be at that, my dear."

When we arrived at home, I said goodnight to John and to Mama, and I went straight up to bed, thinking no more about John's ideas. It had been a wonderful evening, and I would allow nothing to spoil it for me. I fell asleep with expectations of pleasant dreams, but I woke to something quite different. My cousin John had fled in the middle of the night, and nobody would tell me why.

- 39 -

Mrs. Jenkinson

On the Perils of Eavesdropping

After seeing my young lady settled that night, I had started downstairs, intending to return her tea things to the kitchen. Halfway down, however, I was arrested by what I heard emanating from the drawing room. Not all the words were clear to me – the door was only slightly ajar – but the identity of the two voices involved was unmistakable. It was Lady Catherine and Colonel Fitzwilliam, and they were engaged in heated conversation.

"Did my brother not say anything at all to you about it, then?" Lady Catherine demanded.

If the colonel answered, I could not hear.

"Well, he certainly should have!" her ladyship continued. "And failing that, you might have put two and two together yourself. Otherwise, what did you think you were coming here for?"

"I *thought* it was just as you said in the summer, that you desired my help with easing Anne back into society. Apparently it was foolish of me, but I took you at your word, Aunt. I never *dreamt* there was more to it than that!"

"With all my marked attentions? I do not throw these compliments away lightly…" Here her voice dropped.

I next heard the colonel saying, "And to tell anybody else before you were assured of my consent? It was unconscionable! I was never so uncomfortable in all my life. What an untenable position you have placed me in, Madam! And what of your own daughter? Her reputation is at stake here as well."

"You have no grounds to consign all the blame to my account, Fitzwilliam! If your father had done his part, as he assured me he would, none of this would have happened."

"Have no fear, Aunt. I intend to speak to my father forthwith! He shall have his share of the responsibility in the unfortunate affair. No doubt there is plenty of guilt to go round."

"Fitzwilliam, be reasonable."

"I have never felt less inclined to be reasonable in my life, Madam!" With this, he flung the door open, crossed the hall, and barged past me up the stairs, taking them two at a time.

Before I could retreat out of sight, Lady Catherine emerged as well. Her eyes doubtless seeking after the colonel, they alighted on me instead.

"What do you do there, Mrs. Jenkinson?" she questioned testily.

I was caught and had to justify myself as well as I could. "I… I was just taking these things down to the kitchen, Ma'am."

"Then for heaven's sake stop gaping and proceed. You are to forget anything you may have heard or seen here. It is none of your business, and I will not put up with any gossip or interference from you. Do I make myself clearly understood?"

"Perfectly, your ladyship," I said, dropping my gaze and continuing on my way.

"And next time, use the servants' staircase on such an errand," she called after me.

I could not do as ordered; I could not forget what I had heard and seen, and my mind filled with conjecture as to what it might mean. I intended to abide by the rest of her ladyship's instructions, though. I would by no means repeat what I had overheard, however much I might be tempted to do so. My continued employment, I knew, depended on my being discreet. Therefore, when Miss Anne, looking shocked and distressed, put her questions to me the next morning, I had little to say.

"Colonel Fitzwilliam has gone, Mrs. Jenkinson," she told me in a whisper when Lady Catherine was momentarily out of the room. "And without so much as a goodbye or a note for me. What do you suppose could have happened to make him leave Rosings so abruptly?"

I kept my voice low too, though I said nothing treasonous. "I would have no way of knowing, Miss. I am sure it will turn out to have been something perfectly reasonable that has taken him away. Perhaps the colonel remembered some urgent business he needed to attend elsewhere, or perhaps he was summoned home unexpectedly. I trust all will be explained in good time."

The explanation did come, although not as quickly – or to as satisfactory an effect – as one might have hoped.

- 40 -

Lady Catherine

Surrounded by Incompetence

I did not know with whom I should have been the more annoyed – Fitzwilliam for not being perceptive enough to know which way the wind was blowing, or my own brother for leaving the difficult task of informing him to me. I was surrounded by incompetence on every side, which I suppose should have come as no surprise. It was always thus.

Well, Fitzwilliam had gone to sort things out with his father, and Anne none the wiser for it. Apparently Mrs. Jenkinson had remembered her place and valued her living enough to keep her mouth shut. Anne needed to know nothing about the matter until it was settled – settled for the benefit of all, I trusted, Fitzwilliam's as much or more so than anybody else's. Regardless how slow the light was to dawn upon him, my nephew must see reason in the end.

- 41 -

Anne

Receiving a Letter

I did not worry a great deal over my Cousin John's early departure. As Mrs. Jenkinson said, there would likely turn out to be a very rational explanation, and I would know it in time.

Meanwhile, Mr. Essex came again, and I was able to inform him that I had weathered the excitement of the dinner party and the surprise of my cousin's departure without implication to my health.

With my physician present to support me, I plucked up courage enough to mention Georgiana's birthday ball to my mother over dinner. With a third party as witness, I thought she would at least attempt to behave civilly about it.

She stormed at first, censuring me at once for the mere mention of Pemberley (although I had carefully avoided alluding to William and Elizabeth themselves). I persisted, however, speaking in calm and conciliatory tones in the hope that she would be reasonable as well. "Georgiana has done nothing wrong, Mama. You know that is true. And I would so very much like to go to her ball. Think of all the quality people I am sure to meet with there. That must be seen as an advantage."

"It is out of the question," she reiterated. "You *may* meet with some people of quality, it is true, but you will *certainly* meet with those persons against whom I hold the most strenuous and justified objections. Besides, such a long journey would be very taxing. Mr. Essex will agree with me on this."

I did not give him time to do so but plunged ahead. "I am sure Mr. Essex will agree with *me* that I am strong enough now to undertake such a journey, or at least I will be by January if all goes well."

We both looked at the doctor, who froze with his fork halfway to his mouth. He had kept out of the discussion until this point, no doubt in a spirit of self-preservation. But clearly, he could do so no longer. "I… I do," he said. "I agree with you both. Travel can indeed be taxing on the body and even the mind. It is not harmful to one who is well prepared for it, however. With the necessary precautions, I believe Miss de Bourgh might venture into Derbyshire without material danger."

"Cousin John will take me," I said boldly. "I am certain he would if I asked him, Mama, and you have said yourself that his escort gives you the greatest peace of mind."

Mama was silent for a minute, which I hoped was a good sign. It meant that she was at least considering the possibility of allowing me to go.

"Under the *right* circumstances," she said at last, "Fitzwilliam's presence could make all the difference. We shall have to wait and see."

I was satisfied. It was more of a concession than I had expected from Mama on my first approach, and there was still time to sway her. It only remained for John to do his part, to officially throw his weight behind the proposal. From what he had said to me about it before, I had no doubt he would gladly do so.

The next fortnight passed quickly by, and I kept very busy. I had already begun making calls with Mama again, and now I was also getting out on my own as often as possible. Diana Denton came to Rosings one morning, as she had promised to do, staying a full two hours, time she spent mostly with myself alone. Mama remained only ten or fifteen minutes before – somewhat rudely I thought – making an excuse to leave us.

I had almost forgot about Cousin John and his precipitous departure when a letter, come from him, brought the odd episode flooding back. To my surprise, it was addressed particularly to me. To my utter relief (especially after I knew the contents), I was able to spirit it away before Mama had seen it. This is what John had written:

My dear Anne,

I hope you have forgiven me for leaving you so abruptly last month, the evening of the dinner party at the Babcocks. Something astonishing happened later that night – in truth, something your mother said to me – and all I could think was to fly home at once to confront my father over it. Since then, however, I have had time to consider, and my attitude has consequently matured into a calmer, more rational response. Although I still maintain that the method by which I was told was needlessly barbaric, the news itself is not fundamentally unpleasant.

This must sound like pure nonsense to you, but I promise it will all become clear presently. My intent was to proceed with caution in making my explanations to you, to approach the subject gradually lest you be similarly overwhelmed, since I have no way of knowing if you are still as much in the dark as I was that night. And yet, I can think of no way to ease the potential blow.

The simple truth is this. Our honored parents have decided that a match between the two of us would be ideal…

I gasped at the news. A match between John and myself? How glad I was to be alone, for I could never have concealed my incredulity at this announcement! In fact, I took a minute to calm myself before continuing, for I could see there was much more to come.

…My father and your mother agreed on it last summer when we all met at Rosings. That, I gather, was the chief subject of their discussions at the time. Toward that end, I was invited back in October, with the assumption that I would have got used to the idea by then and perhaps even be ready to propose. As you may have guessed by now, your uncle failed in his part of acquainting me with this information. Meanwhile, my aunt apparently let slip the plan to one or two of her friends, speaking of it as an accomplished fact, which resulted in those suspicious remarks and curious looks I noticed at the dinner party. In short, everybody knew about our supposed understanding before we ourselves did.

Have I shocked you, my dear Anne? I hope not. Perhaps you have been more perceptive than I and deduced this information long ago…

Far from it! If he had been in darkness before, I had been in darkness still. If he had been blind, I was blinder, for I had even failed to notice anything amiss at the party.

…You were raised believing you were to marry Darcy, and so I am inclined to think that such a match as this would never have occurred to you. The same was true for me until recently.

Now, however, I can see that from a certain point of view, it makes perfect sense. Forgive me if I speak plainly, Anne, but this is how our parents have it worked out. Your mother is ready to simply exchange one nephew for the other. To her way of thinking, I am nearly as good as Darcy in most respects. As for my father, who had almost despaired of my marrying at all (let alone marrying so creditably), he is overjoyed at the idea. He never expected to be so lucky as to get someone like you for a daughter-in-law.

Please believe me, I am not in favor of allowing ourselves to be bullied, but neither am I so proud as to refuse to do what my father wishes out of pure stubbornness or spite. There is merit to the proposal, which I believe you will see as well, once you have had time to think about it. That is the reason I write to you now – to give you the time to think the matter through.

You know I am extremely fond of you, my dear, and I flatter myself that you find me rather agreeable company as well. Many highly successful marriages begin on less. I am now persuaded it might be just the thing for us both – not a love match, at least not in the beginning, but a union of mutual comfort and convenience. And if we please our families by pleasing ourselves, so much the better.

However, if after due consideration you are dead set against marrying me, Anne, there is an end to it. You cannot injure me, and I promise not to resent you for it in the least.

I will even stand on your side against the plan if need be, for I have made no promises to anyone. That I may discuss these things further with you (or hear your decided 'no' if you had rather), I propose coming to Rosings again before Christmas. Until then, think of me charitably.

With unfailing affection,
John F.

- 42 -

Lady Catherine

Playing the Innocent

I knew within minutes that a letter had come for Anne from Fitzwilliam. Of course I did. Very little goes on in this house that I am not made aware of. As long as it is I who pays them, the servants will be loyal to *me*.

By my instruction, Anne received her precious missive without interference, and she kept it hidden from me ever after, which was very telling. She had lately exhibited a distasteful streak of independence, especially where her future mate was concerned, and I judged that nothing would be more likely to turn her against the plan than for me to press her about it before she had time to become accustomed to the idea. I could be patient when it suited my purposes. So I chose to bide my time and suppress my curiosity, sparing myself the melodramatic scenes that might ensue if I should broach the subject prematurely. Much better to allow my daughter to come to the right decision on her own, if possible.

My brother – along with his apologies – wrote that he believed his son had done that very thing, in short, that he had come to know his own good. Signs had not been promising when he stormed out of here in October, but it was November now, and reason had had time to take its due effect.

Fitzwilliam must have blessed his lucky stars that such a supremely eligible match had been offered him on a silver platter. Only a fool would have refused, and Fitzwilliam was no fool. His letter was evidence of that. Although I had not seen the contents, it struck me that there could only be one reason for his communication. He surely would not have written just to tell Anne he did *not* wish to marry her. If that were the case, no letter would have arrived at all except one from my brother to say that hope on that score was at an end.

I expected another visit to Rosings by Fitzwilliam would settle the affair. In the meantime, I intended to continue playing the innocent while keeping a sharp eye on my daughter.

Oh, to have this matter of supreme importance settled at last! It had been a long road with many disappointments on the way, but now we were on the verge of a successful conclusion. I could feel it.

With Anne healthy again and finally married into the noble family line, as was always the goal, my work would be done. My worries for her future would be at an end. Best of all, since Fitzwilliam had no property of his own – something which would have seemed a disadvantage at first – the newlyweds would naturally reside here at Rosings after the ceremony. So I would not be losing a daughter, as could so easily have happened; I would be gaining a very charming and amiable son. In truth, he was more so than the one I had in mind before. I began to understand that it could not have turned out any better. I had orchestrated the business exceedingly skillfully.

- 43 -

Anne

Debating the Issue

I had never wanted my father's advice more.

There was no one I could talk to about John's offer. Mrs. Collins had gone from the neighborhood, or I might have risked confiding in her. It would not be fair to Mrs. Jenkinson to expect her to render an opinion on such a delicate question, especially when doing so might put her at variance with her employer. And I refused to speak to Mama! I already knew *her* opinion in any case. It now made perfect sense that she had not fought tooth and nail to force me into accepting one of the others. No doubt she already had this better plan in mind by then.

For one mad moment, I considered consulting Mr. Essex. He was a man of sense and education with some experience in the world. I trusted his good judgment and that he always had my best interests at heart. With all the time we had spent together in the past months, we had spoken on many subjects, but never romantic attachments, at least nothing beyond the bare acknowledgment that I had received and declined certain offers of marriage. In spite of the necessarily intimate nature of our friendship, it was hardly a topic into which I could delve more deeply with a man not a member of my family. No, it was out of the question to ask his opinion.

I had to do the best I could by myself, at least until John arrived. So I canvassed the topic back and forth in my own mind, examining it from every angle but to no avail. Coming to a definite verdict is difficult when one can too readily see all sides of a question.

"John would make you an excellent husband," argues my inner pragmatist, trying to convince me. "He would be kind to you and to

your children – an amiable companion. And would it not be a relief to have things finally settled? You know you will never have a moment's peace until you marry somebody. Your mother will see to that."

"What the pragmatist says is true," agrees the self who reasons from the side of emotion. She is not finished with me, though. Having claimed my other ear, she adds, "Your cousin John is a very kind and honorable man. No doubt he would do his best by you. But you have been too used to thinking of him in more fraternal terms. How could you be expected to adjust your feelings so suddenly and so completely?"

"It is not about feelings," comes the immediate rebuttal. "Feelings will sort themselves out properly by and by. You must look at the situation sensibly."

I speak up for myself. "Hold on. I can see well enough the practical advantages for myself in the match; I will be very well looked after. But what does John gain by it? He admits he does not love me."

Emotion pipes up again. "That is true! Although he implies that he expects his fondness for you to grow to more in time, who can say for certain that it ever will?"

"Advantage? You make me laugh!" jeers logic. "Why, there is every advantage to him in this match! Beyond the 'comfort and convenience' he speaks of in his letter, there is the money. Yes, the money! He may be too polite to mention it, but I am not. Marrying you will do away the man's money worries forever! He might even resign his commission and stay at home, no longer risking his life every time another war comes along. That is an excellent benefit as well."

I think a moment. "It would please me a great deal to be able to do that much for him. Still…"

"What are you waiting for, then? Are you expecting Prince Charming to come out of nowhere, riding along on a noble white steed? You have seen all the eligible candidates, and Colonel Fitzwilliam is by far the best of the lot. If you decline his offer, you will end as an old maid or married to that ancient Sir Henry Stanfield. Is that what you want?"

No, that was not what I wanted. Neither did I expect Prince Charming. This round of the ongoing debate went to the pragmatist, but the romantic in me might win the next, arguing that I should hold out for something more than "comfort and convenience." I wanted love and romance, of course. I desired to be swept away by excitement and passion. But I doubted that was very realistic… or even safe?

Again, I thought of Mr. Essex. If I could not ask his advice directly, I could at least ponder whatever he might already have told me that would be pertinent to my deliberations. All I could remember, however, was his admonition against becoming too "stirred up," his counsel to remain well by remaining calm, and taming the emotions in order to tame my headaches. He would no doubt tell me that excitement and passion were the last things I needed, and that I should avoid them like the plague.

In thinking of Mr. Essex, however, I was not looking for an impartial medical opinion, not really. I did not want to hear that I must proceed with caution or that I should view romance as a dangerous substance to be taken only in very small doses. What I would have infinitely preferred from him was the opposite. I would have preferred him to tell me he thought I was meant to have extravagant love in my life, that I was not only allowed but encouraged to experience grand passion, and that I was now well capable of inspiring passion in return, however unlikely that had seemed in the past.

His confidence would have meant the world to me. His belief in my worth as a woman would have given me tremendous satisfaction. For you see, my secret – what I had only recently begun to suspect myself – was that, had the circumstances only been different, had he been the eldest son of a viscount instead of the younger son of who knows what sort of man, Mr. Essex might have been the very one for the job, for he had already proved himself capable of stirring that sort of romantic sensation alive in me.

~~*~~

I attributed these newly discovered sensations to their proper cause. Surely it must be due to gratitude, for how much he had helped to restore my health, and to the special intimacy inherent in our relationship. As my longstanding physician, Mr. Essex had spent more time close to me (in a physical sense) than any other man. I had probably only reacted to him differently from previous doctors because he was young and good-looking, and because of our extended time together. He had become a good friend to me. There could never be more to it than that.

The idea of marrying Mr. Essex was impossible, of course. I needed no pragmatist to tell me that. I should not even think of it. Not only was there no reason to suppose he would desire such a thing, Mr. Essex was entirely unsuitable – his background, his profession, his education, his manners. Well, to be fair, I doubted any fault could reasonably be found with his education, and he was capable of very proper manners when he took the trouble. I had seen that for myself. However, although Mama made due with him at her table when she could get nobody better, she would never consider him good enough to marry her daughter.

No, any romantic feelings I had tending in that direction were therefore only a useless distraction – pleasant fodder for my imagination but that was all. I would do well to redirect my energies in a more productive line. The choice at hand was to marry Colonel Fitzwilliam or not to marry him. Mr. Essex did not enter into the equation either way. Yet, when the doctor came to Rosings five days after John's letter had arrived, I could not help studying his handsome features for some sign, listening to his familiar voice for some new word that would help me with my decision.

We sat half an hour with Mama in the drawing room, where he conversed with her about whatever she liked – ordinary subjects made far too tedious for me by my more-weighty preoccupation. What cared I for the high price of tea or the cut of Mr. Endicott's new carriage when I was teetering on the brink of the most important decision of my life? My other suitors I had dismissed with barely a second thought; John's proposal had to be taken seriously. This was the one that truly mattered. He would be coming soon, and I had to know how to reply to his offer. I had to make up my mind. Should tell him 'yes' or 'no'?

Before me was the man I somewhat irrationally believed held the key to answering the question. Mr. Essex was the one who could have helped me decide, and yet he sat there talking about the health benefits of beet greens! It was most provoking.

At last he turned his attention fully to me.

"Miss de Bourgh, I hope you have saved your walk to take it with me."

"I have, Mr. Essex, as usual."

"Excellent. Do you fancy indoors or out today?"

"Out, I think, if you have no objection."

"That is always my preference, as well you know by now." In keeping with his custom, Mr. Essex extended a courtesy invitation to Mama, and as usual, she declined. Once we were out of doors and on our own, he said, "I should not know how to behave if Lady Catherine ever chose to accept the offer of joining us for one of our walks. What a different character these pleasant outings would take on then. Well, now, which way shall we go?"

"To the orchard," I suggested, pointing off to the left.

"Very well; to the orchard," he said, ushering me in that direction with a light hand temporarily on my back. As we walked, he continued. "I remember the first time we took this way together. Do you, Miss de Bourgh?"

"Yes, I believe I do. It must be several months ago now."

"It is eight months at least. You were not doing nearly as well that day, I recall. You had suffered a setback to your health."

I remembered too. That was the day after Mr. Alderwood's proposal and my subsequent argument with Mama. I had a terrible headache as a result. "I could not bear the light, and you had to lead me about like a blind woman."

"It was no trouble; it was my honor to witness your courage. That is when I knew you would recover. You chose to move forward, even when it was difficult, instead of shrinking back as many might have done in your place. It would have been the end, though. You might never have tried again if once you had given up."

"You must not make me out such a heroine, Mr. Essex. I only agreed to walk a little way hanging on to your arm."

"Ah, but that is not the only example of your bravery I have observed. You had the courage to send away every suitor your mother brought you, defying her wishes. That could not have been easy either."

"I was far from brave, though; I was trembling with fear at every moment."

"That is my point. It is not truly brave to do something when there is no terror attached to it."

"I had not thought of that," I said. "I certainly was terrified, expecting Mama to put her foot down and insist. She did not, however. It seems to me now that Mama did not care so very much about any of them. It would be different if it were something she was quite determined on, a matter of highest consequence. I have the sad example of my cousin to teach me that."

"Colonel Fitzwilliam?"

"No, another cousin, whom you will not have met. He crossed my mother in something of the utmost importance, and she instantly declared him 'dead' to her. We may not have anything more to do with him or even mention his name. That is the real reason she may not allow me to go into Derbyshire for my cousin Georgiana's ball in January. It is with Georgiana's brother that Mama has cut all ties."

"Surely she would not treat her own daughter in that uncivilized fashion, even were you to defy her. She would not refuse to ever see or speak to you again, would she?"

"I honestly do not know, Mr. Essex. She might do worse! The most she could do to my cousin was to excommunicate him. She could *disinherit* me. I would not put it past her."

"So you are left with few alternatives," he concluded.

"While she lives, I must do as she says, at least in the main." Here, I made the decision to inch a little nearer the particular dilemma on my mind. "I must marry someone of her choosing."

"Someone of great wealth or at least great consequence, no doubt."

I nodded to confirm his assumption.

Mr. Essex remained quietly pensive a minute as we walked on, side by side. "There is always another choice, of course. If it were a matter of singular importance, a matter crucial to heart or conscience, you could risk doing as *you* thought right. Perhaps Lady Catherine would behave better than you expect."

This raised my hopes for some positive advice, some insight into his true opinion. "Is that what you would do in my position, Mr. Essex?" I asked. "Is that what you would advise *me* to do in such a case?"

I could not help it; my imagination took immediate flight. While he paused, considering, I imagined what his answer should be.

"Yes, by all means, Miss de Bourgh. I would advise you to follow your heart, never mind what society or your mother may say." He stops and kneels before me. "You must not marry any of those dull fellows that your mother prefers; you must not marry anybody but me. I love you, Anne. I know there is no logical reason that you should take such a risk for me – I have little enough to offer you – but I ask it of you anyway. Will you throw caution to the wind, my darling, and consent to be my wife?"

I looked up expectantly at Mr. Essex as we continued to walk, irrationally hoping for such a proposal and suspecting I would easily succumb to it, ready to say yes if he should ask me. It all depended on him. Did he care for me at all? If so, would he be willing to throw caution and decorum aside himself, in order to say so?

Whatever he might have been thinking, restraint governed the words he expressed. No, that presumed too much. Restraint implied that there had been a struggle between desire and prudence, and I could verify nothing of the kind. Obviously, as with all the rest, any such battle raged only in my imagination.

"I might be willing to risk it for myself," he said. "I have done something similar on occasion – standing by my convictions in the choice of my profession, for example. But I would by no means presume to advise *you*, Miss de Bourgh. I will not be responsible for influencing you to something that could result in dire consequences. No, I would trust to your excellent judgment instead, should you ever find yourself in such a predicament. You have demonstrated nothing but remarkable good sense ever since I have known you."

High praise. Is this not exactly what every young woman wishes to hear from the man she secretly admires – that he thinks she has 'remarkable good sense'? If indeed I had possessed the remarkable good sense he credited to me, I would probably have been highly flattered. But as it was, I could not feel very much gratified by the compliment.

I still had one more chance, however, one more chance to solicit his opinion. Had I been bold enough, I could at that moment have come straight out with my current quandary. *"As a matter of fact, Mr. Essex, Colonel John Fitzwilliam has proposed marriage to me, and I must decide whether or not to accept him. What is your advice?"* Perhaps I should have done so, but I did not. I said nothing about it, nor did Mr. Essex pursue that line any further.

We had by this time arrived at the end of the gravel walk, the path turning to dirt as it entered the orchard. To go farther would be to muddy our shoes, and there was insufficient inducement for that. The orchard was not as cheerful a place in late November as it was in the spring, but dreary instead. Without their leaves and fruit, the trees looked sadly bereft, lifeless skeletons without any flesh to give them vitality or purpose.

"I think we had best turn back," I proposed.

"Just as you like," Mr. Essex answered. We pivoted on the spot and struck out in the opposite direction. After a minute or two, he added, "Oh, I meant to tell you that I must be away for a few weeks. You shall not mind, shall you, Miss de Bourgh?"

I would mind, but of course I could not say so. "This is very sudden, sir. I hope there is nothing amiss."

"No, nothing amiss. I am going into Lincolnshire to visit my family; that is all. My elder brother is getting married."

"Then it is certainly right that you should be there," I said.

"It is some months since I have been home, and I mean to make a proper visit of it, to make up for my long absence. A colleague of mine has agreed to see to my patients in London, and *you* hardly need me anymore. In fact, I should rightly have left off coming so often by now; there is little medical justification for it any longer. But Rosings and its inhabitants are pleasures I am very reluctant to do without."

These words – the last part – were more to my liking, but my spirits were no longer in a condition to fully appreciate them. "You flatter us, Mr. Essex."

"Not at all. I speak nothing but the truth," he said very earnestly.

Just then, the sun burst through the clouds, flashing full in my face before I could defend myself. I turned sharply away, closing my eyes tight in anticipation of the pain I had come to expect at such a violent assault.

"Miss de Bourgh, you are unwell," exclaimed my companion in concern. Not waiting for a response, he took my gloved hand and drew it through to rest on his arm. "Now, keep your eyes shut as you did that other day. I will lead you. Your bonnet will do you no good with the sun in its present position so low in the sky."

In truth, I felt no pain this time, and I was quite certain I could have navigated my way successfully on my own. I had no will to resist his offer, however. It was a cold day, and I coveted the warmth of his nearer proximity if not his guiding sight. Again, I found the sensation of strolling along completely blind and dependant on him strangely agreeable, and it occurred to me that I must take such small comforts while I could. Had he not just said there was no valid reason for him to see me so often anymore?

Presently arriving back at the house, I thanked him and we came inside. While we warmed ourselves by the drawing room fire, Mr. Essex imparted the information of his travel plans to Mama, leaving his direction in Lincolnshire with her just in case we should unexpectedly need him.

Mama seemed not to mind, but I felt a great loss at the idea of Mr. Essex being away so long. He had become such an integral part of our lives that it was difficult to imagine his not being there for weeks at a stretch. I watched Mr. Essex's gig out the window until it disappeared from sight. Then I remained rooted to the spot a while longer, as silent and forlorn as one of those bare trees in the orchard. Of all horrid things, I disliked it most when friends went away.

- 44 -

Lady Catherine

On Meeting Expectations

We should see no more of Mr. Essex for at least a month. With Anne doing so well, I did not object when he said he intended to go away to visit his family. In fact, I told him to take as long as he wanted. In truth, the timing of the doctor's absence was quite fortuitous. Fitzwilliam would be arriving soon, according to his letter – one that came addressed to *me* this time – and it would be as well to have everybody else out of the way.

Anne, the sly creature, betrayed nothing when I told her of Fitzwilliam's plan to come – no hint whatsoever that this could be anything more than a routine visit. But we both knew it *was* more, much more. Though he wrote nothing definite to me, Fitzwilliam was already convinced and ready to marry Anne or he would not have been traveling to Rosings again so soon. I was inclined to believe Anne was leaning in the right direction as well, otherwise she would hardly have been able to hide her anxiety at the prospect of confronting another unwelcome proposal.

Once again, Anne's good fortune impressed me. She had been very well treated compared to what happened so often in my day. She would not be marrying some near stranger about whom she could know nothing but rather a person she had been acquainted with from infancy. And I had had years to observe Fitzwilliam's character myself as he grew up before my eyes. It did not seem consistent with his nature to be duplicitous, so there was every reason to hope he would be faithful to my daughter. My brother assured me that although there had been various women in his son's life, none of them represented a serious attachment. That boded well. He would be marrying Anne by choice, not by coercion, only pretending to give up some other woman he might prefer. *That* was a recipe for certain disaster, as I knew too well.

It all would soon be settled. All my work and trouble would be rewarded, and then perhaps, with my duties as a mother faithfully discharged, I would at last have some time for myself. I might do as I pleased for a change.

Meanwhile, there were one or two other important matters demanding my attention, the most pressing of these was the situation with the new rector and his wife. Although I had given Mr. and Mrs. Chesterfield the same benefit of my generous guidance that I had always given the Collinses, I was not completely satisfied that they had received my advice as they ought. They were behaving entirely too free for people in their dependent position, I found. Mr. Chesterfield did not feel the need to ask my opinion of his sermons before preaching them, and Mrs. Chesterfield was no better. When I showed her the parsonage, she almost turned up her nose at the shelves I had taken the trouble to have installed in the closets. Then all she could say about the garden was that it was a shame there were so few flowers – a comment I could not help but think betrayed a dangerously frivolous streak.

I could see I should have to take a firmer hand and make it unmistakably clear what was expected of them. That might require more effort than I anticipated when I gave Mr. Chesterfield the living. What an infernal nuisance it was, especially when I had been anticipating having fewer responsibilities weighing on my shoulders. Mr. and Mrs. Collins were far more easily tractable.

45

Anne

Making a Sensible Decision

Once Mr. Essex left us, I immediately took myself to task over the wild imaginings and irrational romantic notions I had been indulging on his account. It was a very good thing that he had gone away, I decided, so that I could without distraction consider what was really important: Colonel Fitzwilliam's proposal. That is what rightly demanded my full attention and clear thinking. Again, I reminded myself that I was not in the position of choosing between two very different men, for only one of them had asked me. Simply put, my choice was either to gamble on an uncertain future or accept the worthy gentleman who had generously offered me his name and his protection.

When John arrived in the middle of December, I felt strangely shy at first seeing him again and embarrassed knowing the purpose of his visit. Although if anybody should have been uncertain, it was he, for he did not yet know what I meant to say to his proposal.

Instead of a formal exchange of bow and curtsey, I offered John my hand when he came in. He held it, giving it an affectionate shake, saying, "Anne, how good it is to see you again."

"I feel the same," I returned warmly.

Although there was nothing more intimate to our greeting than that – nothing more than what we had said and done a dozen times before in the past – Mama smiled in a way that revealed she believed it held extra significance this time. Her look bespoke the self-satisfaction of one who had already won her point. Though I knew she probably had, I was determined to leave her in some doubt of victory as long as possible. I daresay it was rather small minded of me to desire to deprive my own mother the pleasure of being right, especially when I had come to the very same conclusion she had, that marrying Colonel Fitzwilliam would be the best thing for me. I had nearly reconciled myself to that fact. I only wanted my decision confirmed by talking it through with John face to face.

Mama was more than willing to provide us as much time in private as we required to sort things out. That was certainly her unstated purpose in leaving us alone while she tended to some supposedly urgent household business that first day, in recommending we walk together while the weather was fine the second, and in sending us by carriage on an errand to the village the third. Why we continued the pretense, I cannot exactly explain. I knew she must have a very good idea why John was there; after all, it had been her idea. But somehow I did not like to admit I knew that she knew.

On that first day, John approached the question delicately. Drawing his chair closer to mine, he began by saying, "Well my dear, I suppose we should take advantage of your mother's absence to discuss our situation. If you are ready to talk, I am ready to hear whatever you may wish to say on the subject raised in my letter to you last month."

I had organized my thoughts in preparation for this moment, so it was only a matter of taking a deep breath and beginning. "I thank you most sincerely for the honor of your proposal, John, and I must tell you that I am favorably disposed towards it. Yet before I give you a firm answer, I wish to hear from your own lips why you believe this is best – not for me, you understand, but for yourself. I am not looking for flattery. As you acknowledged in your letter, this is not a love match, so I trust we may be completely honest with each other."

"By all means, Anne. I will be as honest as I am able, and I want the same from you. There is nothing to be gained by dissembling."

"I agree. Our best chance of success lies in dealing with one another openly and frankly."

"Quite. Well, you already know that I did not at first receive the idea of the match between us with perfect equanimity, not because it seemed unpleasant but because it was far from something I had ever considered as a possibility. Yet the more I thought about the arrangement, the more sense it made to me.

"You will understand all too well what it means to feel the expectations of a demanding parent." Here he paused for my assent, which I gave with a nod. "With every passing year, my father's insistence that I must marry, and to a very high standard too, grows louder and louder. I am expected to choose a lady of good breeding, and I am *constrained* to choose one of good fortune, since I have very little money of my own. You must forgive me for mentioning it, but we did promise to be completely open."

"Of course. You must not imagine me ignorant of practical matters, John."

"Well, then, you see my problem. It is not that I have been unwilling to do my duty; it is only that I have never run across the young lady who will both suit myself and at the same time satisfy my family. Some voices – again, I shall be plain with you that I refer to the voices our cousin Darcy and his wife – advocate holding out for love…"

I interrupted. "Stop a moment, John. Do you mean to tell me William and Elizabeth know of our delicate situation? How mortifying!"

"Allow me to explain. When I fled Rosings so abruptly in October, I desired to go straight to my father with my questions, but I was obliged to stop overnight at Pemberley along my way. Forgive me, Anne, but I was in such a state of turmoil that I could not hide my unrest. Consequently, Darcy and Elizabeth did hear from me the reason for my perplexity – the plan your mother and my father had hatched between them. However, the Darcys did *not* hear of my subsequent decision to propose to you, nor has anybody else. You are the first and only one privy to that information, if that makes you feel any better."

"Much, yes. This must be settled between the two of us, first and foremost."

"Indeed. Then as I was saying, Darcy and Elizabeth not surprisingly counseled that both you and I should hold out for love. No doubt they want all of their friends to know the same exceptional felicity in marriage that they themselves enjoy. However, I am of the opinion that a true love match like theirs is, sadly, out of reach for most of us. I have known many attractive and charming women in my time, but I have never come close to being in love with any of them. I may not be capable of more than deep affection, and *that*, my dear girl, I already feel for you. As to the other considerations, I cannot hope to find anybody who would better fill the bill.

"I believe we would deal very well together, Anne. In any case, it seems to me it is time to stop procrastinating and take action. I am grown weary of the uncertainty and of being a perpetual disappointment to my father. I wish to have things finally settled. If you agree to marry me, I shall count myself a very fortunate man."

John had given me exactly what I asked for: an honest recital of the advantages to himself in the match, without flowery words, flattery, or any excessive sentiment. It struck me immediately that all the same arguments he made applied equally to myself – well, all except the one about money, of course – and most were things I had already been thinking. We were in nearly identical situations, and we were of the same mind. That augured well. Like John, I also grew weary of the indecision. The solution was obvious, and the advantages were advantages to us both.

Over the course of the next two days, John and I thoroughly canvassed every aspect of the question again. We talked about where we should live if we married, and how we should conduct our lives. We talked of children, of faith, of aspirations for the future. We talked of politics and family. I appreciated that he listened to all my opinions and seemed to count them of equal value to his own. By the third day, we had come to a definite understanding.

"So we are agreed?" John asked. We were sitting side by side in the small parlor we had adopted as our own, where we were always given complete privacy. "We shall be married in six months' time."

"Yes, the second week of June," I added.

"Well, then, that is settled. Yes… good."

For an awkward moment, neither of us knew what to do next. I was afraid John would try to kiss me to seal the pact we had made between ourselves, but he did not. He only took my hand for a moment before releasing it again and asking, "Do you wish to tell your mother or shall I?"

In the end, for me it had come down to what I had promised myself before (and in my heart, promised my father). I would have been entirely content to wed William Darcy as originally planned. Failing that, I swore I would refuse to marry at all unless somebody equally admirable asked me, someone I could like just as well. I had kept my promise; John was such a man, and I was perfectly convinced that I should be as happy with him as I ever would have been with William. Perhaps happier, for John's manners were more to my personal taste.

My mother's jubilation at the announcement may well be imagined. Here again, it was not so much what she said as the exultant look in her eye that offended me. But I tried to remember what John had written in his letter, to copy his more mature attitude expressed therein. "*I am not in favor of allowing ourselves to be bullied, but neither am I so proud as to refuse to do what my father wishes out of pure stubbornness or spite.*" We had not been forced into this decision. We chose it for our own reasons and in our own best interests. The fact that it happened to make Mama nauseatingly triumphant as well could not be helped.

There was some good even in this, however. It seemed Mama's supreme satisfaction with herself at the success of her plan put her in charity with all the rest of the world, at least temporarily. She even granted my well-timed request for permission to travel to Pemberley for Georgiana's birthday ball in January. Perhaps she did not mind my seeing my cousin Darcy again if it were only to gloat over how well we had got on without him.

Although John and I did expect to tell the Darcys of our engagement in January (as well as my aunt and uncle Fitzwilliam on the same trip), it would be done very discreetly, and we had Mama's promise not to announce it to outsiders in the meantime. Family should be informed first.

I made one tiny exception for Mrs. Jenkinson, however, who was more family than not, at least in my view. "If you ever wanted to ask Mama a favor," I told her teasingly the next time we were alone together, "I advise you to do it today, by all means, Mrs. Jenkinson, for I think you will find her in an especially benevolent mood."

"Why is that, Miss Anne?" she asked in some confusion.

"Because I have just given her the very thing she wanted most in the world; I have agreed to marry Colonel Fitzwilliam."

She drew in a sharp breath of surprise and then broke into a wide smile. "Have you, now? Well, that is excellent news indeed! Colonel Fitzwilliam is a fine man, and I am sure you will be very happy together."

"I am of the same opinion, Mrs. Jenkinson, or I would never have engaged myself to him. The wedding will be in June."

Her expression changed from joy to uncertainty. "And then what, Miss?" she asked.

"Hmm? How do you mean?"

"Where shall you and the colonel live once you are married?"

"Oh, yes, of course. I see your point. This may affect you as well, you are thinking. In any case, I have no definite answer for you. There are many things still to be decided, and you may be sure Mama will have much to say about the matter. I should think we shall simply stay here, at least at first, since Colonel Fitzwilliam does not have an estate of his own. He is a second son, you know, so he will not inherit. But never fear, Mrs. Jenkinson. I could not possibly do without you. You shall always have a home with me, wherever I go."

As I lay abed that night, waiting for sleep to claim me, I congratulated myself on making a wise and well-considered choice for my future. This was monumental progress, and I looked forward to the weeks and months to come. There would be preparations and parties, and telling our friends the news. No doubt they would all be very pleased for me.

Then I thought of Mr. Essex, wondering how and when I should impart the vital information to him. I did not deceive myself into thinking he should care very much one way or the other. It was simply that, as a kind of extended member of our household, it would be difficult to keep the news from him. And besides, I might need his help to safely manage all the excitement the upcoming events would entail. This idea was confirmed when I woke the next morning with a fearful headache, my first in weeks.

- 46 -

Lady Catherine

Triumphs

Nothing is better than success – to conceive a plan, strategically advance it step by step, and see it come to fruition at last. Perhaps this is how God felt about his creation before mankind rebelled and it all went horribly wrong. Nothing like that was likely to occur to *my* creation, however. The match was too perfect. The pieces fit together flawlessly. All parties unanimously agreed.

I considered that as soon as Anne and Fitzwilliam were married, I should leave them on their own at Rosings – newlyweds must have their privacy – and take myself off to town. That would be just the thing. There was no earthly reason I might not now spend more time partaking of London society than what Anne's health had allowed in the past. I was still in the prime of life and of a very attractive age. That charming Count Deering remarked on it every time I saw him.

"My dear Lady Catherine," he said the last time, bending over my hand, "you are an ageless beauty. I cannot understand it. The rest of us grow older while you remain fresh and eternally youthful."

Yes, he would be very pleased to know I was in town again.

And he was safe. We were *both* safe, I should say, since he made his situation plainly understood to all. I believed Count Deering found the arrangement quite convenient. A wife permanently exiled to a mental institution never gets in the way, and her existence must be the very best protection against unreasonable expectations being raised that ever there was. Any woman imagining herself becoming a countess must look elsewhere.

Were all current impediments removed on both sides, however, I still maintained that I should never marry again – the Count or another. I would not willingly surrender my independence a second time for *any* man. So I might enjoy Count Deering's company with no obligations, and he might enjoy mine on the same terms. And soon too, if I had my way, which I fully intend to.

Anne had fallen into line in the end, just as I predicted she would. It showed she had inherited some of my practical good sense. Her long-term compensation, I trusted, would be a highly successful marriage. She garnered a more immediate reward for her compliance, however, in securing my permission to attend Georgiana's birthday ball on Fitzwilliam's arm. It was generous of me to grant her wish; that is true. But I had other motivations as well. Since I could not possibly go there myself, I expected to have a full report from Anne about what transpired at Pemberley.

The young man who was once my nephew looked well enough when I caught a glimpse of him at Mr. Collins's funeral services, but how would he fare, I wondered, once he heard his dear friend Fitzwilliam had freely chosen the fate he thought himself above accepting? Perhaps his own marriage was not as satisfying as he had expected. By this time, he might well have discovered the folly of marrying outside his sphere and against the wishes of those who were in a position to know what was best for him. No doubt his inferior little wife had shown by now how ill-suited she was to take my sister's place as mistress of that great estate! The decline in the dignity of the place must be everywhere apparent.

My other unwitting informant in the situation would be Mrs. Collins, whom I had asked to correspond. Now that she was settled so near Pemberley, she would have a close and frequent view of what went on there. Of course, she would be too loyal to her friend to be of much use to me; she would never gossip about any disharmony or faults in management. Still, I thought she might occasionally let slip something worth hearing.

Here is Mrs. Collins's first letter from Derbyshire:

Dear Lady Catherine,

Thanks in part to all your helpful advice about our route and the best inns to frequent, Mrs. Sanditon and I traveled safely and fairly comfortably north into Derbyshire. There is nothing one can do about the condition of the roads in

December, however, and the many little delays and inconveniences mud creates.

Reddclift is a fine estate (although nothing compared to Rosings Park, of course), and Ruth's brother-in-law has been exceedingly obliging to us. Although the cottage he has given over to our use is not quite as large as Hunsford parsonage house, I am certain we shall be very content here. The needs and wants of two widowed gentlewomen are few.

We have already dined twice at the great house, where we enjoyed expansive views from the drawing room windows, very fine food and drink, the company of our generous host, and the delight of seeing his two young offspring – daughters of ages two and four. Mr. Sanditon has also offered us the use of a carriage whenever we might have need of one. Here again, our wants are few: an occasional trip to the village shops and church in Kympton on Sundays. We have already met Mr. Thornton, the rector of the parish, who was so kind as to call at the cottage to welcome us almost immediately.

I was surprised to find another message of welcome waiting when we arrived at the cottage. You will please pardon my mentioning it, but the message was a note from Mrs. Darcy, to which I have now responded with my heartfelt appreciation and assurances of my intention to call on her soon. It is a very easy distance from Reddclift to Pemberley, I am told.

I continue to be astonished at my own good fortune, to have discovered so many blessings coming quick upon the heels of a tragic loss. I shall certainly lack for nothing here, especially friends, having brought my sister-in-law with me, having discovered new friends in my new home, and looking forward to a reunion with the one oldest and dearest to me.

All these things have eased my sadness at leaving behind my life in Hunsford and my equally kind friends there. I shall never forget your generosity to Mr. Collins and myself, your ladyship, and I remain your humble servant,

Charlotte Collins

I supposed I should have to take the bad with the good when it came to Mrs. Collins's correspondence. If I wanted news from Derbyshire, I should have to put up with the annoyance of hearing my adversaries praised a great deal more than they deserved.

I also received a communication from Mr. Essex a week before Christmas, asking after Anne's health and saying that, if we had no particular need of him, he intended to stay on with his family a while longer. Although the additional company might have made the atmosphere at Rosings a little more festive, Anne continued well and we had Fitzwilliam now. With their engagement to celebrate, we needed nobody else.

- 47 -

Anne

Regarding the Distant Event

"We have not seen Mr. Essex in weeks," I remarked to Mama the day after Christmas, which we had spent very quietly – John, Mrs. Jenkinson, Mama and myself. "When was he expected to return?"

"Oh, did I not tell you?"

"Tell me what?"

"He wrote a week ago to say he meant to stay in Lincolnshire a while longer if we had no particular need of him. It was something to do with his mother being ill, I believe. So I imagine we shall not see him until at least the second week of January, possibly not before you return from Derbyshire."

Had Mama asked me if I needed Mr. Essex, I would probably have said I did not. There had been only that single headache so far, and one does not like to admit a weakness or be the cause of inconveniencing another person. Still, one likes at least to be consulted.

"May I write to him, Mama? He may wish to give me some medical advice about how best to avoid trouble when I travel."

"That will not be necessary. I happened to mention your engagement and your travel plans to him in my reply. If there should be anything particular he wants to tell you, I am sure we will hear from him again soon."

Thus, I was spared the questions of when and how to tell Mr. Essex about my marriage plans. He knew already, thanks to Mama.

I could not help wondering what his opinion was, especially when many days passed without any further word from him. Would he think I had accepted John's offer because my courage finally failed me, that I was not willing to stand up to Mama one more time? Surely not. Surely he knew enough of Colonel Fitzwilliam to judge that an offer from him held more merit than all the previous offers combined. The last time my doctor was at Rosings, he had expressed confidence that my sense would always guide me right. I hoped he would see accepting John as the latest proof of that good sense. For some reason, it seemed terribly important that I should preserve Mr. Essex's high opinion of me if at all possible.

His letter finally came the first week of January. I would much have preferred to speak to him in person, but his written word was better than no word at all. Mr. Essex had addressed the brief missive to Mama – for propriety's sake, I supposed, which seemed the height of irony to me. Considering all the time we had spent alone together unchaperoned in months past, could there really be some greater danger in his writing to me directly? But I was promised to another man now; perhaps that made the difference. At least I was allowed to read the letter for myself after Mama had finished.

Dear Madam,

Thank you for granting me leave to stay longer away and for the information you were so good as to send me. I shall be much obliged if you would pass along my heartiest congratulations to Colonel Fitzwilliam and to your daughter upon their engagement. Until I can do so myself, please assure them that I wish them both joy.

As for her travel plans, I have every confidence in Miss de Bourgh's being capable of managing the minimal risks very well. If Mrs. Jenkinson is to travel with her, so much the better. It is mostly a case of maintaining the healthful habits that are by now well established. I would, however, recommend limiting the hours of travel. Adding an extra day to the journey to avoid excessive strain on body and mind will be well worth Miss de Bourgh's time.

I shall plan to see you both after I have returned from Lincolnshire and Miss de Bourgh from Derbyshire. Until then,

My Very Best Wishes,
Mr. Hiram Essex, esq.

It seemed a bit impersonal to me. Short, too. Not the easy way we had of talking to each other under ordinary circumstances. It was probably only the fact it was a letter. I had noticed that oftentimes a person's style of writing was considerably different from his or her style of speaking, usually much more formal. This was the first letter of Mr. Essex's composing I had ever read, and no doubt he had taken into consideration that my mother would see it also.

In any case, the letter answered my original question by making it quite clear that I would not see Mr. Essex again until the end of the month. It was not at all as I had hoped but perhaps for the best. My future husband deserved all my attention now.

John stayed on at Rosings so that we could travel north together in the middle of January for Georgiana's ball. We had both agreed to a six-month engagement to allow for making plans and adjusting our ideas to fit our changed relationship. Those early weeks should have given us plenty of time to do so, confined together mostly indoors by abysmal weather as we were. However, neither of us could seem to settle to anything serious. Perhaps it was precisely because the event loomed so far in the distance. We could not see it properly. It did not yet seem real. When the formal announcement was made the first of February, that would all change. Then there would be no more excuse for delay. There would be plenty to do in the short months that remained.

For the time being, though, we talked of other things and found what diversion we could in Mrs. Jenkinson's music and in a little company now and then. John even offered to help refresh my memory of the dance steps I would need for the ball. Still, it was a gloomy time of year, and I think we were all feeling somewhat oppressed. Although John was as good-natured as anybody I knew, I believed the unnatural confinement wore upon him as well.

It would be different once we were married, I considered. If we resided at Rosings, my husband would find his own occupations, indoors and out. He would discover where he could take a hand in helping to manage the estate. He would have all his own things about him as well – guns, horses, dogs – and no doubt he would see to a billiard table being installed at once. None of these diversions were currently available, however, and with my blessing, John finally took himself off to London for a few days. It was a relief to me as well in that I no longer felt the need to always try to entertain him.

If only I had had the chance to pursue music like other girls, I thought as I stared out the window at the mixture of snow and rain pelting down. I could then have done my part to relieve the tedium of such days for myself and others. Nothing was quite so cheerful as music after all.

A new thought occurred to me, and I asked abruptly, "Mrs. Jenkinson, do you suppose you could you teach me to play the piano-forte?"

- 48 -

Mrs. Jenkinson

On Being Needed or Not

We had been sitting quietly in the drawing room all afternoon. With Colonel Fitzwilliam gone to town that morning, it was only the three of us again. When conversation lagged, Lady Catherine turned her attention to a book. I moved closer to a window with my work basket, hoping for better light to do a bit of mending by. Anne, who seemed restless, got up to take a turn about the room, stopping a minute at a window near me before bursting out with a question.

"Mrs. Jenkinson, do you suppose you could you teach me to play the piano-forte?" she asked.

I was taken completely unawares. "Well," I said, "it is more difficult to learn as an adult, but I certainly will be glad to teach you, if your mother has no objection."

Lady Catherine, who had looked up from her book, merely shrugged.

"Then may we begin at once?" Anne asked eagerly. "Perhaps I shall even be ready to play something for Colonel Fitzwilliam when he returns. How surprised he shall be!"

"Very well," I said, putting my work away. Anne started for the piano-forte in the next room. Thinking it better to get through the elementary instruction where we would not try Lady Catherine's patience, I added, "Let us begin on the instrument in my apartment."

"A much better idea, Mrs. Jenkinson," said her ladyship. "Anne may play for me another time, when she is ready."

So up Anne and I went, both grinning with excitement. She was an enthusiastic pupil, and not devoid of natural ability, I discovered. With some review, she quickly remembered the little she had learnt before as a child – the meaning of the notes on the page and where to find them on the instrument. Execution of what was written there took much longer. Still, when we quit to dress for dinner two hours later, Anne could play a scale and a simple tune, one note at a time. I was well pleased, and she seemed satisfied also. The last week had been trying for her, and it was good to see her in better spirits.

"May we resume my instruction tomorrow, Mrs. Jenkinson?" she asked.

She had clearly got the bit between her teeth and would not let go. Her determination for conquering this new challenge reminded me of the way she had attacked improving her health under Mr. Essex's direction.

"Just as you like," I told her. "I am completely at your disposal, as always, and it will be pleasant to have lessons to pursue together again."

It gave me a ray of hope that perhaps I had not yet outlived my usefulness, that I might still have something left to teach my young lady. And yet despite Anne having said she could not possibly do without me, I felt that things would inevitably change once she was married. She would move on into her new life, and I might well be left behind like an old garment that no longer fit. When we reach adulthood, we all discard the outgrown trappings of our youth.

I had known this day might come. I had worked for it, even prayed for it – prayed for the recovery of her health which made all other things possible, and for a gentleman worthy of her. Now my prayers had been answered. In less than six months' time, Anne would be wed, becoming Mrs. John Fitzwilliam. He was a good man; I had no doubt of it. He was also a man of consequence, the importance of which could not be overrated. I hoped they would be happy together. I thought their chances equal to or better than most people can boast at the outset.

Upon the return of her betrothed from town, Anne proudly played the little song she had been preparing for him. When she finished, the colonel clapped enthusiastically, laughed with delight, and praised her efforts. "Clever girl," he said more than once.

I am not certain it was altogether the reaction Anne had been hoping for. No doubt Colonel Fitzwilliam meant to be kind, but I am afraid it may have sounded to Anne as if he had dismissed as child's play what she had worked on so seriously – a pat on the head instead of true admiration, a treat rewarded to a clever dog who had performed a trick correctly. Still, I hoped this would not deter her. Seeing what she had been able to accomplish in just a few days, I felt she could go far with continued application.

Furthering Anne's musical pursuits would have to wait until later, however, for there was the trip into Derbyshire to accomplish next. I was very pleased to have been given leave to attend Anne thither, to see something of a new part of England and to witness, albeit from a discreet distance, the spectacle of the Pemberley ball – the grandeur, the pageantry, the display. Through Anne, I would experience it all.

I knew the ball was given in honor of another, but it seemed to me it was an event equally momentous for Miss Anne. In many ways, this ball represented her coming out into society. She had missed so much in the years she had been closeted at home by ill health. And even now, she would never have the thrill of a proper London season because she was already engaged. This ball – while she was well and not yet known to be spoken for – would have to serve for all the dances and parties she had ever missed from age sixteen to twenty-one.

Instead of taking a maid, Anne insisted I go with her to Pemberley. "I must have Mrs. Jenkinson with me," she had declared to her mother. "And you know that is Mr. Essex's advice as well, Mama. I want no maid. Mrs. Jenkinson will look after all my needs very ably. She will be nurse, maid, and chaperone all in one."

I was very gratified by this testimonial, but in truth, there was little enough for me to do in the beginning. Although the journey north was inconvenient and tiresome, as travel always is, it presented no significant threat to safety or health. Anne weathered it all without nursing from me. I did of course serve as her lady's maid at each stop along the way, helping her dress, styling her hair, and so forth. As for my role as chaperone, I doubt I was much needed there. It was bound to change over time, but Anne and Colonel Fitzwilliam still behaved towards each other as they ever had, more like disinterested cousins than young lovers. To all appearances, they might have ridden alone together all the way to Pemberley and back without any compromising mischief taking place between them.

- 49 -

Anne

At the Ball

Moonlight is known to play tricks on the eyes and the mind. Nevertheless, as we approached Pemberley, I earnestly scrutinized the ghostly scenery passing by outside my window, watching for some point of familiarity. It was more by way of a calming exercise than for any other reason, for my nerves were threatening to unravel.

I was not particularly concerned for my appearance. We had dressed for the ball at the inn where we had last changed horses. There, I had appraised my reflection in the glass when Mrs. Jenkinson finished with me, and I had been satisfied. I was not so vain as to think myself truly beautiful, but I knew it would take very little to impress my Darcy cousins and Elizabeth, none of whom had seen me in above a year. In that time, my appearance had so materially altered (for the better) that I thought it possible they would not at first recognize me.

When they *did* know me, though, would they be glad to see me? The closer we drew to our destination, the more I worried over what kind of reception I should receive. I looked to John for reassurance once again, asking him, "Are you quite certain we have done the right thing by telling nobody I am coming with you to the ball? I begin to worry I will not be welcomed after all."

"Do you give your cousins so little credit?" he asked. "I will vouch for it; they will be overjoyed to see you, the more so for its being a surprise, as all birthday presents should be."

"I hope you are right, John."

"I *know* I am. Think nothing more about it."

"Very well. And we are agreed that we shall say nothing of our engagement until the moment is right, not until at least tomorrow. This is Georgiana's night, and we must not rob her of any of her feathers."

"Agreed. No one at the ball – no one except perhaps Darcy and Elizabeth – will ever guess our secret. I shall pass myself off as a bachelor this one last time, and I encourage you to flirt to your heart's content with every gentleman you meet. Charm them all. I will only trouble you for a dance or two myself."

John was correct about one thing. My arrival on his arm was a tremendous surprise.

William, Elizabeth, and Georgiana were waiting in the great hall to receive their guests. At first glimpse of them, my heart leapt in nervous excitement. Then the people they had been speaking to moved away, and three sets of eyes fell upon us. There was a long pause, during which I watched a range of sentiments – from interest and confusion to sudden recognition – play across their faces.

Elizabeth recovered her composure first. Stepping forward to offer me her hand, she said, "Why, Anne, how wonderfully well you look, and how splendid, Colonel, that you persuaded her to accompany you. We are so pleased to have you both with us tonight."

When the others followed with similarly gracious sentiments, the moment of awful suspense was over.

"Thank you for receiving me," I responded. "Fitzwilliam said you would not mind."

"Mind?" repeated Elizabeth. "We are delighted!"

John joined in cheerily, "As you see, Anne is now strong enough to undertake such a journey, which is another cause for celebration, is it not?"

"Indeed it is," said Cousin William, locking eyes with John for a long moment as they shook hands. Then, turning to me, he continued, "Anne, you look quite recovered. I understand the credit for your newfound health belongs in part to a clever young physician."

At this reminder of my dear doctor and all he had done for me, my eyes involuntarily dropped. "I daresay I owe my recovery almost *entirely* to him," I said. "Mr. Essex is an uncommonly kind and learned man. I shall be forever in his debt."

"Then *I* am grateful to this Mr. Essex as well," said Georgiana, "since it is apparently due to his care that we have the pleasure of your company now."

Truly touched, I smiled and thanked her sincerely. Then it was time to move on to the ballroom as others came in the door behind us.

"What did I tell you?" said John. "They were all overjoyed to see you."

I was mightily relieved by the warm reception, and I would have liked nothing better than to spend much more time in conversation with those three whom we had just left. I knew, however, that in such a large gathering, their attentions would be spread very thin.

At the entrance to the palatial ballroom, we stopped a moment to take in the sight. I had seen the room before in my many visits to Pemberley, but it had always been deserted in recent years, since Lady Anne had died – an elegant setting waiting for something beautiful to happen. Now it lived up to its purpose once again – lit by scores of candles sparkling through crystal sconces and chandeliers, and filled with fashionably dressed ladies and gentlemen milling about in anticipation of the official commencement of the ball. It was quite a sight to behold.

"Ah, there is my sister," John said, giving a little wave.

"Lady Deborah?" I asked in excitement. "Yes, I see her! She is coming over. Did you know she would be here, John?"

"I thought she might, but I did not wish to give you false hope by mentioning it in advance."

Smiling radiantly, Lady Deborah kissed her brother's cheek. "Hey ho, John," she said before turning to me with a light embrace. "And Anne, I cannot tell you how pleased I am to see you again. My brother has told us how well you do, but I hardly expected this! Let me look at you." She stepped back a pace. "Why, John, our cousin has turned into quite a beauty."

"She has indeed."

I could feel my face growing warm. "You are too kind, Lady Deborah," I protested. "I do not deserve such extravagant compliments."

"Nonsense. *I* say you do! And what is this 'Lady Deborah' business? I wish you would call me Dodo like you did as a child. Then I would know you are still my friend."

"Of course I am!"

"Where is Fortin?" asked John.

"Oh, heavens!" she said with a lilting laugh. "My handsome husband is somewhere about, but you must not charge me with keeping him in tow. He may do exactly as he pleases tonight as long as he grants me the same privilege."

Just then, the orchestra played the chords signaling the beginning of the ball. People made way for the first set to form for the minuet. An older gentleman I did not know – undoubtedly someone of high rank – led Georgiana to the top. Georgiana looked very grown up for eighteen with her tall figure swathed in an elegant, blue gown. Her countenance glowed with excitement… or possibly embarrassment. Which, I could not be sure. My guess was that Georgiana did not much relish being made the center of everybody's attention. Like it or not, however, that must be the case for her this one night at least.

Next in the set were William and Elizabeth with their respective partners, followed by many other couples.

"Let us not be shy," said John. Offering me his arm, he led the way to where we could begin a second set, and soon the ball was underway.

The minuet was traditional but not my favorite. Still, since I knew the dance well enough to not worry about forgetting the steps, it was a comfortable way to begin. When it finished, John bowed to me and took my hand. "Thank you, my dear," he said. "But now I suppose we had best go our separate ways, lest our true situation become too obvious. Ah, here comes a new partner for you."

I turned to see William and Elizabeth approaching.

"Will you dance with me, Anne?" he asked.

"Thank you, yes," I said. We moved to take our places, and John stood up next to us with Elizabeth. He gave me a surreptitious wink as we started off.

With my being so badly out of practice, William's taciturn habit actually came as a kind convenience, allowing me to give the dance my full attention at first. When I became more confident, however, I hazarded a little conversation, fitting it around the movements of the dance as best I could. "How well Georgiana looks tonight," I said, glancing in her direction. "She is very much the fine lady now."

William followed my gaze. "Yes, she is a child no longer. It should not surprise me, but somehow it does."

Having come to the bottom of the set by this time, we had more leisure for talk while we stood idle a minute. "I hope she will not find the attention too overwhelming," I continued. "I believe I might in her place."

"Georgiana is naturally shy, as you know," William said seriously. "Elizabeth had a few words with her to settle her nerves before coming down, however. And now that things are successfully underway, I hope she may forget her self-consciousness." As we started to move again, he asked, "How is your mother?"

"She is very well, I think."

"Quite frankly, Anne, I am amazed Lady Catherine allowed you to come to Pemberley. I thought she had forbidden all contact between us."

I hardly knew what to say to this, since I could not yet reveal that which had made the difference – my engagement to Colonel Fitzwilliam. Fortunately, the demands of the dance gave me an excuse to delay before replying. "It was not easy to convince Mama, but I did so want to attend Georgiana's ball. Time has passed, and perhaps she is not so angry anymore as she once was."

"While I am happy if her restrictions on you have eased, Anne," William said at his next opportunity, "you must know that your mother was not the only one made angry. It will be a long time yet before all insults can be forgiven and forgotten… at least on my side."

"I understand. Mama was not kind to you."

"Say nothing of that. It is for the insults to Elizabeth that I must have some redress." Parted once more, he changed his tone when we came together again. "Forgive me, Anne. Tonight is meant to be a night for celebration, not recriminations."

We ended our dance near Georgiana, and her partner required an introduction. That is how Sir Frederick Clark came to ask me for the next dance, and so on from there. In fact, I was never without a partner except occasionally by choice. Although I was stronger than I ever had been, I was unaccustomed to dancing all the night long.

Since I chose to sit out the last dance before the supper break, I had to fend for myself as to dinner companions. But then I spied Charlotte Collins motioning for me to come take an empty place at her table. Before my arrival, I had not thought to see Mrs. Collins at the ball. As Elizabeth's dear friend, however, and a near neighbor once again, of course she would have been invited. She wore half mourning and did not dance, but I was very pleased to see her looking so well otherwise. We had only exchanged the merest greetings earlier, so I was glad to have more time with her now.

"Do sit here beside me, Miss de Bourgh," she said, "and relate to me all the news of Hunsford. I have had only one letter from your mother, and it was not very informative."

"There is little enough to report," I said, considering it a necessary falsehood. Mrs. Collins would hear of my engagement in due course. In the meantime, a change of subject was in order. "How very happy I was, Mrs. Collins, to hear you are so well pleased with your new arrangements here in Derbyshire."

"Yes, I still cannot believe my luck in finding such an agreeable situation. I should not say that I found it, though, as if I could take any credit, for the offer fell into my lap like manna from heaven. But, my dear, you must tell me how you ever induced Lady Catherine to allow you to come tonight. I gather Colonel Fitzwilliam escorted you; I suppose that he may have something to do with it."

I looked at her sharply, wondering if she could possibly have guessed the truth, but her eyes were wide with innocence. So again, I was forced to be evasive in my answer. "I asked Mama's permission when she was in a particularly good humor, I suppose. Now, who is here of your acquaintance that I should know?"

"Have you met Elizabeth's sister Jane?" Charlotte asked. "She is at the next table, there – the one in pale pink with the fair hair and skin."

"I have not. My, she is just as beautiful as I had heard."

"Yes, and perhaps even more so now that she is with child. And there are two more sisters to Elizabeth," Charlotte said, nodding in the other direction. "You will have heard of Lydia, who is now Mrs. Wickham," she added with a significant look. "The one with the rather showy feathered headpiece, laughing so merrily."

Remembering all I had heard about that lady and her infamous husband, I answered, "Ah, yes, I see."

"And beside her is Miss Kitty Bennet, the second youngest next to Lydia. I expect you will have some chance to become acquainted with her, since I understand Kitty is staying here at Pemberley for a time."

Beyond, I noticed John. He had kept his word to disguise our real situation by playing the bachelor. After our first dance together, he had not returned to me for another. Now, during the intermission, he kept away from me still. I saw him across the room entertaining a group of ladies, no doubt with something from his vast inventory of droll stories, most of which I had already heard. I would not begrudge him his enraptured audience, however. We were not married yet, and even when we were, I hardly expected his gregarious nature to change. I did not intend to be the sort of wife who smothered the life out of her husband.

While I was speaking to Mrs. Collins, a noisy disturbance erupted out of sight, from the direction of the entrance hall. I turned in time to see Cousin William hastening in that direction, John and a couple of male servants following. William returned a few minutes later to make explanations to the wondering crowd.

"My dear friends," he said once people had quieted. "I do apologize that the evening's entertainments have been so rudely interrupted. It was only a harmless local rascal under the influence of too much ale. The poor soul wished to come in and make merry with you." Following William's lead, people laughed at this. "He has now been sent on his way. I beg you would return to your supper and to your companions, and think no more about it."

Somehow William's light remarks did not ring true to me, and I was sure there was more to the business than he led us to believe.

When it was nearly time to return to the ballroom, John caught my eye and came briefly to my side. "I promised I would dance the next with Georgiana," he said. "Will you reserve the one after that for me?"

I smiled. "If you like," I said, feeling very pleased with him.

"I *do* like. See you soon." With a quick squeeze of my hand, he was off again. Just when I had begun to feel the tiniest bit neglected, John had shown me I had no reason for self-pity.

The orchestra swelled, and a nice young man called Mr. Heywood asked me to dance. He did not require much of my attention, however. His eyes kept straying, following Georgiana, I suspected, since that is who he spoke of when he did take the trouble of conversing at all. *Was not Miss Darcy the most accomplished of young ladies... the most elegant dancer... the most angelic in appearance?*

"Georgiana has made at least one conquest tonight," I told John when he returned to me for our dance. "My last partner could not take his eyes – nor his mind, I daresay – off her while you two were dancing. What did you find to talk of with her?"

"Nothing much – my compliments to her, to her dancing, to our hostess, to the orchestra – all well deserved but not terribly original thoughts. Oh, and we talked of you too," he added as the Scottish reel got underway.

"Of me? What on earth could be of mutual interest there?"

"Everything, my dear, I assure you," he said with a smile. Then he spun away from me and back again. "Georgiana wonders where your future will lead, now your health no longer holds you back... and what ambitious plans your mama may have for you. There, you see, she was treading a little too near forbidden territory, and I had to be rather circumspect answering. I am sure she thought no more about it, however. On a night like this, there are much more important things to occupy her mind and time."

The lively nature of the dance had made even this much conversation difficult to accomplish – one word or a short phrase at a time – so we gave up the effort entirely for a while. But later, I said what I had been thinking about in the interim. "You have had the advantage over me, John."

"How do you mean, my dear?"

"Georgiana is my friend too, and yet we have been limited to only a few letters exchanged between us in over a year. And now tonight, while you could reserve time with her, I have mostly been obliged to talk with strangers whom I shall never see again. Is that fair?"

"I suppose not. Hmm. I have never looked at it quite that way before. I think perhaps you are on to something, Anne. What is needed is a fundamental revolution in the way balls are conducted – less dancing and more talking – and one may reserve time with whomever one likes, man or woman. What do you think? Will the idea catch on?"

"I think you tease me, sir."

He laughed. "Guilty as charged, madam. Then, since we cannot solve the problem tonight, I advise you to find time in the next day or two to renew your friendship with your dear cousin."

"That I most certainly shall do." The dance ended, and I asked my next question with more privacy as we left the floor together. "Now what was that earlier business about? That disturbance during the supper?"

John looked conscious and leant closer. "Very well, but you must never say a word about it. It was just as Darcy explained except he did not name the so-called 'harmless rascal.' In truth, it was Mr. Wickham, steeped in drink and trying to force his way in where he was not wanted. He has been subdued and will bother no one else, at least not tonight. Poor Darcy. It seems he will never be rid of that scoundrel."

It was probably true, I considered. Once a man is made a brother by marriage, he is a brother to the end. One might do one's best to keep at a distance, but family ties – for better or for worse – were tenaciously binding. I could only hope that Mr. Wickham would be changed by time and the settling tendency of marriage into a more responsible and less troublesome creature.

Other than the minor flaw of Mr. Wickham's creation, however, it was a delightful evening, underscoring the sort of thing I had missed by being so long confined to home by illness. Even as a married woman, however, I could continue to enjoy such entertainments if my health remained good, so there was much to look forward to. But for now, in consideration of my health, I decided to cut this particular evening short. Although, in preparation for this late-night affair, I had gradually adjusted the time I retired to bed, I did not wish to press my luck too far. I preferred to sacrifice seeing the fireworks display rather than risk a relapse.

So I slipped out before the end and was directed by one of the servants to a guest room assigned to me for the night. There I found my trunk and Mrs. Jenkinson to assist me.

- 50 -

Mrs. Jenkinson

Discussing the Ball

Although I would not say so to my young mistress, I was as nervous as she had been for the idea of arriving to Pemberley without proper notice. I need not have worried, however. The household staff was apparently trained to be gracious and efficient when dealing with the unexpected. I gathered that as soon as Miss de Bourgh walked in the front door, Mrs. Darcy sent word to make accommodation for us. Our trunks were taken up to a very nice bedchamber with a small adjoining anteroom for me, and I was told when and where I could get my supper.

Later, before returning to the room, I found a place out of sight where I could linger a while to enjoy the music and a limited view of the ballroom. It was a bittersweet sight, reminding me of another day, long gone by. When the orchestra played, I found my mind anticipating the movements of the familiar dances and my body longing to respond. I had known such grand evenings once, when I was an invited guest and not merely a paid companion. I had looked my best, felt myself admired by more than one gentleman, and danced with spirit, much like I observed Miss de Bourgh doing now. It was *her* turn to shine. My place was in the shadows, and I could do no more than remember – remember and sway with the strains of the music.

Anne had promised not to stay too late at the ball, and she was true to her word. "Ah, good. There you are, Miss," I said when she came in. "If you are ready to retire, I shall ring for your tea."

"Yes, thank you, Mrs. Jenkinson. It was a lovely night, but I am tired."

I went to the bell cord. "You enjoyed yourself, then?"

"Oh, yes. Very much so."

She told me all about her partners and the fine supper while I was helping her to undress. And then her tea arrived.

"Plain tea tonight, I suppose," she said, looking the tray over.

"No, Miss. When I was downstairs earlier, I told them what you required, and they said it would be no trouble at all. So you have your prescribed tea as usual." I poured it out and passed her the cup.

"How clever you are to have arranged it, Mrs. Jenkinson. It would not have seemed right to end the day without this one nod to Mr. Essex." She drew the steam deeply in through her nostrils. "I can never smell this distinctive aroma without thinking of him."

"Yes, Miss," I said without further comment, not wanting to encourage this line. I was taking down her hair at the dressing table when she continued it on her own.

"I wish he could have been here tonight."

"Who do you mean, Miss?"

"Mr. Essex, of course."

I studied her reflection in the glass. "I hope you did not feel yourself in need of medical attention at any point."

"Not at all. I was only thinking that he might have enjoyed the dancing. You know what a proponent of physical exercise he is. And I would have enjoyed dancing with him too, I daresay, instead of so many gentlemen I did not know and could ill pretend an interest in. Besides, it has been entirely too long since we have seen Mr. Essex. It is not surprising that I should regret his continued absence, is it?"

"But you have Colonel Fitzwilliam now, Miss," I said evenly, beginning to brush out her dark-blonde hair. "You should not need Mr. Essex or anybody else for company."

"If the colonel and I were openly engaged, it would have been quite different tonight. I could have danced with him a good deal more than I did, eaten my supper with him, and been introduced by him to all his friends. I believe he must know nearly every one of the guests. As it was, I only wished I had a few more of my own acquaintances, like Mr. Essex, about me."

"He would hardly be the sort of person invited to a society ball," I reminded her. "Even if the Darcys knew him, I shouldn't think his connections were anywhere near lofty enough."

Anne turned about to look directly at me. "Mrs. Jenkinson! What a snob you are," she teased. "I never would have suspected it of you."

"Not at all, Miss. I like Mr. Essex very well indeed, but it is wisest for all concerned that we should remember his place. That is all. Now, allow me to finish."

Anne turned back to face the glass again. "You are quite mistaken in any case, Mrs. Jenkinson. Although I did see persons of the highest social order tonight, there were others not particularly exalted – Mrs. Collins and also the rector of the parish to name two. In the proper evening clothes, Mr. Essex would not have seemed one bit out of place."

Mr. Essex in evening clothes: that was a picture I hoped Anne would not dwell on too long. "Ah, Mrs. Collins," I said, seizing on the opportunity to change the subject. "How does she do?"

This was a fresh cause for the uneasiness I had felt before about the blurring of distinct lines where Mr. Essex was concerned. Anne seemed to have grown entirely too fond of the man, too dependent on him, and I feared a patch of difficult ground ahead when the break must inevitably occur. But other than a few mild words of caution, such as I had already given her, there was very little I could do.

After Miss de Bourgh was settled for the night and I retired as well, I chided myself for my unreasonable qualms. Anne would hardly have time to consider Mr. Essex, much less miss his presence, once this engagement was announced. As she herself had said, that would make all the difference. Colonel Fitzwilliam would very naturally succeed to the central place in Anne's life. She would be so fully occupied with wedding preparations and then wifely duties that she would soon find out she could do very well without her physician's constant attendance, if she remembered to think of him at all.

- 51 -

Anne

Finding the Right Moment

I came down to a very late breakfast the next day in time to hear Elizabeth asking Georgiana's opinion of the ball.

"I never danced so much in my life!" my cousin responded. "I am thoroughly exhausted, and it may take me a week to recover, but I could not have asked for a better birthday. It was altogether wonderful, was it not?"

"It was indeed," I agreed. Coming to briefly embrace her, I continued. "I am so pleased for you, Georgiana, and so pleased to have been here to witness it as well. You and your ball were a resounding success."

I had a few more minutes' conversation with Georgiana while we helped ourselves to the tempting things on the sideboard. We were far from alone, however. The Heywood family had been housed overnight at Pemberley as well as Elizabeth's sisters, Mr. Bingley, and his sister Miss Bingley. All these slowly drifted down from their rooms in various states of mind and body – some a little better and some much worse for the wine consumed the night before.

The entire Bingley party, which included Mrs. Wickham, departed shortly after breakfast, but their numbers were soon replaced by others who drove back out for the day from their lodgings in Lambton.

John came over to me at one point to voice what I was thinking as well. "Clearly, we shall have no opportunity for a private word with our cousins today," he said. "Our announcement must wait a little longer."

"True. There can be no question of attempting it in this company, especially when we have some reason to expect the news will not be universally rejoiced."

"Never fear, Anne. Darcy and Elizabeth will come round in time. But, yes, we had much better make our explanations in private. Tomorrow, perhaps."

"I do hope so," I said. "I cannot be comfortable with this concealment. Though necessary, it somehow seems underhanded to withhold the truth from our friends so long."

Conditions were more favorable by the next day. All the others had gone before noon, leaving only William, Elizabeth, Georgiana, and Kitty Bennet besides ourselves. With Kitty staying on at Pemberley indefinitely, this was as small as the family party would be in the foreseeable future.

The moment was clearly at hand. John looked at me for my concurrence, and then he began. Clearing his throat first, he said, "Excuse me, but might I have your attention please?"

I heard the slight tremor in his voice, which informed me I was not the only one suffering from nerves.

"Perhaps we should all sit down," continued John. "I have some news to share."

Everybody sat as John had bidden them. I took the seat next to my betrothed at his invitation, feeling increasingly embarrassed. It seemed to me that by now it must be so completely obvious what John meant to say that the words themselves were hardly necessary. I glanced from face to face, deciding I was correct where William and Elizabeth were concerned. But Georgiana looked quite unsuspicious, and I believed the same was true of Miss Bennet.

"Dear friends," the colonel began when they were settled. "I am glad you are all here, for I have something very important to tell you. I know that some of you may have already guessed what it is," he said with a nod to William and Elizabeth. "For the rest, it will probably come as quite a surprise. Regardless, I hope you will share my joy at my good fortune." Taking my hand, he revealed, "Anne and I are engaged to be married."

For a long moment, no one seemed to move or breathe. Only Kitty Bennet looked prepared to celebrate our happy tidings, but even she held back, probably sensing the hesitation of the others who knew the situation far better. I felt my face going scarlet. I had not expected adulation, but this stunned silence was mortifying.

Georgiana suddenly jumped to her feet. Looking at the floor and not at us, she mumbled, "Let me be the first to wish you joy, Cousins. Now, please excuse me." She hastily left the room.

Miss Bennet soon followed, closing the door behind her and leaving us with only William and Elizabeth. They recovered quickly enough, having no doubt anticipated what the other two had not. Obligatory words of congratulation followed, although I could see that neither of them was sincerely happy at the news.

My mortification only increased, and I could not bring myself to speak.

John stepped in where I could not. Cutting to the heart of matter without delay, he said, "I apprised Anne of your sentiments in the matter, and we discussed your counsel at length. Darcy, Elizabeth, I know this course is not what you recommended, but I hope you will try to be pleased for us nonetheless."

This roused William to action. Looking earnestly at me, he said, "I want it clearly understood that my disapprobation is in no way meant as a slight to you, Anne. Quite the reverse. It is precisely because of my high regard for you *both* that I opposed the idea. To me, such an alliance seemed to hold so little chance of success."

"It must be your decision," added Elizabeth. "We only wish you to act according to what will constitute your own happiness, without reference to the ambitions of others."

At this, my discomfort diminished somewhat, and I knew I must speak. It was important to me that these dear friends understood. "Then let me set your minds at ease," I said with as much self-assurance as possible. "Fitzwilliam and I have made our decision without undue pressure or persuasion from anyone else. We are satisfied that this will be for the best."

"What Anne says is correct," John agreed. "We have made our own choice for our own reasons. If it pleases our families as well, is that not a good rather than an evil?"

"Naturally; that goes without saying," replied William. "Peace in the family is to be maintained whenever possible. If this marriage is truly what you both want, we will respect your decision and wish you joy."

"Yes, of course. I will pray for your every happiness," promised Elizabeth.

~~*~~

Georgiana did not return to us, and we shortly received word by her maid that she was indisposed with a sudden headache. I was sorry to lose her company, but her plight and its effects were things all too familiar. She would have nothing but sympathy from me. Elizabeth ventured upstairs more than once to check on her condition, returning to say that Georgiana was sleeping and that she had not thought it right to disturb her.

It left only five of us at dinner and to entertain each other throughout the evening afterward. Thankfully, with Miss Kitty Bennet present, we could not and did not return to the debate over the wisdom (or lack thereof) in the engagement between John and myself. It had taken many, many hours of consideration for me to come to the conclusion I had. I would not have thanked anybody who persisted in casting doubt on that decision.

It seemed to me an altogether safer subject would be to ask Mrs. Darcy more about her family. Much had changed for them since I had last seen Elizabeth in Kent, after all.

"I was very gratified to meet with Mrs. Collins again at the ball, Mrs. Darcy," I said during dinner, "and to see three of your sisters as well. I understand Mrs. Bingley and her husband now reside in the north also, like yourselves."

"Yes, it is a joy for me – for both of us – that Jane and Mr. Bingley are recently settled so near. They are within thirty miles of us, in Staffordshire, at a place called Heatheridge. We expect to travel back and forth quite often, especially when the weather improves."

"It is a very easy distance," William added.

"My other sister, Lydia – Mrs. Wickham, I should say – is staying at Heatheridge temporarily, she and her husband. That is how it happened that she was able to come to the ball. And with Kitty here, you have met us all, Miss de Bourgh – all except Mary, that is. Mary does not care for a ball, and Mama says she simply cannot spare her from home in any case. Mary has made herself quite indispensable, it seems."

"And you, Miss Bennet," I said, turning to Kitty, "how long will you be staying at Pemberley?"

"That, I cannot tell you, Miss de Bourgh," she said lightly. "I have *not* made myself indispensable at home, and my mother can do without me very well. Consequently, I am free to go visiting as often as I like. I was at Heatheridge from Christmas until now, and I may be here at Pemberley some weeks, if Mr. Darcy does not mind." William gave only a wry smile at this, and then Kitty went on, addressing her sister. "Lizzy, perhaps Papa may pay you another surprise visit and take me home to Longbourn on his return."

"Perhaps, or failing that, it may be Mama instead. She has vowed to come in the spring to be with Jane when the baby arrives." Elizabeth turned to me. "This will be Mama's first grandchild, you see, and she is very eager."

"Naturally."

"Are you musical, Miss Bennet?" John asked Kitty presently.

"No, not at all, Colonel."

"That is regrettable," he replied. "With Georgiana indisposed, who will play for us tonight? Elizabeth, can we prevail upon you? It would be a bleak evening indeed without any music at all."

"Certainly, if you like. You know my limitations, but I am happy to do what I can."

"Thank you. I would ask Anne, but I think she would tell you she is not yet ready for an audience." He turned merry eyes to me. "Is not that so, my dear?"

I was too embarrassed to respond. Having heard Miss Darcy play so brilliantly for the company the night before, I now had a much better idea of what John had been used to hearing. It was painful proof of the feebleness of my own attempt.

"Why, Anne," said William in surprise. "Have you begun to learn?"

"Only just," I said, not meeting his gaze. "Mrs. Jenkinson gave me a little instruction while John was away in London. It is nothing to boast of, as his words correctly implied."

"Well, I think that is simply marvelous!" said Elizabeth. "You are to be highly commended, Miss de Bourgh. Sometime when you are ready, I should love to hear you. You need not be ashamed to play for me, since you know I am certainly no proficient either."

Elizabeth's playing that evening, although not nearly as accomplished as Georgiana's had been, still seemed so far above me as to be completely out of reach. It was like comparing a sapling to a tall tree. The difference necessarily encompassed many long years. One would hardly expect to grow an acorn into an oak in a matter of weeks or months. Similarly, it seemed pure folly that I had thought I could learn enough, starting so late, to be at all worthwhile.

I tried to put that thought aside, however, and simply enjoy my last night at Pemberley. We were leaving the next day, bound for Eastchapel, the seat of the Earls of Matlock and consequently John's family home, which I had visited several times as a girl. There, we would impart the good news of our engagement to those whom we thoroughly expected would receive the announcement with more enthusiasm than it had met with at Pemberley.

That next morning, we looked for Georgiana at breakfast, but we were told she was still not well enough to come downstairs.

"I am sorry not to see Georgiana again before we go," John told our hosts as we were about to depart.

"As am I," I added before he continued.

"She did look frightfully pale yesterday, poor thing, but I trust she will soon recover. If you would be so kind as to give her my warmest regards, Elizabeth, I would be much obliged. You know how fond I am of her."

"I surely shall, Colonel."

I thanked William and Elizabeth profusely for their hospitality and bid them farewell.

- 52 -

Mrs. Jenkinson

On Completing the Tour

Although my observations of any place beyond Rosings Park were somewhat limited, I had been used to believing there was no estate better for seeing everything done just as it should be. I knew this was Lady Catherine's opinion and that she credited her own good leadership and strict discipline for it.

"One must take a very firm hand, Mrs. Jenkinson," she had told me on more than one occasion. "I tolerate no folly, and I deal with insubordination quite ruthlessly. I have no alternative, otherwise unruliness would spread like an infectious disease until it threatened to bring down the whole house."

I had considered that Lady Catherine might be correct, especially where a great estate like Rosings was concerned and especially where there was no master to exert his strong influence. I could not disprove her theories by my own experience at least. When I was married and had managed my own household, it was on such a smaller scale as to make any comparison useless.

Now my eyes had been opened. A great estate could thrive and prosper just as well with a different style of leadership... and possibly with happier servants and staff for being better treated. At Pemberley, I had observed loyalty based on genuine respect for the master and mistress rather than fear of what they might do. Power was used with a benevolent touch rather than wielded by an iron fist, from what I had lately observed. I was sorry to leave it behind.

We were then on to Eastchapel, where the quality of everything was equally exceptional but I suspected a more repressive air generally reigned – as similar to Rosings as a presiding brother and sister cut from the same cloth could be.

I gather the announcement of the engagement went a long way toward improving the atmosphere, however.

Miss Anne told me, "It was just as I had imagined it would be, Mrs. Jenkinson. The earl and his lady looked very satisfied indeed with the arrangement. And why not? Their younger son marrying an heiress of the same noble line as himself, and all that lovely money staying in the family? They could not have been more pleased. I am quite certain my Aunt and Uncle Fitzwilliam never liked me half so well before."

I hoped they would soon come to appreciate their niece and future daughter-in-law's other estimable qualities as well, however.

Then, after a four-day stay at Eastchapel, it was back to the road for the long return trip to Rosings. But perhaps the journey only seemed especially long for how conversation began to lag as we progressed, mile after tedious mile.

As entertaining as Colonel Fitzwilliam can be, Miss Anne seemed to have already heard most of his stories… at least those fit to tell in the presence of a lady. To break a long silence, he might start by saying to Anne, "Did I ever tell you about the time I…?" And regardless how he continued – whether it was his sojourning in Newcastle, becoming lost in the woods near Pemberley, or going sea bathing at Sidmouth – Anne would nod and finish his thought for him. Then it was her turn to try, but she had no better luck. No, he had not read the book she mentioned, and he never really had any particular desire to visit the Alhambra (or the other places she longed to see).

Silence fell again, and there was nothing to do but look out the windows at the wet and dreary scenes of gray passing by. I almost found myself wishing for Lady Catherine's presence, for although her conversation was not always to my taste, she certainly knew how to fill a silence.

I made a vow to myself, then and there, to avoid all further travel in the winter. It simply was not worthwhile. The inherent discomforts were too much to overcome.

- 53 -

Anne

On Adjusting to New Circumstances

That first week at home again – the first week of February – was a veritable whirlwind of activity. There were calls to be made, announcements given, and invitations for an engagement party at Rosings extended, all of which I enjoyed.

The engagement party itself was the largest, most festive and extravagant affair held at Rosings in years – in truth, since before my father died. Everybody who was anybody came, prepared to celebrate our good news with music, sumptuous food, and quality wine, all at my mother's expense. I felt happy, laughing and dancing the night away with John by my side. It was on such occasions that his true talents shone. There was no one more convivial, no one fonder of telling a joke or indulging in general merriment. And I was carried along on his accommodating coattails.

Through it all, I surprised myself by discovering that I was not as shy as I had always believed. Perhaps I had only disliked being looked at and talked about for the wrong reasons. After all, there was nothing admirable in being sickly, pale, and unaccomplished. And there was little satisfaction in being acknowledged as an object of pity either.

Now, all that had changed. Now I received compliments on my fine appearance and attention for making an excellent match. John and I were toasted wherever we went. We were told what a handsome couple we made. Everybody predicted that our marriage was destined to be a glorious success. These things, as it turned out, I did not mind hearing in the least.

The continual round of merrymaking could not last forever, though.

"Go," I told John cheerfully when he proposed his departure. We had spent nearly every day of the last two months together, and I knew we were both ready for at least a brief intermission. "Mama and I have work to do in any case, work best done without a man's interference. What do you know about planning a wedding?"

"Not a thing!" John proclaimed. "I am sure you are correct; I should only be in the way, making a nuisance of myself."

"Exactly."

"Very well, my dear, I shall go now while I am not wanted here. Then, once I have settled my affairs, I will put myself completely at your service again. Perhaps you will find some small, useful task for me by the time I return."

So John bid us farewell, and without him it became impossible to maintain the pleasant charade any longer. One cannot live forever on a cloud, after all; sooner or later, one must return one's feet to solid ground. The gaiety surrounding the announcement of our engagement was one thing; the looming reality of marriage was quite another.

I could not have admitted it to John or anybody else, but I suddenly felt like I had been playing at being someone I was not, as if I had been carried along by one of my vivid imaginings all this time, only pretending at being John's betrothed. But perhaps all prospective brides experience similar sensations. I had never been on the verge of becoming somebody's wife before. Small wonder, then, that it should seem like make believe in the beginning.

But I knew this was real, not some sort of fanciful game. There would be no changing the rules whenever it suited me or stopping altogether if I grew weary of playing. While a boulder rests at the top of a mountain, various outcomes are possible, including maintaining the status quo. Once it is set in motion, however, the outcome is inevitable. Nothing can stop the ponderous rock from rolling down to the valley below. I had started the boulder rolling myself, and now marriage would follow betrothal just as surely. The sooner I accustomed my thinking to that true state of affairs, the better.

It was simply a matter of overcoming foreignness with familiarity. Perhaps it would be helpful to picture the scenes in my mind, I thought one morning, alone in my room. If I envisioned my wedding over and over again (as I had done in my adolescence, when I thought I would marry William Darcy), the prospect of soon being made John's wife would no longer feel so strange. It was time I put my overactive imagination to some practical use.

It is a beautiful, sunny morning, of course, for Mama would never put up with anything less for such an important occasion. I see myself clearly as I enter Hunsford church. I am wearing the gown that has already been ordered made for me. It is the palest shade of bluish-gray imaginable, like the soft hue of a dove's breast, which Mama says brings out the color of my eyes.

Holding myself erect and feeling confident, I raise my face to look for my groom in front of the altar. He has his back to me at first, but then he turns and I see John's familiar face. He is smiling at me as I slowly make my way up the aisle to meet him. And there we stand, side by side. As Mr. Chesterfield reads the service from the Book of Common Prayer, we look at him for a few minutes, we glance at each other with shy consciousness, and then back again to the rector.

I have heard the words many times before, read for other couples on other days, so everything is familiar to me. I know the part where we will take our vows is coming next. John makes it through without any trouble. But when it is my turn, I open my mouth to speak and nothing comes out. I try again with the same unsatisfactory result.

"What is the matter with her?" I hear someone murmuring from one of the pews behind me. "Does she want to marry the man or not?"

The church walls begin to close in on me, and the vision melts away.

My first try was not a great success, but I was confident I would do better the next time, making it all the way to the end of the ceremony and beyond. I wondered if John was having the same trouble adjusting his thinking. Probably not, I decided, for he seemed to take all life's events in his easy stride and always with a dash of humor to smooth the way.

With my thoughts so unsettled over the upcoming changes in my life, I looked forward to resuming the comforting routine of Mr. Essex's visits. I looked forward to finding him exactly the same as he ever was and our friendship still strong. I should have been the only one altered. Although I am sure I had thought of him every day in the interim, my foolish attachment to him *must* have been weakened by our long separation and the fact that I was now engaged to another man.

Instead, when Mr. Essex finally came in the middle of February, he appeared the one most changed. He had retreated behind an unfamiliar mask of formal reserve, holding himself at a greater distance – physically and in every other way – as he performed his usual duties.

"Look this way… now the other. Very well. Now your diary, if you please, Miss de Bourgh… Yes, I see. Anything new to report? No? Then it is time for your exercise…"

He might have been talking to a person he never met before in his life, one in whom he took nothing more than a professional interest. All I could think was that he severely disapproved of my engagement (although it was never mentioned between us beyond what he had said in his letter), or there was something else bothering him.

I did not like to say anything while Mrs. Jenkinson was present, but later, when we walked the halls and passageways of the house together, I asked Mr. Essex what was wrong. "Is it your mother?" I inquired with concern. "Mama said that, according to your letter, you stayed on in Lincolnshire longer because your mother was ill."

"It is true; she was ill," he said as formally as before. "But she is fully recovered now. You must not concern yourself. There is nothing whatever the matter with me."

I did not believe him, but neither did it seem fair to accuse him of withholding information when I myself had already done the same. He claimed to have detected some change in me – some negative alteration in my health. When he asked me about it, I dismissed the idea, saying that he must be imagining things, for I was every bit as well as when he had last seen me.

It may have been better if he had not come. I believe the encounter did neither of us any good.

When Mr. Essex had gone, I put him from my mind and refocused my attention. Since I was alone in my rooms again, I took the opportunity to close my eyes and make another try at envisioning my wedding. This time, however, I was even less successful.

The day is fine. The church is full of well-wishers. I make my entrance as before. But when my groom turns to smile at me, it is not Cousin John's face I see. Mr. Essex waits for me at the head of the aisle.

Disaster.

- 54 -

Mrs. Jenkinson

With Reasons to Worry

Although Anne seemed to enjoy it all (the Pemberley ball, the travel, the parties, etc.), I think these extra exertions may have taken some of the stuffing out of her. Or perhaps it was only what could be expected: the inevitable let down after so much celebration, or the fact that Colonel Fitzwilliam had gone away for a few weeks. But when the culminating engagement party was over, Miss Anne started to slip into a spell of something akin to lassitude. It was barely noticeable at first, just enough that I recognized a definite difference.

I asked her about the wedding plans, thinking that would be a subject sure to animate her.

"Mama has everything well in hand," she said. "My help is not needed."

"Well, then, if you are at your leisure, let us resume your music lessons," I suggested, hoping to rekindle the excitement she had originally displayed at the idea. "You made such a good beginning before our travels."

"There seems little point, Mrs. Jenkinson." she said. "I will never achieve anything worthwhile, starting so late as I have."

"I disagree, Miss. Perhaps you may never be a true proficient or feel comfortable performing in company, but what of it? I am confident you could learn enough to bring pleasure to yourself – and your husband, once you marry – by playing a little cheerful music of an evening, when no one else is about to hear or criticize. That is a worthy goal, in my opinion, and reason enough to continue."

"I doubt my husband will receive pleasure from anything I could play for him. It should be more likely a painful sensation to his ear after being entertained so much better by other women of his vast acquaintance."

"You must not say such things, Miss Anne. Music is like a gift; half the enjoyment comes from one's fondness for the giver. Because of his great affection, Colonel Fitzwilliam must appreciate what he hears from you more than anything from the most accomplished stranger."

I may not have fully convinced her, but Anne consented to continuing her lessons at the piano-forte, making good progress despite the fact that I felt her heart was no longer entirely engaged in the effort.

I was glad that Mr. Essex, after some further delay, was finally coming to see her again. She had been doing so well before, and I hated to think she might be losing even a little of the hard-won ground she had gained. Perhaps she would benefit from her physician having the chance to assess the situation and encourage her. And now, with the engagement firmly in place and announced all the way from Derbyshire to Kent, surely there was no more danger on that head.

Mr. Essex came in the middle of February. As usual, he reviewed the notations in Miss de Bourgh's diary, performed a cursory examination of her person in my presence, and then walked with her at some length. As the wet weather dictated, they were confined to the indoors, pacing up and down the passageways.

Miss Anne chose to return to her apartments when they had finished, and I escorted Mr. Essex back downstairs to take his leave of Lady Catherine. He paused along the way, however, to talk a moment with me in private.

"Mrs. Jenkinson," he began. "Forgive me, but I must ask for your advice. I could not help but notice that Miss de Bourgh did not seem quite as well as the last time I saw her, before Christmas. She would not admit to anything being amiss, but you must know what I mean."

"Yes, certainly I have noticed. It is a subtle alteration, but not much about Miss de Bourgh escapes my detection."

"That is just as I expected, Mrs. Jenkinson. So, to what do you attribute this change?"

"I trust it is nothing serious, sir, only the result of overexertion and the natural anticlimax after an extraordinary period of gaiety. You did not find anything more, did you?"

"No… No, nothing physical," he said, shaking his head. "It is the apparent downturn in her spirits that concerns me, and as we have discovered, spirit and body are deeply intertwined in Miss de Bourgh's case. But you know her better than I do, Mrs. Jenkinson. What is your opinion of this engagement to Colonel Fitzwilliam? Is Miss de Bourgh entirely satisfied with it? If she harbors some regrets…"

"Regrets? Oh, no, Mr. Essex. There, I think you are quite mistaken. Such an idea would never have come into your head had you seen Miss Anne at the engagement party, laughing and dancing away as merry as could be. And she thinks the world of Colonel Fitzwilliam. In fact, I shouldn't be surprised if it were his going away that has her a bit downcast now. No doubt she misses him terribly."

"Yes. Yes of course, Mrs. Jenkinson," he said soberly. "I daresay you are correct. That could certainly account for what I observed in her today. How long will the colonel be away?"

"A month or more, I believe. The wedding is not until June, after all, and he has some business to attend to first. I expect we will have him back among us by Easter, though."

"Very well, Mrs. Jenkinson. I have done what I can to encourage Miss de Bourgh, and I know I can depend on you to do the same. Try to persuade her to take more vegetables in her diet; that might be of some use. And be sure she continues the other measures that have brought us this far. I shall return a fortnight hence."

When he did so, only to find Anne no better, Mr. Essex confided in me further. "I am very concerned about Miss de Bourgh's apparent decline. It may be nothing, but I would prefer to err on the side of caution. Keep a close watch, Mrs. Jenkinson. And you must not hesitate to send for me, night or day, if anything the least bit alarming should develop. I will drop whatever I am doing and come at a run if she needs me." Upon finishing this impassioned speech, he looked conscious and began to color. "If I am needed, I should have said. I am very devoted to my patients, you understand, Mrs. Jenkinson."

Oh dear, I thought. *I believe I do understand.*

- 55 -

Lady Catherine

Receiving Surprising Correspondence

I had held nothing back; it was no occasion for economy. I had ordered everything the best that money could buy for Anne and Fitzwilliam's engagement party… and certainly everything was a degree or two finer than what the Babcocks had done for their daughter. It was all a great success. Everybody said so. The same would be true for the wedding itself and the breakfast following: no expense would be spared.

My plans were already well underway, too. I had tried to interest Anne in taking on some of the more minor tasks, but she only made delays and excuses. So I had to undertake the business myself, which may have been just as well. My taste is undoubtedly superior, and Anne keeping out of it saved me the trouble of overruling whatever questionable choices she might have made. Much better that she should occupy herself with inconsequential things, like her lessons at the piano-forte with Mrs. Jenkinson or walking the corridors with Mr. Essex.

Yes, the bright, young physician had started coming with some regularity again. But now that all was firmly settled, I judged that his renewed presence could do no harm. He would hardly have the effrontery to interfere with an established engagement. His influence with me and with my daughter were not absolute, after all.

My correspondence with Mrs. Collins turned out to be very unsatisfactory. She never wrote but to tell me of some unpleasant news from Pemberley, where she had established herself as a frequent visitor. It had been bad enough listening to Anne's glowing account of Georgiana's ball without having every detail repeated in Mrs. Collins's enthusiastic letter shortly afterward. And then in

March, she delivered something worse still. According to Mrs. Collins, it was now generally known that an addition to the Pemberley family was expected. I suppose with everything so favorably arranged for Anne with Fitzwilliam, I should have been less bothered by such information. Yet I had sanguinely anticipated that disgraceful marriage would produce nothing more than shame and disappointment for the parties involved. The best I could hope for now was that this child would be the first in a long succession of girls, which must be a severe frustration to any proud man.

Even considering what Mrs. Collins had told me, nothing prepared me for the shock of the correspondence I received a few weeks later. No doubt, on principle, I should have thrown the letter straight into the fire as soon as I recognized what hand had addressed it. It was from my nephew – the one whom I no longer acknowledged to be my nephew, that is.

I did debate whether or not to open it. My curiosity was extreme, however, and I ultimately decided there could be no harm in reading it. Knowledge conferred power, and whatever the letter contained would undoubtedly give me more of an advantage than ignorance would. I could always pretend afterward that I had not read it, if that seemed advisable.

For no reason I could fathom, my heart set to pounding as I broke the red Pemberley seal and unfolded the expensive paper. Here is what was written inside.

Lady Catherine de Bourgh, Rosings Park, Kent
Madam,

Allow me to offer my congratulations on the engagement of your daughter Anne to Colonel Fitzwilliam. My wife and I have the highest opinion of them both and wish them all possible happiness in their marriage.

Much as you are looking forward to this addition to your family circle, Mrs. Darcy and I find that we are expecting an addition to ours by a different means. This blessing causes me to reflect on the importance of maintaining (and restoring, where necessary) peace and unity within my extended family. I regret the disagreement that has broken that bond in our case. Although I will make no apologies for a marriage in which I have been supremely happy, I am sorry that the accomplishment of it occasioned you pain. My hope is that the success of the match now made for your daughter will produce a degree of felicity eclipsing any pleasure lost by a disappointed former plan.

Though I am amenable to conciliation, what passed between us – especially uncharitable words spoken and written against my wife – cannot be easily forgotten. However, if after the passage of time you have experienced an alteration in your position to the extent that you now find yourself able to make some reparation, I am willing to hear whatever you have to say on the subject. The matter is entirely in your own hands, Madam. I remain, respectfully,

Your nephew,
Fitzwilliam Darcy

Righteous indignation flared at some parts of what I read, and yet at others, I felt a faint softening. Darcy – now that he had taken this first step, I thought it permissible to say his name again, at least to myself – had been such a favorite with me that I had to admit the idea of a reconciliation between us held some deep-seated appeal.

But there would be no groveling on my part, no instant giving in. As for the reparation he proposed, that was out of the question. After all, *I* was the injured party, and my pride would not be toppled by a handful of fine-sounding words.

He had left the matter in my hands, and I saw no need to rush any response. Much thought would be required. First I had to decide if I would answer his letter at all, and then what to say if I did.

While I sat in deep thought, considering these questions, Anne came in and asked what had arrived in the post.

"Oh, this?" I said dismissively, folding the crisp paper again and tucking it away out of sight. "It is only a letter from Lady Ethel. Nothing that would interest you."

~~*~~

It was a relief when Fitzwilliam returned to us in April. I had sent for him when I saw that Anne's spirits seemed to flag in his absence. Besides, I felt it was important to include him in the wedding plans, at least in a nominal way. The event was less than two months off by then, and there was still much to be done.

Always, at least in the back of my mind, lingered the question of what to do about Darcy's letter. Finally I decided that, for my dead sister's sake, I could be magnanimous. Without false penitence or admitting to being the one in the wrong – which, of course, I certainly was not – I was willing to take at least a small step toward healing the breach. After long and careful thought, I composed my response.

Mr. Fitzwilliam Darcy, of Pemberley, Derbyshire
My Nephew,

I confess that I was very much surprised, but not displeased, at receiving a letter from you, sir. Although I am not entirely satisfied with your tone in parts, I can appreciate the exertion and compromise of pride required of you in writing it.

I thank you for your compliments concerning Anne's upcoming marriage, for which I too have every expectation of success. I believe Colonel Fitzwilliam will treat my daughter with the respect she deserves. Anne is a treasure, and I think he fully comprehends the honor she does him by consenting to be his wife. I trust that he will prove worthy of this privilege, a privilege that another gentleman chose to cast aside to his discredit.

As for this estrangement between us, I must admit that it is a matter of some regret for me as well. I am sure no one respects the value of family connections more than I do myself. Although I have not yet learnt to repent of the conviction that you acted wrongly in marrying beneath you and against the wishes of all your relations, I concede that my own behavior subsequently was not above reproach.

Some of the frank sentiments I expressed at the time would, perhaps, have been better left unsaid. The words proceeded from a sense of indignation based not simply on an offense to myself, but also for what I perceived to be an injury to my daughter. You will soon understand that in defense of one's child, of any age, one is apt to do things one otherwise would not. This must be my excuse.

In future, should you call at Rosings, I shall receive you. You may bring your wife as well, if you wish. As I recall, I once found her rather entertaining.

Lady Catherine de Bourgh

I assumed that these concessions, which were clearly more than what Darcy deserved or had any right to expect from me, would be sufficient to bring him crawling back, begging my forgiveness. Then all would be well again. For my sister's sake, I was prepared to accept her son back into the family fold, despite the piece of disagreeable baggage he would bring with him. By such means, I would once again demonstrate for all to see that I really was exceptionally high-minded.

However, I soon found that achieving reconciliation between our two families would demand an even higher price from me – one I was unsure I should be willing to pay.

- 56 -

Mrs. Jenkinson

On Remaining Watchful

All this time, I had worried Miss Anne might become too attached to her physician, and now it appeared it was the other way round. I was sorry for Mr. Essex. Still, there was no danger to my young lady as long as the unfortunate attachment was only on his side.

I resolved to remain watchful nevertheless. I could not bear to see Anne make the same enormous blunder I had; that is what was on my mind. I could not bear to think she might lose her focus and throw away everything by marrying the wrong man based on fleeting passion mistaken for love. My husband had been every bit as handsome and charming as Mr. Essex… and probably every bit as poor too. Affection had quickly faded, and I had been left with nothing when Mr. Jenkinson died.

I did not wish that fate for Anne. She had money now but might be, like I had been, cut off without a single sovereign to her name if she went against parental wishes.

I never could forgive my father for disinheriting me. However, now I saw what I had been to blind to when I was young. I saw that I would have been better off in the end had I married the man he had chosen for me – an older gentleman of real consequence – instead of the one I chose for myself. I might still be a widow, but I would be living in the style of Lady Catherine instead of as one of her paid staff.

To my way of thinking, Colonel Fitzwilliam was the perfect match for Anne – amiable, well-connected, parentally sanctioned, and not an old man by any standard. I stood ready to do whatever I could to make sure she stayed the course.

That spring, Rosings, which should have been a house in cheerful anticipation of a much-touted wedding, seemed to have turned into a house of ennui.

There was now no question in my mind but that Anne's health and spirits had generally declined in the colonel's absence. Although she only occasionally complained of a headache, some of the other symptoms had reappeared. Her appetite was off, and her energy on the wane. She did spend time daily at the piano-forte, but I could not seem to interest her in any other kind of occupation. She had even lost some of her enthusiasm for her health regime. A walk out of doors, with its refreshing air and signs of spring abounding, failed to put color in her cheeks or a smile on her face.

Throughout the month of March, I told myself that things would turn round when Colonel Fitzwilliam came back to Rosings. His return at the end of the month did not remedy the situation, however, and he can be forgiven for not understanding my concern.

"I notice no great difference in her, Mrs. Jenkinson," he told me when I raised the issue. "Compared to what she once was, she still looks remarkably well to me."

This much was true, and if it had not been for Mr. Essex's agreeing with my opinion, I might have convinced myself I was only imagining things.

I could by no means accuse the doctor of neglect, for he hovered attentively close at hand, coming to see Anne at least once a week again, as in the beginning, and doing what he could. But with what ailed him (and I fancied I knew what that was), he had little encouragement to spare for his patient. His own youthful vitality and positive ideas seemed on the decline as well.

The two of them now dealt with each other more formally, I noticed, which was only right. Anne's engagement had naturally changed things between them. She had an obligation to her betrothed to hold other men at a distance. Mr. Essex also had a duty, a duty not to interfere. For the most part, I was pleased (and relieved) that they both faithfully respected these boundaries. I must admit, though, that I felt some small measure of sadness at their loss of close friendship, and especially if it should exact any further toll on my young lady's health.

Anne's trend for the worse continued. Although her deterioration was not yet severe, my conscience demanded action before it should become permanent. I could not bear to remain idle, watching the life slowly draining out of her one drop at a time. Something had to be done, and soon. Since it appeared that nobody else was prepared to, I resolved to get to the bottom of whatever was troubling Anne myself – for her sake and for my own peace of mind. But when I did, I was no happier for it.

- 57 -

Anne

Confessing the Truth

Mrs. Jenkinson confronted me at a moment of weakness. That must be my excuse, for I would never have made such a disgraceful confession otherwise.

I had utterly failed in my resolve to accustom myself to the idea of marrying Colonel Fitzwilliam. Although I still believed in all the rational reasons that had convinced me to consent to the arrangement in the first place, I had made no progress beyond. That being the case, I began to regret the six-month engagement John and I had agreed to. The waiting had become a torment rather than a way to ease the transition to married life. And since I knew there was no possibility of going back, it would have been better to move forward and have done.

To make matters worse, my inconvenient feelings for Mr. Essex had stubbornly refused to fade away as I had intended they should. How could I banish thoughts of him when he continued to hover about so closely? Yet it seemed I would never be rid of him. The more I saw him, the more I could not help thinking about him. The more my mind dwelt on him, the more distressed I became. And the more distressed and poorly I felt, the more often Mr. Essex insisted on coming to Rosings, concerned for my health. I was stuck in a trap of my own making, sinking in quicksand I could not escape.

Mama seemed oblivious to all this and deaf to my few feeble attempts to elicit her help. It would have been in her power to send Mr. Essex away at the very least. When I suggested it, however, she only looked at me shrewdly and said she thought that "inadvisable."

Mrs. Jenkinson had been wringing her hands over me for weeks. I believe she had even reverted to counting the mouthfuls of food I consumed and surreptitiously checking the fit of my gowns, worried that I might have lost an ounce or two. Although I had steadfastly denied there was anything the matter with me, by early April even *I* did not believe that anymore.

I was feeling particularly low that evening. Mr. Essex's manner had again been very distant when he came, and after he had gone, I had taken my disappointment out on John, cutting him short when he had innocently asked if the doctor's visit had been helpful. I promptly apologized, but I returned to my room very dissatisfied with everybody, especially myself. Curling up on the settee and opening a book I had no interest in reading, I indulged myself in a few silent tears instead, although I could not have sensibly justified them or even defined what specific sorrow they were meant to address.

Unfortunately, my watchdog was not far behind me. This time she let herself in without bothering to knock. "Oh, dear," she said upon finding me in such a sad state. "Has it come to this? You *must* allow me to help you, Miss. And no good telling me there is nothing wrong this time; I will not accept that answer."

She stared down at me with motherly concern, and I knew I owed her as much relief from anxiety I had it in my power to give. Controlling my tears as best I could, I presently replied. "Very well, Mrs. Jenkinson. I will not pretend there is nothing wrong, but neither is there is anything you can do to help. I must get the better of this thing myself, and I am determined to do so."

"At what cost to your health, Miss? Forgive me, but I cannot keep silent and watch you slip back to the way you were before. You made me Mr. Essex's deputy, remember? And you charged me with watching over you in his absence."

"It seems to me, Mrs. Jenkinson, that he is *never* absent," I said miserably. "He was here only this morning, and doubtless he will return in a day or two. Why not leave the doctoring to him?"

"Have you told him what the trouble is?"

I made no answer.

"I thought as much. Nor the lovely gentleman downstairs who wants to marry you, I would wager. But you must tell somebody before it is too late, Miss – before this decline goes too far."

"The lovely man downstairs who wants to marry me," I repeated sadly. "Colonel Fitzwilliam deserves much better. He deserves a wife who will love him with all her heart… or at the very least, one who is not already in love with somebody else."

"What?" cried Mrs. Jenkinson, one hand flying to her mouth in alarm. "I certainly hope you do not mean Mr. Essex!"

"Who else?" It was such a relief to finally admit the truth, but then of course regret instantly followed – regret and dread that the information should go any further. Desperately, I grasped Mrs. Jenkinson's free hand and pulled her over to sit beside me. I bade her, "Oh, please forget what I said, dear lady! There is nothing to be done, and it would be mortifying if Mama or Colonel Fitzwilliam should ever hear of it. You *must* promise not to tell them!"

I gazed into Mrs. Jenkinson's face with a pleading look, trying for several seconds to discern what she was thinking. There I read a jumble of feelings – shock, pity, concern, disappointment, and possibly even distaste at what she had heard. I could not be sure of any of it. Although I did care what she thought, the most urgent thing at that moment was to extract her promise of secrecy.

Finally she said, "I will not tell either of them, Miss. You can depend on it. Oh, but how dreadful! I am very sorry for it. What bad luck! Still, I hope you mean that you intend to go through with the wedding just the same."

"What choice do I have? I would never go back on my promise to my cousin, and a future with Mr. Essex would be impossible in any case. You know it as well as I do. He is entirely unsuitable, and Mama would never allow it."

"Very true, Miss. You would be putting *everything* at risk."

"I simply must conquer my feelings for Mr. Essex; that is the only solution. Perhaps you could help me to convince my mother he should not attend me any longer. His continual presence only makes the situation more difficult for me."

Mrs. Jenkinson sighed. "Hmm. I wish I had so much influence with your mother. I think the most effective persuasion would be for you to show her you are lively and cheerful again. Remember how glad Lady Catherine was to do without Mr. Essex all those weeks in the winter, when she was convinced you did not need him."

I was mightily relieved to have Mrs. Jenkinson's assurance that she would keep my secret. I knew I could trust her to do so. And there was wisdom in what she said. Perhaps if I could force myself into at least the appearance of excellent health again, I could be free of the constant reminder of my straying affection, once and for all. Then my health might indeed improve. But I was afraid I might already have sunk too far for that, that I had not enough strength left to attempt such a resurrection.

~~*~~

Thanks to Mrs. Jenkinson's patient efforts, I graduated from the piano-forte in her apartments to the grand instrument in the music room. My skills had progressed to the point where hearing me was no longer too tedious for Mama. In fact, she occasionally tossed a word of mild praise my way, never failing to add to it the admonition that I must practice every day if I expected to achieve anything worthwhile. Considering it was the same advice she had given Elizabeth once upon a time, I took it as a compliment indeed.

I was occupied in this manner – practicing my latest musical challenge – when Mr. Essex arrived one afternoon a week or more after I had made my foolish confession.

"That was quite good, Miss de Bourgh" he said, clapping lightly and coming into the room when I had reached the end of the piece. "I hope you do not mind, but I paused to listen. I am most impressed."

"Oh!" I said in surprise. "You must excuse me, Mr. Essex. I did not know you were there or I should have left off sooner. My playing is hardly worth listening to."

"I disagree, Miss de Bourgh. It is a long time since I have heard anything I enjoyed half so much."

"Then I pity you, sir. Do you really have so few accomplished ladies amongst your acquaintance?"

He smiled. "Skill is one thing; musical expression is quite another. Besides, knowing how diligently you have worked and how far you have come in a short time added immeasurably to my pleasure in hearing you play. You have my utmost respect and admiration for your efforts, Miss de Bourgh. Will you play another for me?" he asked. "Please."

"Very well," I said. "Since you have already heard a sample, you will know not to expect too much." I pulled out another simple piece and tried to do my best. Feeling Mr. Essex's eyes on me completely upset my concentration, however, and I was not yet skilled enough to play acceptably under duress.

"Never mind," he said when I gave up in the middle. "It was perhaps unfair of me to ask for an encore. Another time, perhaps. Now, shall we take our walk?" he asked, extending his hand to me. "It is a fine spring day."

I am afraid I stared at him, bewildered. This was not the aloof Mr. Essex I had come to recently expect. This was the man of old, the man of warmth and sincerity. I wondered what had made the change and if it would last… or even if I wanted it to. As painful as it had been to see him distance himself, I had accepted that it was for the best. That unsociable man, I could more easily resist. This one, I was in love with.

"Yes, of course," I said, shaking off my brief reverie and rising from the instrument without the use of his proffered hand. As tempted as I was to take it, I thought it wisest to avoid his actually touching me if possible. I could not avoid agreeing to walk with him, however. That was a confirmed part of our every appointment together. And he was right about the inviting weather; the April afternoon could not have been finer.

As was also our custom, I gave him the choice of destination. "What would you prefer today, Mr. Essex? – the orchard, the lane, the rose garden, the shrubbery, or the groves?"

"The orchard, I think. I am quite partial to that walk, and perhaps we will see some of the earliest trees in bloom. By the way, where is Colonel Fitzwilliam? Perhaps he would care to join us."

"No, John has gone into town on business. He will not return until tomorrow."

"Ah," he said as we started off down the familiar gravel walk.

Although we continually varied our routes, we had carried on together so long that there were few new places left to explore. As for this particular path, I daresay by then we could *both* have found our way to the orchard and back blindfolded.

Mr. Essex continued his friendlier conversation as we progressed, almost making me believe we had slipped back into our old, comfortable ways. But then he fell silent as we neared the orchard, at the point where we usually turned back toward the house. When I stole a glance at him, he looked very grave indeed. Suddenly, he said, "May we sit down here for a few minutes, Miss de Bourgh?" indicating a bench placed where it gave onto a fine prospect of the park. "There is something very particular I must speak to you about."

I sat as he requested. Mr. Essex did also, remaining silent, only staring out at the view as if he had nothing whatsoever on his mind. When I presently asked what he had wished to speak to me about, he shot to his feet and began feverishly pacing in front of me, a few steps one way and then back again. His hand worked over his mouth as if alternately trying to assist and then block what he meant to say. In some agitation myself, I waited, having no idea what might come next.

Finally, he said, "First, I want you to know, Miss de Bourgh, that I have struggled with this dilemma for weeks, perhaps months. I have wrestled with the question of whether or not to tell you certain things, whether I had any right to do so. Who was I to impose on you – a treasured friend, a lady in delicate health – what may turn out a very unwelcome weight upon your shoulders? And so I have repressed my feelings and kept quiet. But lately, I was encouraged... That is, I have become convinced that greater harm could result, to more than myself, by my staying silent. Therefore, I must risk it, if you will permit me. Will you give me leave to speak freely, Miss de Bourgh?"

He waited for my answer. But with such an ominous preamble, what was I to think? He was my physician, after all. Was he going to tell me I was dying and there was nothing to be done about it? Was he going to say there was something terribly wrong with my mother? In fear and trembling, I granted him permission to continue.

"I thank you," he said with a little bow. "Please believe that I will be as considerate of your feelings as possible. My intent is not to injure you in any way; quite the reverse. And yet I hardly know what your reaction to my news will be; I only know that I must find out, and there is not another minute to lose."

That is when Mr. Essex told me the most surprising thing; he told me that he was in love with me and that he had been for quite some time.

- 58 -

Lady Catherine

Making Necessary Concessions

Fitzwilliam was in London, and Anne had gone out walking with Mr. Essex when that final letter from Darcy arrived. I was glad to have solitude to read it by, especially when I discovered the tenor of the content, which was not at all what I had expected.

Madam,

I must thank you for your kind invitation to call on you at Rosings Park. Unfortunately, the present circumstances make it impossible for my wife and I to accept your hospitality, although I shall continue to hope this will not always be the case.

In fact, I should very much like to see Rosings again. I remember with fondness many of my visits there, especially those when my uncle was still with us. To this day, I mourn his loss and question the upsetting circumstances surrounding his abrupt end. Surely, I must not be the only one still wondering about that tragedy.

It may interest you to know that Mrs. Darcy, Georgiana, and I will be staying for some weeks at our house in town beginning the middle of May, giving Georgiana a London season. Should you sincerely wish to restore a state of peaceful family relations, I would strongly recommend that you consider calling on Mrs. Darcy there some afternoon. As you cannot deny, a bride visit to her is long overdue.

If all goes well, such a step on your part should effectively clear away the last obstacle. My sister and I shall await the outcome. Perhaps we – as well as Anne and

Fitzwilliam, if they are available – could join you and Elizabeth afterward. As before, I once more leave this matter in your hands. Let your good sense and your conscience be your guides.

Fitzwilliam Darcy

Well, this was very disagreeable! Instead of Darcy crawling back to me, he apparently expected me to be the one doing the groveling. He tells me I must wait upon his no-account wife; evidently, *that* was to be the price of the reconciliation we both wanted.

As I read between the lines, I discovered even more subtle coercion used on me. Mentioning his uncle was a stroke of pure genius; he must have known what effect that would have. Frankly, it amazed me that Darcy had it in him to be so devious. I should probably have admired his skillful maneuvers if he had been working his machinations on somebody else.

What was I to do about it? That was the question. Could I swallow my pride and dance to the tune he had ordered? I could do anything I set my mind to, of course, but at what cost to my dignity this? On the other hand, I had to consider what the cost might be of refusing his terms. No reconciliation, obviously. But might there be an even greater price if Darcy made good on his veiled threat about Sir Lewis?

My unenviable task was to choose the lesser of the two evils… if only I could determine which one that was.

- 59 -

Anne

On Being Too Late

While I sat in silent shock at his declaration of love, not knowing what to think, Mr. Essex hurriedly went on.

"Do not say anything in return," he requested. "I know you are not free to do so, even if you wished. Only hear me out, I beg you.

"Please be assured that it is you yourself and not your fortune that I wish to make my own. If the way were ever made clear for us to marry, I would gladly renounce all claims to your inheritance. You should know that my own financial situation is not nearly as desperate as you may believe. I am well able to maintain myself and a family… in a modest but respectable style. Of course Rosings is another matter, but that would be up to you to decide… Wait!"

I had got to my feet and made for the house in haste.

He ran after me. "Forgive me, Anne," he was saying.

"It is 'Miss de Bourgh' to you, sir!" I called back over my shoulder.

"Yes, of course. Forgive me, Miss de Bourgh. Perhaps it was wrong of me to speak, but I was convinced you had the right to know the truth… before it was too late."

"It is already too late, Mr. Essex, although I by no means wish to imply that it would have made the slightest difference. As you very well know, I am engaged to Colonel Fitzwilliam, and I intend to keep my promise to marry him."

"Even if that does him more harm than good in the end?"

"What?" I asked indignantly, wheeling about to face him. "Do you truly believe that being married to me would be the worst thing that could happen to the man?"

"No, of course not! Only that if you care for me at all…"

I turned and strode away from him again.

"Allow me to put it another way, then. If you sincerely care for the colonel, do not you think you owe it to him to be honest? A little pain now would be kinder than all of us living with a mistake for a lifetime."

These words ringing in my ears, I ran into the house so he would not see my tears. *Too late. Too late!*

~~*~~

In abject misery, I refused to see Mr. Essex again that day or even to emerge from my rooms until I was assured he had left the premises. I loathed the man for burdening me with such untimely news. Did he expect me to be gratified by the admission of his love when I was in no position to accept it? Should I have thanked him for telling me I could have had what I wanted, if only… For knowing how close we had come… Now these things would torture me forever. I might never forgive him for that.

An hour later, Mrs. Jenkinson came to tell me, "He is gone, Miss, and not to return until a week hence unless sent for sooner, he says." Here, sighing and looking quite put out, she drew something from her pocket. "He asked me to deliver this to you. I probably should have refused, but…"

"Give it to me!" I demanded, interrupting her and snatching the letter out of her hand. "You may go now, Mrs. Jenkinson. Thank you," I said without taking my eyes from my prize. As soon as I was alone, I opened it and hungrily read the contents.

Dear Miss de Bourgh,

Forgive the liberty I take in writing, but since you will not see me, I have no other choice. I cannot in good conscience leave Rosings without making some attempt at explanations and reparations.

First, my dear, I regret that my declaration has apparently made you unhappy. That was not my intent, and I still believe you had the right to determine your future course based on all the information available, not only part. So I offer you what I can: the fact that I love you. It is for you to decide whether or not that particular piece of information will make any difference in the end.

If you care nothing for me, then the decision is an easy one. You will go on as before, as if I had never spoken. You may proceed with your plans to marry Colonel Fitzwilliam without one word of criticism from me. Or, I acknowledge it is possible that you will prefer to marry Colonel Fitzwilliam despite harboring some feelings of affection for me. He is a good and honorable man, I believe, and without question a man of superior consequence. With the benefit of mutual affection, he will no doubt make you a very satisfactory husband. No one would fault you for choosing him over me. Traditional wisdom and the standard claims of duty will support you.

In either case, I will not hound and bully you to change your mind. I will not resent you for being unable or unwilling to return my ardor. My friendship is steadfast, my genuine concern for your well-being unconditional. I will continue to respect and serve you as your physician if you will allow me, or recommend someone to replace myself if you prefer not to see me again. The choice is entirely yours, and if it goes against me, I shall endeavor to accept it.

There is another option, however, one I dare to hope you will consider if indeed you do care for me.

Do you remember our discussion in November, when we were out walking? Could you have failed to understand my wishes even then? Oh, how I now curse my stupidity for not having spoken plainly at that opportune moment! Instead, I considered I had no right to put myself forward as your lover. I told myself you could not care for me in any case. I exercised what I thought was prudent restraint, and the next thing I heard, you were engaged to somebody else. But I digress.

That day in November, I suggested to you that in a matter of singular importance, a matter crucial to heart or conscience, you might dare to do what you thought right instead of what your mother or society demanded. This is that moment. If you love me as I love you, then consider the possibility that marrying anybody else would not only be wrong but possibly dangerous. If your mind has failed to warn you, then perhaps your body is trying to do so. Perhaps your current decline results from a troubled spirit. If so, and the decline were to continue, what kind of wife will you make for Colonel Fitzwilliam?

Excuse my being so blunt, my dear Anne, but I could not bear to let you sacrifice yourself to an unhappy marriage, not if I could have prevented it. I cannot bear to see you bound for life to a man you do not love, regardless how otherwise good and highly eligible he may be. If it ruins your health and makes you both unhappy, your sacrifice will have been for nothing – a noble but empty gesture.

But perhaps I am completely mistaken – led astray by my own vain wishes. If so, please forgive me and disregard my ravings. If not, I beg you would reconsider your engagement. I know there is no logical reason you should risk everything for me, but I dare to ask it of you anyway, my darling. If you love me, say you will throw caution to the wind and be my wife. Your devoted...

H. E.

P.S. – Have no fear. When I come to you next, we need not speak of these things. We will be as we were before unless you choose otherwise. I place my fate into your benevolent hands.

How was I ever to recover from such a letter? The words penetrated deep, stirring heart, piercing conscience, and destroying my peace.

Before, I had been resigned. With no reason to believe that Mr. Essex could return my affection, I was convinced a life with my cousin would be the best I could hope for, that I would be content and in time learn to be happy. Now, however... Now, even that modest goal seemed done away with forever, attainable no longer. Now I would always have to live with the knowledge that Mr. Essex had in fact loved me and would have married me if I had encouraged him to think it possible.

But it never was possible; that had not changed by Mr. Essex's declaring it should be otherwise. There had always been Mama's indomitable will to contend with, compounded now by my promise to John. As for Mr. Essex's assertions about my declining health and what would be kindest for everybody in the end… Although I thought of little else, I came to no useful conclusions. No matter what I did, it seemed I would be in the wrong.

So I did nothing. In a kind of pathetic paralysis of the mind, I slid along towards the date that would seal my fate forever, feeling panicked at times and yet powerless to change the outcome or even to decide if I should try to do so. John – such a kind and decent man – remained dutifully by my side. From his great solicitude, I knew he could see that I was struggling. I would not tell him what ailed me, though. How could I? As for Mama, she carried on as usual, keeping charge of everything including every aspect of my upcoming wedding, having no doubt by this time given up on my contributing anything useful to the process.

And so the last days of April slipped inexorably away, and now May seemed to be galloping on at a perilous pace. June would be upon us in the blink of an eye.

The weeks came and went; Mr. Essex came and went. I said nothing to him about his declaration or his letter, and he kept his word about never raising the question again. He monitored my waning health from a respectful distance. There was grave concern – sometimes exasperation or even desperation – in his tone as he counseled me what I *must* do to become stable again. But he never spoke of love. Only occasionally in a pleading look did I read the eloquent renewal of his offer, the impassioned request that I should answer it with word as well as decided action.

At such times, I had to look away lest he apprehend my true feelings. It was better that he should think I did not care.

I preferred, if possible, to at least preserve his good opinion of me. I preferred he never knew what a coward I was. I was not courageous, as he had once declared me to be. I was not brave enough to find out what Mama would do if I crossed her on something so vitally important. I did not feel adventurous enough to learn what it might be like to live in a "modest but respectable style," should my mother disinherit me. I could not do it… not even for Mr. Essex.

At my high point, I might have considered something bold, but no more. Whatever nerve I might have had then had faded along with my strength.

- 60 -

Lady Catherine

On the High Cost of Getting One's Way

There was nothing for it but to make up my mind to doing what needed to be done. I would call upon Mrs. Darcy, I had decided, regardless of the injury to my pride it would require. My nephew might have dictated the terms of the reunion, but I would have the satisfaction of getting what I wanted in the end. There was no denying it; what I wanted was my nephew and niece back in my family. I was the matriarch, and I would restore harmony. This was no different from so many of the other tasks I undertook. A job might rightly be somebody else's responsibility, but it fell to me in the end because I was the only one who could properly carry the thing off.

Very well, then. If I must, I could behave with civility to the former Miss Bennet, the undeserving new mistress of Pemberley. I could pretend to humble myself for the brief time it would take to achieve my goal. Then I would be duly rewarded.

Once I had decided, I wasted no time. There was no point in putting off something unpleasant. Delay only increased and prolonged the pain. Better to get the thing over with quickly, before the wedding in this case. Perhaps when we were on cordial terms again, I would ask Darcy to give the bride away, since her father was obviously unavailable.

Fitzwilliam wanted Darcy in attendance, of course; I knew that already. Consequently, I assigned Fitzwilliam the chore of writing to his friend.

"Tell him I will call on his wife on Friday," I said. "I want to be sure to find her at home so that we can accomplish the necessary visit while we have to be in town anyway. I will send you and Anne on an errand while I make peace with Mrs. Darcy. Then you can both join us afterward."

So that was settled.

At the appointed day and time, my carriage pulled up to the curb in front of Darcy's house in Berkeley Street.

"Do not be too long about your business," I told Anne and Fitzwilliam before alighting. "I shall expect you back in no more than one hour. We cannot remain here all day."

"Yes, Mama," said Anne quietly.

"Never fear, Madam," added Fitzwilliam. "We shall return promptly."

The footman handed me out, and as the carriage drew away, I steeled myself for the unpleasantness that lay ahead. Then, with my head held high, I marched up the stairs, was let in, and announced.

Elizabeth rose to formally greet me. "Lady Catherine. Good afternoon."

She looked somewhat different from what I remembered – a little thicker about the middle, for one thing. But it was more than that. It was in how she held herself with what seemed a greater dignity than I had noticed when she was a mere Miss Bennet – a nobody from nowhere. Or perhaps it was only the expensive cut of her clothes. She could never have afforded such a quality gown before.

"Good afternoon, *Mrs. Darcy*," I returned. Oh, how it pained me to address the young usurper of my sister's title by that name! It is a testament to my unconquerable will that I was able to do so with relative good grace.

"Please, do sit down," Elizabeth invited. "How good of you to come all this way to call on me."

"It was no trouble; I was in town already," I said rather dismissively. This constituted a slight misjudgment on my part I realized as soon as I saw Elizabeth stiffen.

"I see," she said icily. "I am so glad that you were not put to any inconvenience on my account, Madam."

Inwardly, I sighed. Now a further exertion was required of me. "I beg your pardon, Mrs. Darcy," I said in a more placating tone. I even dropped my eyes a moment, which I thought was an inspired touch, to demonstrate my supposed contrition. "I would have come to pay my respects regardless, and I do hope you will be good enough to forgive the tardiness of my visit." There, that should do it, I thought.

"Of course," she said, surprisingly graciously. "I trust your ladyship is well."

"I am, thank you. And allow me to compliment you on your... your obvious good health. Darcy informed me of your expectations. You must be very happy."

"Yes. *Very*."

She held my eye for a minute to carry her point home, or possibly defying me to contradict her. I would not take the bait, however. I only smiled slightly and nodded. When she was apparently satisfied, she resumed her usual livelier manner again.

"What brings you to town, Lady Catherine? Besides your intention of calling on *me*, that is?"

"Wedding business, mostly. Anne had a fitting at the dressmaker's yesterday, and I have sent her and Fitzwilliam on with the carriage today to Bond Street for various and sundries. There is so much to do, as anybody knows, to prepare for a wedding, at least any wedding of importance."

"Indeed. I do hope they will have time to step in for a bit when they return for you. We have not seen Anne since January, and we never tire of Fitzwilliam's company. I have ordered some refreshments prepared for that possibility."

We carried on in this way, talking about mostly inconsequential things – the weather, the roads, how they were enjoying the London season, and so forth. I even deigned to ask after her family. All the while, I was careful to keep my countenance impassive and censor my speech of anything that could reasonably be construed as criticism. All that was important on this occasion, I reminded myself, was that Elizabeth should be content I had met her husband's requirements.

She could have demanded more, I suppose, knowing I was in no position to argue. At the very least, she could have kept me in suspense much longer than she did if she had chosen. To her credit, however, after only about ten minutes she rang the bell to ask that Darcy and Georgiana should join us. Moments later, in they came.

Ah, this was what I had been after; this was my reward for my act of contrition, for doing my penance so convincingly!

Darcy looked much the same as when I had caught a glimpse of him at Mr. Collins's services. But my eyes quickly slid from him to Georgiana, and there they stayed. I was transfixed, and I believe I actually began to tremble. I saw not the adolescent I remembered from two years before (and who I had unconsciously expected again); I saw my long-dead sister standing before me, young but fully grown.

Getting hold of myself, I said, "Georgiana, come here." Closer inspection only confirmed my first impression. "My heavens," I continued. "Yes, you have the true look of her now, your mother that is. Of course, you were too young when she died to remember much about her, but you will have seen her portrait in the gallery at Pemberley. That likeness was taken when she was just your age, the year she married your father. The resemblance is quite distinct. Have you not remarked it yourself?"

"Oh, but my mother was so beautiful!" she exclaimed quite innocently. "I cannot see that I look a thing like her, Lady Catherine."

"You are too humble, child; you underestimate yourself. Nevertheless, I am very happy to see you again, my dear." I tipped my head to allow her to kiss my cheek. Then I turned my attention to Darcy, saying, "I am pleased to see you also, nephew. Are you well?"

"I am, and let me say how gratified we all are by the extraordinary improvement in Anne's health. I hardly knew her when she came to Pemberley in January."

"Yes. Dr. Essex is a clever physician, and he has done wonders for Anne. I have very high hopes for her now that her health no longer holds her back. She has such natural talent and taste; they have only wanted proper opportunity to develop."

"Is Anne enjoying all the wedding preparations?" Georgiana asked me.

"To a degree," I said. "Although, since Anne is modest by nature, it is an adjustment for her to be the focus of so much activity and attention. She has not the strength of spirit to carry it off, you see, so I have had to step in and manage the arrangements myself. I did assign Anne and Fitzwilliam an errand on Bond Street today, though," I continued. "They are to return here when finished. I do hope they are not too long about it. I always insist upon being back to Rosings before dark. It is so perilous to travel at night, and I am excessively attentive to all details of safety. I was telling Lady Metcalfe only the other day that she would do well to follow my example in these matters. I was appalled to learn from one of my servants that she did not return from her excursion to Hastings until long after sundown. There *was* a tolerable moon that night, I believe, but still it was most imprudent." I then turned to Elizabeth with something I had planned in advance to say. "Mrs. Darcy, I hope you will do us the honor of calling at Rosings Park before you return to Pemberley. Perhaps the three of you could drive down one day soon. There is still time before the wedding."

Mrs. Darcy hesitated, apparently not confident enough to speak for them all without consultation. "Possibly," was all she would say. Then she was asking about the chance of meeting Mr. Essex. And Darcy was on about how his wife's singing, accompanied by Georgiana on the piano-forte, was something not to be missed. I had to be polite, so I said, "Of course, I should be glad to hear you sing, Mrs. Darcy… some time or other."

I believe they were on the point of actually imposing on me to listen to her, then and there, when Anne and Fitzwilliam arrived. The promised refreshments followed, and as soon as it was civil to do so, I made our excuses to leave. I had accomplished all I had come for. It was skillfully done, too, though I say it myself. If I could get these relations of mine to call on me at Rosings again, I felt my triumph would be complete.

- 61 -

Anne

Answering an Ultimatum

As Mama had informed me, we were all going to town, John included. It did not surprise me that she had wedding business on the agenda, but I was amazed when she said that before coming home on Friday, she intended to pay a bride visit to Elizabeth Darcy!

Of course, I dared not question her; I consulted John instead. "After all her ranting about never speaking to any Darcy again, after her disparagement of poor Elizabeth, what can Mama mean by calling on her?" I asked him.

"I wish I knew! Lady Catherine can be none too happy about it, though. Did you notice how she was gritting her teeth quite hard together when she talked of it? Perhaps one day we may hear the truth, but for now I am simply glad for what it will mean for us. Reconciliation would nicely clear the way for continued close fellowship between our two households. I was afraid that, to avoid upsetting your mother, we might always have to sneak off to Pemberley in secret."

Despite the promise of a spectacle – Mama paying deference to William and Elizabeth – I could not feel enthusiasm for a trip to London. I could not feel enthusiasm for anything, only deepening despondency as the wedding day grew closer.

Mr. Essex had all but given up on me, I had decided because of how he stayed away so long. That should have pleased or at least relieved me, but it did not.

Poor John, though. He could not turn a blind eye to my continued decline, like my mother seemed able to do. He could not escape my circle of misery, like Mr. Essex. He was forced to stay and watch as my spirits sank lower and lower until he had finally seen enough.

"This must stop, Anne," he told me when we drove away after depositing Mama on the Darcys' doorstep in town that Friday.

"What do you mean, John?" I asked, although I actually had a pretty good idea.

His tone was firm, determined but not unkind. "We cannot go on like this. I refuse to stand by and watch your health – your very life! – slipping away day by day. You need not say anything now. However, I am putting you on notice. Tonight, when we get home to Rosings, I expect you to tell me what the trouble is. In fact, I will insist on it!"

"But, John…" I feebly objected.

"No, Anne. I will not hear any excuses. I will soon be your husband, and you *will* obey me in this."

Though he was a military officer, in friendly society I was accustomed to John joking and cajoling, not commanding. In truth, I had never heard him use such language and such a dictatorial tone before, certainly not with me. He did so now only reluctantly, I perceived. He was not angry; he was afraid for me. He was afraid for *us*. I could not fault him for that.

I was glad to see my cousins and Elizabeth again when we returned to Berkeley Street to rejoin Mama, although we did not stay long. Elizabeth had arranged for some refreshments, of which I could eat very little. I spoke very little, too, other than to once give John a mild reproach for teasing Georgiana.

Mama talked enough for everybody, though. It seemed whatever had transpired before John and I arrived had successfully carried away the remainder of her reserves. The period of estrangement was forgotten, and she was back to behaving towards the three Darcys nearly the same as she had been used to doing before the trouble began. Although sitting in another woman's house, Mama presided like a queen, and it seemed as if everybody else had the manners to overlook her presumption.

All through the day – ever since hearing John's ultimatum – I had been preoccupied, and I really was quite fatigued when we at last arrived home to Rosings that evening. Nevertheless, I knew I still had to face John's questions.

It seemed I had three choices for what to say to him. First, I could continue denying there was anything the matter. John would not believe me, but he could hardy force me to speak either. Still, defying his reasonable request for information seemed an inauspicious way to approach marriage, especially when we had expressly agreed at the outset that our best hope of success was to be open and honest with each other. It occurred to me that I could invent a falsehood to explain my despondency. There were two insurmountable problems with this idea, however. I had been unable to think of an even remotely convincing story and, as before, I would be violating my pledge of honesty.

That left only one option: confess the truth. This seemed as impossible as the others. I hated to admit what a fool I had been; worse still was the thought of hurting John.

~~*~~

Mama retired directly, leaving us to ourselves. Taking me by the hand, John led me to the little parlor that had been the scene of so many of our frank discussions. Once he had closed the door, he did not even have to repeat his earlier question. I was by this time so weary, so tired of bearing my weight of guilt and wretchedness alone, that I began unburdening myself before we could sit down.

"Oh, John!" I cried. "I have done the most despicable thing to you! I have treated you so very ill!"

He came to me immediately, pulling me into a comforting embrace and saying, "There, now, Anne. I doubt that very much. Come. Let us sit down over here, and you can tell me all about it. Nothing can be so bad as you make out."

"But it is, John! I shall not blame you if you despise me forever. I despise myself for not being able to get the better of the thing in all this time."

"Whatever it is, I promise not to despise you. Now, out with it."

And so I told him. Along with an ocean of tears, I poured out my guilty secret before him. I told him that I did not love him, and worse still, that I might never learn to love him because of my obstinate attachment to a different man.

"I suppose it is Mr. Essex," John said gravely.

I nodded as another sob erupted from my throat, already raw from what had gone before.

John got to his feet and strode across the room and back, head down and arms clasped behind his back. "I have observed the two of you together, of course, noting that there was some undeniable bond between you. I thought it was simply friendship and your gratitude over what he had done toward restoring your health."

"Yes. So it began. I intended that it should amount to nothing more. When I thought the affection was only on my side and entirely impossible, I believed it would fade away in time."

He looked at me intently. "But now you do not think so; now you no longer believe the idea impossible?"

"No! I still believe that! My promise to you and most especially Mama's disapproval… You can imagine what she would do."

"What has changed, then?"

I dropped my eyes and my voice. "I no longer think the attachment one-sided."

"Oh, I see." John took another circuit about the room before continuing. "Has Mr. Essex actually spoken to you, then?"

I nodded again. "A few weeks ago." I hurried on. "You must not think ill of him, John. I beg you would not. He saw how unhappy I was and thought I should know all the facts before it had become too late, in case I should wish to reconsider…" I trailed off self-consciously.

"Reconsider marrying me and marry him instead, I suppose."

"Yes, but I told him very firmly that I would not listen to him. You must believe me, John! I said I intended to abide by my engagement, and I gave him no reason to hope I would change my mind. We have not spoken of it since, I swear."

"An honorable response. Yes, a very honorable response." He sighed, concluding heavily, "And yet you are miserable."

I could not deny it. I dropped my head into my hands and sat quietly weeping, awaiting whatever John would say.

It was five more minutes before he gave up his pacing and returned to me. Sitting down beside me, he said, "Look at me, Anne."

I obeyed, turning to face him and whatever judgment he would deliver.

"That's better. Now listen carefully. First, let me assure you that I do not despise you… and not even Mr. Essex, although perhaps I should. I know that neither one of you set out to land us in this muddle. And I believe you when you say you intended to honor your commitment to me. What is to be done about it, though? That is the question. Now, tell me this. Would you marry Mr. Essex if you were free to do so?"

"Oh, John," I said with a different kind of tears in my eyes. "You are too good."

"Never mind all that," he said with a dismissive wave of his hand. "Answer my question. Would you marry Mr. Essex if you were free?"

For one brief moment, I allowed myself that flight of fancy. I imagined Mr. Essex and I were man and wife, joined forever by fervent love and by the authority of the Church of England. From there, it was an easy leap to all the rest. My enlivened mind pleasantly embellishing the picture with every detail required for connubial bliss.

Then it all came crashing back to earth again.

"How could I, John? Insurmountable obstacles remain. Mama would surely put a stop to it. Or if she could not, she would disown me. Then there is the problem of Mr. Essex's lack of financial competency. If Mama cut me off, what on earth should we live on? Besides he probably hates me now."

Presently, John stood up again and pulled me to my feet as well. Returning to his usual cheerful manner, he said, "Go to bed and rest well, my dear. Leave this situation entirely in my hands. Tomorrow, you and I are going up to London."

- 62 -

Mrs. Jenkinson

Noticing a Change in the Air

Something was different. I cannot rightly say what, but there was a change in the air, especially as concerned Anne. I first noticed it when she finally came up to her rooms on Friday night. I knew she was tired – what with their visit to the Darcys and the travel home – and I could swear by her blotchy red face that she had been crying. And yet there was that spark of life back in her eye, the one that had been sadly missing for weeks.

"Will you take some tea?" I asked her. These days, I never knew if she would or not, she had grown so remiss in following her health regiment and resistant to my attempts to enforce it.

"Essex tea? Yes, please," she said with conviction. "And then I am off to bed. I must get my rest because Colonel Fitzwilliam is taking me up to London in the morning."

"But you only returned from there two hours ago!"

"I know. This time it will be just the two of us… on a secret errand." Her eyes grew wide as she said this.

"A secret errand? My, my."

"Someday, I hope to tell you about it, dear Mrs. Jenkinson. But not now. I will just ask you to pray that all goes well tomorrow. I have a feeling my entire future depends on what transpires then."

So pray I did! The wedding was only a week away now, and I prayed all would transpire as intended.

I could feel an undercurrent of excitement between Anne and Colonel Fitzwilliam at the breakfast table the next morning. Then the colonel spoke up. "Lady Catherine, your daughter and I are bound for town today."

I daresay her surprise was as great as mine had been the night before. "Going to town again?" she asked, sounding quite incredulous. "How absurd. Fitzwilliam, what are you about – some kind of fool's errand?"

"I assure you it is not a fool's errand, Madam. Just a little outing of pleasure. And surely you can spare us. We can take Mrs. Jenkinson with us, though, if you think we require a chaperone. Mrs. Jenkinson?"

"Yes," I said, hoping to be included in this mysterious mission. "I would be happy to go. Why, I can be ready in five minutes."

Lady Catherine rendered her ruling. "No, Mrs. Jenkinson, you are not needed. You may stay here. What I question, Fitzwilliam, is your dragging my daughter out on the road again. Travel is so fatiguing, and it seems to me she is not looking quite as well as she used to."

"But I am not the least bit tired, Mama. I slept very well last night, and I feel quite rested and refreshed. Besides, I want to go."

"The truth is, Aunt, I wish to get Anne a little wedding present."

"Oh, John!" said Anne. "How lovely."

I thought so too.

"It should have been a surprise, my dear," he continued. "I freely admit it. But I would not have your mother needlessly worrying. And in truth, I want you to have the chance to pick something out for yourself. Whatever you like. My taste is very questionable, especially when it comes to finery."

With this explanation, Lady Catherine gave her blessing.

I was not so easily satisfied, however. I could not imagine how my young lady's "entire future" could depend on an errand just to choose a present.

When she returned that night, I asked if I she would show me what Colonel Fitzwilliam had bought as her present.

"My present?" she asked as if she could not at first understand what I meant. "Oh, yes, my present. But I mean no; I may not show it to you, Mrs. Jenkinson. I am to forget I ever saw it myself! The colonel means to wrap it up and give it to me after we are married. It is a wedding present, after all."

"Yes, of course."

I was quite sure there was much more to the story. However, I hardly cared. What mattered to me at that moment was the mischievous smile I saw flitting across my young mistress's lips, the lightness of her spirit as she prepared for bed – she was actually humming! – and the heartiness of her appetite the next morning. Whatever the errand to London had entailed, I was simply grateful for its beneficial effects.

- 63 -

Lady Catherine

On Plans Coming to Fruition

It was only a few days until all my plans would come to fruition.

However frivolous it seemed that the young people had wanted to run off to London again, I could not help being pleased about Fitzwilliam's devotion and Anne's enthusiasm. I had been waiting and waiting for my daughter to show some sign of joy over their upcoming nuptials, some acknowledgement of her good fortune, and some proper gratitude for my arranging it all. Now at last she seemed appropriately cheerful.

As it turned out, we were to have some company before the big event. A message from Darcy came on Sunday saying that the three of them had decided to drive down to Rosings the next day after all, which I was gratified to hear. Then later, another message arrived, this one from Mr. Essex. After quite a lengthy absence, he was coming on Monday as well. With Mrs. Jenkinson, we would be eight: enough for a stately dinner party.

I considered that I could make it ten if I invited the Chesterfields over from the parsonage. But then I quickly discarded the idea. I still could not always depend on them for their support; I could not count on their opinions always falling into line behind mine, as they should. Occasionally (and quite surprisingly), I still found myself missing Mr. Collins and his wife in this regard.

Staying with the original eight, my mind set to work designing the menu for the occasion, planning where each one should sit, how I would conduct the meal and entertainments. The Darcys would witness the fact that Rosings and I went on just as before. Mrs. Darcy would see how a real lady of good breeding organized a fine dinner and showed her guests an enjoyable evening. If the Darcys knew how to live well, I knew how to live better.

I looked forward to hearing Georgiana play, which never failed to put me in mind of my sister's musical gifts. Now, with two more years of instruction and practice, I reasoned my niece must be very accomplished indeed. I supposed I would have to put up with Elizabeth singing as well – her husband had seemed determined to put her forward – but that could not be helped.

Oddly enough, Fitzwilliam began to laugh when he heard what company we were to expect. "Darcy coming Monday as well?" he exclaimed. "And Elizabeth and Georgiana? Oh, what fun! Do you hear that, Anne? We never thought to be so lucky, did we?"

"It is good news, I suppose," said Anne in some confusion.

"Good news? It is the best! I can think of nothing finer. How fortuitous they should happen to come the same day as Mr. Essex. Why, Mrs. Darcy had just expressed on Friday her interest in meeting the good doctor, and now her wish will be granted Monday. Yes, I call that highly fortuitous."

Although I could not understand what Fitzwilliam was on about, I thought it a good sign that he was prepared to set the tone for a convivial evening. We would show our guests the happiness of our circumstances and the superiority of our hospitality.

- 64 -

Anne

Taking a Stand

I felt as if something far larger than myself had been set into inexorable motion, like the wheels of a heavy carriage rolling downhill. It only remained to be seen if I would be run over in the street by that carriage or taken to the place in the world I most wanted to go. Those were the only two outcomes I could envision: complete happiness or utter ruin. There could be no middle ground. There could be no going back.

With so much at stake, I could not help being on edge when the Darcys arrived in the middle of the day. I knew Mr. Essex would not be along until later, and so there might still be hours of suspense to be got through first.

Mrs. Jenkinson and I took our customary places in the drawing room, and the others filled out the circle with Mama sitting in the most prominent position in her high-backed chair, prepared to preside over the conversation.

"How was your drive from town, Darcy?" she asked after everyone was settled.

"Quite tolerable. The roads were dry," he answered.

"I understand that you brought Mrs. Collins with you from Derbyshire."

"Yes, your ladyship," said Elizabeth. "She was good enough to accompany us as far as Hertfordshire. She is visiting her family there and will come into London on Thursday so that she may drive down with us for the wedding on Friday."

"It was very charitable of you to convey her so far," continued Mama. "I doubt that she could have afforded such a journey otherwise, with her modest resources. I shall be glad to see her again. She and Mr. Collins always suited me so much better than the *new* rector and his wife. I find Mr. and Mrs. Chesterfield entirely too independent for persons in their situation. Why, only last week I discovered that they have made changes to the parsonage – removing shelves from the closets and rearranging the furniture – all without my permission. And Mrs. Chesterfield has recklessly converted some of the garden from the growing of vegetables to the purpose of raising flowers! I would have been glad to advise her against such foolishness if she had had the courtesy to consult me, but neither of them can be troubled to call at Rosings above once a week. I am quite put out by the way Mr. Chesterfield neglects his duty."

"He is still new to the position, Aunt. Perhaps he does not yet understand what is expected of him and of his wife," suggested John.

"How does Mr. Chesterfield do at his other responsibilities?" asked Elizabeth. "Does he have more aptitude for preaching than he does for obeisance, perhaps?"

"I suppose he does," Mama conceded. "I have no complaint against his sermons. They always seem correct and well-considered."

"He also spends a great deal of time visiting the poor and infirmed," I said in the clergyman's defense. "I have heard good reports of that sort from many people in the parish, and Mr. Essex says that he often encounters Mr. Chesterfield as he makes his rounds among the sick."

"From what you say, Anne, I am inclined to think well of the man," said Cousin William, "despite his shortcomings," he added dryly.

"He sounds a lot like our good Mr. Thornton," said Georgiana.

With that line of conversation not going her way, Mama tried another. "Mrs. Darcy, when I saw you lately in London, you expressed an interest in making the acquaintance of Mr. Essex. I am pleased to say that he will be returning from town this very day. He sent word that we should expect him by dinner if not before. So, you may have the pleasure of meeting him after all … *if* you would care to stay."

"Yes, do stay," John encouraged, amusement in his eye. "It will certainly be worth your while."

This, the Darcys consented to do. So it was then quite definite; whatever followed – triumph or annihilation – there would be witnesses. Unlike John, I could not yet be convinced of that being a good thing.

When the conversation flagged, Mama called for some music. Elizabeth and Georgiana, apparently prepared for the request, passed through the wide archway to the instrument in the adjoining room. Georgiana took her place at the piano-forte directly, and Elizabeth stood beside it to sing.

They began with a piece I recognized as *Voi Che Sapete* from *The Marriage of Figaro* by Mozart. I was enjoying it very much (as were the others, I daresay) until Mama, quite rudely, began speaking to poor Mrs. Jenkinson about something or other that could no doubt have waited for another time.

John left the drawing room circle first, moving into the music room with the excuse of needing to turn pages for Georgiana. William went next, and I dared to follow in his wake. The two of us took seats there, where we could hear the performers better.

Despite her continued inattentiveness throughout the three songs that followed, Mama apparently felt fully capable of rendering an authoritative judgment as to the quality of the performances. She generously praised Georgiana's playing. But for Elizabeth, her compliments were more tempered.

"As for your singing, Mrs. Darcy, I must allow that it is not altogether lacking in value. I would go so far as to say that you possess a fine, natural voice. Clearly, though, that potential was never properly developed. Use of the voice is like the playing of any other instrument. One must be continuously schooled in it from an early age under the guidance of an expert. No true excellence can reasonably be looked for otherwise. Your parents should have engaged a master for you. Then, with faithful practice, you might have been a true proficient instead of merely adequate."

After hearing this speech, William abruptly stood and declared, "Well, I for one enjoyed the music immensely. Now, however, I could really use some fresh air. Elizabeth, Georgiana, will you join me for a turn in the garden? It begins to feel a bit close in here."

John said, "I agree. Come along, Anne. You look like you could do with some exercise. Your physician is coming later," he added with a wink, "and I know you want to be able to give him a good report."

"Yes, certainly I will come," I agreed.

Mrs. Jenkinson took this as her cue. "You must all excuse me now. Lady Catherine, my apologies, but I cannot join you for dinner after all. I will just have a little something sent up to my room, for I really have the most frightful headache."

"I hope not, Mrs. Jenkinson. You will put my table quite out!" Mama said in a huff.

"Once again, please forgive me, your ladyship. Goodnight to you all."

While Mrs. Jenkinson made good her escape, the five of us of the younger generation quickly took to the out of doors where we strolled through the formal gardens at the front of the house. No one appeared in any hurry to return to the confines of the drawing room.

Soon I heard the unmistakable sound of an approaching carriage of some kind. Looking up, I said, "It is Mr. Essex. He is come." My heart fluttered at the sight.

Mr. Essex pulled his gig to a halt nearby. Climbing down, he came towards us with long strides, smiling.

John performed the necessary introductions, and then William said, "You are a miracle worker, sir. I have long wished to make the acquaintance of the man responsible for my cousin's transformation."

"I was only too glad to help. I am sure my predecessors did their best, but it is high time medicine advanced beyond the dark ages. Patients like your cousin, Mr. Darcy, deserve all the benefits modern science has to offer." Mr. Essex then turned his attention to me. "I hope you are feeling especially well and strong on this *particular* day, Miss de Bourgh."

"I am well," I said. "Whether I am *strong* enough or not, we shall soon discover, shan't we? But, now you are come, I feel up to any challenge."

"And you have a surprising number of companions here to lend you their support," he encouraged.

"Aye. They are loyal friends, and I am grateful to have them with me, especially today."

No doubt this exchange raised a certain curiosity among my fellows, as did perhaps the fact that John handed me off to Mr. Essex and offered his arm to Georgiana instead. But I did not care. All would be explained soon enough.

"Well now," John said decisively. "Shall we all go in? Dinner will be a memorable experience; I think I can promise you that."

~~*~~

The dinner looked very fine indeed, although I barely tasted it. I was far too nervous to eat. I was waiting for the right moment to set our plans into motion. I was waiting for Mama to take an intermission from talking long enough for me to find my courage and my voice. When she stopped to sample the roasted pheasant, I saw my chance. Mr. Essex gave me an encouraging nod from across the table, and then I did not hesitate.

"Mama," I said as boldly and confidently as I could. "I have something important to tell you."

Mama looked up immediately, detecting a threat from an unusual quarter. She stared suspiciously at me through narrowed eyes. Then, in her well practiced tone of intimidation, she asked, "What did you say, Anne?"

I cringed out of habit, but I had been prepared for this, and it only stumbled me for a moment. Then I set my jaw, stood, faced my mother, and repeated my declaration with even more resolve. "I said I have something important to tell you."

"Anne, where are your manners? Sit down at once and hold your peace!" Mama insisted. "We have guests, and I will not have our dinner disrupted."

The weak and sickly Anne de Bourgh might have felt unable to resist her mother's force of will. Even a few days before, that sad young lady might have meekly complied. But I was not entirely helpless anymore. Thanks to Mr. Essex and to John, I had found my strength again. I had started to believe I had a future worth living, and that I could take an active part in deciding what that future would be.

"If I have your full attention now, Mama," I said, "I *will* sit down. But I am quite determined to have my say; I will not be put off. As for our guests, there is no reason they may not hear; it will be common knowledge soon enough anyway."

"Good heavens, child! What *are* you about?" With unpleasantness now clearly inescapable, Mama dismissed the servants with a wave of her hand.

Emulating the proud pose I had seen my mother use so often, I slowly sat down, my back ramrod straight and my head held very high. A hushed anticipation stole over the company. Every eye was on me, including Mama's. I enjoyed that moment, feeling for once in my life that *I* was in control. I also savored it as the calm before the storm. I knew that my next words would turn everything upside down. I could not worry about that, though. There would be occasion to deal with the disarray later. It was time to say what must be said – simply, calmly, but with unwavering assurance.

"There has been a change of plans, Mama. I have broken off my engagement to Colonel Fitzwilliam and consented to marry Mr. Essex instead." That done, I smiled and reached across the table to take my beloved's offered hand.

- 65 -

Lady Catherine

On Discovering Duplicity

The force of the blow momentarily staggered me and deprived me of the power of speech. I was not the only one horrified, I am sure. I heard gasps and then stunned silence. When I had sufficiently recovered, I declared the obvious truth in my most commanding voice. "What utter nonsense! Why, the very idea is scandalous; every feeling revolts. Mr. Essex, unhand my daughter this instant! Anne, apologize to Colonel Fitzwilliam and our guests, and never speak another word about this madness again. Do you hear me?"

This should have been the end of it, but I regret to say that Anne failed to repent. She failed to respond to my justified censure. In fact, she remained inexplicably calm, saying, "I hear you clearly enough, Mama, but I have not the smallest intention of yielding. I am of age, so there is nothing you can do to prevent me from marrying whomsoever I choose." Then there was some nonsense about when and how and a license before she concluded. This part I remember very precisely, though. She said, "I *shall* marry the man I love, Mama. Anything else, I now realize, would be impossibly perverse."

"Well said, my dear," uttered Mr. Essex.

In the cold light of total detachment, I myself might have agreed with him. I might have been able to admire Anne's demonstration of a strength of will not unlike my own. However, this was a most inappropriate manner and a most inopportune moment for my daughter to suddenly develop a backbone. I cursed under my breath and looked about the table for an ally, but nobody seemed prepared to come to my aid. Then I remembered the one person who must be on my side.

"Fitzwilliam, do something!" I ordered. "You are the injured party here. Can you not make my daughter see reason?"

Instead of looking correctly outraged at what was taking place, I could almost swear he was enjoying himself.

"I fear it is a hopeless business, your ladyship," he said lightly. "She is determined to have her own way, and I am quite convinced that neither you nor I will be able to change her mind. You are correct about one thing, however. I am indeed the injured party, and, as such, I am entitled by law to compensation for my loss."

It grew worse and worse. In disbelief, I cried, "Heaven and earth, Fitzwilliam! You would not bring a legal action against us, surely."

Now his manner turned very serious indeed. "Lady Catherine," he said, "let us *both* carefully consider how we are to react to this surprising development. For my part, I am convinced that if you can find the charity to accept Anne's choice, I will be persuaded by your good example to likewise forgive the offense without prejudice."

So that was his game, and skillfully played too. "I see," I said sharply, apprehending the implication of the colonel's veiled threat. There would be no help for me from him, clearly. On the contrary, Fitzwilliam appeared to be in league with the others to thwart me at every turn. I was the victim of duplicity on every side.

"Well, now," said Fitzwilliam, getting up from his chair. "I believe there is nothing more for me to say on the subject, so I will leave the three of you principally involved to work out the details. Darcy, Elizabeth, Georgiana – I suggest that we diplomatically withdraw."

I had not the strength or inclination to object, and so they went, leaving me alone with Anne and her professed lover, the ungrateful doctor.

"*This* is how you repay me for all my kindness and hospitality?" I accused him. "You steal my daughter right out from under my nose! I suppose that was your plan all along. You could not resist the money. Well, let me tell you, sir; you shall never get your hands on a single penny! I would rather see my daughter living in poverty than to give you the satisfaction of taking control of her fortune."

"I do not want your daughter's fortune, Lady Catherine," claimed Mr. Essex. Anne had come round the table to sit by him – no doubt so they could flaunt their distasteful affection in front of my face with more convenience. "It is she herself that I treasure. And there was no premeditation involved, I assure you. I did not plan to fall in love with Anne, much less did I have any idea that she could care for me."

"It is true, Mama. Neither of us planned this, and we both resisted the idea as long as we could, in part because we knew it would displease you. But there is danger marrying in one place when heart and passion are pulling one elsewhere. Would not you agree?"

What did she know of such things? Was it a general statement, simply meant to support her current position? Surely, it could be nothing more. Nevertheless, there was some truth in what she said, as I had learnt from bitter experience with her father.

"Besides, Mama," Anne continued, "this match is more eligible than you might think. Mr. Essex has lately told me more about his situation and family. He may not be as well connected as Colonel Fitzwilliam, it is true, but it is not an association you need be ashamed of either. And as to fortune, you must admit that Fitzwilliam has little enough himself."

"Lady Catherine, as I have told you before," said Mr. Essex, "my father truly is a gentleman – a baronet, in fact. And although, I am the second son, I have a little money of my own, as well as some significant expectations from an uncle. All these things your solicitor can verify, as has Colonel Fitzwilliam already. In short, I am well able to keep myself and your daughter in respectability, even without her money."

Glaring back at him, I then played my trump card. "I could disinherit her for this, you know. The de Bourgh fortune is still in *my* hands, and no one would blame me for punishing a disobedient daughter."

"But there would be much talk if you did, Mama," Anne said. "Perhaps even a nasty scandal. You know how people delight in seeing a noble family torn down. And John would not take such a move on your part kindly. He has been a darling about this whole affair and very protective of me. I would not put it past him to retaliate with a suit if you decide to be vindictive. I am sorry, Mama, but that is the truth of the matter."

Scandal? Lawsuit? It would only increase my misery. I was suddenly extremely weary, and it seemed the fight had drained right out of me. I sighed deeply, and without meaning to, I murmured, "Then what is to be done?"

They had come prepared with a well considered plan, I soon discovered, and with ready answers for all my questions and objections. Everything was to be managed as quietly and tastefully as possible. The originally intended wedding was to be cancelled at once, and then another circumspectly planned. Rather than Hunsford church again, it was determined that a new location might be more discreet. And it seemed Mr. Essex had in fact already acquired a license in London. It would be a small affair – just family and a few close friends.

Anne explained, "Mr. Essex means to make no difficulty about the marriage settlement – whatever your solicitors draw up. And then after the wedding, we will probably want to divide our time between Rosings and London… if that is acceptable to you, Mama. Otherwise, if you want to be rid of us altogether, we can stay at his house in town. I have seen it, and it is perfectly respectable."

"What! Are you now in the habit of visiting men's houses unchaperoned? This is not how I raised you, Anne!"

"I was not unchaperoned; Cousin John was there. That was our true errand in London on Saturday. We called on Mr. Essex, and soon all was settled."

"It seems you have thought of everything," I said miserably.

I do not recall agreeing to the litany of particulars laid before me at the time by my daughter and future son-in-law, but I suppose I must have. I was still in control of my faculties enough to see I had little choice in the matter. Anne clearly meant to go ahead with her plans, with or without my consent. My threat to disown her made no difference.

I had to acknowledge – to myself at least – that *that* drastic measure was an empty threat. It would be cutting off my nose to spite my own face. If I had learnt one thing from the painful estrangement from Darcy, it was that I valued the company of my closest family members more than I cared to admit. I would not give up my only child, even if she had most inconveniently turned out to have a mind of her own.

- 66 -

Anne

On Finding One's Happiness

Mr. Essex and I, now arm in arm and aglow, rejoined the others, who were standing in the drawing room in a nervous huddle awaiting the outcome of the dining room conference. "Mama has gone to bed with a sick headache," I told them.

"That, I can well believe!" said Cousin John. "But what did she say before that, if you do not mind my asking? How were things left between you?"

I could not stop smiling. "She has agreed to everything, at least in principle."

"Yes," said Mr. Essex. "It was touch and go there for a while, but she eventually came round. Anne and I are to be married as quickly and quietly as possible in London."

"Mama says we may return here to live if we wish, although I believe we will want a place of our own before long. Hiram has great ambitions as to his career," I announced proudly, using my intended's Christian name aloud for the first time. "It would be far too limiting for his future prospects to be confined to Rosings Park."

Hiram smiled down at me. "Dear Anne, my greatest wish has already been granted; my greatest ambition is soon to be realized. I can ask for nothing more. My career may take care of itself."

Just then, I saw through the drawing room's open doors two footmen carrying a large trunk, which I thought I recognized.

"What is this, John," I asked.

"Darcy has called for his carriage, and I am going as well, I am afraid. After the part I played in this afternoon's insurrection, my face will be the last Lady Catherine wants to see across the breakfast table tomorrow morning. And so I must take my leave of you for now, but, fortunately, not without first having seen your victory secured. My heartiest congratulations to you both." He shook Mr. Essex's hand and kissed my cheek.

More congratulations followed from William, Elizabeth, and Georgiana, as well as their promises to attend the wedding.

My heart overflowed with goodwill and gratitude for them all, but especially for John. He was about to climb into his carriage when I stopped him by laying a hand on his arm. I wanted to explain my great affection for him. I wanted to expound on my appreciation for all he had done to secure my happiness. But I could find no words. "Fitzwilliam, what can I say? I am forever in your debt."

"Nonsense!" he exclaimed. "Glad to be of service, my dear. My reward is seeing you made so happy. And I suppose I must confess some small satisfaction in beholding my aunt's rather remarkable countenance this day as well. Should I live to be a hundred, I doubt I will ever forget that extraordinary sight!"

In another few minutes, they were all gone, leaving me and Mr. Essex alone. We had been alone together many times, of course, but never before as acknowledged lovers, as a newly engaged couple. We stood there on the front porch for a long time, only a few inches apart, just looking at each other. I was trying to take in the fact that this was real, not one of my wild imaginings, though it seemed just as improbable.

It astounded me how much had changed in so short a time. Only three days before, I had been excessively downcast, thinking Mr. Essex, away in London, had been lost to me forever. Now here he was with me at Rosings again, my betrothed, gazing into my eyes with undisguised love and admiration, all obstacles to our future happiness suddenly removed. I was ecstatic but slightly bemused at finding myself in uncharted waters.

"What do we do now?" I asked at last.

Hiram laughed. "Do you mean this minute or for the rest of our lives?"

"Both, I suppose. So much led up to today's events, and now that we have achieved our goal, I feel a little up in the air, at loose ends."

"Very well, then. I suggest we start by not worrying about the rest of our lives just yet. As for the here and now, let us put your feet back on solid ground – quite literally – by reenacting the familiar." He continued with a playful air. "Miss de Bourgh, will you walk with me? There is plenty of daylight still, and outdoor exercise is highly beneficial to your health, you know."

Catching the spirit of his banter, I responded in kind. "Yes, I do know. My physician always tells me so. Which way would you like to go, Mr. Essex? We have many fine walks and lanes roundabout. Do you prefer the orchard, the rose garden, the shrubbery, or the groves?"

"Oh, the orchard, most definitely. There is a certain bench there, I believe, conveniently placed for a fine prospect of the park. It is a destination I am quite partial to."

"As you say, there is a bench with a fine prospect. I would not have thought your memories of it would be quite so fond, however. Are you sure it is a place you care to revisit?"

"Ah, I understand what you mean, Miss de Bourgh, but that is precisely why I wish us to return. You see, I intend to rectify the situation by making a different ending. Do you think I shall be successful? When you are seated on that bench tonight, and I tell you once again that I love you, do you think I will receive a more favorable response?"

"I believe so, Mr. Essex. In fact, I think I can promise that I will not run away this time."

"Excellent! I am very glad to hear it, for if you will stay a minute, I have a feeling I should very much like to kiss you on that spot."

"Which spot do you mean? On the orchard bench?"

"No, I think I should much prefer to kiss you on *this* spot," he said, placing the tip of his finger on my lips. But then, he could not wait; he kissed me for the first time where we stood – a light and teasing kiss. "Now, shall we make for the orchard?" he asked afterward.

"Oh, yes, Mr. Essex," I said eagerly, "with all possible haste."

Once there, we replayed the scene that had gone awry before. This time when he told me he loved me, I told him his affection was returned in full measure. Then he kissed me again as promised – a thorough kiss, pulling me up into his arms and lifting me off the ground. I discovered that this kind of 'up in the air' I quite liked.

Sometime later – much later, in fact – I said reluctantly, "I should go in now, Hiram. I promised Mrs. Jenkinson I would finally tell her everything tonight. I do hope she will not be too disappointed. I believe she was nearly as set on my marrying Colonel Fitzwilliam as was Mama."

"Oh, I shouldn't worry," he said confidently. "Something tells me she will not much mind the change. She only wants to see you happy, you know. Who do you think it was that encouraged me to reveal my heart to you in the first place?"

- 67 -

Mrs. Jenkinson

Witnessing a Wedding

"Oh, Mrs. Jenkinson!" Anne exclaimed when she burst into my room. "I am so happy, and I find it is all due to you! When Mr. Essex told me, I had to come to you at once."

Nothing could have been more gratifying – witnessing her joyful countenance and knowing I had played a part in achieving it. "Everything went well, then?" I asked, although I could clearly see that it had.

She started at the beginning, filling in every piece of the puzzle I did not already know: how Colonel Fitzwilliam had finally coerced a confession from her; how he then generously released her from their engagement; how it was also he who had designed the plan for breaking down Lady Catherine's resistance; how they had gone to see Mr. Essex in town to confirm his constancy, his solvency, and be assured of his cooperation; and finally how the scene had played out at the dinner table, from which she had asked me to absent myself.

"We are to be married just as soon as it can be arranged!" she concluded. "But what I do not understand is your part, Mrs. Jenkinson. I thought you were violently opposed to my attachment to Mr. Essex, wanting me to marry Colonel Fitzwilliam as Mama arranged that I should. How is it that you came to change your mind?"

"I hardly understand it myself, Miss. I admit at first I saw in Mr. Essex a picture of my late Mr. Jenkinson – handsome and charming but not a practical choice for a husband – and I worried for your future if you should marry such a man and end like me. But then I could not bear to see you so unhappy… and him too – Mr. Essex, I mean – for I truly have always liked him. There you were pining for him and him pining for you, each one unbeknownst to the other.

"Well, I finally decided it was not my place to keep the two of you apart. It was not fair to impose my history on anybody else. It should be up to you to write your own story, make your own choices. I at least wanted you to know there *was* a choice. So I encouraged Mr. Essex to speak up before it became absolutely too late. I hope I did the right thing."

Anne touched my arm. "Dear Mrs. Jenkinson, I plan to show you years and years of positive proof that you did."

"I fear there will be a terrible price to pay with your mother, Miss Anne. If she ever learns I had a hand in this…"

"Never! I shall never tell her and neither shall Mr. Essex. In any case, I intend that it will soon be *I* who provides your living, and then you will have nothing left to fear from Mama."

She had remembered her earlier promise to me. Even in the midst of her excitement, she suggested again that she intended to keep me with her always. That is what I wanted more than anything else in the world, whether it meant staying at Rosings Park, living in town, or moving to Lincolnshire, where Mr. Essex's family made its home. I would have no grandchildren of my own, but I should take it as a great consolation to count myself an honorary grandmother to Anne's offspring – to see her made a mother with sons and daughters growing up about her.

Perhaps I was wrong when I had thought it impossible that I could ever be any kind of true family to her. After all, I had also once thought it impossible that she could marry Mr. Essex.

~~*~~

I had the privilege of helping Anne dress for her wedding less than a fortnight later in London.

"How are your nerves this morning?" I asked her as I made a few final adjustments to her hair and her veil.

"They are as jumpy as hailstones dancing on a slate roof! I think I may swoon, Mrs. Jenkinson. How does any woman get through it?"

"Breath deeply," I recommended. "And keep your eyes on Mr. Essex. That faithful compass will see you right."

I gave my advice confidently enough, but I was not sure I could follow it myself. For days I had only just been able to keep sentimental tears at bay. Now that the climactic moment was upon us, I wondered how I would get through it without completely breaking down.

At the church, I sent the bride up the aisle on Mr. Darcy's arm before I slipped into one of the back pews, pulled out my handkerchief, and prepared to witness the scene through watery eyes. With plenty of life and color back in her complexion now, Anne looked truly beautiful in her pale, silvery-gray gown (the one she originally intended to wear for Colonel Fitzwilliam). The color looked much more becoming draping her willowy form than it did on her mother, whose skin was a remarkably similar shade of gray, I noticed.

I could pity Lady Catherine… at least a bit. However cold and dictatorial her manner, however unreasonably harsh her demands, I felt sure that somewhere, deep down, she did love her daughter and wanted what *she* believed best for her. After all her extraordinary efforts to secure a brilliant match for Anne, this must have been a dark day for her, the final outcome a bitter pill for her to swallow. She sat at the front, posture rigid and unsmiling, as if stoically enduring the unjust punishment of twenty lashes.

Anne only had eyes for Mr. Essex, I observed. I must say he made quite a dashing figure, his wedding clothes setting off his fine, tall frame to advantage. Miss Georgiana, in her assigned role as bridesmaid, stood up beside Anne. And I could see Mrs. Darcy sitting with Colonel Fitzwilliam a few rows back. Of the others gathered, some I recognized and some I did not. It was not a large crowd by any means. The guest list had been deliberately limited due to the last-minute change of plans. I believe it was decided that the fewer people making comments on the switch from one groom to another, the better.

I certainly saw nothing scandalous in the proceedings myself. Anne did not swoon as she had feared. Mr. Essex played his part so well that no one unacquainted with the facts would have guessed he was not the man originally cast in the role. And even Lady Catherine managed to make it through the ceremony without overtly demonstrating her displeasure or raising an objection at that part where the rector gives opportunity. She did look very unsteady when she attempted to rise at the end, however. Her two nephews quickly offered their support, but she rejected them both in favor of the arm of another distinguished but unidentified gentleman, whom I later learnt was a certain Count Deering – a particular friend of Lady Catherine's, apparently. He had the honor of escorting her ladyship from the church and to the place nearby where the wedding breakfast was held afterward.

From my seat at the back of the church, I had taken it all in, savoring the sights and sounds as treasures to tuck away and remember always, like the Virgin Mary who *kept all these things and pondered them in her heart.*

From my particular vantage point, I believe I also saw one thing nobody else did. I am probably the only one who noticed a second mystery man – a bearded gentleman, also somewhat past his prime. He slipped in across from me just as the ceremony began and slipped back out again as it was ending. He was there uninvited, I guessed, and yet something about him looked familiar. Unlike in Count Deering's case, however, it would be weeks before I learnt his identity.

- 68 -

Lady Catherine

Rising Above Disaster

The wedding was a severe trial, under the mortification of which I bore up with remarkable courage. When the rector asked the question if anybody could show just cause why the two before him should not be joined in holy matrimony, one may imagine how I felt. I could have recited chapter and verse on that subject. However, I did not. I held my tongue, quite literally biting it between my teeth lest it should get loose and have its way after all. Anne would never have forgiven me for that.

Knowing Count Deering was close at hand gave me strength. I kept him nearby at the wedding breakfast as well, where things were much more agreeable. I could not control the particulars at the wedding (at least not the most important element: the identity of the groom), but the breakfast was another matter. I made sure everything there was just so, and people told me that they had never seen such an affair done better. By the end of it, I felt quite revived.

With the passing of time, I have somewhat recovered from the initial blow of Anne's rebellion and her choice of husband. The newlyweds stayed the first week at his small house in town (although I had offered them the use of my much larger one), and then they journeyed into Lincolnshire to spend a month with his family. Now Anne has written to ask if it would be agreeable to me for them to return to Rosings Park for a time. I have generously granted my permission.

The house has seemed rather empty with them gone – and Mrs. Jenkinson too for the last four weeks, for Anne insisted on having that lady with her when she traveled north. It will be good to have my family all at home again, even Mr. Essex, I suppose. In truth, I always found him excellent company. If I can overcome my resentment against him – and with my indomitable will, I can do anything I set my mind to – then I may even learn to enjoy his companionship again.

For my own sake, I have put a good face on what has happened. When anybody asks, I say that I am very pleased with the match, and that the pair asked for and received my consent to marry. After all, I cannot have anybody thinking I was outmaneuvered by my own daughter.

It is not quite so bad as I had first thought. A son of a baronet is not a *complete* nobody, and if his elder brother should die... Well, these things do sometimes happen. In the meantime, I suppose Mr. Essex will keep occupied with his career, since unfortunately he seems to have no intention of giving it up. Although on the surface this appears a very challenging point, I admit, it really is a matter of how people can be persuaded to look at the thing. I had been used to believing that a gentleman taking up an occupation (anything other than the few accepted genteel professions) committed social suicide. But ideas change, helped along by forward thinkers like myself.

Mr. Essex is by no means a lowly apothecary; he is a university educated physician, a man of science and superior intelligence, a man on the forefront of progress. Yes, in the right hands, much can be made of that idea. And people who already know him seem to hold him in high esteem. His presence might not ultimately disgrace the family. In fact, with my guidance and patronage, he might go far indeed.

In any case, I am hardly beaten down to where I cannot rise again. Heaven forbid! Anne's marriage is not the end of the world. As I frequently remind myself, I fare far better than if it had been my son who married. At least I will not be required to make way for some upstart daughter-in-law, who would see me moved to the dower house even before her arrival. Rosings is still mine and will remain so as long as I live. For whatever duration Anne and Mr. Essex reside here, they will do so on *my* terms.

The same privileges of ownership apply to my house in town, where I can go any time I like. If my daughter and her new husband do not always go with me, so much the better, for then I will be free to consort with certain other especially interesting friends nearby, such as a certain count. Now that my time is my own, I intend to make the most of it.

- 69 -

Anne

On the Past and the Future

I still can hardly believe I am a married woman. But when I wake up to find the same half-naked man in bed beside me every morning, I begin to be convinced! Sometimes his eyes are open, looking at me with similar wonder to what I feel looking at him. Sometimes, especially after a night out late seeing a patient in crisis, he still slumbers. Then it is my treat to watch him unawares, to study the interesting contours of his face, to admire his manly beauty and marvel at my great good fortune that he is my husband.

And so I am becoming quite domestic, learning wifely duties and delights. Our living arrangements are still unsettled. For now, we live like vagabonds, dividing our time between London and Kent, since Hiram has medical clients in both places. Mrs. Jenkinson moves about with us wherever we go. She is indispensable to me in so many ways – practical, but primarily personal. And, since we have an instrument even in our small house in town, I am able to continue my lessons with her at the piano-forte. Hiram likes to hear me play, and I am quite proud of the progress I have made.

Whenever at Rosings, I still feel myself a child, an underling to Mama, even if she is not there. But at the smaller Essex house in town, I am mistress of the place. I organize things as I please. I direct the servants as *I* see fit. It has been a revelation to have some say in my own life and in my own home for a change. Were it not for the constant reminder of my domineering mother's bad example, I might need to guard against going mad with the power of it! As it is, there is no danger; I plan to be a very different sort of mistress, a very different sort of wife and mother.

My health has rebounded nicely, my recovery beginning as soon as the stress of fearing I would marry the wrong man was relieved. Not that John Fitzwilliam is a 'wrong' man; he just would have been the wrong husband for me. I like him much better as my cousin and dear friend, and I hope to see him also happily married one day soon. Having already heard rumors of a surprising new but fervent attachment, my guess is that event might not be very far off. This new attachment of his is one more confirmation that we did the right thing by not keeping to our engagement.

After the surprising events that led to my marrying Mr. Essex, I did not think it likely I should experience anything so unexpected again, not for a very long time at least. I was quite wrong, however. Three months after we were married, Hiram brought me a strange request while we were in London. "I have a patient I would like you to meet," he told me as we were preparing for bed one night.

Thinking it quite an odd thing for him to have said, I naturally asked him to explain.

"It might be more correct to say he wishes to meet you."

"He? What is the gentleman's name, and why on earth should he wish to know me?"

"Anne," Hiram said, coming to me and placing his hands lightly on my shoulders. "You must prepare yourself for a shock, although I hope it will be a pleasant one in the end."

I swallowed and looked him full in the face.

"It is something I have known for a long while, something I stumbled upon quite by accident. I have only been waiting for the proper time to broach the subject with you. Now that you are strong again and we are settled, I believe that time has come."

I had no idea what my husband meant to say, but he looked so grave that I began to tremble. "No more of this suspense, Hiram. Just tell me straight out, whatever it is."

"Very well. It is someone of your past acquaintance, someone who was once very close to you. When he heard that I knew you, he asked me to arrange a reunion. Anne, my darling, it is your long-lost father, Sir Lewis de Bourgh."

I could not support myself under this shocking news. Hiram caught me as I began to sink. "He is alive?" I managed to ask after a minute.

"Yes. He is definitely alive, although I cannot say he is well. That is how I came to meet him; I was called in to attend him in his illness."

New questions and fears raced through my mind. "Is his illness serious?" I asked in alarm. If my father had been alive all these years – and I still could hardly believe it – I could not bear to lose him again so soon. "Is he dying?"

"You must remember he is almost an old man now, nearly sixty, and anything at that age can be considered serious. But, no, I do not believe there is any immediate danger. Still, it seemed imprudent to put this off any longer. Will you see him, Anne? I think that you should, although I can understand why you might not want to."

It took me two days to answer that question. My heart had at first leapt with joy at the thought of seeing my beloved Papa again, but then the inevitable doubts and questions assailed me. If he were alive, why had he left us? Why had he left *me*? Where had he been all this time, and why had he never made any attempt to contact me before? And in light of that question, why now? Also, what did Mama know of this business? Was she just as much in the dark about it as I had been?

When I tried asking Hiram, he would only say, "I wish I had the answers for you, my dear. These are questions you must put to your father."

So with great excitement and equally great trepidation, I agreed to see this man who had deserted me nearly nine years before. Hiram drove me over in his gig – a long drive to a less fashionable part of town. The house itself was respectable enough, however. It was something more on the order of our own modest dwelling than Mama's. When we were let in and I saw him, I did not know what to do or say.

"Anne, here is your father," Hiram said to get us started.

I walked toward this man, who was older and wearing a graying beard but still recognizable. He was my father; there was no doubt in my mind about that. As I extended my hand to him, I noticed there were tears in his eyes. Then I was in his arms being rocked back and forth.

"Annie, my girl," he repeated over and over again. "My own Annie. How I have longed for this day! You cannot imagine."

By then, I was crying too, saying, "Oh, Papa! I have missed you so."

When at last the tide of emotion had been sufficiently stemmed, we three sat down. I looked at my father in wonder and expectancy, waiting for his explanation.

"It is a hard thing to tell, Annie, my girl. It has been a harder thing to live. Nevertheless, you deserve to hear the truth. I hope you will listen with a heart that is open. I am a flawed man, and I have lived a flawed life, which has forced me to make some very difficult choices. Where I have failed you, I ask you to look for the charity to forgive me.

"I did not die when my carriage overturned nine years ago, as your mother has told you, but it was nearly so. What you have presumably never heard, is that I was not traveling alone that night. I was on an errand of mercy, attempting to save a lady and her infant son from great danger. I do not mean to make myself out a hero, though. I was never that, for the lady did not survive. And to my shame, I must also confess that she would have needed no rescuing in the first place were it not for my own earlier actions. The truth is, Annie, the lady – a married woman – was my mistress, and her infant was your half-brother, my illegitimate son."

He paused, allowing me necessary time to digest.

My head was awhirl with what I had learnt so far. Then, thinking back to those awful days, I recalled the grief and chaos that had engulfed our household. But it had not been only *our* house in mourning; there was another at the same time... "Diana's mother," I said when I had put the pieces together. "It was Mrs. Denton. She was with you and died."

"Yes," he said quietly, dropping his head. "We had been sweethearts since we were children, but we were not permitted to marry. My father had grander plans for me. I was to marry into a titled family – the daughter of an earl."

"Mama."

He nodded. "And Henrietta married Mr. Denton. Years later, when their family happened to move to Kent, we met again. The attachment between us was still strong, and eventually, while her husband was away on an extended journey, we gave in to temptation. When he returned to find his wife with child – one he knew could not be his – he threatened bodily harm if the baby turned out to be a boy. He would not have another man's bastard as his heir, he said. So when the time came, I carried mother and child off in the middle of the night to hide them away in London. Only it was a dark night and there was a storm. The accident…" He trailed off. "When I woke from my injuries hours later, I learnt Henrietta was dead."

"The child!" I cried. "What about the child?"

"Yes, miraculously, he survived. Annie, my girl, you have a brother. His name is Harry."

Again I needed time to comprehend this. I had a brother, something I had always longed for… but under different circumstances. I had a brother, who would presumably be nine years old now. "Where is he, Papa? May I meet him?"

"All in good time. I have sent him off with his nurse so that we might have some privacy and so as not to overwhelm you all at once. You must allow me to finish my story, though, my dear."

"Of course. There are still questions to be answered, such as why you did not return home."

"Exactly. Well, I faced a dire dilemma. I had intended to keep Harry and Henrietta safe here in town, away from harm and from gossiping tongues."

"And away from Mama."

"Quite. Except for the accident, she might never have known. But when she came to London and discovered the true situation, she was incensed, for which I cannot say that I blame her. Her reaction was particularly harsh, however. She told me that if I expected to come home to Rosings, I must give up my son – leave him in a foundling home and never see him again. Otherwise, I should be dead to her, and that is exactly what she would say had happened – that I had been killed in the accident. To ensure that the story was believed, I must stay away, never showing my face and name anywhere I could be recognized.

"Neither choice was acceptable, but still I had to choose. To fight your mother on this, to attempt to bring Harry home to Rosings with me, would have been to bring scandal and disgrace upon us all… and upon Henrietta's memory."

"So rather than give up your son, you left. You gave *me* up."

"For a time, Annie. Only for a time! Harry was a helpless babe. He was my responsibility, and he had nobody else. The foundling home would have been little better than a death sentence. I could not do it to him. You and I had already had fourteen years together, and I knew you would be well looked after. I was determined that when you were grown, when you were out from under your mother's control, I would find a way to meet with you again. And so I have, thanks to your fine husband. In the meantime, Harry and I have lived abroad; we have had a good life in the West Indies. My solicitor has sent me regular word of you and of your mother, and whenever I returned to English soil, I looked for a chance to at least catch a glimpse of you unawares. I was at your wedding, you know."

"Really? How was it that I did not see you there?"

"You seemed to have eyes for no one but young Mr. Essex, here. Besides, I was very unobtrusive in the back. Only Mrs. Jenkinson espied me, I believe, but even she did not suspect."

So that is how I got my father back... and acquired a brother too. Hiram and I see them both frequently, and Papa has asked us to look after the boy should anything happen to him. The gift of Harry – for a gift to me he truly is – has become my consolation for the years lost with my father. At least for the time being, their near proximity and the fact that I have seen them must remain hidden from Mama. She has endured enough trauma for one year.

A mere hint at this family secret had already proved sufficient to unnerve her. Hiram stumbled quite innocently upon this useful fact the first time he came to Rosings. Though he did not know the story then, he saw at once what effect mentioning Papa had on my mother. He soon learnt that if he needed her cooperation with anything, all he need do was drop the name of Sir Lewis de Bourgh and she was suddenly all obliging.

~~*~~

I believe I fall more and more in love with my husband every day. And he with me, so he says. Now that all constraints have been removed, we are free to do and say what we like with each other. I had no idea marriage could be like this.

As long as we can be together, it matters very little what we do. One night we may be happy staying quietly at home and the next we are just as pleased to be going out somewhere. We are equally keen to explore the verdant countryside or the architectural and cultural advantages of London. At some point in the future, we plan to travel farther afield too. Scotland, Venice, and the Alhambra of Spain are on our definite list.

We speak of books, and music, and even medicine, which I have discovered to be very interesting. Sometimes I pick up one of Hiram's books and try to decipher the meaning of the foreign-sounding words and concepts it contains. It is like discovering a new universe, one inside the body instead of out. I can certainly see how it captured Hiram's imagination to where he wanted to be a part of its practice – for the relief of suffering and in the furtherance of scientific knowledge.

He has visionary ideas for how medicine must progress, as well as for the role he would like to play in the process. This I found out early in our marriage. Mama had decided to spend some time in town – "for a change of scene and society," she said – and so we had Rosings to ourselves.

As we took our daily walk, arm in arm, Hiram looked up at the imposing front facade. "What a great pile this house is," he said, "a monument to what can be achieved if one has more money than one knows what to do with."

Puzzled, I said, "You sound as if you do not like it?"

"Oh, it is a fine display of architectural genius, no doubt, but not to my taste. I prefer something of more modest dimensions for a comfortable family life. Even if we should have twelve children…"

"Twelve children!" I cried in alarm.

"Have no fear, dear Anne. I have no intention of putting my wife through such a strain as that. My point was going to be that we cannot begin to fill all these rooms – not unless you aspire to house and entertain great groups of friends and strangers month after month."

"Not at all. The idea does not interest me in the least."

"I am glad to hear it. Then in that case, this house will remain nearly as empty as it is now. Why, the entire east wing has never been used once since I have known you! Presuming your mother does not disinherit you next time you or I displease her, it will one day be for you to decide what to do with the place."

"What do you mean 'do with it?' It is a house; one uses a house to live in. What else should one do with it?"

"Exactly!" he said, his eyes lighting up. "That is what I have been asking myself. What else might one do with an enormous place like this?"

"I hardly know," I admitted. "You have the advantage over me since I have never thought on that question before. If it were up to you, Hiram, what would you do with Rosings?"

"Very well, since you ask. If it were mine, Anne, I would like to see Rosings put to better use than for housing a small family and a host of servants, many of whom exist only to keep clean dozens of rooms that are never used." He stopped and looked up at the house again. "I can envision at least half of this grand building converted for some superior purpose, more specifically, a medical purpose: a medical school, a hospital of some sort, perhaps for the dedicated research and treating of one specific type of illness, or an asylum for rehabilitating injured soldiers returned from war. Imagine the possibilities."

I stared up at the familiar edifice, seeing it for the first time through different eyes. As I did so, my mind leapt ahead to catch up to Hiram's, to begin imagining the possibilities he had been speaking of, the possibilities held by this marvelous house that had been my home all my life. Instead of barren, I suddenly saw it alive with activity – children playing on one side, people of purpose coming and going on the other. A thrill ran through me.

"Nothing could be done while Mama lives," I said, stating the obvious fact. "We dare not even mention such an idea."

"Why? You think your mother would disapprove?" he teased. "Oh, I can just hear her now." With voice raised an octave higher, he continued. "Is such a thing to be endured? It shall not be! Every feeling revolts at the very idea. I would rather this house were torn down until not one stone stands upon another than to see it fall into the hands of the undeserving! I would smash every one of the sixty-four windows myself before I would have unwashed strangers peering through them!"

I was near helpless with laughter at this point. "Enough!" I cried. "I can scarcely draw breath."

Hiram's tone returned to normal. "You know I have the greatest affection for your mother, Anne. I truly do, despite her foibles. But she is of the old school. Regardless what she might say about being forward thinking, this idea would be too radical for her. The world is changing, though, and we must be prepared to change with it when it is our turn to lead. Those who possess greater resources – of mind, education, and finance – must expect to bear a greater responsibility than in the past for how those resources are used."

This is another reason I love and respect Hiram Essex so very much. It is not only that he is tender and considerate with me, and that he makes me laugh every single day. I love that he cares for the rest of the world as well. He is not all for what he can get for himself; he is conscience-bound to do what he can for the benefit of others round about him.

I often wished I had been taught something useful, not only how to behave in society and to superintend a manor house. Now I am learning from my husband what I had always suspected myself, that there is indeed more to life and that I might have a meaningful role to play. I have a sound mind and now a sound body. I have expectations of a sizable inheritance – enough to do some real good. Perhaps together (in addition to raising a family, I hope), my husband and I will accomplish something important – or at least worthwhile – with the blessings we are given. These are dreams for the future, and the future looks very bright.

I used to wonder what might have happened had Elizabeth Bennet never come to Rosings. I used to envy her vivacity, her siblings, her father alive, and finally, her happy marriage. Such desires no longer occupy my mind, however, for these very things are now wishes fulfilled. I have my father again, a sibling of my own, and a marriage surpassing whatever felicity I had imagined then. As for vivacity, I flatter myself I have gained a measure of that as well, although in a slightly different style. For what does vivacity mean but to live life with spirit? And that I most certainly intend to do. In truth, I have already begun.

Thank you for reading *The Ladies of Rosings Park.*
If you enjoyed it, please consider the rest of this series:

The Darcys of Pemberley
Return to Longbourn
and
Miss Georgiana Darcy of Pemberley

~~*~~

Shannon Winslow's other novels:

For Myself Alone
The Persuasion of Miss Jane Austen
Leap of Faith
Leap of Hope

~~*~~

Learn more about Ms. Winslow and her books at
www.shannonwinslow.com

Printed in Great Britain
by Amazon